FOUND

Nervously he picked up the phone on the second ring.

"Is this Greg Nielsen?" a man's voice asked in French.

"You must have the wrong room," he replied, trying hard not to disclose the tension in his voice.

"I know that you're Greg Nielsen," the caller persisted.

"You're obviously mistaken. There's no one . . ."

"I would urge you not to play games with me, Mr. Nielsen. Be in front of the Bristol at six tomorrow morning."

David's mind was focusing on the accent of the caller. Clearly Parisian, he decided.

"Did you understand what I said?" The caller sounded annoyed. "Tomorrow at six."

"And if I'm not there?"

"Certain people in Washington will be very interested in knowing where you are, Mr. Nielsen."

The phone clicked dead.

SPY
DANCE

ALLAN TOPOL

AN ONYX BOOK

ONYX
Published by New American Library, a division of
Penguin Putnam Inc., 375 Hudson Street,
New York, New York 10014, U.S.A.
Penguin Books Ltd, 80 Strand,
London WC2R ORL, England
Penguin Books Australia Ltd, Ringwood,
Victoria, Australia
Penguin Books Canada Ltd, 10 Alcorn Avenue,
Toronto, Ontario, Canada M4V 3B2
Penguin Books (N.Z.) Ltd, 182–190 Wairau Road,
Auckland 10, New Zealand

Penguin Books Ltd, Registered Offices:
Harmondsworth, Middlesex, England

First published by Onyx, an imprint of New American Library,
a division of Penguin Putnam Inc.

First Printing, November 2001
10 9 8 7 6 5 4 3 2 1

This book is dedicated to my wife, Barbara,
who never stopped believing.

PROLOGUE

Dhahran, Saudi Arabia

At ten minutes past midnight, Greg Nielsen stormed into the makeshift wooden building and slammed the door so hard it nearly tore off the hinges. His face was flushed with anger, and his heart was pounding like a drum.

Outside, under a full moon and star-laden sky, a strong wind whipped through the oppressive desert air and swirled the sand into small mounds. Even crickets didn't venture out into the forbidding atmosphere. Meanwhile, the window air conditioner chugged and whirred loudly, as it did twenty-four hours a day, fighting a losing battle with the sweltering heat in the middle of August.

Tacked above the entrance to the building was a small sign that said U.S. AGRICULTURAL MISSION. It fooled no one. The lone sentry on guard confirmed what everyone knew: this building on the outer edge of the huge American military and commercial complex in Dhahran, in the heart of the most productive oil field in the world, was the Saudi Arabian outpost of the Company, as the CIA was euphemistically called.

"Brad and I had a real shouting match," Nielsen exclaimed to Bill Fox, his assistant. "We almost came to blows."

Fox was seated at one of the two battered gray metal desks in the large, drab room. He looked up anxiously from a thick pile of computer runs and asked, "Does he know that you've been talking to Colonel Azziz?"

"I told him the time for pussyfooting is over."

Fox sucked in his breath and blew it out in a whoosh.

"Don't worry," Nielsen added. "He doesn't think you're in this with me. In fact, he wants the Company to can me as station chief of this hellhole, and for you to get my job. So you'll come out of it smelling like a rose. How do you like that?"

Fox looked guilty but relieved. Ignoring him, Nielsen turned his thoughts back to his meeting in General Chambers's office. He had refused to be intimidated. He'd learned long ago that military men like Chambers preferred to tell Washington precisely what the President and his advisers wanted to hear.

"Must have been a helluva discussion," said Fox, staring at Nielsen through heavy black-framed glasses. Only thirty-three, Fox was five years younger than Nielsen, but he looked ten years older. His thinning and prematurely graying hair and an expanding forehead gave him a mousy look.

"Oh, it was. When he gave me the usual shit that 'the Saudi royal family is America's great friend and ally,' I laughed in his face. I told him that they were one of the most corrupt, repressive and autocratic regimes in the world, and that they only supported us if it was in their own self-interest."

"They also happen to be our largest supplier of foreign oil. It won't be a great day if people back home turn on a light switch and nothing happens."

Nielsen smiled. The lack of creative thinking by people like Fox had doomed the Company to its current state of rigor mortis. "Jesus, Bill," he said. "That's the whole point: how to maintain a secure source of Saudi oil for the people back home."

"And you think that dumping the Saudi king is the answer?"

"Wake up and open your eyes. The radical fundamentalists are getting stronger here, as they did in Iran under the Shah. It's only a question of time until they topple the royal family and seize control. Then they'll be in a position to cut off our oil spigot."

"I'm not sure you're right, and I hate like hell betting all our marbles on Colonel Azziz."

With his distinctive off-kilter walk, pronounced now, as it always was when he was tired, Nielsen crossed the room to the small refrigerator. He desperately wanted a cold beer, but he had to settle for a Diet Coke because of the Saudi royal family's prohibition of alcoholic beverages. He pulled out two cans, tossed one to Fox across the room, snapped open the top on the other and sipped greedily. Then he leaned back in his desk chair and put up his feet, encased in rugged high-cut boots covered with dust. He was still feeling the surge of adrenaline from his argument with General Bradley Chambers, and his deep blue eyes were alert, shining with intensity. He ran his hands through his closely cropped cinnamon brown hair, coated with a layer of wind blown sand, thinking about his next move. To preempt Chambers, he'd go to Washington tomorrow. He'd get support from Hugh O'Brien, the director of the CIA. He'd persuade O'Brien to escalate the issue to the Oval Office.

"Listen, Greg, don't get pissed," Fox said hesitantly. "But maybe you should try to see General Chambers again tonight. Figure out a way to make peace with him here before it gets out of hand."

"The hell with that, Bill." Greg was a nervous bundle of energy, talking fast and gesticulating, as he did whenever he was excited. "I've spent fifteen years of my life trying to safeguard the flow of Middle Eastern oil to the U.S. We lost out in Iraq and Iran, and I'll be damned if I'll sit back quietly and watch the same thing happen here. Chambers is dead wrong. It's not in our national interest to support the Saudi monarchy against Azziz and his fellow officers if they're planning a coup."

"You don't make policy, Greg," Fox said gingerly. "You've been telling them what you think in Langley. So far they've refused to take you seriously."

Nielsen wasn't listening to Fox. He was deep in thought. "If Chambers does manage to get his way with Washington and have me tossed out of here," he said, "I think I'll quit the Company. I've had enough. I'll go someplace and use my computer expertise. Maybe it's time I worried about myself instead of playing the role of an American patriot."

"If you're serious about that, I just might join you," Fox replied. "Alice called me tonight. She won't move here with the kids." He looked discouraged. "My marriage is going down the tubes faster than a stone in a lake. And I haven't gotten laid in months. Hell, I'll follow you anywhere as long as there are women I can screw without running the risk of getting my nuts chopped off."

Nielsen still wasn't listening to his colleague. "I'm not worried about myself. It's Colonel Azziz. He's a good man. If Chambers reports to the king on my contacts with Azziz, they'll kill him in a second."

"You know what I think?" Fox asked.

Nielsen looked up at his assistant. "What's that, Bill?"

Fox never had a chance to respond. At that instant a huge explosion erupted outside with an intensity so fierce that it blew the glass out of both windows in the office. Instinctively, Nielsen and Fox hit the concrete floor and rolled under their desks to take cover from flying glass and other debris.

As soon as the room was still, Nielsen bolted up and sprinted for the front door. Fox was right behind. Outside, they saw a huge fireball shooting high into the air about a mile away.

"Jesus," Fox said, "we were lucky. We got the pressure wave. Not the direct hit."

"Oh, shit!" Nielsen screamed. "That's the Khobar housing complex. Let's move it."

Quickly, they climbed into a jeep and roared across the dirt road to the housing complex.

Minutes later, Nielsen pushed through the barriers cordoning off the scene of the bomb blast. He said to an MP, "I'm going inside to pull out people." Fox was two steps behind his chief.

Together, they worked with rescue units, struggling to bring out the wounded and dead from a twisted eight-story concrete-and-steel structure before portions of it began to collapse. Others tried to put out the half-dozen fires that were still raging.

It was risky work in tight quarters. As the rescue effort became more organized, those who were trained to do it urged Nielsen and Fox to stand back and let them do the work. Fox acquiesced but not Nielsen. By now he was wearing a dark green military helmet, which he had found on the floor next to a corporal whose chest had been blown apart. He moved carefully from room to room, not wanting to disturb the constantly shifting debris. He called, "Anybody here?" and then listened carefully for muffled sobs or cries for help. He slung bodies over his shoulder and carried them out, moving his lame right leg as fast as he could. All the while he could feel their blood oozing down his neck and arms. His face was soon black from the charred ruins of the building, and his arms ached with weariness.

He picked up a small girl, maybe five years old, in shock. Her right arm had been severed at the elbow, and her glasses had been smashed against her face, bloodying her eyes. He thought about his own sister, Betty, when she had been hit by a car while riding on her bike and had broken her glasses. He could still remember her tiny fingers digging into his neck in terror as he carried her to the hospital.

Outside, he deposited the girl's limp body with the waiting medics. He found he had tears trickling down his face, and he wiped them away with the dirty sleeve of his shirt. All around him he heard the words "huge bomb in a truck . . . suicide bomber . . . just like Oklahoma City . . . wait'll we find out who did it . . . we'll kill the bastards . . ."

Nielsen didn't have to wait to find out who did it. About a month ago, he had infiltrated an Iranian-backed Hezbollah terrorist cell operating in the Shiite region of eastern Saudi Arabia. He had learned that they were planning something big aimed against the American military, on the assumption that the Saudi royal family could remain in power only as long as it had the support of the Americans. If terrorist acts could induce the Americans to leave, as they had in Lebanon and Somalia, the radicals could wrest control from the despised Saudi royal family and establish an Islamic republic that would control the largest oil reserves in the world. Nielsen was never able to find out who the mastermind was behind this operation or when and where the attack would come, because his source had not shown up for a meeting last week. Instead, Nielsen had found a small metal box waiting for him at the desert crossroads that had been their meeting point. When he opened it, he found a picture of the man who had been supplying him information and, covered by insects and maggots, what were unmistakably male genitalia.

Taking the information to General Chambers, he had argued for stepped-up defenses at all American military installations. But Chambers had scoffed at his warning.

The sun was starting to rise quickly in the eastern sky, bringing with it the blazing desert heat. It was only five-fifteen, and yet Nielsen felt he was in a furnace as he gently carried a pregnant woman with burns on most of her body.

He was on the verge of collapse from exhaustion, but he made himself move back toward the devastated building. "One more time," he told himself. "Do it one more time."

This was precisely what he had told himself on the last five trips. As he started toward the building, he felt a tug on his arm. He wheeled around to face Major George Hawkins, one of General Chambers's aides.

"The general wants to see you," said Hawkins.

"Later. Tell him I'm busy saving lives."

"General Chambers said 'on the double,' Mr. Nielsen."

"Fuck him. This is more important."

"Others will do the rescue work." Hawkins pointed at the rescue party, which had grown. Television trucks and cameras had arrived on the scene with their ubiquitous microphones shoved in front of anyone who would make a statement.

Nielsen knew there was no point arguing with Hawkins. In weary resignation he followed the major across the Dhahran complex to a building that had remained intact. It was the base headquarters, which had been built to withstand anything except a direct attack.

They rode the elevator to the third floor, where Major Hawkins deposited Nielsen in a large conference room. Standing alone with his back to the door, the general was studying a map on the wall, while puffing on a large cigar. The air-conditioned room was such a contrast to the outdoors that goose bumps erupted on Nielsen's skin. Unobtrusively, the major exited and pulled the door shut behind him.

As if the sound of the closing door was a cue, the general mashed the cigar under his boot and whirled around. He gave Nielsen a cold stare of contempt. The rows of medals on his tan army jacket sparkled in the sunlight pouring in through the windows.

"Are you proud of yourself, mister?" Chambers barked in his booming voice. His western North Carolina accent had an icy edge.

"What are you talking about?"

"Thanks to you, Azziz and his ga'damn buddies managed to kill more than a hundred Americans tonight. With over two thousand Americans living in that complex, it's a ga' damn miracle the casualties weren't ten times that amount."

Nielsen felt the anger rising in his body. "Azziz had nothing to do with that bomb."

With his jaw firmly set, Chambers moved in close to Nielsen. "How much did you tell Azziz about our defenses here at Dhahran?"

"What are you talking about?"

"All the times you met with him. You must have told him plenty about our defenses."

Nielsen was incredulous but also wary. Chambers was a snake. Nielsen understood what he was doing: trying to set up a scapegoat for his own failure to maintain adequate security at the base.

"Not one fucking word," Nielsen replied, raising his voice. "The subject never came up. If I wanted to help someone strike a blow against the royal family, I sure wouldn't do it by killing Americans. Hell, I was the one who developed the computer systems that govern security at the king's palace and in the oil fields. All I'd have to do is give those computer programs to the dissidents. They would have the keys to the palace, for chrissake."

"I'm asking you one more time. What did you tell Azziz about our defenses?"

"And I'm telling you, nothing."

"I'd like to ask Azziz, but as soon as the bomb went off here, I told the king about his relationship with you. I was promised that his head would be on display in Riyadh by noon today."

Nielsen gave a low curse. "You bastard."

"They wanted you, too. But I said you were ours. I'm shipping you back home to stand trial before a military court as an accessory to the murder of the more than one hundred Americans who were killed here today."

Nielsen could hardly believe his ears. "You're what?"

Chambers repeated what he'd said. Then he pointed at a wooden chair next to the conference table. "Sit down, mister," he ordered Nielsen. "I'm going out to get a couple of MPs to arrest you."

"Like hell you are," Nielsen shot back. He walked swiftly toward the door.

Moving to cut him off, the general stationed himself ten feet in front of the door. He was powerfully built, two hundred and twenty pounds and a couple of inches above six feet. With a barrel chest and powerful arms, he'd always reminded Nielsen of a tank. At the age of fifty, Chambers, a former champion wrestler at West Point, was still in incredibly great shape.

"I gave you an order, mister," the general barked. "Go back and sit down."

"Fuck you. I'm not under your command."

"It's a military zone, mister. Everybody's under my command."

Nielsen feinted left and then moved sharply to the right, hoping to get around Chambers. He was halfway to the door when Chambers grabbed his left arm and twisted it behind his back. "Let go of me," Nielsen cried out. He couldn't break free.

Chambers slammed him against the wall and kept

applying pressure to his arm. While Nielsen struggled, Chambers used his fifty pound weight advantage to keep him pinned against the wall.

"You were resisting arrest, mister," he shouted. "Now you're mine."

To make the point, the general pulled away for an instant, and then slammed Nielsen hard against the wall. A jolt of searing pain shot through Nielsen's body.

"Let's try that again," Chambers said sadistically.

Before the general could smash him against the wall another time, Nielsen gathered his right hand into a fist. The frustration and anger he had felt all night were surging to a crescendo. With a sudden jerking motion he slammed his fist into Chambers's face. The general never saw the blow coming. Nielsen felt the bridge of Chambers's nose disintegrate and some teeth give way.

Blind with rage, spitting blood, Chambers grabbed Nielsen's throat with both hands. As the general kept squeezing, Nielsen felt himself weaken. He knew that Chambers meant to kill him. From deep inside he summoned the strength to bring his fist up one more time. He slammed it so hard into Chambers's face, he heard the crunch of the general's jaw breaking. This time Chambers screamed in pain. Releasing his hold on Nielsen, he dropped to the floor, clutching his face and gasping for breath. Blood was pouring from the general's nose and mouth.

For good measure, Nielsen kicked him once in the balls and bolted for the door of the conference room. He opened it slowly and peered out. From his vantage point, at the end of a long corridor, he saw Major Hawkins in the third-floor reception area, about forty yards away, casually chatting with two MPs and a corporal, a good-looking young woman, on duty at the reception desk. The MPs must be there to arrest him—just waiting for a signal from the general, who was on the floor writhing in pain. Other than those four, the floor seemed deserted. Across the corridor from the conference room was a red EXIT sign marking an inside staircase.

Nielsen waited until the four were looking in a different

direction, and then he slipped across the hall and into the stairwell. He didn't know if it was locked on the first floor, but it was the only choice he had.

As he raced down the three flights of stairs, he tripped at a landing, tearing his pants at the knee. Then he picked himself up and kept on running. At the bottom, on the first floor, he tensely grabbed the doorknob with a moist hand. The door opened.

Peeking out, he saw pandemonium at the front entrance. A score of reporters were badgering the base press officer. In the glare of television lights, a CNN reporter was reeling off a series of preliminary statistics: "One hundred and eight people dead, one hundred and eighty-two wounded, and . . ." Nonchalantly, Nielsen walked in the direction of the front door. In the confusion, he slipped among the milling crowd and through the front door.

Once he was out in the intense heat and bright sunlight, a wave of fear overtook him. What had he done? Now he was a dead man. Before the attack on Chambers, he could have defended himself at trial.

But what could he do now? In a matter of minutes, Chambers would get help. The whole U.S. military in Saudi Arabia, as well as the Saudi police and army, would be looking for him. Every exit from the country would be sealed. Border police would have his picture. They would have orders to shoot to kill.

He would have to call someone who could make him disappear.

CHAPTER 1

July, Five Years Later

David Ben Aaron sipped an espresso, leaned back in the black leather chair and closed his eyes, savoring the feeling of a great dinner at Arpege. There were only twelve well-spaced tables in this temple of haute cuisine on the Left Bank—not far from Napoleon's tomb. Suddenly, he was aware of a stockinged foot moving up and down between his legs. Across the table, Maria Clermont, blond, beautiful and braless, leaned over to scoop some chocolate soufflé out of her dish. She picked up the spoon, rolled the soufflé around on her tongue and gave him a sensuous smile that fit with her hair falling seductively over one eye.

He could hardly believe that this was the same woman he had spent five hours with today in a conference room with half a dozen Renault executives. David had been trying to sell the French carmaker a new computer program his kibbutz had developed. Then, Maria, the high corporate official, had been wearing a loose-fitting gray suit, hemmed long to look professional, no makeup or lipstick and her hair tied back tightly. Her voice had been serious, she listened intently and took copious notes, never giving any indication whether she favored the transaction he was proposing.

Yet when she walked through the doorway of the restaurant, he was dazzled, as were all the other men in the room. She was stunning, wearing a black silk sheath dress cut tight and short to display her high, full breasts, narrow hips and long, beautifully sculpted legs. Around her neck hung a

gold chain with a pendant made of a large round cabochon
emerald surrounded by diamonds that sparkled against her
suntanned skin. Her lipstick and nails were a dark red, and
the aroma of Patou's Joy followed her as the maître d' led
them to their table.

Her voice had a deep throaty tone that hadn't been there
this afternoon, and she accompanied it with a robust, earthy
laugh. Even her mannerisms were different. No longer the
prim and proper executive, she relished the raw oysters,
picking up the shells and erotically licking the juice. He
had watched with amusement as she ate clean the bones
from the exquisite herb-crusted rack of lamb they had
shared with a bottle of 1985 Clos la Roche by Dujac.

Hoping to prolong the evening's pleasure, he asked,
"How about a cognac or an Armagnac?"

"I have a bottle of 1945 Chateau de Laubade at home,"
she replied. "Most people think that was the best year of
the century."

He didn't care about the year of the Armagnac. He was
just relieved to hear that he wouldn't have to invite her
back to the Normandy, his fleabag hotel on the Left Bank,
which definitely would have chilled the mood.

"But if that doesn't suit you, I have some '49 and '53
as well."

"I'm impressed."

"Don't be. When I gave Michel a divorce, I insisted on
keeping the wine cellar as well as his Armagnac collection.
He cried like a baby." She gave a short, caustic laugh. "If
he hadn't decided to marry that tart, he could have continued the old arrangement. Having her on the side while
being married to me. I would never have found out. God,
men are such fools."

David nodded slightly to a tuxedo-clad waiter and silently
mouthed the word "*L'addition.*" Seconds later a check
appeared.

"Speaking of being impressed," Maria said, "I'm blown
away at how well you handled yourself at this three-star
Paris restaurant for a . . ." She stopped in mid-sentence.

"For an Israeli," he said, "or for a Jew, you mean."

She blushed and looked indignant. "I didn't mean that at all," she protested. "I meant for someone who's not a native Frenchman. You people are always so sensitive."

"History in this part of the world hasn't been kind to us, but still I'm sorry I misunderstood you," he said gracefully, wanting to let her off the hook. It was eleven o'clock in the evening of a very long day. At this point he had one objective, and that was to get her out of that black dress and into bed. They could fight about politics and bigotry some other time . . . if there was another time.

In the cab, he put an arm around her shoulder, and she snuggled up to him. The air from the open window of the taxi blew against both of their faces, scattering the thick, curly black hair on his head. He closed his eyes, enjoying the moment.

Behind the cab, a gray BMW sedan was following them, carefully maintaining a twenty-yard distance on the mostly deserted streets. Neither David nor Maria had any idea it was there. If the taxi driver did, he didn't pay it any mind.

"What's your wife going to say about this?" Maria asked devilishly.

"She died a year ago," David replied tersely.

She stiffened. "I'm so sorry. Really I am. Michel always says I put my foot in my mouth."

"What about your colleagues at Renault? What will they say?"

She raised a finger to her lips. "Shh. They can't know, or I'll be sacked. It's a company rule. We can't consort with vendors or prospective vendors."

"You're kidding."

"No, I'm dead serious, and they enforce it."

"So you're taking a helluva chance for me."

"Let's just say I'm betting you're going to be a good lover and worth the risk."

He gave a devilish smile. "I'll try not to disappoint you."

She laughed. "You're so damn self-confident. That's what I liked about you the first time I met you. You can do anything you want. And when Jean-Pierre left to take that phone call, and we were standing alone at the coffeepot, you simply said, 'What time would you like to have dinner with me tonight?' Not whether I would, but what time."

"Well, you have to try things. You never know what will work. Plus, I figured you had clout in at least one good Paris restaurant, and I wanted a good meal while I was here. Do you have any idea what the food's like in Israel?"

She stroked his cheek. "That's not all you wanted from this evening. Your eyes let me know that."

Tired of her chattering, he reached his hand under her silk skirt. To his delight he found that she was wearing stockings and a garter belt, rather than those annoying panty hose. He stopped on the soft, moist skin on the inside of her upper thigh.

On the outskirts of Paris, Maria gave the driver directions for a series of turns on narrow roads until they rolled up a gravel driveway that led to a huge stone house. It was lined with tall evergreens and had a well-manicured lawn. David whistled involuntarily.

"Part of the payoff from the divorce," she said. "Rich men shouldn't fool around. It can get expensive."

"You must have had a good lawyer."

"Ah, they're worthless. I did the bargaining myself."

"I didn't realize you were so talented."

"You haven't seen anything yet. Now kiss me."

And he did. It was the first time he had kissed a woman in a year, and he enjoyed it.

As he learned minutes later, Maria lived alone in that grand house. There was no one to awaken during the loud session of lovemaking that began just inside the front door.

"I'm going to rip off all of your clothes," she said as she tore at the buttons on his shirt.

It ended an hour later in the bedroom with her third cry of ecstasy. Then she turned onto her front and fell into a deep sleep. He pulled the sheet up over her naked body and moved the unfinished snifters of Armagnac away from the edge of the night table so she wouldn't hit them if she swung her arm.

For David, sleep wouldn't come. He lay on the bed looking at the full moon through the open curtains of the second-floor bedroom window. The evening had brought back haunting memories. Next week it would be one year since Yael's death.

He had never thought it possible to love someone as intensely as he had Yael. He could still see her light blue eyes, sparkling with life, as if there were tiny sapphires buried in the centers. Combined with her intelligence had been the bold drive of a risk taker. She'd been someone who knew what she wanted from life. Someone for whom life and love were exhilarating.

Yael had kissed him deeply, holding him tight, that last morning before she left to go to Jerusalem. She had lingered for a moment to squeeze his hand, as if she had an awful foreboding of what was ahead. Then she raced off, late for her ride, her blond hair cascading down on her back, her body still trim and athletic, her long legs well formed from running, sensuous where they joined together at her small, tight rear in khaki slacks that hugged her skin.

It was a picture that would stay etched in his mind. In the last year, his celibacy had been a form of mourning for Yael as well as a part of the life he had so carefully constructed for himself after her death. But as the end of the year approached, he realized that he couldn't bring her back. Before this trip to Paris he had made a decision that the time had come to get on with this part of his life as well.

Suddenly, he thought he heard a noise downstairs in the house. He bolted up to a sitting position and listened carefully. First there was nothing, then a slight sound.

Light footsteps on a wooden floor?

What could it be?

A pet?

She hadn't said anything about one.

Was he being paranoid?

He heard another sound.

There *was* someone downstairs. Now he knew that for sure.

He slipped out of bed and quickly took stock of the house, as he remembered it in a mind foggy with alcohol. There were two sets of stairs leading up from the floor below: the wooden back stairs from the kitchen that they had used this evening, carrying glasses of Armagnac, and the carpeted center staircase.

Instinctively, he looked for his clothes, but then remembered that they were scattered with hers downstairs just inside the front door.

He needed a weapon. As his eyes scanned the bedroom, he didn't see anything he could use.

Suddenly, he remembered that in the kitchen, she had half a dozen knives hanging on the wall, next to the pantry. As quietly as possible he crossed the room, naked, to the wooden back staircase. Stealthily, he tiptoed down the stairs, partially illuminated from a light they had left on in the kitchen.

When he reached the kitchen, he heard footsteps going up the center hall staircase toward Maria's bedroom. He quickly surveyed the knife rack and grabbed a boning knife with a black handle. Clutching it tightly in his hand, he crossed the oriental carpet in the living room and climbed the center staircase.

It was dark on the second floor and very still.

Perhaps the noises were all his imagination.

Or paranoia?

He climbed slowly, holding the knife in his hand now moist with perspiration.

Suddenly, without warning, he heard the unmistakable sound of an automatic weapon being fired across the bedroom.

He ran wildly. At the entrance to the bedroom, he saw the wide back of a black-shirted man gripping an Uzi and surveying the damage he had caused. Instinctively, David threw the knife at the assailant. It plunged into the back of the man's neck. The assailant started to raise his gun and turn around, but he abruptly collapsed to his knees, dropping the Uzi, which skidded harmlessly across the polished wooden floor. The man was propped against the wall, with the knife still stuck in his neck.

Ignoring the assailant, David turned on the bedroom light. He took one look at the bed and knew it was hopeless for Maria. Enraged, he turned his attention back toward the killer, who was writhing in pain. David picked up the Uzi and aimed it at the man.

"That was meant for me, you bastard, wasn't it?"

The man's eyes told him that he was right.

"Who sent you?" he demanded.

The man started to raise his hands to pull out the knife in his neck, now surrounded by spurting blood, but they fell down weakly. "The knife . . ." he mumbled.

"Tell me who sent you, and I'll take it out."

The killer closed his eyes. It was futile, David realized. The man had lost too much blood. He would never be able to talk. David was tempted to fire off a few rounds and put the killer out of his misery, but after what he had done, he deserved to die a slow death.

Sadly, David examined what was left of Maria's beautiful body. Her head had been blown apart. Brain and tissue were splattered against the mahogany headboard.

"I'm so sorry," he said. "So sorry you brought home the wrong man tonight."

He brought his clothes upstairs and dressed quickly but carefully, making certain that he didn't leave anything of his in the house. Then he grabbed a white monogrammed washcloth from the bathroom and meticulously wiped every surface he had touched, including the handle of the knife. When he was finished, he dropped the washcloth into the sink and let it soak in hot water.

He glanced at the pink princess phone next to the bed. For an instant he considered calling the police, but quickly rejected the idea. He didn't want to leave the sound of his voice, which might be recorded. It was a risk that he couldn't afford to take.

Chances were that no one had known she was having dinner with him tonight. She had said that she was too worried about her job to tell anyone.

The reservation at Arpege had been made in her name. No one knew him at the restaurant. He might be able to slip away, after all. At any rate, he had to take the chance. He couldn't risk dealing with the police.

CHAPTER 2

It was one of those gorgeous sunrises that characterize the eastern Mediterranean in the summer, when the red ball of a sun rises across the desert against a perfect azure sky without a single cloud in sight. It didn't seem right to have such a beautiful morning. It should have been damp and gloomy with the heavens gray and cloud-laden to match their mood.

They walked together, arms around each other, a man and a woman in her mid-twenties, up the hill, toward the cemetery of kibbutz Bet Mordechai, on a rocky plateau in western Galilee. They had come to observe the one-year anniversary of the death of the same woman, but their relationships with her in life had been so separate and different. Only in the last year, since her mother's death, had Daphna formed a bond—in part through shared grief—with this Russian.

Daphna could still remember the first time she had met him. Four years ago, she had come home from Shabbat leave in her last year of military service, as a helicopter pilot in the Israeli Air Force. Mother had been radiant—no, she shouldn't call her Mother, even in death she should call her Yael, as her mother had wanted in life. In the small kibbutz house that Yael occupied, she had told Daphna, "I want you to meet a new immigrant from Russia tonight at dinner. David Ben Aaron is his name. I'm going to marry him."

He seemed nice enough that night—a scholarly looking Russian, her mother's age, with thick coal black curly hair, deep black eyes and wire-framed glasses, who tried so hard to communicate with her in Hebrew, until she finally felt sorry for him and shifted to the Russian she had learned in school. But she didn't have the faintest idea why her mother had decided to get married for the first time after all of these years. Not that it mattered to her, or so she told herself. After all, didn't Bruno Bettelheim write that one of the results of kibbutz living, with separate living arrangements for children and parents, was a severing of strong parental emotional bonds?

Yet here she was approaching her mother's grave, weak in the knees, overcome by the grief that had shrouded her for the last twelve months, ever since a friend had pulled her out of a class in English literature at the Hebrew University to tell her: "There was a bomb on a bus . . ." She shuddered thinking about it.

She squeezed her arm more tightly around David as they neared the small gravestone. "Professor Bettelheim, you were wrong," she mumbled to herself between clenched teeth. The last twelve months had been hell for her. She would dream about her mother and wake up in a cold sweat. For hours on end she had roamed the streets of Jerusalem, expecting to find her mother, to learn that it was all a mistake, that Yael hadn't boarded Bus 18 that day, that the buyer from Saks Fifth Avenue she was supposed to meet in Jerusalem, to sell him furs from the kibbutz, had been detained in New York.

The buyer had wanted to meet Yael in Tel Aviv, but her mother insisted on Jerusalem because Daphna was there. That way she could have dinner with her daughter that evening after she finished with the buyer. Her mother had been so happy in those days. For the first time in her life she was happy. She had so much to live for. She . . .

Daphna couldn't choke back the tears any longer.

They flowed freely. The gravestone was ten yards ahead, and they slowed their pace.

She had managed to finish the year in school, barely working, rarely going to classes. Professors liked her and felt sorry for her; they gave her passing grades.

She had known she couldn't remain in Israel any longer.

Suddenly, it had become too small for her. She had needed money to go abroad, and had spent the summer waiting tables at the Hilton in Tel Aviv, working as many hours as she could.

In September, she had left Israel and a lifetime of friends. She traveled in Scandinavia, where her mother had gone twice a year buying fur pelts for the kibbutz to convert into designer coats. Her mother had started the business for the kibbutz when oranges and grapefruits, their original economic foundation, became no longer profitable. In Denmark, Sweden, Norway and Finland, Daphna had roamed the streets and visited fur dealers expecting to find her mother. If she saw a familiar woman's form in front of her, she would rush up and accost the stranger, then back away apologetically.

In October she traveled to Paris and enrolled in the Sorbonne, studying world literature. She lived in a hovel on the West Bank—Left Bank—she always made that mistake. She was desperately trying to reinvent herself, to try to find a reason to get up in the morning.

The gravestone was dignified and small. Just her mother's name, Yael Bat Avraham, and the date. Daphna did the math in her head. Forty-five years . . . far short of the biblical three scores and ten.

She released herself from David's grip and stood with her hands folded in front of her. Tears flowed freely down her cheeks. Her body shuddered with pain.

She glanced over at David. He was kneeling, close to the stone. His face was in his hands, but she could hear his muffled sobs of grief. He had loved Yael, she thought. Daphna was happy that at the end, for the last three years of her life, her mother, this independent spirit, this hard-driving kibbutz leader, who had single-handedly forced the other members of the kibbutz to develop what became a profitable fur business, had found someone to love her. For the happiness he had given her mother, she would always be grateful to David.

In Hebrew eighteen was a lucky number. It meant *chai* . . . life. It wasn't lucky for Yael that day.

Daphna knew that they were supposed to say prayers on the anniversary of Yael's death. She didn't know about David, but she wasn't religious. She wasn't sure if she even believed in God.

David was mumbling something softly. Maybe he was praying. If so, that couldn't hurt.

For her part, Daphna knelt down and picked up a few pebbles. She placed them gently on the gravestone. They marked her coming. Her mother would know that she had been there.

The hot sun beat down on their bare heads. Tears flowed down her face faster than the sun could dry them.

David helped her to her feet. Then he enveloped her in his arms, letting her tears wet his shirt.

She offered to take a *sherut* from Haifa to Ben Gurion Airport for her return flight to Paris, but David insisted on driving her in one of the kibbutz's old Ford pickups, which coughed and sputtered until they hit the open road.

Even with the windows down, it was stiflingly hot in the cab of the pickup. She lit up a cigarette and blew the smoke toward the open window.

"When are you coming back?" David asked.

"I don't know," she replied weakly. "Maybe never."

"You like Paris that much?"

"There's nothing here for me. What can I do with a degree in world literature at the kibbutz?"

"You could always take over the family fur business," he said, trying to lighten the mood.

When she didn't respond, he added, "Or teach literature at a university in Israel."

"Teaching's not for me. At the end of the school year, I might go to New York, to Queens."

He looked over at her. "Why there?"

"Why not? There are more Israelis in Queens than anywhere else except Tel Aviv. I'll marry a rich American who plays football, drives a Cadillac and brings me breakfast in bed. What do you think about that?"

"You've been watching too much American television. That's what I think."

He wanted to help this troubled young woman, puffing intensely on her cigarette, who meant so much to him, but he didn't know how. He didn't know what to tell her.

"You know what's weird?" she blurted out.

"What's that?"

"I'm totally an orphan. I don't have a single living relative that I know about."

Immediately she sensed his hurt. "A blood relative, I mean. I shouldn't have said that. I do feel close to you, David, but it's not the same thing. You know."

When he didn't respond, she continued, "She would never tell me who my father was. Just that she would tell me one day. About all I know is that he was a military man, a war hero, a commander of a tank unit. He was married at the time. They fell in love when she was in the army. He would have gotten a divorce, she said. But he was killed in the Yom Kippur War in 1973 in a tank in the Sinai. Burned alive inside, when his tank took a direct hit. She was four months pregnant. So she came to live on the kibbutz. That's absolutely all I know."

She tossed her cigarette out of the window and paused to light another.

She smokes too much, he thought. I should tell her. But how can I, today?

"I could have half brothers and sisters," she said bitterly.

He raised his eyebrows. "What do you mean?"

"Well, if this tank commander had other children with his wife. She would never even tell me that. That's the one thing I'll never forgive her for."

"That's not fair, Daphna. Nobody should live their life as if each day will be their last."

"What did she tell you about my father?"

He hesitated for an instant. "Only what she told you. One day she planned to give you the whole story."

"When?"

"She didn't say."

From the sound of his voice, Daphna felt he was hiding

something that Yael had told him, something she didn't know, but grief had sapped her will to pursue it. "It's too late now," she mumbled softly.

He shook his head. Her pain was his pain. He was sorry he couldn't help her.

"Maybe I'll go to Russia and look up your family," she said.

"I've got no family there," he replied softly.

"What happened to your parents?"

"Dead. Both of them."

With horror, she imagined his parents dying from years of forced labor in a Siberian work camp.

He looked at her gently. "Like you, I'm an orphan."

At Ben Gurion Airport, she grabbed her bag, resting between them in the front of the pickup. As she was about to jump out and head into the terminal, he reached under the seat and handed her a small box. "A present for you," he said.

"What's this?" she asked, surprised.

"Open it."

Inside was a beautiful miniature chess set with the chessmen carved from ivory and onyx. "It's the one we played with last night," she said.

He nodded. "I want you to have it."

She was taken aback. "But it's your favorite. You said it was hand-carved in the time of Czar Nicholas II. It's the most valuable thing you brought when you came to Israel. I couldn't possibly take it."

He looked at her beseechingly. "Please, it would mean a great deal to me."

She searched his dark eyes. He was a nice man, this Russian. In the last year as she had gotten to know him, she had come to like him. Then she looked down at the chess set.

"I'll take it under one condition," she finally said.

"What's that?"

"You'll come to Paris and play chess with me there."

"Or you'll bring it back to the kibbutz, and we can play

here." She looked stricken. "Paris is fine. And in Queens, too," he added quickly.

"You've been watching too much American television," she said, trying to mimic his words and tone from a few minutes ago.

He laughed. "Go, or you'll miss your plane."

She tucked the chess set into her bag and hugged him.

He sat there and watched her walk away. She looked so much like her mother. Not just her face and the long blond hair, but the tall, thin figure that moved gracefully through the crowds milling in front of the terminal. She also had her mother's peculiar distance. He had known Yael so well, and sometimes he thought he hadn't known her at all.

A cop came over and tapped on the windshield of the pickup. "Let's go. Move on."

Driving back to the kibbutz from Ben Gurion Airport, David felt a gaping emptiness. The visit to Yael's grave and the painful ride with Daphna had left him depressed.

He had loved Yael so much. Three years they had lived together as husband and wife. Three years—that was all. The best three years of his life, but so little time. What a shame. He knew that he should be grateful for those years, but he couldn't. He was sorry there weren't more. Sorry that she got on that bus. Sorry he didn't get to Israel earlier. Sorry that . . .

Ah, what was the use? He had gone through all of that over and over again, grieving and crying for an entire month after her death, unable to think, unable to work, unwilling to eat. Then his grief had turned to cold fury and a desire for revenge. He wanted to know who was responsible for the attack, and if the legal system couldn't impose punishment, then he would find a way himself.

Repeatedly, he had gone to Jerusalem seeking information, but to no avail. The most that Shin Bet or the Mossad had established was that the perpetrators came from outside of Israel and PLO-controlled territory. Polite bureaucrats had said, "We're still working on the case. We'll let you know if we have a breakthrough." But they never did.

During this awful time, the members of the kibbutz consoled and supported him, while always leaving him distance to mourn. The kibbutz was a community—an entity greater than himself, not perfect by any means, populated by people with egos and petty jealousies like any other society, but still something that on balance made life for him worthwhile. He had come to respect these people and their way of life. He was grateful that it was now his life as well.

What had surprised him was how these gruff kibbuzniks, most of whom had spent their entire lives on Bet Mordechai, had been willing to accept him as a newcomer. Perhaps it reflected the measure of their love and regard for Yael. But he'd earned some of it on his own. As director of the High-Tech Center of the kibbutz in the last two years David had developed a computer software package for the automotive industry. He had already entered into a million-dollar-plus contract with Ford in Detroit. In the last six months, he had met with Toyota officials twice in Japan and Renault once in Paris. He was pessimistic about his chances with the French company, but Toyota was close to signing a two-million-dollar deal. That would mean a new dining room and maybe even a new swimming pool for the kibbutz.

At the next exit, he turned off the highway, and onto the pitted blacktop road that led into the kibbutz. Bouncing along in the pickup, he passed the litchi trees that had been retained when orange and grapefruit groves had been destroyed for economic reasons, because of cheaper product flowing into western Europe from Spain and Brazil. Litchi, persimmon and other exotic fruits still found a lucrative market.

The road went up a hill. He passed the old kibbutz swimming pool, constructed on a small mound. In front, a magnificent view spread out before him. He could see the rest of northern Israel and well into southern Lebanon; to the right rose the rugged Golan Heights.

He parked the pickup in front of the main administration building—the original wooden structure that marked the beginning of the kibbutz in 1952. He walked across the dusty center courtyard to the spanking new cinder-block building that housed the High-Tech Center.

Pushing open the door, he nodded to Batya, who doubled as a secretary/receptionist. Curt as usual, and without so much as a greeting, she announced, "Gideon was here. He wants to see you. He said go right to his office. Nowhere else."

David found Gideon, the director of security of the kibbutz, sitting behind a battered wooden desk in the security building, another makeshift shed twenty yards from the administrative building. He was reading the morning paper when David walked in. A founding member of the kibbutz, who had fought in Israel's wars in 1948, 1956 and 1967, Gideon was well into his seventies.

David had grown fond of the wizened old character with creased, leathery skin and a mop of brown hair that stubbornly refused to turn gray. His mind was as sharp as a tack, and he loved telling stories about the country in the good old days. Gideon was also a fabulous chess player, and though David had improved noticeably in the last year while playing with him, he still hadn't won a single match against the security director.

Despite his wooden leg, the result of an Egyptian land mine in the Mitla Pass in June 1967, Gideon got up immediately when David walked in.

"You've got a visitor," Gideon said. "He's waiting in the administration building."

"A foreign customer?" David asked hopefully.

"No, a police detective from Haifa."

David's immediate thought was of Paris and Maria's death after their dinner at Arpege. She must have told someone she was having dinner with him, and the French police had asked the Israelis to interrogate him, as a prelude to requesting his extradition.

With Gideon, he decided to tough it out. David looked puzzled. "Well, I was driving fast this morning. They must have picked me up on the radar."

"No, it's not that."

"What, then?"

"He insisted on telling you himself. He wants to talk to you alone."

David smiled. "But surely you dragged something out of him?"

Gideon nodded. "But of course."

"And?" David held his breath.

"All he would say is that it has to do with somebody stealing dental records from Dr. Elon."

"In Haifa?"

"Yeah."

The news hit David like a sledgehammer blow to the stomach. His mouth went dry, and his heart began to race.

Then quickly he gathered all of the inner strength he could muster. Don't panic, he told himself. Don't show even a hint of concern. Gideon's smart, very smart, and the policeman may be as well. Gideon's also tied into Shin Bet and the Mossad. You've been here only four years. They still regard you as a foreigner. They won't care what you say. They'll be watching to see how you say it.

This day had to come. You knew it would. You trained yourself to deal with it. Now do it.

Gideon was staring at David. He was his friend, and yet he was still the director of security for the kibbutz. The next few seconds would be critical.

"I plead guilty," David said, his face lighting up with a smile.

"Guilty?"

"Yeah. I stole my dental records so that sadist won't remember I'm a patient. He won't be able to send me any of those notices to remind me it's time for him to start drilling my teeth again."

Gideon pretended to chuckle. He was a bad actor.

"I know why you're laughing," David said, playing along.

"Yeah, why's that?"

"He's taken out every one of your teeth already. He can't do anything else to you."

"That is certainly true." Gideon opened his mouth to show a gaping hole on the right side.

David left the security building and walked slowly across

the courtyard to Administration, trying to appear calm. He didn't dare turn around. He could feel the eyes boring into the back of his head. Gideon was watching him through the window.

David knew immediately that, unlike Gideon, the detective wouldn't even pretend to laugh. He was an intense-looking man in his late thirties, who spoke Hebrew with a South African accent, David deduced. He was dressed casually in a white shirt open at the neck and khaki slacks. His face was dominated by heavy brown-framed glasses with Coke-bottle-thick lenses and a high forehead that gave way to thinning mud brown hair.

He had commandeered an office, and he asked David to sit across the desk from him. In front of the detective was a steaming mug of coffee.

David knew that the detective would do the interview by the book. And he did, first pointing at a tape recorder that he turned on, then introducing himself as Ephraim Goldberg, with a dour expression on his face. He crisply stated the time and date, carefully writing it down in a bound notebook. David decided he'd better play it serious. This wasn't Gideon he was dealing with.

"Please state your name."

"David Ben Aaron."

"And how long have you lived in Israel, sir?"

David suppressed a smile. Surely, Goldberg had obtained the information from the central police records. "Approximately four and a half years."

"And before that?"

"I lived in Moscow, where I was born."

"Occupation in Russia?"

"Computer engineer."

"And your last position of employment?"

"With Novosti Chemical Company in Moscow."

"Where did you live when you first came to Israel?"

"On an Ulpan in the Negev."

"Which one?"

"Ha'emek."

"Then you moved to this kibbutz?"

"Correct. About four years ago I met a woman who was a member of this kibbutz. We were married, and a short while after that I moved here."

"And your wife? Does she still live on the kibbutz?"

The idiot was either grossly insensitive, or he hadn't done his homework. David forced himself to reply calmly. "A year ago she was killed on bus eighteen in Jerusalem. You remember, the suicide bomb."

Goldberg was human after all. He looked down at his hands. "I'm sorry," he said weakly. "I had a friend on that bus as well. He didn't die, but I'm not sure that was a blessing."

The detective suddenly remembered the tape recorder and looked abashed for his outburst. "What kind of work do you do here on the kibbutz?"

"I'm the director of the kibbutz's High-Tech Center. We've developed a new computer software package that provides twenty basic safety checks on an automobile each time the ignition is turned on, and alerts the driver if there's a problem. Ford successfully tested the program in Detroit, and we've already received a large contract from them."

"Are you dealing with any other foreign companies?"

Instinctively, David decided to omit Renault. Even a moderate degree of checking with Paris might turn up Maria's death on the same day she had met with him. But what if the detective already knew about Maria?

Watching him closely, David responded, "I've had an initial meeting with Toyota in Japan, but so far no contract."

Goldberg didn't react but moved on. "Have you used Dr. Elon in Haifa as a dentist?"

"Yeah. Everybody at the kibbutz does. We have a contract with him."

"Have you ever used any other dentists in Israel?"

"No." David decided a lack of humor at this point might make the detective suspicious. "Finding dentists to drill my teeth isn't one of my great joys in life. One is quite enough, thank you."

Goldberg didn't crack a smile.

"Can I ask you what this is all about, Detective?"

"There was a break-in at Dr. Elon's office last evening about nine P.M. Some dental records were stolen. Where were you?"

"Here. In the kibbutz dining room. My stepdaughter flew home for her mother's unveiling. The kibbutz had a small ceremony remembering Yael—that was her name. It was taking place at nine o'clock. Anyone from the kibbutz can verify that story."

David waited for Goldberg to finish writing. Then he asked, "I assume that my records were among those stolen?"

Goldberg stared coldly at him. "They were the only ones taken."

Having been afraid to ask, David was glad Goldberg had volunteered the information. He felt his heart thumping, but he looked at Goldberg with a bewildered expression.

"Why would anyone be interested in my dental records?"

"That's what we'd like to know. And why yours alone? Any ideas?"

Looking mystified, David shook his head. Running through his mind, though, was the thought: whoever did this was a rank amateur. He didn't even have the sense to steal a score of records, including mine.

"You have any suspects?" he asked gingerly.

"I can't tell you that," the detective replied.

David felt his life unraveling in front of his eyes.

When the detective left, Gideon didn't say anything to David about the visitor. As David expected, he waited until they were playing chess that evening.

"So what happened with the Haifa detective?" Gideon asked fifteen minutes into the game, right after he surprised David by taking a rook.

"Trying to break my concentration?"

"You're so far behind, it doesn't matter whether you concentrate or not."

David recounted for Gideon everything that had happened in the interview.

When he was finished, Gideon said, "The police don't have any suspects yet. Goldberg told me that. But why would somebody want your dental records?"

David shrugged.

"And why only your records?"

"Goldberg asked the same question. It's been going through my mind all afternoon."

"And?"

"I have no idea. Maybe the thief mixed my name up with someone else. He could have pulled out the wrong records. After all, David Ben Aaron is not an uncommon name."

Gideon stroked his chin thoughtfully and gazed at David, then down at the chess board.

"Perhaps," he finally said.

David knew that Gideon wasn't convinced.

"We close in ten minutes," the owner of a small café near Jaffa Gate in the Old City of Jerusalem said to his only patron, a young olive-skinned Israeli who had been nursing a cup of coffee for the last hour.

Kourosh nodded to the owner and checked his watch. It was ten minutes to one, almost time for him to be leaving. He reached into his pants pocket to examine one more time the small handwritten map he had been given in Rome, but he changed his mind. There was no need for that. He had the route fully memorized.

He picked up his navy blue windbreaker and put it on. He flattened down the dental records in a side pocket to make them less obtrusive, to avoid any questions from police he might encounter. Then he gave the owner a ten-shekel note and quietly left.

The cobblestone pedestrian pathways of the Old City were well lit as he started in the direction of the Jewish Quarter. The recently renovated and restored buildings had a bizarre old-new look as the bright helium lights reflected from the Jerusalem stone. Acting as if he were going home,

Kourosh nodded to a security policeman who examined him casually, holding an Uzi at his side. The policeman looked bored, cursing his luck for drawing the graveyard shift.

Three blocks later, Kourosh glanced over his shoulder. The policeman was looking the other way. Kourosh quickly darted to the left and walked swiftly along the narrow road which led to another world—the dark and winding alleyways of the Muslim Quarter. He slowed his pace, not wanting to make a wrong turn, fearful that someone would jump out of one of those closed buildings and attack him.

Shops were boarded up for the night, but the pungent smell of spices, cooked lamb and overripe melons lingered in the air. Homes were shuttered. The streets were deserted except for a scrawny old dog who sniffed at Kourosh briefly, lost interest and headed away. From one second-floor window he heard Arab music. From another, the cries of a baby. He was terrified of being alone here at night; his heart began to thump and his knees wobbled. He was looking around so much that he stumbled on the uneven cobblestones, tripped and skinned his knee. Still, he pushed on, following in his mind the route he had committed to memory, convinced that he could save his parents, that he could get them out, that he could do for them what they had done for him.

He wasn't an observant Jew, but with fear came mumbled prayers. He walked up an inclined cobblestone alley. The map had said it was a right turn at the first alley. That put him into a tiny dead-end path that was almost pitch dark. He looked at the numbers on the buildings. Number seven was the third building on the right, as the map had said.

It had an old battered wooden door, with blue peeling paint. He knocked three times, as they had told him. His whole body was shaking as he waited for someone to answer. What if no one was here? What if . . .

Suddenly, the door opened, and strong, grimy arms pulled Kourosh inside an entrance hall lit by only a single candle. The door was quickly closed behind him. Two men dressed in the style of Arabs of East Jerusalem, with their standard head covering and graying beards, were watching him carefully. One said in Persian, "Did you bring the dental records?"

Kourosh reached into the pocket of his windbreaker, removed a brown envelope and handed it over. The man took the envelope, moved over close to the candle and studied the contents. Then he nodded with approval.

"When will they be released?" asked Kourosh nervously.

Those words were the last he ever uttered. The other man grabbed Kourosh around the head and mouth to keep him from screaming and then drove a sharp knife into the young man's chest again and again.

When Kourosh's body stopped convulsing, they kicked him outside into the alley and raced away.

CHAPTER 3

Israelis compulsively read newspapers. Journalists, encouraged by their large and engaged audience, respond with diligent and aggressive reporting. Psychiatrists frequently speculate about why the tiny country leads the world in published newspapers per capita. It's free press carried to an extreme.

So from the time of his interview with Detective Goldberg, David had searched the three largest national dailies—*Ha'aretz, Ma'ariv* and *Yediot Aharonat*—for any information about the theft of his dental records. He hoped to find bits of evidence that the Haifa police had leaked purposefully or accidentally. The day of the interview with the Haifa detective, he hadn't seen anything at all in the newspapers. But the next morning, another grisly story dominated the front page of *Ha'aretz*. As he sat reading the newspaper with a cup of coffee in the kibbutz dining room, David's level of anxiety was rising fast.

There in the center of the front page was a picture of a good-looking young man with dark hair from Haifa. Underneath was an article that identified him as Kourosh Hareri. His dead body, stabbed a dozen times, had been found late the night before in a narrow alley in Arab East Jerusalem. Despite Arab protests, the area had been sealed off, and a door-to-door search was under way. So far the police had no suspects.

Inside the newspaper was a profile of Kourosh. He had been twenty-eight years old and employed as a clerk at Bank Hapolim in Haifa. When he was twelve years old, immediately after the fall of the Shah, he had come to

Israel from Iran by himself. His father had owned and operated a bank in Tehran. They were among the affluent upper class, including some Jews, who had waited too long to escape from the country. Once the Ayatollah's people slammed shut the doors to the outside world, Kourosh's parents knew that they had no chance of getting out. So they concentrated all of their efforts, and what jewelry and other possessions they had been able to conceal, toward smuggling Kourosh, their only child, across the border into Turkey. According to the newspaper, the police had no idea what Kourosh was doing in East Jerusalem late last night.

David studied Kourosh's picture and shook his head sadly. Suddenly, he became aware of Gideon sitting down across the table with a cup of coffee in his hand.

"A gruesome story, isn't it?" Gideon said.

"What would he be doing there late at night."

"Did you know the boy?"

Startled, David said, "Why do you ask that?"

Gideon hesitated. "Well, I thought with him living in Haifa and so forth . . ."

"C'mon, Gideon, don't play games with me. What does 'and so forth' mean?"

Gideon coughed, clearing his throat. "I got a call from a friend of mine with the Haifa police department. After Kourosh's body was found with his wallet in his pocket, they searched his apartment. They found notes he had made for himself and other materials indicating that he was the one who stole your dental records from Dr. Elon's office, but they couldn't find the records anywhere. Isn't that peculiar?"

David's face remained cold and unemotional, but his mind was churning. So whoever had put Kourosh up to the theft had killed him after he handed off the records. David wasn't surprised that they had decided to eliminate Kourosh as a witness. He was of no more use to them, and it was safer that way. What David found mind-numbing was that someone wanted his dental records badly enough to kill for them.

"What do you think of all that?" asked Gideon.

"I have no idea. East Jerusalem is a rough neighborhood for a Jew at night."

Gideon's eyes narrowed. "Wait, it's more complicated than that. The Mossad has taken over the case."

David considered the implications of what Gideon had just said. In Israel, the police and Shin Bet handle domestic security issues. The Mossad gets involved only if there's a foreign component.

"The Mossad?" David asked incredulously.

"It seems that Kourosh flew to Rome last week on a sudden one-day round trip. From the available evidence in the boy's apartment, he apparently was promised that his parents would be released and flown to Israel if he provided someone with your dental records. Isn't that something?"

Knowing that Gideon was close with Mossad people whom he had commanded in the army, David was surprised that he was divulging this much information about the evidence. Then the reason came to him: The Mossad had deputized Gideon to tell him these facts and to gauge his reaction, before he had a chance to digest the news or to develop a response. David decided communications were a two-way street. He would use Gideon as well.

"Look, Gideon," David said slowly, staring squarely at the director of security, "I've thought about this a great deal. The explanation I gave you the other night has to be right. David Ben Aaron is a common name in Israel. Whoever organized this effort mixed me up with another David Ben Aaron. If I were the Mossad, I'd be checking out all of the other David Ben Aarons in the country."

"That's a possibility," Gideon snarled, and he walked away.

David sat at his computer in the High-Tech Center trying to work, but he couldn't concentrate. Distraught, he kept thinking about Kourosh.

He remembered the knapsack under his bed. There was no point trying to use it now. Gideon had stationed himself in front of the door of the High-Tech Center. For the time being, escape from the country was impossible. He had no choice but to tough it out.

He looked up at the clock on the wall. It was already five minutes after ten. The Mossad bureaucracy must be cumbersome these days. He had expected them an hour ago.

They arrived fifteen minutes later—two strapping young men in their twenties. One clean-shaven, the other with a sandpaper beard. After they had shown him their identification, the bearded one told him harshly, "We'd like you to come to Jerusalem for questioning." In the car, they didn't talk. They were the pickup and delivery team. The clean-shaven one drove; the sandpaper beard was in the back with David. He made no effort to conceal the gun in his shoulder holster.

They drove toward Jerusalem, as David expected. After riding about an hour, when they were still about ten miles from the capital, they pulled off the highway onto an unmarked gravel road that led back into the hills. At the end of the road David saw a small three-story structure built with Jerusalem stone during the British occupation. A high barbed-wire–topped chain-link fence surrounded the building. At the checkpoint where the gravel road passed through the fence, their car paused for a second before one of the three armed guards quickly waved them through.

David thought about asserting his legal rights—the right to counsel, the right to appear before a magistrate and so forth—but he brushed those aside. As he had learned in the last few years, Israel has no written constitution. Emergency regulations for dealing with security issues imposed by the British before 1948 were still in place, and they gave governmental authorities wide latitude in dealing with suspects, even citizens.

Before getting out of the car, the man in the backseat asked David to put his hands behind his back, and he clamped on a pair of handcuffs. David smiled faintly. They know I won't try to escape. They're trying to intimidate me, to make me feel vulnerable.

The two men led him up the stairs to a third-floor room that had two wooden chairs and nothing else. One was empty. In the other sat a large, powerfully built man with a blond crewcut, bloodshot gray eyes and a pug nose. He was in his forties, David guessed. Probably a high-ranking official if he was still with the Mossad at that age.

In one hand he held a hard rubber police baton. The windows were open, and olive trees fluttered outside in a gentle breeze. It wouldn't matter what sounds came from the room. No one would hear them.

Keep calm, David told himself. Don't show fear. Never show fear.

The driver pushed David into the empty chair and said, "We'll be outside, Yosef. Call us if you need us."

More intimidation. David didn't smile this time. He decided to go on the offensive. "Why am I here?"

Yosef sneered, "Because you killed Kourosh Hareri. But you don't need me to tell you that."

David managed to conceal his surprise. That wasn't the answer he had been expecting. He thought they would focus on why his dental records had been stolen. He wondered if this Yosef really believed the murder charge, or whether it was part of the intimidation routine to get him to talk. But then a terrible thought flashed into his mind: the Mossad had had a couple of serious embarrassments in recent months, which were being widely discussed throughout the country. Would they charge him with Kourosh's murder and try to make it stick? A quick arrest would repair their public image. David could feel a knot in the pit of his stomach.

"But I didn't kill Kourosh Hareri," he declared.

"Then where were you last evening between ten P.M. and three A.M.?"

"Asleep in my bed at kibbutz Bet Mordechai."

"Does anyone else know that?"

"I live alone."

"Then you don't have an alibi."

"I don't need an alibi."

Yosef extracted from his jacket pocket a three-by-five

black-and-white glossy photograph depicting Kourosh on the ground where he was found. He walked over and handed it to David. Then he returned to his chair while David studied this grim reminder of how cruel people could be.

"A helluva job, you did," Yosef snarled angrily.

"I didn't do it."

"You're a liar," he shouted. "We have witnesses who place you in the area at the time."

"You can't have witnesses. I wasn't there."

Yosef frowned and slapped the baton against the palm of his other hand. "We can do this the easy way or the hard way," he said. "What I want is the truth. What I want is a confession from you."

David stared back coldly, sending the message: you can beat me if you'd like, but I won't be intimidated. "I didn't kill Kourosh Hareri," he responded, "and what's more, I didn't have a motive for killing him."

"He stole your dental records. That's a motive."

"The records don't mean that much to me. I can get new X rays taken. It's not that difficult."

Yosef scowled, "A real comedian you are."

"No, I'm being serious. Why should I want them back?"

"To prevent them from falling into someone else's hands—someone who hired Kourosh to steal them."

And who the hell was that? David wanted to know. He tried to get Yosef focused on the records. "Then where are they?"

"You destroyed them after you got them back."

"Why would I do all of this in Jerusalem? Why not in Haifa?"

"To make it look like Arabs killed Kourosh."

Investigators generally share very little of their theory, but David realized that Yosef was so proud of the murder case he had constructed that he wanted to expose it to David to see if he could punch holes in it, which Yosef could later correct. This guy is a real piece of work, David thought.

Yosef rose from his chair and began slapping the baton

against his palm as he walked slowly and menacingly toward David. Watching him, David held his breath. He clenched his hands together behind his back and stiffened his body, making it easier to absorb the blows.

Yosef narrowed his eyes and stared at David harshly. He stopped about a foot away. In a threatening tone he said, "Are you ready now to confess?"

David shook his head. "I didn't do a thing."

As Yosef raised his hand with the baton, getting ready to bring it down, David kept his eyes locked with the man. The agent could strike him if he wanted to, but he would know it was a person he was beating, not an inanimate object.

Abruptly Yosef lowered his arm, turned and walked away toward one of the open windows.

He's not going to hit me, David decided with relief. He had seen enough interrogations in his lifetime, and he had learned to tell the difference. Those who got pleasure out of beating suspects did so early in the process. They couldn't wait to do it. For others, like Yosef, it was a game of intimidation and bluff. That conclusion made David feel better.

"So let's talk about your dental records," Yosef said. "Who put Kourosh up to the theft?"

"I have no idea."

"Why are you lying to me? Of course you have some idea."

David repeated the explanation he had given Gideon about many David Ben Aarons in Israel.

Yosef didn't buy it. "Don't take me for a fool. It infuriates me."

A long, heavy silence settled over the room as Yosef's hard, cruel eyes bore in on David. "I can wait all day if I have to."

David knew that he meant it.

After several moments, David took a deep breath and said, "When I was still in Moscow working as a computer programmer for Novosti Chemical Company, the Russian organized-crime gangs were just gaining power. One of the gangs approached me and forced me at gunpoint to do some work for them. They were computerizing their gambling and prostitution operation. I worked for them for about a month at nights. They paid me only a fraction of what my time was worth."

"Well?" Yosef asked impatiently.

"Then my visa for Israel came through. You know how arbitrary the Russian authorities are. You hear nothing. You hear nothing. Then one day it's just delivered to you in the mail."

Yosef nodded.

"So I worked for the gang that night, and I skimmed off some money that I needed to leave the country. Just enough for that. Far less than they should have paid me. After all, I'm no thief."

"And?"

"Anyhow, I left Moscow the next day, and of course I didn't show up for work that night. I made my way to Odessa and changed my name. Then I flew here from Odessa. Now I think they've caught up with me. They have my dental records in Moscow. To make sure it's me, they wanted to get the records here and make a match."

"But why did they use the Kourosh kid for the robbery?"

David shrugged. "Who knows? Maybe they bought him for money. After all, it's not so easy living here on a bank clerk's salary."

"And if they got a match on your dental records, you think their plan was to have someone kill you?"

"One of their members who's living in the country, helping them extend their reach to Israel."

Yosef shook his head in irritation. "You Russians are such trouble," he said contemptuously. "No other group of immigrants has been like this. I can't wait for the next generation. We'll be able to shape them up. But you people! Ech! You're as bad as those religious nuts who come here from the United States. Hundreds of you are coming here with suitcases filled with dollars that they got illegally in Russia like those gangsters you worked for. Thousands of you aren't even Jews. Thousands won't learn the language, but they want handouts from the government. You Russians will destroy this country."

Now visibly angry, Yosef pounded the baton against the windowsill. David kept quiet. He had learned that Yosef was echoing sentiments shared by many Israelis.

Suddenly, Yosef realized that David had managed to sidetrack him. He returned to the matter at hand.

"You better be telling me the truth," he said. "I have ways of checking your story. Records in Russia. Interviews with people here. This story of yours about gangsters and prostitutes better be right."

"It is. I promise you."

"But even if it is, it just helps the case against you. Then you did have a motive for killing Kourosh—to keep him from giving those dental records to the Russian thugs."

"I've told you the truth about Russia, and I didn't kill Kourosh."

"Then who did?"

"If I knew, I would have told you long ago. You think I'm enjoying this?"

"You're lying. If you confess now to the murder, you'll get a light sentence. I'll see to it."

"But I didn't kill Kourosh."

Yosef stared at him. "Enough," he barked finally, and he summoned his colleagues, who led David down four flights of stairs to a basement that had been carved into the stone. On the way down, he listened for the sounds of other prisoners, but the building appeared to be deserted. In the basement was a tiny windowless cell with a dirt floor and a hole in the ground for a toilet. The air was stifling. A single dim light was recessed into the ceiling. The men unsnapped the handcuffs and took David's wristwatch. Then they pushed him roughly into the cell and locked the door.

"Call us when you're ready to confess," one of the men shouted to David through the small barred opening.

David sat down on a wooden bench chained to the wall and evaluated his situation. Though he had hoped not to become involved, even after his dental records had been stolen, he realized how futile that hope had been. He felt his world crashing down around him.

His situation wasn't hopeless, he knew that. He had chips to play. Information he could yield to get out of this cell, but he was afraid it would land him in an even worse situation, although that hardly seemed possible right now.

He sat calmly, trying to preserve his strength. Israelis prided themselves on being more humane than other people. They would give him food and water, and if they didn't beat him or torture him today, they probably wouldn't tomorrow. As for the cell, he had been in solitary confinement before. These Israelis were no match for some of the sadistic bastards he had seen. He could survive here for a very long time. All he had to do was not self-destruct with terror or panic. Keep calm. Keep focused on something else. Something pleasant. Yael. Yes, Yael and their incredible days and nights together.

CHAPTER 4

Without his wristwatch, David had no sense of time. He hadn't been questioned since his arrival at the stone compound. He hadn't been physically touched. Guards had passed him three meals by opening the door briefly, then returning an hour later to retrieve the tray that had held his food, which was adequate—fruits, vegetable, meat, pita bread and water. He did push-ups and ran in place to keep up his strength. He slept, and he waited.

Finally, he heard the sound of two men approaching down the stairs, talking loudly to each other. From their voices he could tell that they were the two who had driven him from the kibbutz. Perhaps they were bringing him back to Yosef for another session. He tried to steel himself for the interrogation.

He heard a key in the lock, and the prison door opened wide. For an instant he had difficulty adjusting to the bright light in the corridor outside.

"We've come to release you," the sandpaper beard said. "It was all a mistake. We're sorry."

"You're sorry?" David replied.

"That's right. You can apply to the government for compensation, if you want."

David could hardly believe his ears.

In silence, the two drove him back to the kibbutz, where Gideon was waiting at the gate. Together, they walked up the dirt road, David with his twisted leg and Gideon with one wooden leg. The mid-afternoon sun was hot and unyielding.

"What happened?" David demanded to know.

"Read the newspapers. Sharansky and your Russian party kicked up a political storm, claiming that there was no evidence against you, that you were being used as a scapegoat for Kourosh's murder, and, as usual, a Russian was being blamed for everything. There was even a protest on your behalf in Tel Aviv. So they had to release you."

Gideon had said it so unenthusiastically that David replied, "You obviously thought they should continue to hold me."

"Not because I think you killed Kourosh. You didn't. I would have known if you had left the kibbutz that night."

"I appreciate your not sharing that information with the Mossad." David said sarcastically.

Gideon bristled. "Look, David, I'm responsible for security here, which is a serious matter. We're living literally in the scope of Syrian guns. Obviously there are things in your past that you're hiding. For all I know, you are a KGB agent who slipped into Israel as part of the huge wave of Soviet immigration."

"That's preposterous, and I resent your saying it. I've been a loyal member of this kibbutz. My computer programs have brought us millions of dollars in contracts."

They were approaching the center courtyard of the kibbutz.

"That's all true," Gideon replied, "but those contracts pale in the face of security concerns. I came out here to warn you. You'll find things different for you now. I want you to know that so you won't be surprised."

"What do you mean, different?"

"There was a vote taken when you were gone. Whether to expel you from the kibbutz."

David was stunned. He had done so much for the kibbutz in the short time he had been here. "I can't believe that."

"People are scared. Still, you won, but barely. So it really is in your interest to tell me the whole story. The next vote might not turn out the same way."

"I'll take my chances," David said, and he turned away from Gideon, crossing over to the High-Tech Center.

As he walked into the door of the building, Batya raised

her thin eyebrows and looked at him with a mixture of fear, concern and bewilderment.

"I'm glad you're back," she stammered. "I never thought that . . ." She left her thought hanging in the air, uncertain as to how she should finish it.

"I was a murderer," he said, completing her sentence.

She blushed. "I didn't mean that. I even voted for you."

"I appreciate that. Really I do, Batya."

As he headed back toward his office, he considered calling a meeting of the entire staff of the High-Tech Center and clearing the air with them. The difficulty was that he couldn't—or more accurately, wouldn't—answer the questions that these bright people would undoubtedly ask. And he refused to lie to them. So, reluctantly, he decided that wasn't an option.

At his desk, David looked at a blank computer screen and tried to ponder his options. Quickly, he reached one conclusion: he wouldn't sit still and wait for the next blow to come. That wasn't his nature. He was a man of action, someone who controlled his own destiny.

Lacking any better avenue, David turned back to the press. In addition to the three major Israeli daily newspapers, which referred to Kourosh's murder and the theft from Dr. Elon's office as the Dental Affair, he began reading the *International Herald Tribune* and *The New York Times,* because of the Rome connection with Kourosh.

For two days he scoured those five newspapers from one end to the other, searching for any little piece that could help him decipher the complex jigsaw puzzle someone had created.

In the meantime, he was constantly aware that his recent arrest had made him an object of suspicion among many on the kibbutz. He could sense the questions that pervaded the small community, the whispers that stopped when he approached a group of people. Some made a point of telling him that they never doubted his integrity and loyalty, but their expressions of support were forced. Others simply walked away when he approached; and he couldn't blame them. For decades, security in northern Israel had hung by a thread. The possibility of a KGB agent in their midst had to be terrifying.

On the third day, when he was reading the *International Herald Tribune* in the kibbutz reading room, he saw an announcement in the personal ad section: "Tonto seeking Lone Ranger." A London telephone number was given.

David stared at the words, tapping his fingers on the table and thinking. He read the message again. And then a third time. Was it meant for him? How could he know for sure? Reruns of American television westerns had circulated widely throughout the world for decades. Plenty of others could have used those names in referring to themselves.

And if it was intended for him, what then? Was the man who referred to himself as Tonto trying to warn him about something that was being planned by those responsible for Kourosh's theft and murder? Or was Tonto part of a scheme to flush David out and then to crush him once he was exposed? The idea of relying on Tonto made David very uncomfortable. He had no doubt that Tonto would sell him out for a string of wampum.

Yet further speculation was pointless. He was floating at sea after a shipwreck, and a rope was being offered. He had no choice but to grab for it and later find out who was holding the other end.

He'd have to be careful. He had no doubt that the Mossad was still watching him. They might not let him leave the country, and if they did, they would be certain to follow him.

David picked up the phone and dialed the London number from the newspaper. He got an answering machine with a recorded message. In English, a woman's voice said: "No one is here to take your call. Please leave your message after the beep." The accent was British. Northwest England, he guessed. Birmingham maybe. Working-class. That didn't tell him a thing. Tonto could have paid any London prostitute a few quid to record the message.

He waited for the beep and then left his message:

"The Lone Ranger will meet Tonto August 27 in Lon-

don. Time: thirteen hundred hours. Place: Green Park. The
Piccadilly side. If I'm not there, wait fifteen minutes and
return in one hour."

He felt better making this move, but he was still left with
the glaring question of how he could leave the country to
keep the commitment. After considerable thought, he decided to create an elaborate ruse, first calling Detroit to
ask his contact at Ford for a reference at Jaguar in England,
which Ford now owned. The Ford contact enabled him to
set up a Jaguar meeting in England on the 27th.

Then he walked out to the reception area in the High-
Tech Center. "Batya," he said to the receptionist, "call
the travel agent and get me an airplane ticket to London
next week on the 26th in the morning and back on the
29th."

She pulled back in surprise and puzzlement.

"Don't worry," he told her. "I'm not trying to run away
with state secrets. I have a meeting with officials of the
Jaguar Motor Company in England. Ford's given me an
introduction."

She blushed with embarrassment. "I'm sorry," she
stammered.

David smiled at her. "It's hard to act normal when you
have a killer in your midst."

"I didn't mean that."

"I know. Don't worry." His tone was kindly. He couldn't
blame her. Like many others in the tight-knit community,
she had lived here her entire life. He was the outsider Yael
had brought in. And now this.

"What about a hotel?" she asked, changing the subject.

"The Jaguar people will take care of that."

As he left the reception area, he glanced at his watch. It
was 8:35.

Back in his own office, he called the Park Lane Hotel
on Piccadilly in London.

"In on the 26th and out on the 29th," he told the reservations clerk, "and I want a room on a high floor facing
the park."

He booted up his computer and waited. At 8:50, Gideon

was standing in the doorway to his office. Fifteen minutes, David thought, not bad.

"I hear you're going to London next week," the director of security said, leaning more weight on his good leg.

"News travels fast."

"Why are you going?" Gideon demanded.

David was tempted to say none of your fucking business, but he knew how vulnerable he was. With a single phone call the Mossad could pull his passport and hold him in the country. He wanted this trip to London and the answers it could provide too badly to take the risk. In a polite matter-of-fact voice, he said, "I'd still like to make some money for the kibbutz. I have a meeting at Jaguar, in England."

Gideon coughed. "I didn't mean you shouldn't go."

"Then what did you mean?"

"I wonder if this is a good time to go with all that's happened, and it's not over yet."

"What am I supposed to do? Sit here like a clay pigeon?"

"Why not give the Mossad time to find out who killed Kourosh? Let them dispose of those people before they can get to you."

But David stubbornly refused to cancel the trip, telling Gideon that he had worked too hard to develop the new computer project. "We already sold Ford. They own Jaguar. If I get another large contract, it'll mean a new dining room for the kibbutz, and I'm determined to get it."

"I'm not saying delay indefinitely. It's a question of timing."

"Courage, Gideon," David responded. "We can't live our lives like that. We're Israelis. Normal is always our pose."

Gideon bristled. "You're lecturing me about the Israeli character?"

David forced a laugh, "Sure, but so what?"

"Where will you stay in London?"

"Oh, I don't know. Wherever the Jaguar people put me."

That was all he intended to tell Gideon. All Gideon would be able to report to Jerusalem.

* * *

David arrived at terminal three at Heathrow, where he spent a full hour wandering around in the baggage-claim area before going through customs. Then he crisscrossed the main terminal several times, darting into rest rooms and shops, before boarding a bus for terminal two. From there he took another bus to terminal four. He took the Underground into London, changing trains twice and boarding each time at the last instant. Neither time did he see anyone trying to board quickly with him. By the time he emerged from the Underground at Green Park Station and walked along Piccadilly toward Knightsbridge, he was breathing a sigh of relief, pleased that he had lost whatever tail the Mossad had sent.

It was almost seven o'clock when David got to the reception desk at the Park Lane. Room 804 had been reserved for him, facing the park, as he had requested. He remained in the room only long enough to inspect the view from the large double windows and check for bugs. Satisfied, he went back down to the lobby, purchased an international calling card and walked along Piccadilly until he found an empty red calling box. As he dialed the number in Lausanne, Switzerland, he had long ago committed to memory, he held his breath, hoping Bruno would be home.

He was relieved to hear the familiar "Yes, please," in Bruno's unmistakable French with a Swiss German accent.

David answered in French, "Bruno, it's a voice from your past."

"And your French hasn't improved."

"Should I talk in Hebrew?"

Bruno chuckled. "You could do that, but I wouldn't understand a word. So how are you, joker?"

David smiled. "Joker" had been Bruno's nickname for David. "In trouble again."

"Why did I have a feeling that was the case when I heard your voice? What can I do for you?"

"I need a contact in London. Someone who can supply me with necessities."

"Give me a minute," Bruno replied, now all business. "I'll check my little black book."

Waiting for Bruno, David glanced at the walls of the calling box. About two dozen cards had been posted—suggestive pictures of scantily clad women with phone numbers and enticing descriptions, like "hot and busty."

When Bruno came back on, he said, "Dial 171-555-8746. Ask for John and use my name. Now, what else can I do for you?"

With everything that was happening, David needed Bruno's advice. "How about buying me dinner later this week? Say Friday?"

"I'd love to. But with all of that wonderful Israeli food you've been eating, would La Rotonde in the Beau Rivage still be good enough for you?"

"That's real funny."

"I hope you'll stay at my place in Montreaux."

"I'd be delighted."

"Good. Call me with an arrival time, and I'll have Rudolph pick you up."

David's next call was to John, who answered in a cockney accent. "Empire Ticket Service. John here," he said in a cheerful voice.

"I'm a friend of Bruno's. He said you could help me."

"Anything for Bruno," he replied, now sounding tense.

"I need a Beretta with a silencer."

"Tonight?"

"Tomorrow morning will be fine."

"At ten o'clock, go to a boutique at number Ten Glen Street in SoHo called the Turtle. Ask for Clyde. When you buy a sweater, your Beretta will be packed in the box. When you're finished with it, dispose of it however you'd like. It won't be traceable."

The next morning, a perfect London summer day with a gentle breeze cooling the warm rays of the sun, the kind of a day that occurs about ten times each summer in London, David spent an hour at the Jaguar office on Berkeley Square, meeting with Richard Highsmith, whose name he had been given by a contact at Ford. Then he visited a special exhibition of Russian art at the Royal Academy Museum on Piccadilly before going to the Turtle on Glen Street in Soho, where Clyde helped him pick a sweater his stepdaughter would like. He returned to his hotel via Piccadilly, stopping at Fortnum & Mason for a jar of orange marmalade and then a cappuccino at a small shop on the street. Periodically, he glanced over his shoulder, but he didn't think he was being tailed.

It was twelve-thirty when he walked back into the Park Lane. The time for playing the tourist had ended.

At ten minutes to one, David stood in front of the window of his eighth-floor room with a pair of high-powered binoculars focused on Green Park. A row of hedges separated the park from Piccadilly, and on the far side there were four empty benches. David expected Tonto to sit down on one of them, but so far there was no sign of him. David scanned the park. Two mothers wearing light summer dresses, with babies in prams, were chatting, taking advantage of the pleasant weather. A young man and a woman in a halter top were hugging and kissing on a blanket on the grass. A midday jogger in shorts and a T-shirt ran across one of the diagonal paths that crisscrossed in the park.

He glanced at his watch and focused on those four empty benches.

At exactly one o'clock, David watched the man who referred to himself as Tonto walk slowly and cautiously along a path that led from Buckingham Palace to Piccadilly, constantly turning his head like someone being hunted. Tonto walked back and forth twice in front of the four empty benches before sitting down on one at the end. Even then his head and eyes remained constantly in motion, twitching as he looked around.

As instructed by the Lone Ranger, Tonto waited fifteen minutes, got up and left the park. David scanned the area carefully. No one followed him. David was relieved.

For the next half hour, David continued to watch the park, but he didn't see anything unusual.

*   *   *

Eight floors below, under the large Japanese flag at the Japanese Cultural Information Center, Shauel kept one eye on the entrance of the hotel and tried to look unobtrusive—always one of a spy's hardest tasks. The gray checked suit he had worn was too heavy for the day, and he was perspiring. He was also annoyed because this entire assignment was a stupid waste of time, particularly when he had planned to be on vacation with Zippora and the children in the lake district of northern England.

Suddenly, the cell phone rang in Shauel's pocket. He moved a couple of paces away from the hotel and held the phone up to his ear. As he had expected, it was Sagit in Jerusalem, and she sounded irritated.

"What's happening? You haven't called in."

"There was nothing to report."

"What do you mean, nothing?"

"He's acting like a typical tourist. He shopped and went to a museum. This whole effort is a ridiculous waste."

"Does he know you've been tailing him?"

Shauel sighed in resignation. Once Sagit had her mind set on a course, there was no turning her around. "I doubt it. I used a three-man tag team, as you suggested. It's diverting resources from other activities. The ambassador's angry at me."

"Too bad. Tell him to call Moshe. It's all been approved by the prime minister. Finding out what happened to Kourosh is now a top priority in Jerusalem."

"I was hoping I could break it off."

She snapped, "if you don't do the job right, you could end up like Yosef."

"The old man really sacked Yosef? With all of Yosef's friends in the Knesset, I couldn't believe he did it."

"Moshe's in a state these days. Heads are going to roll, and both of ours could be included. So, if you're smart, you'll stick with the subject and call me if anything happens."

Suddenly, Shauel saw David walking through the front entrance of the hotel. "Gotta run, Sagit. Subject is on the move."

*   *   *

David waited until Tonto was seated on a bench before he crossed Piccadilly to the park.

Hearing the sound of footsteps, the man on the bench shot to his feet and watched David coming closer. David reached into his pocket, pulled out a small black mask to cover the eyes, and tossed it to the startled man.

"Don't say a word," David told him softly. "Sit back down on the bench, slowly. Then we'll talk."

David waited until Tonto followed his instructions, and sat down beside him. Even though no one else was within earshot, David still whispered, "I've got a loaded Beretta in my jacket pocket. If this is a setup, whatever else happens, you're dead."

Beads of perspiration broke out on Tonto's forehead. "Jesus, Greg," he said. "I wouldn't ever have believed it was you if it weren't for the limp. How the hell'd you change yourself so much?"

"Look, Bill, this isn't a reunion, and we're not here to play twenty questions."

"But where are you living now?"

"One more question from you, and I'm out of here. I ask the questions. I want to know, who's interested in my dental records?"

Bill Fox looked puzzled. "I didn't know anyone was."

"You're lying," David replied, pushing the gun against Fox's rib cage through the cloth of his jacket.

"No, I'm not. I swear it." Fox took a handkerchief out of his pocket and mopped his forehead. As David watched him, he was struck by how different Fox looked now from five years ago. The heavy black-framed glasses were gone, replaced by contact lenses. The gray in his hair had been colored. A trim beard had been added, which Fox no doubt thought made him look debonair, although to David it looked comical. These changes made David guess that whatever else was happening, Fox had something going with a much younger woman.

"Then why did you want to see me?"

"Things are falling apart in Saudi Arabia now, just as you predicted five years ago," Fox said.

David snorted. "That's no big surprise."

"Actually, it's even worse. The country's on the verge of bankruptcy. The bills are now coming due for their recent spending binge for expensive new military equipment they can't use, and for factories that aren't functioning. The huge living stipends from the king that thousands of Saudi princes get each year are expanding exponentially." Fox slid a couple of inches along the bench, away from David and the pressure of the gun. "When the price of oil took a dip last year, they began reaching into their foreign reserves, which are nearly depleted. The Saudi king knows he's in big trouble financially. He's even stopped covering the debts of some of his close family members."

"How do you know that?"

Fox looked uncomfortable. "I just know."

"So how do the fundamentalists fit in all of this?"

"The Hezbollah terrorist leader, Mohammed Nasser, is organizing for a violent revolution similar to the overthrow of the Shah. I figure he'll move in six months or so."

David shrugged. "All of this is a real tearjerker, but don't waste your time telling me about it. Go tell them in Washington. Margaret Joyner's a lot smarter than Hugh O'Brien ever was. She should be sympathetic."

"I already tried, but I got nowhere. She included General Chambers in our meeting. I don't know how much you've followed this stuff, but your old buddy Chambers managed to persuade some of his friends in the Senate to lean on the President for Chambers's appointment as chairman of the Joint Chiefs."

David had read about Chambers's appointment in the newspaper. "Why are you surprised? He could always be a political animal if he thought it served his purposes."

"Well, he sure managed to manipulate Margaret Joyner in our meeting. I couldn't believe that she listened to him when he told her to disregard everything I was saying. Besides, she made it clear that her top priority right now, and until November 6, is President Waltham's reelection. One thing she doesn't want is a foreign policy crisis. So, I decided to place the ad in the *Herald Tribune*. It was a real long shot. I didn't know if you would even see the ad. If you did, would you remember after five years that I used to call you the Lone Ranger, and myself Tonto? Then, among the fifty or so crank calls I received, I heard a voice that sounded like yours, and the type of message you would leave."

Fox had piqued David's interest. "But why did you want to get in touch with me?"

"You're the only one I could think of who might be able to stop the fundamentalists from taking power."

David shook his head in disbelief. "That's why you went to so much trouble?"

"I have a lot of respect for you." His eyes were open wide, pleading with David for help.

What was really driving Fox? David wondered. "I'm flattered, Bill, but five years ago I was a different person in a different life. I'm not in that business anymore. I frankly don't give a rat's ass whether the American people pay three dollars a gallon for gasoline or thirty-three. I gave almost twenty years of my life to my country, and I ended up a fugitive. I don't have that many more years left, and I'd like to enjoy them as best I can."

"That's not the Greg Nielsen I remember."

"Yeah, well, lots happened to me since the bomb blew up on the American complex five years ago. You may not believe it, but it's possible to find contentment in a world not dominated by Langley. Since you came all this way to meet me, I'll give you some advice and make the trip worthwhile."

"Yeah, what's that?"

"Quit the Company yourself. You might like spending time with Alice, Ned and Mary Ann."

"It's too late for that. My marriage is history."

"Sorry to hear that." David sounded sympathetic. He remembered how broken up Fox had been when Alice refused to move to Dhahran. "But why do you care so much about what happens in Saudi Arabia? You did your job. You raised the warning flags for Washington, just as I did. If they won't listen, that's not your fault."

Fox squeezed his hands together and stared at a mother playing on the grass with a two-year-old girl with gorgeous blond ringlets. Knowing Fox, David realized there was something else here. He waited for Fox to tell him. Maybe that held the key to the theft of his dental records. All the while, his eyes darted around the park looking for anything suspicious.

Fox again wiped his forehead. David watched the sweep second hand of his watch make one complete revolution while Fox remained silent. Then David said, "You don't have to tell me, but I'm leaving."

He started to rise.

"No, don't do that," Fox said plaintively, tugging on David's arm. "Please help me."

The man was practically in tears. David sat back down. "Okay, what the hell's going on?"

"About six months ago I became friends with a Saudi woman, Princess Misha'il. She's a writer who was educated at Oxford. I figured she would be a good source for information. She's very outspoken in the country on women's issues."

"You mean, she thinks women should have lives of their own. Maybe even go out in public themselves or drive a car. Radical ideas like that?"

"Yeah, that kind of thing. She's not married, and she's the daughter of one of the king's cousins. So they tolerate her. Well, anyhow, she has a close childhood friend and relative, Jameelah, who's in a bad personal situation."

Fox hesitated.

"Go on," David pushed, his eyes scouring the park again. The young couple was still making out on the grass. The blond girl was drinking juice from a bottle. The two women rocked babies to sleep in prams while they gossiped.

"I mean, she's married to a real slimeball. She's one of his four wives. Her father forced her to marry him two years ago. He's a lot older, a fat slob, who happens to be a nephew of the king. In contrast, she's just gorgeous and intelligent, and a really decent person who—"

David interrupted him. "Jesus, Bill. You're not having an affair with this Jameelah, a married Saudi princess, are you?"

Fox squeezed the handkerchief in his hands. "We're in love," he finally said.

"Love? Are you kidding? You're out of your fucking mind." He stared hard at Fox. "If her husband finds out, his family will kill both of you just like that. They'll cut off your dick and stuff it in your mouth. Then they'll chop your head off. The women in the family will stone her. I've seen it happen." He watched Fox trembling as he spoke. "How old's this Jameelah?"

"Twenty-three," Fox said weakly.

"Well, if you really love her, break it off with her before it's too late."

Fox knew as well as David what their fate would be if her husband found out, but he had refused to break it off with her. He was almost forty, but his hormones were raging as if he were twenty. It wasn't just sex—made all the better by its forbidden character—but love, he told himself.

For Jameelah there was another component as well. She was rebelling against a society and a life in which her father had forced her as a young virgin to become the third wife of a fat middle-aged man who viewed her as his plaything for whatever he wanted. He disgusted her, and what he demanded of her sexually was loathsome. With Fox, she was making an intellectual statement, albeit a dangerous one. Saudi women should be free. But he wasn't just the vehicle for her rebellion, Fox believed. Jameelah was deeply in love with him as well. He intended to sneak her out of the country where they could be free to love each other.

"Breaking it off with Jameelah's not an option," Fox said stubbornly.

"Then what do you want with me? I'm not Ann Landers, for chrissake."

"You don't understand. If Nasser and his group stage a
fundamentalist revolution, they'll kill all the royalists. It'll
be like 1917 in Russia. They'll kill her husband and all of
his wives and children. Nasser's made that clear, and his
people are ruthless. After all, they're doing God's work.
They've got their power center in Hezbollah cells deep in
Shiite areas in the eastern part of the country, and the
Iranians are pouring in arms, money and people as fast as
they can be absorbed. It's a question of months until they
make their move to take over the country."

"You've clearly got a problem," David said.

"Please help me. Please. You're my only chance."

Fox's hands trembled as he thought about the risk he
was taking in coming to talk to Nielsen. In his Washington
meeting with Joyner and Chambers, the general, who kept
rubbing his jaw, set and reset in two long rounds of plastic
surgery, had made clear his hatred of Nielsen. With an
awful menacing look in his eyes, he had told the CIA director, "Listen, Margaret, I don't believe for one second the
CIA conclusion that Nielsen died in the Saudi desert trying
to escape. That was only your people protecting one of
your own. Now that I'm chairman of the Joint Chiefs, I'll
use the DIA to find that bastard. If he happens to be shot
trying to escape, well, that'll be a real shame." Then after
the meeting, when Fox had stopped at a bar in Georgetown
to take stock of his alternatives, an Army major on Chambers's staff had delivered a note from the general that said,
"If I ever hear that you're still involved with Greg Nielsen,
I'll make sure that Jameelah's husband finds out about
your relationship."

Fox looked at David beseechingly and continued, "You
have to understand how evil this Nasser is. He's already
been responsible for gunning down six royalists, cousins of
Jameelah's husband, in their beds and hacking up their
bodies. He's launched an attack on the American embassy
in Kuwait. He was responsible for a terrorist bomb on a
bus in Jerusalem about a year ago, last August, I'm sure
you read about it wherever you live. It killed—"

David sat up with a start, reached over and grabbed the

lapel of Fox's jacket tightly. He pulled Fox toward him. "What did you just say?"

Startled by David's burst of emotion, Fox repeated what Nasser had done.

"How do you know he was responsible for the Jerusalem bus bombing?"

"The Saudi secret police got the information during their interrogation of suspects after the murder of the six royalists."

David moved his face in close to Fox. "And they never told the Americans?"

"Nope."

"Bastards." He released his hold on Fox. "How'd you find out?"

Fox took a deep breath and looked at Greg with fear. He had never seen such hatred in a person's face. "I planted a bug in Jameelah's house with the aid of a servant whom I bribed. I wanted an early warning in case her husband found out about us. On the tape, I heard her husband talking with one of his brothers after the interrogation. They laughed and said the Jerusalem bus bombing was the only good thing Nasser ever did. Killing all those Jews."

"But now that the terror's being aimed at them, they're not so enthusiastic."

"They're scared shitless."

"Serves them right."

"But what can I do to stop the fundamentalists or to get Jameelah out of there?"

David didn't hear Fox's question. He was too consumed in his own thoughts, reliving his own grief for Yael.

"So what can I do?" Fox repeated.

"Let me think about it. When I have some information for you, I'll use the London answering machine. If there's a reference to Portland, Oregon, you'll know it's me. You got that?"

Fox nodded. "Please, Greg, you're my only hope."

David looked around as he and Fox stood up. In the far corner of the park he saw something he didn't like. A jogger in a black warm-up suit had just come through the wrought iron gates of the park and was running toward them along a diagonal cement pathway. It was too hot for a warm-up suit unless you wanted to conceal something. David watched the jogger getting closer. He had thick, curly black hair and olive skin. Suddenly, he reached into the pocket of his jacket. Out came a metallic object that sparkled in the sun.

As soon as David saw it, he pushed Fox down on the ground behind the bench. He dropped next to the dazed Fox, reaching for his Beretta at the same time. The jogger came closer and closer, raising a gun with his hand. He got off the first shot, aiming at David, but it sailed high over the bench. The mother with the blond girl screamed. The couple making out shrieked.

David raised the Beretta and aimed at the jogger, who suddenly stopped to fire another round. Before he could pull the trigger, David fired. His shot caught the jogger square in the heart. As blood oozed through the jacket of his warm-up suit, the gun fell out of his hand, and he collapsed onto the path.

More screams.

"Take off," David barked to Fox. The CIA station chief jumped to his feet and ran toward the park exit leading to Knightsbridge. David wiped his prints from the Beretta, tossed it into a trash can and ran in the other direction, toward Piccadilly Circus. By the time he heard the sound of a distant police car, he had already blended into the crowds. Slowly and calmly, he walked up to Shaftsbury, then to the left into the streets of Soho. He found a porno movie theater and settled into a seat—only one of three men in the grimy theater—close to an emergency exit.

He tuned out the moans and groans of the copulating couples and tried to evaluate his options. What bothered him was that the jogger had two possible targets, but his first shot had been aimed at David. He was the target, not Fox. Somebody had found him. It was an assassination attempt, plain and simple.

Going back to the Park Lane for his bags was dangerous. On the other hand, leaving them there and not returning to the hotel was a worse choice. It would seem suspicious and cause the hotel's management to notify the police in view of what happened.

He left the theater and wandered in the crowds along the Strand to make certain he wasn't being followed. He took a circuitous route to the Park Lane, approaching the hotel from Mayfair.

Back in Room 804, he packed his small suitcase quickly, then took one more look outside with his binoculars. The park was filled with bright lights as the police combed the grass for evidence. He scanned in every other direction, but didn't see anything suspicious—until he looked down at the sidewalk close to the hotel. There, he saw a man in a gray checked suit with a receding hairline, in his mid-thirties, David guessed. He was standing about ten yards from the hotel entrance with his eyes continually jumping from the front door to a Hebrew newspaper he was reading. Well, well. So the Mossad had finally decided to get into the game. It was about time.

With his next thought David went pale. The checked suit could have been here since yesterday. He might have seen everything David had done in the last twenty-four hours. When he had arrived at Heathrow, he had been so worried about avoiding a tail that he had overlooked the fact that if someone knew he was staying at the Park Lane ahead of time, they could easily keep tabs on him by watching the hotel. And it would be simple enough to find his hotel, though he had made the reservations himself. All they had to do was check with the Israeli phone company all outgoing international calls made from the kibbutz. How could I have been so stupid? he chided himself. But he knew the answer to that question. After five years his trade craft was rusty. Besides, he was getting too old. Spying was a young man's game.

Still, he wasn't beaten yet. From the checked suit's presence, it was obvious that the Mossad had no interest in turning him in to Scotland Yard or MI5. So, after paying his hotel bill, he walked outside the Park Lane, and went directly up to the agent, who quickly, awkwardly folded his newspaper.

In Hebrew, David said to him, "Do you work in the cultural section of the embassy or some other department?"

Though embarrassed that he had been caught, checked suit couldn't conceal a small smile. David hailed a cab, and as he expected, checked suit hailed the next cab. When David got out in the heart of crowded Trafalgar Square, he moved quickly up and down the narrow streets, packed with pedestrians, until he was certain that he'd lost the tail. To be doubly sure, he took the Underground, waited until the last second to board, and saw that the platform was deserted. By now, adrenaline was surging in his body. I may be rusty, he thought, but don't count me out.

He spent the night at a tiny bed and breakfast in Chelsea, operated by a gray-haired British spinster who must have been deaf, based upon how loud she played the telly. As he tossed in bed, waiting for her to turn the damn thing off, he developed a plan to escape from London and elude the Mossad as well as the people who had sent the jogger. He knew how the game was played. The Mossad would be watching Heathrow and Gatwick airports and checking the reservation lists of all international carriers by accessing the airlines' computers. That was always the first priority. He doubted if they had sufficient resources in England to check surface transportation as well, and he was prepared to bet that they wouldn't share their knowledge with the British authorities. So he decided that early tomorrow morning he'd be on the Chunnel train to Paris.

In the morning, as an extra precaution, he went into a local Boots drugstore and purchased a woman's blond hair dye and makeup. He took them into the men's room off the lobby in the Carlton Hotel, where he lightened his hair and made his skin pale.

Satisfied with what he saw, he took a taxi to Waterloo Station. There, he dodged around enough to convince himself no one was following him. Again, he waited until the last minute to board.

Once he was on the train, he quickly turned to the three morning newspapers he had purchased at the station. Not surprisingly, the shootout in Green Park was the lead item in all three. The dead man was identified as an Iranian national, but that was all. Scotland Yard said it had no suspects.

Weary from yesterday's encounter with Fox and the nameless Iranian, and having been up much of the night because of that stupid telly, David fell sound asleep as soon as the train started to move.

CHAPTER 5

As David slept on his way to Paris, a sleek two-hundred-foot luxury yacht, custom-built by the Dutch company Feadship and named *Predator,* pulled away from its moorings in the harbor of St. Tropez and moved out into the sparkling Mediterranean. Four burly men from what had once been French West Africa, armed with Uzis, stood on the upper deck beside an Aerospatiale Alouett III, tethered to a helipad. Their eyes darted back and forth as the *Predator* gained speed. On the sundeck, Jacqueline Blanc, the president of Petroleum de France, one of the largest privately owned companies in the country, dressed in a skimpy Versace bikini that showed off her remarkably good figure for the age of sixty-one, put down her espresso cup and impatiently eyed the lawyer, adorned in a dark blue suit and tie. "I want this Greg Nielsen," she said sharply, "and I want him now. Yesterday, to be more precise."

Victor Foch took a deep breath and watched Madame Blanc, as she insisted on being called, gently touch her dyed black hair tied up tightly in a bun, with every hair in place as it always was, even on a boat at sea. He had represented Madame Blanc and PDF for more than twenty years. Though she paid him handsomely, he didn't like her. He doubted if anyone did. Still, he had a great deal of respect for her, and he knew that she was never to be underestimated. In the war her parents, both Catholics, had bitterly divided over politics and survival. Her father joined the Vichy government and was ultimately executed by De Gaulle's forces after the war. Her mother took little Jacqueline and joined the resistance, conducting hit-and-run attacks against the Nazi occupiers. A month before D-Day, the Germans caught her mother and made Jacqueline watch while they tortured and killed her. After the war Claude Dessault, one of her mother's colleagues in the Resistance, who became a confidant of General De Gaulle and ultimately finance minister in the French government, adopted her and became her mentor. She grew up hearing about the new France and its vibrant economy. He made certain that she attended the Sorbonne, where she studied economics. After that, she earned an MBA at Wharton. Once she completed her education, Dessault used his contacts to aid her rapid rise to the position of a powerful industrialist. Throughout her business career she had gone to great lengths to keep her name out of the media, but Madame Blanc was both feared and revered in top French economic circles.

Victor was used to her demands, but he still insisted on giving her advice. Whether she followed it or not was a different matter.

"Let's talk about Greg Nielsen," Victor said. "I don't think it's a good idea to include him."

She sneered at him with annoyance. She didn't like anyone questioning her decisions. "Why not?"

"Because we won't be able to depend on him."

"What makes you say that?"

Victor reached into the black leather briefcase resting on the deck, set the numbers on the combination lock and snapped it open. With long, thin fingers he pulled out a blue bound folder and clutched it possessively in his hand.

Victor said, "It's a complete dossier on Greg Nielsen from his birth in Aliquippa, Pennsylvania, to what he was doing last week. We even found the cause of that limp, that distinctive walk of his that allowed Khalid to spot him in Paris. In high school he was playing American football, and a big player from someplace called Beaver Falls landed on his right leg during his senior year. That injury kept him out of the war in Vietnam, though he tried to enlist."

"Did you also cover the facts about his battle with General Chambers five years ago?"

"Absolutely. They were drawn from the secret report of the Senate Intelligence Committee that Margaret Joyner then chaired. I obtained a copy from a Senate staffer, and I've had a psychiatrist look at it. He confirmed professionally my instinct that Nielsen's not a team player and that we won't be able to depend on him even if, and it's a big if, we can get him on board."

She held out her hand. "Let me have the report, Victor. I'll form my own opinion."

Reluctantly, he handed her the folder, then watched while she lit up a Cohiba cigar and read the document. He was hoping to see a frown in her face that showed she agreed with him. Together, they had developed a plan so daring and brilliant that he could barely restrain his excitement. And now, just because that Arab had accidentally spotted a man who walked with a bad leg in Paris, they were about to put the entire plan at risk.

When she finished reading, she tossed the report back to Victor.

"Well?" he asked, hoping for agreement.

"This Daphna, the stepdaughter, is a valuable pawn for us." Her voice was cold as steel. To her Daphna wasn't a person. She was an object to be used. "He's soft on her because he's transferred his love for the mother to the daughter. And the best part is that we can easily get to her in Paris."

He was sorry that he had included any mention of Daphna in the report. Predictably, it had only served to whet her appetite. "Somehow I knew you'd pick up on his relationship with Daphna."

"Well, the man has obviously worked hard to create a new life for himself," she said in a matter-of-fact tone, "and now we're going to destroy it."

"We don't have to do that, you know. There's another option. Ignoring Nielsen and moving ahead."

"That's not an option. Colonel Khalid wants him, and that decides it for me. At least for now."

"But what can he really contribute?"

She leaned forward, pressing her forefinger hard against

Victor's chest for emphasis as she responded. "Khalid says, and we've confirmed, that Nielsen developed and installed the computerized security system at the king's palace in Riyadh five years ago when he was still with the CIA."

"But they must have changed it ten times since with developments in technology."

"Khalid says no. He says the Saudis aren't like the West that way. They're not continually updating their systems. They follow the third world approach of installing a system and leaving it in place. If we can neutralize that system before an attack, casualties will be lighter and the whole operation will go that much easier."

"Why do you care about their casualties? Suppose Khalid loses ten thousand men in an attack on the palace. Big deal."

She was losing patience with Victor. "Personally, I don't care," she replied sharply. "But for now my main objective is to keep Khalid happy. He's always been a reluctant partner. If he walks on us, we have nothing. Don't ever forget that," she said, showing total contempt for Victor and his obvious lack of intelligent analysis. "We lose a deal worth an absolute minimum of $500 million per year for several years. We're talking about billions of dollars. And you're getting a five percent cut. So my conclusion is that we get Nielsen on board; we use him for our purposes; we watch him carefully; and when we're finished with him we dispose of him."

She tossed the barely smoked Cohiba into the water to illustrate her point.

Victor knew it was hopeless. Stubbornly, he persisted. "It won't be easy to get him to work with us. You know that?"

"That's why I pay you so much money. To do the hard things. If you can't do this for me, I'll have to find somebody else who will, and rethink our relationship." She paused for a moment, letting her words sink in. "Now," she added, "how quickly can you get him to join us?"

Victor frowned. "One of the pieces is already in place, the Israeli dental records. I can move up on the other one right now."

"Then do it!"

"Do you want to know the details?"

"That's your job. Just get it done, and as soon as possible."

Victor gave a deep sigh of resignation. Having anticipated her decision, he pulled the cell phone from his jacket pocket and punched in the Washington telephone number he had memorized. "You may proceed with the transaction," he said in English for the tape on the telephone answering machine.

"And one other thing," Madame Blanc said to Victor in a threatening voice.

"What's that?" he asked nervously.

"I'll be very unhappy if anything happens to Greg Nielsen before our operation takes place." She reached over and grabbed the front of Victor's shirt just below his neck, pulling it tightly. "I'll hold you personally responsible. Do you understand?"

"Clearly," Victor replied, gripping his deck chair with white knuckles.

He wondered if she had learned that he had attempted to arrange Greg's execution at Maria Clermont's house. This Greg Nielsen was clever. He had somehow managed to escape and kill Maurice, an experienced hit man, in the process. Victor knew that he had been taking a risk, trying to kill Greg Nielsen, but from the minute he had learned about Khalid's request to include Greg Nielsen, he had been worried about the success of their operation. All of his instincts told him that this Greg Nielsen would somehow wreck their plan, although he wasn't sure how. In view of what Nielsen had done to Maurice, Victor was even more worried. But he didn't dare try again. Not after what Madame Blanc had just said. He would have to follow orders and get Greg Nielsen on their team. No matter how much he detested the idea.

Clint Merrifield drove cautiously across the 14th Street Bridge from Washington to Alexandria, Virginia, watching the headlights in the rearview mirror. Tonight's job was simple enough, and yet something about it bothered him. He couldn't put his finger on it, but after five years of doing burglaries and murders for hire, he had developed a sixth sense that told him which jobs shouldn't be taken because they could go south on him. Tonight's was like that.

The trouble was, the money was so good: $100,000 all in cash. The bald-headed man with the bushy brown beard had already given him twenty this afternoon. And he was looking to get out of the business, to go back home, on down to Durham, and start being a father and a husband again. With this hundred thousand clams, he wouldn't have to work again for a while, and that would suit Dee just right.

Following a gray van, he drove past National Airport and entered Old Town. At Queen Street he turned left, parked about two blocks away from Dr. Walter's office and climbed out of his car. It was a few minutes before midnight, and the street, filled with small redbrick three-story town houses, a combination of private homes and small professional offices, was deserted. It had rained about an hour ago and would rain again soon. The air was damp and heavy. Police cars routinely cruised the area, and, fearful he would stand out in this rich shiny-ass district, he told himself, "Walk fast but not too fast." He wanted to get off the street as soon as possible.

The next building on his left had a sign in front that said DR. FREDERICK WALTER D.D.S. Merrifield knew a little about real estate prices in the Washington area, and he concluded this was a high-rent area for a dentist's office. That fucker must have a lot of rich patients, Merrifield decided.

At their meeting this afternoon the bald-headed man had told him about the layout of the building and even provided a drawing. Merrifield had quickly decided to go in through a ground-floor window in the back. He slipped on a pair of thin black leather gloves and tested the window. The lock would give way with just a moderate degree of pressure. Before going in, he studied the security system through the uncovered windows. He saw nothing on the windows, but there were floor motion sensors. He went in quickly through the window, stood still and took out an electronic neutralizing device with a laser beam. He aimed it at the motion sensor, deactivating the entire security system.

The building was deserted, but from habit, he moved stealthily, on the toes of his rubber-soled shoes. The bald-headed man had told him that the dental records would be behind the receptionist's desk just inside the front door of the town house. Merrifield took a flashlight from his pocket as he walked in that direction.

The information was accurate. Behind the receptionist's desk, he found three rows of gunmetal gray file cabinets. None of them was locked. He found a drawer labeled N–O. Inside that drawer, he scanned the dental records of patients until he found what he was looking for: Gregory Nielsen. It contained an entire manila folder, with X rays and everything. Merrifield folded it up and stuffed it into the pocket of his leather jacket. In a matter of seconds, he was out of the building and back onto the deserted sidewalk.

From Alexandria, he drove across the bridge and into Washington, then north and west through Rock Creek Park. It was raining hard, with bursts of thunder and lightning. As he drove cautiously, he decided that he had been wrong about this job. It was a piece of cake. Easiest big money he'd made in a long time. Just past the Broad Brand Road cutoff, he saw a sign that said PICNIC GROVE NUMBER 16. He pulled off the road and drove toward a small parking lot in a clump of trees. The rain had tapered off to a light drizzle. He turned off his head lamps and parked.

The bald-headed man with the bushy brown beard was wearing a bulky black raincoat. Standing next to his own car, holding a large black umbrella over his head, he looked at his watch.

"You're late," he said. "I expected you half an hour ago."

"The weather. Traffic."

The man grunted. "Do you have what I want?"

"You bet."

Merrifield handed the man the manila folder and watched while he put down the umbrella and examined the records with a flashlight. As he looked, he nodded with approval.

"Now my money," Merrifield said softly. His hand moved close to his jacket pocket, where he had a small pistol concealed. Once, about three years ago, somebody had stiffed him after he completed a job. He had shot the man. It never happened again. Maybe people in the market for his services had their own network.

The man opened his car door, reached in and extracted a brown envelope from the front seat, which he tossed to Merrifield. "There's eighty K in the envelope. Count it if you'd like."

"I will," Merrifield said. He took out his flashlight and set it in place on the hood of his car. Then he began running his hands over the bills—all hundreds. As he counted, he kept looking up at the other man. But for a split second, Merrifield's eyes rested longingly on the money.

The man reached into the pocket of his raincoat and pulled out a black gun with a silencer. Instinctively, Merrifield dropped the money and dove for cover behind his car, going for his own gun. But he was too late. The first shot caught him in the back between his shoulder blades. Merrifield bounced off the car and hit the ground. The bearded man calmly walked over and put a bullet in the side of Merrifield's head.

He checked to make sure Merrifield was dead, retrieved the money, and then he drove away. He had no fear that Merrifield's murder would be tied to the theft of Greg Nielsen's dental records. The two had occurred in separate jurisdictions, and Virginia and D.C. rarely coordinated on law enforcement even if a crime obviously involved both. Besides, the Merrifield murder would just be one more unsolved homicide in the District of Columbia, where there had been 356 last year, and only the easiest ones had been solved. Merrifield's death certainly wouldn't fit into that category.

CHAPTER 6

David was pleased to see that his tuxedo had been left hanging in a closet of the house in Montreaux. He had last worn it two years ago when he had brought Yael for a short holiday along Lake Geneva. He knew that Bruno liked to dress formally for these evenings of dinner followed by the casino, and he didn't want to embarrass his host.

On the way to the restaurant, David thought about the first time he had met the Swiss financier. By January 1979, the final days of the rule of the Shah of Iran, David, as CIA station chief in Tehran, had become quite close with the Shah. Up to the end, the Shah stubbornly refused to leave his country, mistakenly believing that the people would back him against the Ayatollah. He was already quite ill and frail as a result of leukemia, but he loved his country so much that he took a container filled with Iranian soil with him. David had cut through all of the American government red tape to get a U.S. Air Force plane and crew just in the nick of time for the Shah to escape with cash and jewels while State Department officials fiddled in Foggy Bottom. David thought the Shah deserved at least that much for his many years of being a loyal American ally. Doing it earned David a spot at the top of the new Iranian government's hit list.

David flew with the Shah to Geneva—the first stop in what would become the former Iranian leader's agonizing and humiliating odyssey of exile, rejection and death. Waiting for the plane to land at the airport was Bruno, the Shah's friend of many years and personal financial adviser.

That evening, at a quiet dinner at Bruno's house in Lausanne, the Shah introduced David to his host and said, "Bruno, this young man saved my life. If he ever needs anything, please give it to him."

David had been touched by the Shah's words and the sentiment they conveyed. He filed them in the back of his mind, never conceiving that years later, when his own odyssey of exile and rejection began after his fight with General Chambers, he would turn to Bruno because he had nowhere else to go.

As the car sped along the shore of Lake Geneva, David closed his eyes and relaxed. He had no reason to see if he was being tailed. He was confident that he had thoroughly lost the Mossad and anyone else who was following him.

At the restaurant, Bruno was waiting for David at a table with a bottle of Taittinger Comtes de Champagne, 1990, chilling on ice. It had been two years since they had been together, a year since Bruno had sent David a note after Yael's death.

When he saw David enter the room, Bruno rose quickly and gave David a huge hug for a greeting. My God, the man doesn't age, David thought. He has to be seventy, and he looks like fifty, with the same tall, thin, wiry frame, sandy brown hair and ruddy complexion. It's all in the genes.

"I should have answered your note last year," David said, "but it was too painful."

"That wasn't necessary. I'm only glad you brought her here a year earlier, so I got the chance to know Yael, and what a special person she was."

The waiter poured champagne into two Baccarat flutes.

As Bruno raised his glass, he tapped it against David's and said, "To better times."

"To friendship." David responded.

"Okay, so how are you now, my young friend?" Bruno asked.

"I had it tough for a while after Yael's death, but I'm doing better—or at least I was until my life started imploding. That's why I wanted to see you, to get your advice."

The maître d' approached, and Bruno said, "Let's order first."

When he had gone, and as food and more wine arrived, David described in detail for Bruno everything that had happened since Detective Goldberg showed up at the kibbutz, including his meeting with Bill Fox in London. He was excited, and he began talking rapidly, moving his hands as he did. Several times Bruno asked him to repeat what he had said, because it was all coming out too fast in David's barely passable French. With Bruno, he held nothing back. He felt better being able to talk to someone. When he was finished, he said "So, what do you make of all this?"

"Somebody wants you badly. That somebody has plenty of money and brains, but absolutely no scruples."

"Sounds like a great combination. What do I do about it?"

"You could take the easy way out. Go back to Dr. Wilhelm, the plastic surgeon, let him make a few more changes, and I could help resettle you in Venezuela, where the oil business is booming."

David was disappointed by Bruno's words. This wasn't what he came so far to hear. "That's not an option. My God, Bruno, as Bill Fox was rattling on about his personal traumas, he managed to drop that Nasser blew up bus eighteen in Jerusalem. Yael was on that bus. That means Nasser killed Yael."

Bruno shook his head in disagreement. A decision like this had to be made with the mind and not the heart. "You still might be better not to continue."

"Look, Bruno, I hear you, and I respect your judgment more than anyone's, but this is something I have to do."

"It won't be easy."

"I know that, but I'll find a way to get into Saudi Arabia."

Bruno gave a weary sigh of resignation. "Let me make a suggestion, then. If you won't run, at least sit tight for a while. Chances are, the whole dental records business has a Saudi Arabian connection somewhere. Fox already told you that balls are in play over there. Somebody's going to come to you very soon. See what they're offering. It may be a way to get at Nasser."

David weighed Bruno's words carefully. "I won't wait too long," he responded.

Bruno smiled. "I wouldn't have expected you to. Patience was never your strong suit. It's amazing I was able to teach you to play chemin de fer so well."

Laughing, David replied, "You didn't teach me. You introduced the game to me. It's all numbers. I had an instinct for it. You said so yourself. That's why we made our deal."

Bruno didn't argue. When he had first seen how good David was at chemin de fer, he proposed a lifetime deal. He would finance David, and they would split the winnings. That little deal had resulted in David having over a million dollars in a numbered account at a Geneva bank.

"All right, let's go play. We'll test your instincts."

It was a Friday evening, and the casino in Evian-les-Baines, the French spa on the lake's southern shore, was crowded in the main public rooms in front. In the back was a private salon for high rollers, and there was never a crowd at any of those tables. All the men were dressed in evening clothes. The women, heavily jeweled, were smartly dressed in the latest fashions of Paris and Milan.

As they entered the private salon, several players looked up. A couple came over to shake Bruno's hand.

Bruno usually took a seat next to David at the chemin de fer table. Tonight he said, "You play yourself," and he walked over to the blackjack table to sit next to a tall, strikingly beautiful brunette in a black silk dress with a plunging neckline that showed much more than just cleavage beneath a heavily encrusted diamond choker. She was about forty, David guessed, and he was surprised. Bruno, a widower, had a female friend his age whom he saw from time to time, and David had never seen him with a younger woman. From his greeting, he obviously knew this woman well. Good for him, David thought.

He took one more look, then forgot Bruno and the brunette. The key to success at chemin de fer, he had learned long ago, as with other things in life, was total concentration. The room could be on fire, and he wouldn't know it.

He started watching the cards and counting, hoping for that ideal combination of two or three cards that added up to nine, which was the optimum total. Three other men were sitting at the table—a young American who had lots of money and knew little about the game, a heavy red-faced German, puffing on a cigar with a tall stack of chips in front of him, and a grim-looking Frenchman who was cursing his luck.

After an hour, David looked down at the pile of chips on the table in front of him. It totaled $10,200, a mere $200 more than he had started with. But David was patient at this game. He had learned that the secret for successful gambling lay in the Bible—in the story of Josef and Pharaoh—the seven good years and the seven lean years. Gambling, like sports, runs in streaks. Dale Long, a journeyman first baseman for the Pittsburgh Pirates, David remembered, once hit home runs in eight straight games—a record. And an ordinary quarterback will sometimes complete pass after pass on a long drive. So too in chemin de fer. In some runs the bank's hand will win round after round; and in others the player's hand keeps rolling up the wins. The secret to playing chemin de fer successfully, David believed, was to bet relatively small amounts and wait until one of those streaks started and then bid aggressively, following the momentum, while siphoning off a percentage of winnings along the way, thereby avoiding the greed factor. In that way, when the streak came to an end, as it must inevitably, because what goes up must come down, David took home a substantial profit.

So far tonight there hadn't been any streaks of that type. Yet he began to get a feeling—a tingling in his fingers—that told him the time was coming. The Frenchman on his left had the bank and had just lost, so the shoe moved to David, who tossed $8,000 of his chips into the center of the table to buy the bank. On his right, the American bought another $20,000 worth of chips. The German across the table relit his cigar and tapped his chubby fingers lightly on the green tabletop. The American tossed in a bet of $3,000 against the bank, and the German followed suit. The Frenchman picked up the remaining $2,000.

The croupier dealt the cards facedown—two for the other players, who were a unit for purposes of the hand, and two for David, who held the bank. David glanced at his cards. A four and five—la grande—a natural. The best hand you could get. He flipped the cards over, as did his opponents with a three and a two. David had won as banker, and the entire $16,000 remained in the bank. This process was repeated two more times with David prevailing. Now there was $64,000 in the bank.

Under house rules, David now had the option of pulling $32,000 out of the bank and making it a very profitable night regardless of what happened, which was how he usually played. But tonight the German was glaring at him across the table; the Frenchman was cursing; and the American looked puzzled as he continued to draw thousand-dollar bills out of his pocket. David had a feeling in his gut that he could keep riding this wave a little longer. In a move that he would later consider soundly aggressive or unduly reckless, he left the entire $64,000 in the bank.

That move was met with whispers around the room. People who weren't playing at other tables suddenly gathered at the chemin de fer table to watch the excitement. The brunette stopped playing blackjack and moved up to stand behind David. Bruno Wolk remained seated, listening for the croupier's call of the numbers.

The bank was split among the other three players, with the German picking up half and the other two players splitting the remainder.

After two cards were dealt to each side facedown, the player side asked for another card. Dealt faceup, it was a seven. David looked at his cards. He had an ace and a five, totaling six. He would have preferred standing and not having to draw another card, which was likely to push him further away from the optimum total of nine, but that wasn't an option under the rules of the game. The croupier slipped a card faceup out of the shoe. David held his breath and looked down. It was a two. He breathed a sigh of relief. David didn't have to wait to see his opponents' cards. The Frenchman's angry pounding of a fist on the table told him the result.

Now the bank went to $128,000. David looked down at the huge pile of chips in the center of the table. He closed his eyes for an instant, trying to decide what to do. Let it all ride one more time, he decided, as a ripple of tension spread through his body.

Before the other three parties had a chance to split up the new bank, the German shouted, *"Banco"* from across the table, which meant he would bet the entire $128,000 against David.

All the other games in the room stopped as the patrons lined up two and three deep around the chemin de fer table. A heavy tension hung over the room, as the croupier dealt each player two cards.

David peeked at his cards. They were a two and a three. Ugh, he thought, not a great hand.

The German took another card. It was dealt faceup— a four.

Now David had a choice, one of the few times a player ever did. He could stick with his five, or he could draw another card. Possible calculations and percentages ran through his brain as he also recalled and counted mentally the cards that had been played so far from the shoe since they had been shuffled. The brunette was leaning in close to him, looking over his shoulder, but he had no idea she was there. All he could see were the cards. He finally decided that the odds, by a narrow amount, favored drawing another card.

"Card, please," he said to the croupier.

The room was deathly still.

Faceup, the croupier slipped a card out of the shoe. It was a four. David took a deep breath. The worst he could do was tie if the German's cards totaled nine as well. The German was feeling bullish as he turned over his two down cards—a nine and a five, which with the four gave him a hand worth eight points. The only thing that could beat him was a nine. Finally, he thought he had David nailed.

David was totally deadpan when he flipped over his cards. Shouts went up in the crowd.

David had enough. Any more would be letting greed push his luck. He decided to cash his chips. As he collected them, he heard the Frenchman say to a friend who had come over to the table, "Tonight was a bad idea. I should have put all of my money into that long-term contract for Saudi crude."

"That may be pretty risky, too," his friend said.

"Nope. A sure thing. You can take it to the bank."

David thought back to what Bruno had said at dinner. Balls were in play in Saudi Arabia. It didn't surprise him to learn there was a French involvement. Whenever there was money to be made in the Middle East, the French were always involved.

He found Bruno and his friend sipping Armagnac at a small table in a corner of the room. David joined them, and a waiter hustled over with a bottle of 1918 Armagnac.

"Claudia, meet David," Bruno said, "This young man's the mathematical genius I was telling you about. He has a photographic memory for numbers and cards. Anything mathematical."

David blushed. "I'm not so young."

"So how much did we win tonight, partner?" Bruno asked.

"Enough to cover dinner, I'm pleased to report, but not the Armagnac."

Less than two hundred miles away, Jacqueline Blanc thought with contempt, Americans are such fools. Like small children, they can be manipulated, by catering to their egos, to do what you want. So she carefully orchestrated their second meeting. This time in Zurich, a month after they had met in Madrid.

For the venue, she selected the Dolder Grand. From the moment he checked in, he would sense the history in the old stone walls of the hotel. Great men of the world, including Winston Churchill and Albert Einstein, had frequently stayed at this majestic hotel, nestled in a forest high above the lake. He would read the historical plaques and feel like one of them.

She had told him to order dinner from room service, and when the côte de veau arrived, it wasn't accompanied by the pleasant St. Emilion he had ordered, but by an incredible 1982 Châteaux Margaux that she had arranged. Also on the tray was a bottle of fifty-year-old Remy Martin.

Let him ponder his situation while he ate. She was literally holding out the golden ring to him. Did he dare to take it? Still, she didn't delude herself with atmospherics. There were issues of substance as well. In Madrid, he had raised serious operational problems.

At ten minutes before midnight, as she had promised, she tapped lightly on the inside door leading to the adjacent suite. Quickly, he moved to unbolt it. Looking prototypically French, with her dyed black hair tied up tightly in a bun in the back, and dressed in a blue-and-orange plaid suit by Givenchy, she greeted him with a nod. She could have been going to the opera.

As she glanced around the suite, she saw the remnants of dinner pushed into a corner. Very little wine remained in the bottle.

"They took care of you adequately?" she asked.

"I appreciate your planning."

In her hand she held two Cohibas. She flipped one to him. The other she lit for herself, puffed deeply, then walked over to the bar and poured a solid measure of cognac in a snifter.

"You had a good flight from Paris?" he said.

Small talk was over as far as she was concerned. It was time for business now. Brusquely she asked, "Have you had a chance to think about the operation I'm planning for Saudi Arabia?"

"I haven't thought about anything else."

"I need to know now. Are you in or out?"

"I have some serious questions about what you're planning to do." There was hesitation in his voice, tinged with fear.

"This isn't a morality exercise."

"No, I mean operational issues. The ones I raised with you in Madrid."

"I have more details in place now. You want me to run through them with you?"

"Yes, they're important to me. I don't want to be part of an operation that's going to fail."

She looked at him with contempt. What kind of fool did he think she was? "Nor do I," she replied in a cold tone that cut through him.

For the next fifteen minutes, he listened in silence, while she reviewed the newest details of the operation. At the end, she said, "So are you in or out?"

"There are still plenty of loose ends," he said, and he proceeded to tick them off for her.

She shrugged. "Life always has risks. I need an answer tonight."

She could tell he was hesitating, as he rolled the unlit cigar around in his mouth, thinking. She didn't want to push him too hard for fear he'd fall the wrong way. Like a predator held at bay, she walked over to the window and looked out into the thick mist rising from the lake in the city below, enveloping the hotel, which resembled a gray stone medieval fortress. She had spent the last forty years studying men like him. She knew what was running through his mind. He wanted the reward. Were the risks too great? Could he rationalize what she was asking him to do?

She opened the window halfway, puffed again on the cigar and blew the smoke toward the night air outside.

He looked past her through the open window toward the fog outside—so thick you could cut it with a knife. What he would be doing, if he took her offer, was in the best interests of the United States. As for the financial reward he would receive, $60 million was a great deal of money. No question about it. But he deserved it. Every cent. He was entitled to it.

Finally, she heard the voice behind her say in a firm, measured tone, "Count me in."

Trying hard to conceal her excitement, she turned slowly

and said, "Then I can depend on you to deliver Washington on this, as we discussed?"

"Affirmative."

But for emphasis, and to make certain there was no ambiguity, she rephrased the question. "Are you telling me that the U.S. government won't intervene, that they'll sit on the sidelines?"

"That's exactly what I'm telling you."

"And how do you intend to achieve this result?"

"That, Madame Blanc, is my responsibility," he said irritably.

Clearly, she had pushed him to the limit. That's the way she liked dealing with men.

"However, the question of timing is critical," he added. "Schedule the attack for October 6. That's exactly one month before the date of Waltham's reelection, which is all he cares about. That close to November 6, there's less chance of American military intervention. The last thing he'd want is American casualties and the arrival of body bags being shown on the evening news."

She paused to sip some cognac, thinking about what he had just said. He was right, of course. He had good political instincts. She would follow his recommendation.

Satisfied, she handed him two three-by-five white cards with several paragraphs of printing.

"They describe," she explained, "the account I've opened in your name at Credit Suisse on the Bahnhofstrasse in Zurich. You sign one card now and give it to me. I'll see that it's delivered to the bank. The other one's for you. My suggestion is that you memorize the account number and bank regulations. Then destroy the card."

He picked up a pen from the hotel desk and stared for a long minute at the two bank cards. He was aware of the risks in what he was doing, but accepting the money didn't bother him. He believed that what he was doing was right and that he deserved it. With a flourish, he signed one card and returned it to her.

"Tomorrow morning," she said, "the first installment, of fifteen million dollars, will be deposited into the account.

Identical payments will be made on the first day of October, November and December, when the operation will be over. On my books the payments will be shown to Henri Napoleon, which will be your code name should you need to communicate with me." She handed him a small piece of paper with a Paris telephone number. "This is for any urgent communications, although for your sake, I hope that you will never have to use it. Is all that clear enough?"

He nodded.

"Good, then we're finished," she said curtly. With that, she placed her cigar in an ashtray, took a final sip of cognac, let it roll around in her mouth before swallowing and headed toward the connecting door to the adjacent suite.

"You don't have to leave now," he said.

She sneered at him. "If you want some female company, mon cheri, call the concierge. This is Europe, my friend. Even at this hour I'm sure that he'll be able to supply as many girls as you'd like. As for me, I prefer much younger men. They're more dependable. Their pricks rise on demand. That's the way I like it."

Embarrassed, he said, "That's not what I meant."

"With me, monsieur, you have only one task to perform. Since you've already been paid a substantial amount, I'd urge you to make sure that task is performed as promised. If not . . ." she paused for emphasis and rolled her hand into a fist, "well, I wouldn't like to think about what will happen."

The woman's a monster, he thought.

As she crossed through the connecting door, she summed up the situation to herself. First, Khalid and now the American. She needed one more piece to fall into place, the elusive Greg Nielsen, and then her plan couldn't fail. The prize of at least $500 million a year would be hers for the foreseeable future. She would give Victor a little more time to bring Nielsen around. If he couldn't do it his way, then she would turn up the pressure on Nielsen herself.

David took a circuitous route back to Israel: a train to Milan, Alitalia to Athens and Al El to Israel. He didn't want to leave a trail that could be followed back to Lausanne or Montreaux.

It was almost four in the afternoon when he walked into the High-Tech Center of the kibbutz. Surprisingly, the usually dour Batya had a smile on her face. He thought she was almost excited as she handed him a fax that had arrived from Tokyo and another from Paris.

"Good news," she said. "The Toyota people will come here on November 15 for a visit, and Renault wants you back in Paris for a follow-up meeting next week."

Batya didn't feel the need to apologize for reading messages addressed to him. They were a single unit on the kibbutz and in the High-Tech Center. Privacy meant nothing.

"When you got back from Paris the last time, I told you that you were too pessimistic," she said. "Your first meeting with them didn't go as badly as you thought."

He looked at the fax from Renault. They wanted him in Paris for a meeting next Wednesday morning at nine o'clock. All he could think about was Maria Clermont and her death. Was he being set up again? Or was this a genuine expression of business interest on the part of Renault— unrelated to his own past or what had happened when he was with Maria. He wanted to believe that this was just a good business development. He could see signs that pointed to this conclusion. The last time, he had traveled to Paris at kibbutz expense and stayed at a small fleabag hotel on the Left Bank, close to Daphna so they could have dinner. This time Renault had reserved a room for him at the Bristol. The Toyota fax was even better. Four executives would be coming from the Japanese automaker. They had to be close to signing.

As he left Batya, David had almost convinced himself that the contents of both of these messages were good news. He had worked hard to develop this new software package. Ford was a wonderful customer, but the kibbutz needed a second one.

By the time he reached his office and prepared to assemble the other members of the team to convey the news, he had rejected all of his attempts at rationalization. He had learned long ago that when unusual events occur at the same time, it usually isn't coincidence, but manipulation by sinister forces. Kourosh's death, which had involved a trip to Rome, the assassination attempts on him in Paris and London, and now this unexpected summons to Paris on short notice. Then there was the Frenchman's comment in the casino the other night about an anticipated sharp increase in the price of Saudi crude.

Somehow these were related. He didn't think Renault was involved, but whoever was responsible knew somebody at Renault who would cooperate with them to lure him to Paris.

If some type of Saudi oil conspiracy was being developed, perhaps that would be his Trojan horse, his way of getting at Nasser, to repay him for Yael's death. He'd have to be patient, as Bruno had advised, but patience never came easily for David.

As the super-long white Lincoln stretch limo pulled away from the airport in Riyadh, the Saudi prince was alone in the backseat, dressed in a long white cotton *thobe* and traditional headdress. His Savile Row clothes were packed in the four suitcases in the trunk. Up front next to the driver sat the prince's bodyguard, nervously gripping his machine gun. In recent weeks there had been terrorist attacks on members of the royal family, but the prince wasn't worried. He leaned back and closed his eyes. Though it was almost midnight, he wasn't trying to sleep after the long trip from Los Angeles. He was replaying in his mind how much he had enjoyed the last week. His friends liked London, but he much preferred Los Angeles, even though the whole city was run by the filthy Zionists. Since the Sultan of Brunei had taken over the Beverly Hills Hotel, it existed as an oasis in this Zionist world. And what an oasis. He and the six other men with him plus their four bodyguards had taken over an entire floor to ensure privacy. Except for the twenty-four hours they spent in Las Vegas, which had been such a financial disaster he didn't want to think about it, they had hardly ever left the hotel. And there was no need to. Any food they wanted—beluga caviar, the finest steaks, the best chocolates—were brought up to the floor on demand. He had gained so much weight. He must be up to two hundred and forty pounds now.

There had been bottles and bottles of cold Dom Perignon night and day and Lafite Rothschild—another Zionist—with the steaks. The cocaine had been the finest he had ever used, and he considered himself a connoisseur.

Best of all were the girls. Every morning at ten that woman—what was her name? Veronica—would show up with pictures of nude girls. All they had to do was pick as many as they wanted. At twenty thousand dollars for each twenty-four hours, those girls would stay as long as they wanted and do anything that he and his friends wanted, although, he was having trouble getting hard these days, which after all could happen to men after they reach the age of forty. And the girls seemed happy to watch television with him in bed.

The word "bed" made him think of home. He looked out of the car window. They were passing through a lower-income area on the way to the suburb where he lived in a palace with his two wives and eight children. He didn't want to think about the fights that awaited him there.

Even less did he want to think about his financial situation. After this trip—and particularly the unfortunate run of luck he'd had in Las Vegas—he would have no choice but to approach his uncle, the king, for an increase in his allowance. The last time he had to do this—six months ago—the old miser had made him beg and grovel before giving him the money he needed, running on at the mouth with lectures about the middle class and poor people and their lower standard of living and the declining price of oil, as if he cared about any of that. This time he couldn't even be assured of success. In at least two other cases, the king had refused to cover gambling debts of his nephews. What was the world coming to?

The car was slowing to a stop. He turned on the intercom

that connected him with the front seat. "Rasheed, why are we stopping here?" he barked.

"The road is blocked. It looks like road construction. A detour."

"They're crazy. Those people. They keep repaving the same roads," he muttered.

The main highway was deserted. A sign on a wooden barricade indicated they should turn right onto a small back road, into an area of open desert, and the driver took that turn slowly and cautiously because of the length of the car.

The back road was poorly paved, and he drove at a crawl. The car was bouncing. The prince cursed in the backseat.

Suddenly, without any warning, three masked men clutching AK-47s jumped up on either side of the road. They sprayed bullets through the glass windows of the front seat of the car, killing the driver and Rasheed before the bodyguard could get off a single shot.

In the back of the car, the prince flung himself on the floor, hoping to hide. But that was pointless. They knew very well that he was there. He was the reason for the attack.

The rear car door opened, and they pulled him from the backseat shaking, wetting himself and pleading with them. "I'll give you money. My uncle is the king."

"Money," one of the men shouted.

"That's the abomination that drives this country. The answer is Islam. There is our guide, not your money. The House of Saud has lost its way. We won't stop until their rule has ended. Take that message with you to the next world."

He prayed he could die a quick and painless death like Rasheed and the driver, but these were Nasser's people. They had already killed twenty members of the royal family—a fact that had been kept out of the press.

"Please," he begged. "I'll do anything."

But they ignored his words. They tossed him down roughly on the sand on his back—spread-eagled. They drove four stakes into the ground and tied each of his arms and legs to one. With a large knife, one of the men hacked away at his genitalia, then cut off each of his limbs.

They shouted, "Nasser is doing justice. God is great."

Then they turned and walked away, letting him die a slow, exceedingly painful death.

CHAPTER 7

David had an aisle seat in business class. With only ten minutes until takeoff, the window seat next to him was still empty. On the assumption that there would be a Renault meeting, he reached into his briefcase and pulled out his presentation. He had worked hard on his French over the years, but it was still far from perfect. He wanted to sound smooth tomorrow.

Two minutes before departure, a dark-complexioned woman with a large white hat, tortoiseshell sunglasses and a black Chanel bag slipped into the window seat. She was dressed casually but smartly in a white skirt, blue-and-white-striped blouse and navy blue blazer that was unbuttoned to reveal her full figure. Chic was the word that popped into his mind. She looked as if she were in the Côte d'Azur rather than Tel Aviv. About forty years old, he guessed. She wasn't beautiful, but she exuded a sensuality that excited David. His gaze moved to her left hand. She wasn't wearing a wedding ring. She gave him a cursory hello, barely glancing at him. Then she settled into her seat and began reading a copy of *Le Monde*.

When the airplane doors closed, he looked around the cabin warily. Israeli security was good, but terrorists had grown more sophisticated. Was there an assassin on the plane to complete the job that had been botched in London, or was someone marking him for killers in Paris? And if so, who? He had no way of telling. For all he knew, it was the woman sitting next to him.

As he studied her out of the corner of his eye, while pretending to work on his presentation, he became more persuaded that she was the one. There was just something about her that bothered him. Could they be so crude as to resort to the honey pot? The oldest trick in the book. Did they think he was so gullible? But maybe he was becoming paranoid.

He waited until the plane had leveled off at thirty-five thousand feet, and they each had had a glass of champagne before he began talking to her.

"Are you going to Paris for a vacation?" he asked her in Hebrew.

She put down the newspaper. "I live in Nice. I'm just changing planes at Charles De Gaulle."

"So you were visiting Israel as a tourist?"

"I'm sorry, my Hebrew's not so good."

He repeated the question in French, happy for a chance to practice. She replied, "I have a brother in Jerusalem. He's a doctor."

"Has he lived there long?"

"My parents originally moved from Morocco to Nice in 1948. My brother was a Zionist, and he moved to Israel after the '67 war."

"And you?"

She laughed. "I was in love with a Frenchman at the time. Or so I thought. By the time I realized that wasn't the case, I owned two boutiques in Nice. That Zionist business never meant much to me. Besides, I didn't feel like moving again."

"How long were you in Israel on this trip?"

"Why do I feel as if I'm being interrogated? Are you a policeman?"

Outwardly he smiled. Inwardly he cursed himself for being so clumsy and rusty in tradecraft. He reached over and shook her hand. "David Ben Aaron."

"I'm Gina," she replied, smiling as if she liked him. "Pleased to meet you."

"Gina what?" he wanted to ask. But he didn't, of course.

"Now it's my turn for interrogation," she said devilishly. "What do you do in Israel?"

"I live on a kibbutz."

"That's not the callused hand of a farmer I just shook."
He laughed. "Computers are my field. It's the new high-tech age."

As they continued their conversation over lunch, he found that Gina was a fascinating woman. She was obviously intelligent, well read and knowledgeable about art and fashion. She was a serious photographer who had exhibited in Cannes. "And, no, I don't do weddings or bar mitzvahs," she said, smiling, as her mouth turned up softly. She had traveled extensively, and she had distinct views on political issues concerning Israel, the Middle East and Europe. She tore into the current Israeli government for being too soft in the peace process and the French government for giving away the country's independence to a bunch of "German-dominated cone-headed EC bureaucrats in Brussels." She was witty, and she made him laugh.

Without pressing, she asked him what he did on the kibbutz, and he described the high-tech operation in very general terms. He told her about life in Moscow and the breakdown of law and order with the rise of the Russian mobsters.

"The stupidest people in the world are the Jews who refuse to get out of there," she said in her typically blunt way.

As the flight attendants cleared the luncheon trays, he decided that he hadn't enjoyed talking to a woman so much since Yael's death. Besides everything else, he found Gina physically attractive in a sensual, erotic way. As she spoke, from time to time she gently touched his hand, occasionally pausing to rest hers on top of his. He liked her so much that he almost forgot she might be part of a hit squad trying to assassinate him.

Reality set in when the pilot announced they would be landing in another thirty minutes. Fun's over, he thought grimly. Now the war begins.

She went to the lavatory, taking her Chanel bag with her. While she was gone, he developed a game plan.

"When's your plane for Nice?" he asked on her return.

In the air wafted the aroma of the perfume she had just added.

She glanced at her watch. "In about two hours. Why?"

"Well, I have a crazy idea. My meeting's not until tomorrow. You think those boutiques of yours will survive one more day without you? I'd love to have dinner with you tonight in Paris."

A twinkle appeared in her eye. "Dinner would be wonderful. But I don't have a place to stay in Paris."

He smiled. "The rooms in the Bristol are large. They could easily put in a cot for you."

"And you don't snore?"

"Never have."

"It's a deal, then."

She bit too easily, he thought. He wasn't that charming and attractive. She must be thinking that he had just fallen into the trap they had set for him. That was good. That's what he wanted her to think. If they made their move soon after his arrival, he could use her as a shield. At best, it would buy him time and complicate their task.

In Charles De Gaulle Airport, as he walked next to Gina, his eyes constantly swept from side to side. At passport control, she shoved her passport under the glass window before he could see the name. It was clearly a French passport. That much he saw.

Outside the terminal, he looked around warily. No one seemed to be waiting for him. With Gina still next to him, he worked his way to the front of the cab line, then refused the next two cabs, letting them take people behind him, telling her that the third cab in line, a gray Citroën, was larger and would be more comfortable.

On the long ride into Paris he kept looking behind and around the cab, half-expecting a car to pull up alongside and begin shooting. But if Gina was one of them, they wouldn't do that. Unless of course, she was expendable as well.

"What are you looking for?" she asked.

"The scenery," he said, trying not to be so obvious.

They arrived at the Bristol without incident. As soon as he gave his name to the clerk at the reception desk, the assistant manager, with a name tag that said Gilles, bolted out from a room behind the desk and introduced himself with great fanfare. "The Renault people welcome you to Paris, Monsieur Ben Aaron," he said. "I've selected a special suite for you, just as they requested."

David told Gina to wait in the lobby while he inspected the suite. It was huge, with a separate living room and double glass doors that opened to a balcony overlooking the hotel's center courtyard below. A large basket of fruit and cheese rested on the coffee table in the living room.

"One of the finest rooms in the hotel, monsieur," said Gilles.

"I don't like it," David said crisply.

Gilles couldn't believe his ears. No one had ever declined 618 before.

"What's wrong?" he asked, acting personally offended.

"I like to face the street if you don't mind."

"But, monsieur, it's so much noise. I thought . . ."

"Don't think. Show me another room."

David accepted the fourth room Gilles showed him, 210. A small room on the second floor, overlooking the rue St. Honore.

Gina had watched with amusement when he returned time after time with the increasingly flustered Gilles for different room keys.

"You devastated that man," she said when the porter deposited their bags in 210 along with the basket of fruit and cheese.

"You get the closet on the right," he said, dodging her comment.

Moments later, as he was hanging up his suit, and Gina was in the bathroom, the telephone rang. Nervously he picked it up on the second ring.

"Is this Greg Nielsen?" a man's voice asked in French.

"You must have the wrong room," he replied, trying hard not to disclose the tension in his voice. He could feel perspiration beginning to form under his arms.

"I know that you're Greg Nielsen," the caller persisted.

"You're obviously mistaken. There's no one in this room by that name. I suggest you talk to the hotel operator."

"I would urge you not to play games with me, Mr. Nielsen. Be in front of the Bristol at six tomorrow morning. A black Mercedes will pick you up."

David's mind was focusing on the accent of the caller. Clearly Parisian, he decided. "What is your name, please? I'll give it to the hotel operator. Maybe she can leave a message."

"Did you understand what I said?" The caller sounded annoyed. "Tomorrow at six."

"And if I'm not there?"

"Certain people in Washington will be very interested in knowing where you are, Mr. Nielsen."

The phone clicked dead. His hand was moist when he returned it to the cradle.

"Business already?" Gina called from the bathroom.

While he was on the phone, he had forgotten about her. Jesus, that was dumb, he thought. He hoped she hadn't learned much from listening to his side of the conversation.

"They were just confirming my meeting tomorrow," he lied. "The rest of today belongs to us. And the night as well. I'm stiff from the long plane ride. Let's take a walk."

Before they left the hotel, he called room service and ordered a bottle of salmon pink Billecart champagne.

By late in the afternoon, the sky had turned gray, the air cool. As they walked along the rue St. Honore, she slipped her arm through his and moved close. All the while his eyes roved from side to side. He was at red alert, ready to run, or to hit the ground and roll, at the first sign of trouble.

On avenue Franklin D. Roosevelt, at the corner of the Champs Elysées, he asked her to wait while he went into a pharmacy. He bought a package of condoms and a small bottle of chloral. The young woman behind the counter looked at him with amusement, trying to guess what he had in mind. He scowled at the nosy bitch.

Arm in arm, they continued toward the place de la

Concorde. Rush-hour traffic was just beginning, the usual furious honking of horns and shouting by impatient drivers. He completed a circle by turning left at avenue de Marigny.

Back at the Bristol, alone in the small glass-enclosed elevator, he put his arm around her shoulder, pulled her close to him and kissed her, waiting for a reaction. He knew how the game was played. If she was a plant, she would lead him on, but ask him to wait until after dinner to make love, telling him it would be better then, and hoping he'd have so much to drink that he'd talk freely but lose interest in sex.

Her kiss was warm and passionate.

He decided to test her another way. He told her he wanted to wash up. When he was in the shower, she'd think she was free to rifle through his briefcase. He'd suddenly jump out and catch her. Then he'd force her to tell him whom she was working for. He remembered all of the tricks of the trade. He'd get her alone in the bathroom. With the sink and tub running, no one could hear her scream. He'd make her talk in a matter of minutes.

Quickly, he undressed and walked into the large shower stall behind the frosted glass door. As a ploy, he turned on the water, waiting for a minute before he'd jump out and see what she was doing.

From the other side of the door, he heard a rustling noise. Fool, he thought, you've trapped yourself inside a shower stall. Searching for a weapon, he grabbed a bar of soap in a hard green Hermes case and kicked open the door, expecting to see her pointing a gun at him.

Instead she was standing totally nude and adjusting a plastic shower cap over her hair.

"Mind if I join you?" she asked.

Naked, she was far more beautiful than he'd ever imagined. Her breasts were round and full, jutting out to gorgeous dark brown nipples. Her legs, tanned and bronzed, were long and firm, coming together at a triangular thick black mound. His fear gave way to joy and then sexual arousal as she stepped into the shower. I don't care, he thought. I don't care who she is. All I know is that I want her, and I want her now.

As she moved in close, he ran his hand over her back, feeling her warmth. Then he held her tightly, wrapping his arms around her, fusing their bodies. He reached down and kissed her soft, moist lips. As she responded eagerly, he slipped his tongue deeply into her mouth while his hands dropped to her buttocks, and he pressed her tight against his erection. All the while the water rushed over their heads and bodies.

He lifted his hand and stroked her breasts, playing with the nipples until they grew hard. Then he sucked on them greedily, first one and then the other, savoring the taste of her body, while his hand slipped between her legs.

She moaned with pleasure as he found the spot and stroked it ever so gently. He looked down into her eyes, and he saw that her desire was every bit as great as his own.

"My turn," she whispered as she reached down and took his hard cock into her hand. He pushed it away and dropped to his knees, spreading open her folds of skin. With his mouth he found the spot where his fingers had been, and he took her clitoris into his mouth, playing with it with his tongue and sucking it until her whole body shook, and she screamed, "Oh God, yes!"

Only then did he remove his mouth, stand up and hold her tightly.

"I want you inside me," she cried. "Now, in bed."

Dripping wet, he picked her up and carried her out to the king-size bed. As soon as he put her down, she raised her legs high. In a matter of seconds, he slipped inside her. Then she wrapped her legs tightly around his hips, forcing him deeper and deeper. She started to thrust her body, and he moved with her, feeling incredible pleasure, on the verge of a crescendo but holding back, wanting it to last. Her movements came faster and faster, and she dug her finger-nails into his back.

"Bien, bien," she screamed, looking at him with blazing wide eyes. Finally he let himself go. As she felt his release, her whole body shook. *"Très bien,"* she cried. *"Très bien."*

*   *   *

They made love twice more—each time with a passion that startled them both. At the end, she dropped off to sleep, and he stroked her hair gently and watched her sleep.

A wild thought popped into his mind. Maybe Gina will hide me in Nice. We'll make love day and night, and all of this business with Kourosh and the Dental Affair will pass.

The word "Nice" stuck in his brain. She's probably not even from there, he told himself. But what if she is? What if she's the real thing? What if just by coincidence, he had met this fantastic woman on the plane on the very same day that someone called his hotel room and said they knew he was Greg Nielsen.

Don't be an idiot, he told himself. If two incredible long shots hit on the same day, it's not coincidence. The game's fixed. He eyed her large, black Chanel bag resting on the desk. Maybe he'd find an answer in there. He had started to climb out of bed when she woke up.

"You are some kind of lover," she said. "Hold me tight."

"Nope, it's time for champagne. You close your eyes and stay right where you are. I'll pour you a glass."

Telling her he had to rinse the glasses in the bathroom, he poured a little of the chloral deftly into hers, just the minimum amount to do the job, hating himself all the while. Maybe I'm wrong, he thought. Maybe you are really Gina, and you've got nothing to do with any of this, but I can't take a chance. If you're for real, honey, when this is over, I'll come and find you in Nice.

They clicked their glasses together, and she sipped the champagne contentedly.

They went to dinner at Amphycles, a small but wonderful restaurant in the 17th Arrondissement. He asked for and was given the table near the garden, just off the entrance. From there he could watch the door without being seen immediately by anyone who entered.

He figured she would never last half an hour into dinner. He had to admire her constitution. Even with a glass of red burgundy she managed to make it through the luscious crab first course, the chef's signature dish. Midway into a squab entree, the chloral hit her, and it hit her hard.

"I'm so tired," she said lethargically. "I don't know what's wrong."

"Maybe it's the long day. The champagne and wine."

"This never happens to me. It just . . ." Her eyes closed. Her head dropped onto the table.

He apologized for his wife, who had been on a long flight from China today, paid the bill and led her out of the restaurant.

Back at the Bristol, he tucked her into bed. Then he began a meticulous search of her things. Her clothes, including the underwear, were all French. None of them had the names of retail outlets—only the designer or producer. Her shoes were Ferragamo from Italy. Her suitcase contained nothing except for clothes, a couple of junky French novels, and copies of the French editions of *Vogue, Bazaar* and *Marie Claire*. Her bathroom and cosmetic kits were equally prosaic.

He reached into her Chanel purse and pulled out her French passport. The name on the passport was Gina Martin. It had been issued in Nice two years ago. The date stamps in the back showed trips to Israel, Spain and Portugal, and that was all. He pulled out her wallet. There was nothing in it except for a little money—some French and some Israeli—a driver's license and two credit cards, but nothing personal. No notes. No scraps of paper.

He shook his head, thinking about what he had found. It was all too neat and clean. He was now convinced that his first instinct had been right. Gina Martin wasn't a real person. She was phony, created to trick him. But why? Who sent her?

He reached back into the Chanel bag and his hand encountered a good-size metal object, which he pulled out carefully, holding his breath.

When he saw what it was, he breathed a sigh of relief. It was only a Nikon camera with a roll of film partially shot. That at least made sense. On the plane she had told him she was a serious photographer. He rewound the film, extracted it from the camera and tucked it into his pocket, before checking the Chanel bag again. There was nothing left inside.

The red numbers on the digital clock next to the bed showed 11:37 P.M. If he were on the other side arranging the hit, he would move now. The best time was always between midnight and four A.M., when police and witnesses were at a minimum. This was the time he had to be most careful.

He replaced her things as he had found them, sat down at the desk and wrote a short note on hotel stationery.

It was great. Thank you.
I have a business emergency to deal with. Hope to see you again soon.

—D

He placed the note on the pillow next to her, where his head had been. Then he packed his suitcase. Before slipping out of the room, he paused and took a deep breath, wanting to retain her scent and the aroma of their sex as long as possible.

When he had been on the run, he had learned of an underground network in Western Europe that helped former CIA people. As the cold war ended, the Company had made no provision for those foreign nationals whom it had employed over the years. They had been left high and dry—often at risk in their own countries. Many feared an attack by former Soviet, East German or even Western agents who had personal scores to settle.

David hadn't used this underground for more than four years. Now he would find out whether it still existed.

He refused the cab waiting in front of the Bristol, walked down to the Champs Elysées and caught one there. He directed the driver to the Hotel Gironde on the Left Bank. It was a seedy-looking dump. The lobby was deserted except for a man in his late thirties with a shaved head and a large gold earring in his right ear, who sat behind the desk reading *The Stranger* by Camus. Off to his right, below wooden slots for room keys, a small New York Yankees pennant had been tacked to the wood. That was the sign David had been looking for.

The man looked up from his book. "Something I can help you with?"

"I need a room for the night."

"Four hundred francs. Cash payment in advance."

David gave him the money. Then he said, "Glad to see you're a Yankee fan. I was a good friend of Mickey Mantle's. A drinking buddy, to be precise."

"Don't get many of those in here anymore. What can I do for you?"

"How about a room on the second floor facing the street and let me know if anyone's looking for me."

"Will do. What else?"

"I could use a little self-defense."

The man looked around nervously. "Will a Glock do?" he whispered.

"Perfect."

"I'll send it up in an hour."

"Call me. I'll come down."

David reached into his pocket, pulled out the roll of film from Gina's camera and put it on the desk. "Can you have it developed for me by noon tomorrow?"

"Consider it done."

An hour later, David had a loaded gun in his hand. He settled into a desk chair across the room from the closed and chained door, which was blocked by a heavy, filthy red upholstered chair he had moved into position.

It had been a long time since he had had a sleepless night, but the adrenaline and his nerves would keep him awake.

If they didn't come for him tonight, he would deal with them at six A.M.

A black Mercedes was waiting in front of the Bristol when David crossed the rue St. Honore and approached the hotel at five minutes past six, still before sunrise. He

had been standing across the street in a small open enclosure, his eyes continually moving from the car to the street.
He could feel the Glock in a shoulder holster tight against
his chest. His hand was at his side, ready to go for the gun.

Finally satisfied that the driver standing next to the car
was alone, he approached and said, "I'm David Ben Aaron.
I went for a morning walk."

"My name is Rolland. Are you ready to go, sir?" the
driver asked.

"Where are we going?"

Acting as if he hadn't heard the question, Rolland
opened the rear door. Relieved that the long night of waiting was over, and he might now get the answers to his
questions, David took one more look up and down the
deserted street and climbed into the back of the car.

He expected the door lock buttons to snap down, locking
him in, but nothing like that happened. It was still dark, and
the rue St. Honore was deserted. They passed the Palace de
d' Elysées, turned left at rue de Castiglione, and headed
toward the Place Vendome. After a couple of turns, the
car pulled up in front of a gray stone, five-story building.
The driver raced around to open the door for David.

Silently, Rolland pointed toward the entrance, to the side
of which was a small bronze plaque containing the words
VICTOR FOCH AND COMPANY. ADVOCATES.

Tightening his jacket to conceal the gun, David climbed
the stone steps and walked into an entrance hall. Two large,
rough-looking men, one nearly bald and the other with
thick black hair, were standing on either side of a
wooden table.

"David Ben Aaron," he announced. "I'm here for a
meeting."

"Mr. Foch is expecting you," the bald man said. "He'd
appreciate it if you'd leave the gun in your shoulder holster
with us until your meeting is over."

"What are you talking about?"

"There was an X-ray camera in the Mercedes."

"And if I don't give it to you?" David said belligerently.

"Then you won't be able to meet with Mr. Foch," he said calmly.

He wasn't going to win. He pulled the gun out of the holster and tossed it to the man. "What kind of lawyer has two security guards in the lobby and X-ray cameras in his car?"

The bald-headed man shrugged his shoulders and smiled. "A lawyer who has visitors show up for meetings as if they're ready to launch a terrorist attack."

The dark-haired man led David over to a small elevator, rode with him to the top floor and then pointed at a set of wooden double doors. Inside, David saw an attractive young blonde typing at a computer. She rose quickly, showing lots of beautiful leg beneath a black miniskirt.

"Right this way, sir," she said efficiently, and then proceeded to lead him into the inner sanctum—a huge high-ceilinged office with a large oriental carpet in the center of a brightly polished wooden floor. In front of floor-to-ceiling windows was a red leather-topped antique desk. Standing behind it, looking out of the window, was a distinguished-looking man, his chestnut hair showing a little gray at the temples. He turned around when he heard David enter. He was around fifty, David guessed. He was dressed in a smartly tailored three-piece charcoal gray suit, blue-striped shirt with a white collar and Hermes tie. He was tall and thin, with a long, pointed nose. His appearance exuded wealth, success and self-confidence. As David looked closer, he became convinced that Victor Foch wore a toupee—an expensive custom-made hairpiece that seemed natural on his head.

"Thanks for coming," the lawyer said politely in a businesslike tone.

"I have no idea why I'm here."

"It's early. I need some coffee. You want some?"

"Look, Monsieur Foch, there's obviously been a misunderstanding. I want to clear it up as soon as possible. I have important business in Paris."

"You don't have to worry. I know that you're due at

Renault at nine o'clock. I promise you won't be late for your meeting."

David wasn't surprised by the response. This Victor Foch undoubtedly had a contact at Renault whom he had used to lure David to Paris. David was also wary. Everything about the man told him that Victor Foch couldn't be underestimated.

"Okay, coffee then."

The lawyer hit a button on his desk. Seconds later, the blonde in the short black skirt appeared with two cups of espresso, deposited them and quickly retreated.

Victor took a sip and began nonchalantly. "I have a client who has a problem, Mr. Nielsen—"

"There must be a mistake. My name is David Ben Aaron. I'm an Israeli citizen." For emphasis, he pulled his passport from his pocket and held it up.

"I hate playing games, Mr. Nielsen. It's so tiresome, and it wastes a great deal of time, which neither of us have. Let me show you something first so we can bring this dumb show to an end."

The lawyer pressed a button on his desk, and bright lights came on directly behind David, who wheeled around to look. He saw two rectangular screens he hadn't noticed before. Each held a set of full-mouth dental X rays.

"On the left we have dental X rays of Gregory Nielsen taken by Dr. Frederick Walter in Alexandria, Virginia, about seven years ago, and on the right we have dental X rays of David Ben Aaron from kibbutz Bet Mordechai, taken about a year ago by a Dr. Elon in Haifa. I've had three different dental experts look at the two sets, and they're all prepared to swear it's the same person. Why don't you take a look and see what you think?"

Stalling for time, David walked to the back of the room. He didn't look long or hard. He knew what he'd find. They were identical.

He walked slowly back to his seat and swallowed the rest of his coffee in a single gulp. "How did you get these?" he asked.

"A client made them available. I have no idea how the client happened to gain access to the X rays."

"Who's the client?"

"I'm afraid that's confidential. After doing a little research into Greg Nielsen's activities in Saudi Arabia on August 15, five years ago, before his hasty departure from that country, my client thought it might be a good idea to send the X rays to Washington. You know, in the spirit of encouraging Franco-American relations, which are too often strained these days, but then—"

"Cut the crap, Victor. As you said, the time for games is over. How did your people find me?"

Victor wasn't surprised by the directness of the response. From everything in the dossier on Greg Nielsen, he had expected the American to react in precisely this way. "Quite by chance. You obviously spent so much on plastic surgery, on your face, on the color of your eyes, and you even dyed and curled your hair, but you didn't do a thing about your walk, that distinctive walk of yours. When you were in Paris for your first Renault meeting, someone you used to know spotted you from the back, walking along a street, and observed you returning to the hotel Normandy. We did our homework after that."

David was furious at himself. When he had made all of the effort to change his appearance, he never focused on his walk. How could he have been such an idiot? But what could he have done about it? "Who saw me?"

"Sorry, that's confidential."

"And what do you people want from me?"

"Well, as I began to say several minutes ago, a client of mine needs your help, and the client was hopeful that you might want to help if we agreed to destroy all of the dental X rays and forget we ever saw them. You know, a quid pro quo, as we lawyers say."

"And why should I trust you to do that?"

Victor sighed, annoyed that he was being required to spell out the obvious. "I'm afraid you have no choice. If the X rays go to Washington, the Israelis will have to extradite you when Washington demands it. You know what will happen then," he said, pausing. "The Americans will charge and convict you of being an accessory to the deaths of a hundred and ten Americans in the Dhahran bombing, not to mention an assault on an American general. You'll spend the rest of your life in an American prison. Not a pleasant prospect."

"What kind of help do you want?"

"When you were in Saudi Arabia, you developed a security system for the king's palace with sophisticated computer programs. My client would like your help understanding that system. In other words, we'd like to retain you as a consultant."

The puzzle was clicking into place for David. The French gambler at the casino the other night must have gotten wind of what was happening. With what David had already heard, a long-term contract for Saudi crude would indeed be a sure bet.

David said, "So, your client's supporting a coup to take over that country?"

Victor pulled back in his chair. "Heavens, no. We're merely trying to understand how this type of system operates for an installation elsewhere."

David thought about Kourosh. "That's why you've already killed at least one person?" he asked skeptically.

"I resent the accusation. We didn't kill anyone."

David tapped his fingers nervously on the end of Victor's desk, trying to evaluate his options. "I need time to think about it," he said.

"You can give me your decision in a week, when you return for your next Renault meeting."

"I don't have another meeting scheduled with Renault in a week."

"You will when you leave at the end of the day. They're another client of mine, and they'll put you up at the Bristol again. Rolland will pick you up in front of the hotel at ten in the morning a week from today. I assume that you enjoyed the hotel last night."

David wanted to ask Victor if he had arranged for Gina

as well, but he decided not to mention it just in case she wasn't part of their operation.

As David got up and started to leave, Victor said, "I trust that you wouldn't do anything so foolish as miss our next meeting."

"What are you talking about?"

Victor gave a sinister smile. "I just want you to know that we're aware of your stepdaughter, Daphna, a student at the Sorbonne. A very attractive young woman. We have twenty-four-hour surveillance on her. Unfortunately, suicide is the largest cause of death in that age group of women in France. You wouldn't believe how many students jump from the top of a building. We wouldn't want anything like that to happen to her, would we?"

David could barely restrain his anger. He wanted to run across the room and strangle the lawyer. "You bastard," he snapped. "Even the Mafia doesn't use people's families that way."

"You obviously misunderstood me. We're trying to protect her for you."

Furious, David wheeled around and stormed out.

"I'll see you again next week," Victor called after him.

His presentation went poorly at Renault. Still shaken by the morning's events with Victor, and operating without any sleep, he stumbled through his answers to complex questions. Twice his French wholly deserted him, and he had to retreat to English phrases.

By rights, he should never have been invited back. At the end, when he was asked if he could return in a week, he shuddered. Victor and his undisclosed client were powerful people. The tentacles of their influence reached well within one of the giant corporations of France.

From Renault, he took a cab back to the Hotel Gironde to pick up the pictures developed from the film in Gina's camera. They were the most beautiful photographs of a night sky that he had ever seen—a full moon and scores of stars against the cloudless sky. She could easily have taken them in Israel on her recent visit, or in Nice, for that matter. At first he was disappointed they didn't tell him anything about her, but then he began to believe that they confirmed her identity as Gina Martin, the owner of two boutiques in Nice, rather than as an international terrorist.

When he returned to the Bristol, he hoped to find her still there so he could apologize, but there wasn't a trace of Gina in his room. Even her scent had been eradicated by the cleaning of the chambermaids. He called telephone information in Nice, but was told there wasn't a listing for Gina Martin, and he had never bothered to ask the names of her boutiques. He rationalized that plenty of single women have unlisted telephone numbers.

Weary, he slept until it was time to meet Daphna for dinner.

Anxious to know whether she was in fact being followed, as Victor had said, he insisted on meeting her in her apartment, where she greeted him with a warm hug. "I'm so glad you came to Paris, David."

She pointed at his Russian chess set prominently displayed on a coffee table in the living room. "How about a game after dinner?" she said.

As they walked slowly to her favorite bistro in her Left Bank neighborhood, he stopped in various shop windows and asked her about merchandise. That gave him a chance to evaluate the surveillance. Victor's people had both a woman on foot and a man in a car, he concluded. They made no effort to conceal themselves. Victor wanted him to know they were being tailed. David was relieved that Daphna had no idea they were being followed. For now, he didn't want to alarm her.

As he helped her off with her coat in the restaurant, he thought of something Victor had said this morning. She was a good-looking young woman. Growing up on the kibbutz, coupled with three years in the Israeli Air Force, had left her toned and conditioned. The summer after her first year at Hebrew University, they had jogged together five mornings a week on the road outside the kibbutz. He remembered what a struggle it had been for him to keep up with his bum leg. In Paris, she still stuck with a regular work-out program.

Over *moules et frites* with a bottle of *Sancerre,* she said to him, "I'm sorry for being such a whine last week at home. It was a depressing time for me."

He was relieved. It sounded as if she was finally coming to grips with Yael's death. "I'm glad you came back for the memorial service. Something like that makes it easier to move toward closure."

"I'll never have closure. She was in the prime of her life. You know that as well as I do. She was wonderful, but in some ways she must have been a tough woman to live with day and night." She smiled. "Sometimes I had all I could do dealing with her from the sanctuary of the children's dorm. She was so demanding. You know."

"She was very proud of you. She wanted the best for you always. She was devastated when she heard that your helicopter had been shot down—until she knew . . ."

Daphna's whole body tensed. She pulled back away from him. "Please, David, I didn't want to talk about that."

"I'm sorry. On a happier note, when you won the poetry contest at Hebrew University, she not only made an an-nouncement to the whole kibbutz at Friday night dinner, but she read your poem."

"Yeah, I heard. I loved her for that. And a week later she asked me if I was going to do something more practical with my life than write poetry."

There was no bitterness in her voice. That had all passed with her mother's death.

She played with a fried potato, pondering whether she should say what she was thinking. He kept still, letting her decide. Finally she said, "I'm very glad she met you. I could hardly believe the changes in her. She softened. She came alive. They were good years for her, but initially I re-sented you."

"I could tell that."

She could see the hurt on his face, and she was sorry for what she had said. "Well, it wasn't your fault. I wanted my real father, and I didn't want a substitute. Once I gave you a chance, though, I liked you as a person and not just for what you did for her. Then after she died, you were there for me, which I needed because that's a real weakness of the kibbutz. You have the whole community, but you have no one. You know what I mean?"

He nodded. "So where do you go from here?"

She sipped some wine. "Well, funny you should ask. Since I've gotten back here, I've spent a lot of time thinking about things, and . . ."

She paused.

He held his breath.

"I have to get into something more pragmatic and worldly. I'm going to take a journalism course here in the spring. Then, next year maybe I'll go to an American university to get some training in journalism. After that, I'll come back to Israel. If I can get a job writing for one of the papers, helping people understand what's happening all around us in this crazy world, I'll make a difference. The country and the kibbutz are my family. I realize that now."

She sounded so earnest and sincere, the way only young people can, David thought. That boy Kourosh was probably like that, too. David wasn't a religious man, but he said a small silent prayer that Daphna wouldn't end up like Kourosh.

After dinner, they went back to her apartment and played chess. Thinking about the danger he had created for her, he couldn't concentrate.

"Checkmate," she gleefully called at the end. "You're slipping, David. You never even saw that one coming."

CHAPTER 8

Sagit was furious at herself. How could I have been so stupid? she wondered, as she finished describing to Moshe, the director of the Mossad, what had happened in Paris. The air in his office, where the two of them were closeted, was thick with tension and heavy with cigarette smoke.

"What the hell were you thinking?" he demanded to know.

"My plan was to spend the night with him, get up early and stick with him the next day as much as possible. I figured we'd spend a second night together, and I could find out what he had done and search his things to see if he brought back anything from a meeting. Instead, he totally outmaneuvered me, leaving me in bed like a rank amateur."

"It was an absurd idea from the beginning. I can't believe that I approved it and let you use yourself that way."

She bristled. It infuriated her when Moshe later second-guessed decisions they had made together.

"C'mon, Moshe," she said, "you can't play results. It's a tough business. Nobody does it right all the time. Not us. Not the CIA. Nobody."

"We used to be different than everybody else. Better than they were."

Moshe had held his job as director of the Mossad for twenty-two years. As the mastermind behind the daring Israeli raid at Entebbe, he had led the agency in its glory years when the Mossad was the envy of every other intelligence agency in the world. But nothing lasted forever. In recent years he had been presiding over the agency's most demoralizing period, when self-confidence was giving way to self-doubt, and public praise was turning to criticism.

"Maybe we were, and maybe it was only an illusion because our enemies were so incompetent."

"Well, now they've gotten better. We can't afford any mistakes—like the one you just made in Paris."

Slowly and deliberately she reached up to the lapel of her suit jacket, unsnapped her ID badge and tossed it on Moshe's desk. "Don't even think of trying to talk me out of resigning," she said firmly. "I never dreamt that he would try to drug me, but there's no justification for dropping my guard like that."

Moshe stared at her badge resting on his desk. He was angry at himself and angry at her. But resign? He had no intention of letting her resign. He lightened up. "It's called post-coital satisfaction."

She blushed. "Thank you, Moshe." She paused and shook her head grimly. "But the bottom line is that I lost him in Paris. I couldn't follow him to whatever meeting he had, and I didn't get a damn bit of information."

Moshe snuffed out his cigarette, lifted the pack from his desk, took another one out and lit it up. When he returned the pack to the desk, she followed suit.

"I thought you quit smoking."

"Not anymore."

Deep in thought, with a cigarette dangling from his lips, he got up from his desk and walked over to the large floor-to-ceiling windows. Through tired gray eyes, above sacks of flesh, he gazed out at the Knesset and West Jerusalem beyond, remembering it had all been open fields not so long ago.

As Sagit waited for him to continue, she looked up at the wall behind his desk. He'd framed a large blown-up picture of an American black bear that she had taken last year in Yosemite Park, when Moshe had sent her to the United States to develop a working relationship with Margaret Joyner, the new head of the CIA. Sagit had decided that the bear was the perfect symbol for Moshe. On the one hand, the animal was perceived as soft and cuddly—

witness all of the children's teddy bears—and it was generally a peaceful animal. Likewise, Moshe, called Motti in his youth, now with a thick mop of uncombed gray hair and a round cherubic face, wearing a rumpled suit, could pass for the prototype of a gentle grandfatherly figure. On the other hand, bears were short-tempered and got angry quickly. They were fierce, tough, no-holds-barred fighters, who attacked anything that threatened them or their cubs. So, too, Moshe could explode in anger when anyone endangered the people of Israel or when Mossad agents failed to perform up to his high expectations.

"Okay, let's take it one step at a time," he said slowly, in a kindly voice. "I can appreciate your need for self-flagellation, but we all make mistakes. Agencies like ours capitalize on the mistakes people make, but we're human as well. So let's talk about what we lost in this fuck-up of yours. No pun intended. We lost the opportunity to find out what he was doing in Paris. Correct?"

She nodded.

"But you didn't compromise any of our information. Did you?"

"Absolutely not."

"Does he know you are Mossad?"

"I don't think so. I imagine he searched my suitcase and handbag, but I was very careful in what I took, just in case he got access to them."

"So it wasn't such a disaster. Whatever happened is over and forgotten. It doesn't leave this room, and you and I never mention it again."

She glanced at the photograph on the wall again. This black bear had one other facet to its character. If you were one of his favorites, as she had always been since he had recruited her twenty-two years ago, he was willing to forgive mistakes. If she hadn't been, he would have kept her badge and tossed her out of the office, just as he had fired Yosef for arresting David Ben Aaron without any evidence and setting off a political maelstrom.

She still couldn't believe that she had dropped her guard so totally that David was able to drug her. Moshe could say they were all human, but it was a terrible blunder. What made her feel even worse was that she knew why she had been lulled into abandoning all of her experience and training as an agent. She had enjoyed the sex with David so much.

"I don't deserve that much of a break, Moshe," she protested.

"You're right. You don't. But forget about yourself for a minute. Think about me. I'm pragmatic. It's already September. The Knesset Committee on National Security has given me one month to find out what's behind the Dental Affair, and I can't blame them. There's a dangerous conspiracy that involves David Ben Aaron. We've got to find out what's going on. Changing players at this point in the game isn't such a good idea even if it would assuage your guilt."

"But . . ."

"Forget it, unless of course you don't think you can emotionally handle the job after what happened in Paris."

"No, I can do it," she replied in a determined voice. "It was a temporary lapse on my part. He means nothing to me."

"Good. Then let's move on." Moshe puffed deeply on the cigarette and blew a smoke ring into the air. "Where is he now—our Russian kibbutznik who's obviously at home in Paris?"

"He flew into Ben Gurion from Paris this afternoon on El Al 009. I was in the tower with binoculars watching him walk off the plane, a little past two o'clock. I had Customs do a thorough search on him and his bags. Even looking for false bottoms. Nothing turned up."

"And after that?"

"At my request, Gideon Marcos, the chief of security at the kibbutz, met him in front of the terminal, and they went straight back to the kibbutz with two of our surveillance teams trailing them. So as of an hour ago, David Ben Aaron, or whoever he is, was back at Bet Mordechai. We have one surveillance team on the road, just outside the gates of the kibbutz, if he tries to leave, and another about a kilometer away at a key intersection. All agents have his picture. I also took the precaution of placing his name and passport number on the L list at all points of embarkation. He won't be able to leave the country again without your approval."

Moshe nodded his head. "You've obviously recovered from your lapse in Paris. What's your next step, Sagit?"

"I called the people at Ulpan Ha'emek, where he first went to live when he arrived in Israel from Russia, on the chance that they took dental X rays as part of his overall physical."

"And?" he asked impatiently.

"They have a set that someone from the Ulpan's driving to Jerusalem right now. As soon as they get here, I want to take them to Professor Barach at Hebrew University Dental School."

"What are you looking for?"

She had a look of determination in her eyes. She was now hell bent on getting revenge for the humiliation David had inflicted on her. "I don't know. I don't have much else to go on. Just that somebody went to a lot of trouble to get his X rays in Haifa."

"What about fingerprints?"

"When I woke up at the Bristol, I became professional again. I did my best to re-create his end of the telephone conversation, and I placed a couple of items in a clear plastic bag I obtained from a chambermaid, for prints."

"What did he leave behind?" She looked embarrassed. "Well?"

Sagit reached into her purse and pulled out a plastic bag containing a half-empty bottle of chloral and the wrappers from three condoms. As she handed it to Moshe, her face grew beet red. "If you ask me whether it was really three times, I'll kill you, Moshe."

He smiled at her and shook his head. *"Kinahora,"* he exclaimed.

"What the hell's that mean?"

"It's Yiddish for 'you must have had a really good time.'"

"I swear I'll kill you, Moshe, if you ever mention this again."

"At least you should call it a vacation day when you submit your time records." Amused at his own joke, he began to laugh. "I assume you won't tell our fingerprint people how you got these items."

"They don't need to know."

He rubbed his tired eyes. "Did you just tell me that the next morning you made a transcription from a recollection of his part of the phone conversation?"

She reached into her purse and pulled out a folded sheet of Bristol stationery. "I have it right here."

"Read it to me."

Sagit opened up the page and began reading, a Hebrew translation because Moshe didn't understand French. Still, she tried to imitate David's inflection.

"You have the wrong room . . . You're mistaken. There's no one here by that name. I suggest you call back . . . What is your name? I'll give it to the hotel operator. Maybe you can leave a message . . . And if I'm not there?"

Moshe leaned back in his chair and closed his eyes tightly to concentrate. "Read it again," he said.

When she was finished, Moshe asked, "When he first got the call, what was his reaction? Was he surprised, or was he expecting it?"

"Clearly surprised. I was watching him. He was trying to conceal his reaction, but he couldn't."

"That's significant."

"What's it tell you?"

"The caller identified him with a name other than David Ben Aaron. If it was just a code name, he shouldn't have been surprised. But if it was a name he had used at another time in his life and thought he had gotten away from—"

She interrupted. "That's how he reacted."

"The rest of the conversation tells me somebody set an unanticipated meeting for him, later that night or the next morning, which is why he had to get rid of you."

She nodded her approval.

Moshe shifted gears. "How are you coming on the preparation of David Ben Aaron's bio—the bio Yosef didn't have the sense to develop before he arrested the man?"

She had this memorized, and she responded in staccato-like bursts, "David Ben Aaron came to Israel about four and a half years ago. The immigration forms he completed show the following: Born as Anatola Ginzburg in Moscow in 1958. Parents were both sent to the gulag when he was very young. Both died there. Raised in Moscow by a grandfather, Ginzburg, on the father's side. Married and divorced in Russia. No children. Wife's name unknown. Probably not Jewish. Educated in computers. Last employment in Moscow at Novosti Chemical Company as a computer programmer. Port of embarkation: Odessa."

He looked impatient. "Doesn't sound much different than the half million or so others who came from the former Soviet Union in the last decade."

"Stick with me, Moshe. It gets more interesting, I promise you. When he arrived in Israel, he went to Ulpan Ha'emek in the Negev to learn Hebrew, unlike most other Russians."

"So he's smarter than they are."

"While at the Ulpan, he's working part-time for the Dead Sea Chemical Company as a computer programmer. He comes to Tel Aviv one Saturday night. He's sitting in a café in Diezengoff sipping a coffee, and he meets a woman from kibbutz Bet Mordechai. Two months later he marries her and goes to live with her on the kibbutz. He begins working in their high-tech business, trying to get foreign contracts. He's now director of the high-tech operation. They did two million in foreign contracts last year. They just landed a big contract with Ford Motor Company." She paused to look at him. "Nothing I said so far rang a bell for you?"

He rubbed his eyes. "What am I missing?"

"You must be tired, Moshe. You ever know anybody from kibbutz Bet Mordechai?"

He thought about it for a second. "Yeah, Yael Golan, but . . ." Involuntarily his head snapped back. "You're kidding."

A smile formed on her lips. She loved being one step ahead of Moshe. "Nope, you got it."

"Our Russian boychik married Yael?" A long, low whistle broke from his mouth.

"Yep."

While Moshe's mind was busy processing this information, Sagit picked up her analysis.

"Let's talk about Yael now. She volunteered for the Mossad about the same time you recruited me and Leora. From the time I met her in the training program, I hated her. I was green with envy. She was everything I wanted to be. Twenty years old. Tall, blond, beautiful and smart. She also came from a home in Herzilya and a family that was wealthy by Israeli standards at the time. Quite a contrast from me, who was trying to scrounge food for my brothers and sisters when you recruited me in a Tel Aviv gutter."

"None of that's relevant," he replied.

"Yael was also fearless. We used to call her the 'hellcat.' For our first assignment after training, you sent us both to Baghdad. She saved my life when I was lured into a trap by Iraqi intelligence. After that, I didn't hate her anymore. But then you transferred her to Morocco or Yemen or somewhere else in the Middle East, and I lost track of her. Last year I was in Washington for that CIA cooperative project you set up for me with Margaret Joyner when the bomb went off on Bus 18. Otherwise I would have gone to the funeral."

"I went," Moshe said softly, sunk in his own private thoughts about Yael's funeral. Looking at him, Sagit remembered what she had heard when she returned from the United States last year. People said that they hadn't ever seen Moshe so upset. He had taken Yael's death hard. She might have been his own daughter.

Sagit waited a few moments and then continued. "There was gossip in the field that she left the agency in some type of scandal a few years after you transferred her out of Baghdad. Nobody would talk. I think you better tell me what happened."

He squirmed in his chair. "I can't tell you."

"You're joking."

"I swore to her that I would never tell anyone."

Sagit held out her hands in front of her, egging Moshe on to respond. "She's dead now."

"There are survivors who are affected."

"Oh, c'mon, Moshe. We're trying to save lives. One Israeli is dead already, or perhaps you forgot."

He looked at her angrily. "That was out of line."

She was sorry she had made that comment, but she still pressed ahead. "You have to tell me about Yael. It could be critical."

"Why is it so important?"

"Think about what I've told you so far. It doesn't compute. A new Russian immigrant suddenly marries one of our best people, who left the Mossad in a scandal. Supposedly, he meets her by chance in a café. She's never been married before. She marries him two months later. Something's wrong with this picture, but unless you tell me what happened with Yael and the Mossad, I won't be able to figure it out."

"It's irrelevant, and I won't tell you," he snapped. "The subject is off limits. End of discussion."

As Sagit started toward the door, relieved that this humiliating meeting was over, Moshe picked up her ID badge and tossed it back to her.

Professor Barach was waiting for Sagit in a horrendously cluttered tiny office with a glass wall that overlooked a large clinical laboratory. Dressed in a long white lab coat, with piercing blue eyes and a head of thick gray hair, Barach looked every bit the cutting-edge researcher that he was. Decades ago he had been a practicing dentist and professor of dentistry at Hebrew University. Then he became interested in pain. First pain concerning teeth and then facial pain generally. Now at the age of seventy, he was a world-recognized expert on the subject.

Sagit had worked with him several times over the years, after Arab terrorists had bombed helpless civilians, who often died fiery deaths. Dr. Barach became the expert asked to perform the grim work of confirming the identity of the victims in suicide attacks or the perpetrators from their dental records.

"I would like to see you sometime socially," the professor had said to her the last time they performed this grisly task. "You're a charming person, but you only show up at my office for work."

Today when she walked in he was smiling. He brushed a few strands of hair back on his forehead. "Since there was no disaster on the news today, could this be the social visit you've been promising?"

She was all business in her expression and her voice. "Not today, I'm afraid, Dr. Barach."

"Ah, a pity. It's always work with you."

She handed him a light brown envelope.

"Why don't you come with me on Shabbat?" he said. "I'm taking a couple of my grandchildren on a hike up in the north."

"I'm sorry. I'm working this weekend. Another time, perhaps." She would have liked to have gone. He was a fascinating individual and knowledgeable about the land.

"You know you work too much."

"That's also what Moshe tells me."

"I don't like the stories I'm hearing about your leader around town these days."

Alarmed, she asked, "What stories?"

"He's getting leaned on hard by some of the politicians after the death of that Kourosh boy. And Yosef had some important patrons in the Knesset. Firing him may not have been such a good move politically. Word's circulating that the Mossad may have a new director before the end of the year."

Sagit smiled. She knew Moshe and Barach had fought together in the Palmach in Israel's war of independence in 1948. They had remained friends since that time. "We've heard those rumors before," she said.

It always amazed Sagit that on the one hand the name

of the director of the Mossad was so confidential that newspapers for a long time couldn't even publish it, but on the other hand, everything that happened to the director was the subject of dinner table gossip in Jerusalem. Sometimes she thought the country was too small. But was Washington any different? She didn't think so, not after spending time with Margaret Joyner last year.

He looked down at the envelope she had handed him. "What do you have for me?"

"Dental X rays of a male subject. An Israeli citizen. Came from Moscow about four years ago."

"What are you looking for?"

"I don't know. They've become important to some people. We'd like to know why."

Dr. Barach popped the X rays up on a screen, turned on the light and studied the teeth.

"How long did the subject live in Russia before coming to Israel?" he asked, his back still turned.

"His entire life."

"How do you know that?"

"That's what immigration records show."

He wheeled around and stared at her. "You mean the forms he filled out when he arrived in the country."

"Yes, the ones we give all new immigrants."

"Well, he lied on those forms," Dr. Barach said unequivocally.

Sagit was surprised. She had been on a fishing expedition, and it appeared as if she had landed a large one. "What do you mean?"

He picked up a pointer and tapped it on the center of the upper teeth. "Look at this. You see this crown? You see this bridge?"

She nodded.

"This is beautiful work. It's also at least ten years old. At that time work like this could only have been done in the United States, possibly in western Europe or here."

She was excited about Dr. Barach's conclusions. "What about Russia?" she said, her eyes sparkling with intensity.

He laughed loudly. "It'll be another hundred years before they do anything like this in Russia. Well, I don't want to exaggerate. Let's say fifty, to be conservative."

"So you don't think he spent his entire life living in Russia?"

"It's not a question of thinking it. I know."

Barach studied the X rays some more. "Different work was done at different times," he said, "over a number of years. My guess is that your man lived in the United States for a long time."

"Or at least he went there for dentistry."

"Precisely."

As she left Professor Barach's office, Sagit said to herself, "Well, well. David Ben Aaron. So far I have you for one crime: lying on an immigration application. Let's see what else I can get."

Naomi was the Mossad's top expert on fingerprints, and when she arrived personally in Sagit's office, rather than Teddy, her assistant, with whom Sagit had left the plastic bag, Sagit knew they had found something interesting.

Naomi was a no-nonsense professional, and Sagit was glad to see her for another reason. Unlike Teddy, Naomi would never comment on the fact that the evidence included three condom wrappers.

As usual, Naomi had no time for small talk. In Hebrew, spoken with an Irish accent, because she had been born in Dublin, she told Sagit to look at the stack of pages she handed her—each one containing a blowup of a finger or thumb print.

"You notice anything about these?" Naomi asked.

Sagit leafed through the pile. "They're all partial prints." she said, alarmed. Running through her mind was the thought: did I mess up in bagging the evidence? God, I hope I didn't make another mistake in Paris. "Did I smudge the items?" Sagit asked weakly.

"Hardly. The specimens were clear. The prints look smudged because they're partials."

"Partials? I don't understand."

"The subject, a man, had skin grafting about five years ago, probably to remove his fingerprints. The problem is that the prints grow back again and look precisely the same as they did before the skin grafting. What surprises me is why someone who goes to all this trouble to avoid detection wouldn't realize that his fingerprints will grow back."

As Sagit absorbed the information, she began thinking out loud. "Maybe he figured that if he eluded the police, or whoever he was running from for a couple of years, then he was safe."

"But if he truly wanted to be safe, he should have had it redone every couple of years."

Sagit was now persuaded that David was a fugitive. "True. But people develop a new life. They get comfortable. They don't think about their past. I think that's what happened here."

After Naomi left the office, Sagit sat alone at her desk, leafing through the pile of prints. Gideon had told her that he thought David Ben Aaron was, or at least had been, a KGB agent. Well, maybe Gideon had been on the right track in part. Maybe David was a CIA agent, on the run from the agency. Or maybe she was reaching. Maybe he was a civilian American who had committed a crime like tax fraud and taken on a new identity in Israel.

Quickly, she rejected the latter hypothesis. The whole pattern of entry via Russia and grafting fingerprints suggested an intelligence professional. His conduct in Paris was also consistent with that scenario.

No, he had been with the CIA, or one of the other United States intelligence agencies, such as DIA. The longer she thought about it, the more convinced she became.

She tried to decide on her next move. The obvious one was to call Margaret Joyner in Washington. It made sense to tell her everything and then to forward to Washington the dental X rays and fingerprints, to see what light they could shed on the man professing to be David Ben Aaron.

Coordination with Washington required Moshe's approval because the director alone was plugged into the nuances of Jerusalem's usually close, but sometimes strained, relationship with Washington, which could change on a daily basis. Feeling vulnerable because of her misconduct in Paris, Sagit wasn't about to circumvent agency policy, even with the relationship she had developed last year with Margaret Joyner. So she picked up the phone to get Moshe's approval.

While it was still ringing, she quickly hung up.

Informing Washington at this point would be a mistake, she told herself. So far only Israeli interests were at stake. One Israeli citizen had been killed. If David Ben Aaron was a former CIA agent on the run, Washington would focus on him and seek his extradition. But Israel's interest was in finding out who was trying to blackmail him and why; and who had killed Kourosh in Jerusalem. David couldn't help answer those questions from an American prison.

All of those were logical reasons, she told herself, for not asking Moshe to make the phone call to Margaret Joyner. What worried her was that deep down she might have had another reason. After spending time with David on the plane, in Paris, and in the hotel room, did she now like him?

It was preposterous!

She was a career Mossad agent. She had never been married, though she had had several relationships, which she had always broken off because they interfered with her work. Her commitment to the Mossad had always come first. As a woman and a Sephardic Jew, she had been forced to claw her way up the Mossad hierarchy until she became director of Field Operations—the highest position a woman had ever held in the organization. Moshe, her mentor, had described actions she had planned over the years as brilliant, but she thought of herself as competent, hardworking and dedicated. With that perception, she couldn't possibly be developing an attachment for the target of an investigation. It was stupid, and it made no sense. So she pushed it out of her mind.

Still, she rationalized, as long as there was some basis for not throwing David to American wolves, while not sacrificing Israeli interests, she was willing to do just that.

David's fingers moved nimbly over the computer keyboard as his eyes remained riveted on the screen. The High-Tech Center of the kibbutz was deathly still. It was four o'clock on Friday afternoon, and work had ground to a halt for Shabbat.

But David wasn't immersed in the work of the kibbutz. He was using the Internet and every possible source of worldwide information that he could access to expand his knowledge of what had happened in Paris. He began with Gina, who had so fascinated him and whose true identity he so desperately wanted to know. The Internet yielded thirty-two different Gina Martins, but none in the Nice area. French telephone directories provided no useful information. He was resigned to the fact that it was obviously a phony name.

The computer gave him masses of information about Renault, the giant automaker, including sales information, subsidiaries, locations of facilities, contractors, executives and board members. None of it was the least bit enlightening for his situation. Nor did Victor Foch show up in any Renault reference.

Entries for the French lawyer were sparse. His practice was described simply as corporate. His clients were not identified, but designated as "confidential." He made no court appearances. Undoubtedly, Victor was a deal maker—one of those lawyers who functioned in the privacy of boardrooms. David tried to cross-reference Renault and Victor, but he came up with nothing. His best guess was that Renault was not involved in this blackmail scheme and that Victor had used a separate personal relationship with an auto executive.

The French lawyer's name appeared in newspapers on only three occasions—all in *Le Monde*. Ten years ago, he was counsel for a French steel maker acquiring a Czech firm. Eight years ago, he represented a French metals company seeking to import minerals from Russia.

The third entry, though, caused David's weary eyes to lock on the screen. Three years ago, Victor Foch had represented the large French oil company Petroleum de France, or PDF, as it was called, in attempting to acquire Iraqi oil. Ultimately, Washington had persuaded the French government to prohibit the transaction because it violated the stricture against doing business with Saddam Hussein.

David's sagging spirits perked up. It wasn't much, but it was something. He felt a surge of adrenaline as he began to access PDF.

Suddenly, he heard the shuffling of feet in the doorway behind him. Instinctively, he hit the "panic" button, turning off the computer, and wheeled around in his chair.

She was standing there alone, dressed in a khaki skirt and black leather jacket zipped to the neck, a leather bag clutched tightly in her hand.

The words "Oh shit" involuntarily popped out of his mouth.

She was Mossad!

He should have known. How could he possibly have been that much of an idiot?

It was a rhetorical question. He had immediately liked her, and as he had spoken to her on the plane, he had developed a wild, sensual attraction to her. From the time he had seen her standing in the bathroom, naked and adjusting her shower cap, his actions had been directed by his dick—instead of his brain.

There was no hello, no greeting at all. Instead she whipped a Mossad ID card from her jacket pocket and held it up for him to see. It identified her as Sagit Bat Yehoshua.

"I think we have to talk," she said in a curt, businesslike tone, as she put back the ID card.

"Look, I'm really sorry about leaving you that way in Paris. For me it was a question of—"

She cut him off sharply. "Don't flatter yourself. I went to bed with you because it was my job. That's it. Plain and simple."

She paused to let her words sink in. They cut through him like the blade of a knife.

Then she added, "Obviously, I didn't get what I was hoping for. The night was a waste. So now I'm back with a different approach. Right now we have to talk, and you have to provide some answers."

"Not here," he said, pointing to the open doorway behind her. "People sometimes come in to pick up things they've forgotten. Let's go down to the litchi orchard. We'll be alone there."

She looked at him nervously.

"You've got nothing to worry about," he said, resorting to a brusque tone of his own. "I have no interest in anything other than a business relationship with you. Paris was a one-night stand as far as I'm concerned. And, at any rate, you probably have a gun in that bag."

His words had been intended to sting her, and they did. Wanting to show him who was in charge, she reached into her bag and pulled out a pistol. After holding it out to him and letting him know it was loaded, she put it away. "As a matter of fact, I do. I also have two men sitting in a car outside the front gate of the kibbutz, who will come if I hit the alarm button on the pager hooked to my belt."

He chuckled, feigning amusement to conceal his true reaction: dismay that his situation had become precarious. He didn't dare underestimate her. "All of that for me? I'm surprised you don't want me to hand over my passport."

"That's not necessary. Your name, picture and passport number are already designated with a special classification in the computers of Passport Control. You won't be able to leave the country."

"Do you have any legal basis for that action, or do you people do whatever you want?"

She looked indignant. "Don't confuse us with our neighbors. Here we have the rule of law."

"Try explaining that to Yosef the next time he tosses somebody into a prison cell without any evidence."

"Yosef's no longer with the Mossad. He was fired because of what he did to you. That's not how we operate."

"Well, that's at least one good thing. Now, would you mind telling me what your people think I did to deserve all of this attention?"

She snapped her fingers. "Try supplying false information on your application for citizenship, for openers. That's a crime."

David didn't respond. He waited to see what evidence she had.

In the small pickup on the way to the litchi orchard, the two of them rode in silence. She had the gun on her lap, loosely gripped in her hand. She knew that she wouldn't need it, but she wanted to underscore how she felt about him. He turned into the orchard and parked among the trees—filled with ripe, luscious fruit ready to be harvested. The sun was sinking in the western sky, and a light breeze shook the branches.

They climbed out of the pickup and eyed each other warily. She kept her distance, enough that she could go for her gun, or hit the alarm if she had to. Noticing this, David casually pulled a couple of litchi off a branch. He tossed one to her, then peeled and ate the other.

"Amazing they could be so hard on the outside and so soft on the inside," he said languidly.

"Quit stalling and tell me whom you met in Paris."

"You've got no basis to assert that I lied on my citizenship application," he said, hoping to flush her out before he decided how much he'd have to tell her.

"Really? We have a professor of dentistry who's ready to testify in court that all of your dental work was done in the United States, which isn't quite consistent with someone who lived in Russia until four years ago."

He pretended to scoff. "That's not very convincing to me."

"We didn't think it would be, but you left some items in the hotel room from which we got fingerprints."

"Like what?"

"The bottle of chloral." She decided not to mention the condoms.

David was wary now. "And?"

"They were only partial prints. The skin grafting you did is wearing out. You should have had it redone, or not left the bottle behind. That was a mistake."

He smiled disarmingly. "I was distracted."

"We don't think so. We think you're out of practice."

"What's that mean?"

"You were once CIA. You're an exile."

Her words hit him hard. She was smart, and he was impressed. He tried not to show it. "That's total bullshit."

"Listen—whoever you are—I came here today to give you one final chance to play it straight. We're ready to ship what we have to Margaret Joyner in Washington, who happens to be a personal acquaintance of mine. And while we wait for some answers, you can cool your jets in jail, in protective custody, and it will all be perfectly legal."

He realized that she was now holding all the cards. "You can't do that," he protested, exhibiting a false position of strength.

"Just watch us. One of our state attorneys happens to be having dinner tonight at the home of a judge in Haifa. It'll take about thirty seconds to get the attorney on the phone and have the judge sign a detention order, specifying that you're awaiting extradition to the United States. I don't know why, but somehow we're sure Washington will be delighted have you back."

He clenched his hands tightly. She was right, of course. They would love to have him back.

"Well, what do you want?" he asked, still trying to sound bold and self-confident.

"Answers."

"To what questions?"

"For starters, try who you really are, and what happened in Paris after you left me."

Uncertain about how much she knew, he decided to wade in carefully. "Why do you care?"

"An Israeli citizen's dead, because of some type of conspiracy, and you're involved in it up to your neck. We know that from your end of the telephone conversation in the Bristol in Paris."

"And if I answer your questions, then you'll agree that the information about me never goes to Washington?"

"Not a chance. We'll agree that it doesn't go *at this time*. We won't give you any promises about the future. We'll have to see how it unfolds."

"Then it's no deal," he said emphatically.

She gave him a cold smile. "Don't try to bluff me. Before my grandfather brought the family to Israel, he sold carpets in a souk in Baghdad. He taught me well. Nobody outnegotiates me. And certainly not when I'm holding all of the cards."

"Meaning what?"

"You start talking now, or I push the alarm on my watch, and you spend Shabbat in a Haifa jail."

He could see that she wouldn't budge. Meanwhile, an idea was taking shape in his mind. He already knew that getting into Saudi Arabia to kill Nasser would be difficult. Being allied with the Mossad could be a big advantage when he made his move. Yael was one of twelve Israelis who had died in the explosion on Bus 18. The Mossad might be willing to assist him if he played that card at the right time.

"There is something else, though," he told Sagit. "A condition you have to meet before I'll talk to you."

She eyed him suspiciously. "Yeah, what?"

"I have a stepdaughter in Paris."

"Daphna at the Sorbonne. We know all about her."

"What you don't know is that she's in danger because of me. If I agree to talk to you, I want you to promise to get her out of Paris and bring her back home before you take any action based on what I tell you."

Sagit paused to think about what he had said. "That's reasonable," she responded at last. "Daphna's an Israeli citizen. If she's at risk, we'd get her out of a foreign country, even if you didn't insist on it. But I can't commit. I'll have to get the approval of my boss in Jerusalem."

"Call him, then. I'm not answering any of your questions

until I get that assurance about Daphna. And you can tell him, too, that I want the opportunity to have input on the plan you develop to get her out."

His concern for a stepdaughter seemed excessive to Sagit. Was he using this whole Daphna business as a pretext to get back to Paris for some other purpose? She decided to play along with him. "That may be a problem, but I'll make the call. I'm going to tell him the rest of the deal is that you'll agree to answer *all* of my questions completely and truthfully, and if you don't, the dental X rays and finger-prints go to Washington right now."

David nodded reluctantly.

It was twilight, and the air was growing cooler.

"You better take me up to the administration building," she said. "I want to call Jerusalem and get the approval on our agreement."

As he started toward the truck, she added, "After that, let's go someplace quiet where we can talk, and I can take notes."

He looked at his watch. "We're going to be at it awhile. You might as well stay for dinner."

Dinner was a community affair, served buffet style, with kibbutz members and guests seated at long tables. Friday nights brought lots of guests. It wasn't a religious kibbutz, and the Shabbat service was brief.

David simply introduced her as his friend Sagit from Jerusalem. He had not had a guest since Yael's death, and he could tell that Sagit's presence prompted a fair amount of gossip, which was a mainstay of kibbutz life, as in any close-knit society.

At the dinner table, a debate raged about the Syrian government's intentions on peace with Israel. The members were equally divided between those who viewed the Golan Heights as essential to Israel's security, and those who argued that demilitarization and early warning with sophisticated technology could do the job as well.

During dinner, David noticed Gideon watching him from across the room, but the security chief never came over.

After dinner there was singing and then a movie: *Murder at 1600* with Wesley Snipes.

As they started to leave the dining room, Sagit's cell phone rang.

She took the phone into a quiet corner, and he watched her: first talking, gesticulating with her free hand all the while, and then listening. She hung up the phone and returned to him. "He's approved the deal. Where do you want to talk?"

David was relieved to hear about Daphna. "My house."

He saw her hesitate.

"Don't worry, I'll keep my distance."

Walking along the path, lit only by the bright moon, he became conscious of his limp, and cursed that football injury for getting him into this mess. Suddenly, he heard footsteps behind him. David wheeled around quickly. It was Gideon.

"I guess you and I won't be having a chess game tonight," the security chief said.

"Not tonight, but I want to introduce my friend. Sagit, this is—"

"It's not necessary," Gideon said coolly. "I know who she is." He turned to her and said, "You'll give my regards to Moshe?"

David's house, which he had shared with Yael, was a small wooden cottage with two rooms. The front door opened into a combination living room/dining room with a tiny kitchen on one side. In the back was a bedroom, with a double bed and unfinished wooden chest, and a bath. Everywhere there was clutter: books and clothes tossed about, with old newspapers piled on the floor and serving as a makeshift tables for empty soda cans. Half a dozen pictures of Yael and Daphna occupied one wall. None of them with David. As Sagit walked into the house and looked around, she had to resist an instinctive desire to make some order out of the chaos.

They settled down in the small living room. Seated at a square wooden table, Sagit set up a tape recorder, then pulled a pencil and pad from her bag. Across the room, David stretched out on an old frayed sofa, holding a glass of Slivovitz.

"Begin with Paris," she said. "We need to know in detail what happened. Everything."

"Everything?"

She blushed, then looked annoyed. "You know what I mean. You act like a smart ass, and you can spend the rest of the night in jail."

He began with the telephone call he had received at the Bristol. Then he described everything that had happened from the time he left her at the Bristol until he returned home to Israel. He told her about his night at the Gironde, the meeting with Victor Foch, and the meeting at Renault. He talked for a half hour, not leaving out anything, and she interrupted him for small clarifying questions, like when and where his next meeting was in Paris. As he spoke, she tried to take meticulous notes, in case the tape recorder malfunctioned, but he spoke so rapidly that she found herself stopping him from time to time and blurting out, "Hey, slow down. I'm not getting all of this."

When he was finished, he walked over to a small credenza, picked up the bottle of Slivovitz and an empty glass. He pointed them at her, still writing. She shook her head. "Then how about some strong black coffee?"

"That I could use."

He brewed some coffee for her, then refilled his own glass with plum brandy and sat down again.

"Okay," she said. "Now tell us what happened on the fifteenth of August five years ago in Saudi Arabia."

He repeated that story as well, from the time the bomb exploded in Dhahran until his altercation with General Chambers. She was incredulous. "You broke General Chambers's jaw?"

"And his nose, I think. The bastard deserved it, and worse. If he had listened to me and dealt with Colonel Azziz and the Saudi moderates, the terrorist attack would never have taken place."

She was startled by his bold talk. In her experience,

American agents had always been circumspect. He was a breed apart, this Greg Nielsen, now calling himself David. "That's your opinion."

"It happens to be correct. Chambers was a fool."

"It also seems not to have stopped General Chambers from becoming chairman of the Joint Chiefs, which is his current position, as I recall."

Talking about Chambers had put him on edge. "They're a bunch of dumb fucks in Washington. With me out of the picture, he was free to lie about what really happened. So, before a closed Senate Intelligence Committee inquiry, which your big buddy Margaret Joyner chaired when she was still in the Senate, he blamed me for providing him with misleading information."

"How do you know that?"

"I'd rather not say."

She looked up from her pad and shook her head. "Sorry, that's not an option under our agreement."

He was resigned. "Early on, I had a couple of telephone conversations with Tim Donnelly, the assistant director at the time, and an old buddy, but I haven't talked to him in a long while."

"What about your former deputy, Bill Fox? Did you talk to him, too?"

He kept his voice neutral. "Not for a long time."

She was taking notes again. "At least not since you just saw him in London."

How did she know that? he wondered.

As if reading his mind, she said, "You may have given our man the slip after the incident in Green Park, but he photographed you with the man on the bench. We passed it around the Agency, and today somebody called to say they recognized Bill Fox. So tell me about London."

He described for her what had happened in London. He told her that he had taken a circuitous route back via Milan and Athens to avoid a tail, but he didn't mention Bruno Wolk or Switzerland.

"All right, now go back to Saudi Arabia, David, or do we call you Greg?"

"Why do you always have to use 'we'? Why can't you say 'I'?"

"Because I don't want to be personally involved with you."

He was trying to take charge now, to put her on the defensive. His tone was cocky. "I don't think that's it at all. I think, as a woman and a Sephardic, you're afraid of being an outsider in your own organization. I think you need the constant feeling that you belong."

"Thank you for the free psychoanalysis. Now tell me, do we call you David or Greg?"

"I've rather gotten used to David. He was a powerful king, who could have any woman if he really wanted her."

"God, you have sex on your brain." When she glanced up from the pad, she saw him staring at her. A phrase in a novel she had once read popped into her mind: he was "undressing her mentally." Embarrassed, she looked back down. "Forget it, and tell us what happened when you raced out of the building, after you struck General Chambers."

"I managed to sneak out of Saudi Arabia."

"How?"

He hesitated. "I don't think you need to know."

The stony look came over her face again. "We need to know everything."

"A friend flew me out."

"Who?"

"I won't tell you that."

She raised her voice. "Then you're welshing on our deal. The prints and dental X rays go to Washington."

He shouted back. "Let them go. It's not a critical fact. Besides, I don't give a damn anymore."

She slammed her pad shut and stood up.

As he watched her pull the pager from her belt and prepare to activate the alarm button, he thought: Her grandfather must have been one tough negotiator in that Baghdad souk. He hated backing down again, but he had no choice.

"There was a Saudi Air Force captain, a pilot, Khalid was his name. He was a friend of mine, and he supported

Azziz and the moderates. I stole an army jeep and drove to his house. He dressed me up as a Saudi Air Force officer. Then he put me in the cockpit of a plane with him. In all the confusion after the Dhahran bombing, he flew me across the border to UAE. I used one of my backup CIA passports to fly to Geneva, Switzerland, before the State Department could wire other governments with the list of all the passport numbers the Company had issued to me."

"Why Geneva?"

David hesitated for an instant. He'd have to be careful. He wanted his story to sound credible, and yet he didn't want to involve Bruno, who had directed and funded all of his moves from the time he got to Geneva until he arrived in Israel. He decided to tell her the true story and simply omit Bruno's role.

"I had a bank account there with money I had accumulated gambling at European casinos over the years. I'm quite skillful at chemin de fer."

He winked at her. "Money will buy you anything. So I found a good plastic surgeon in the area."

"What's his name?"

"I don't remember. Who cares?"

"We care."

He gave a deep sigh. In a tone of exasperation, he answered, "Dr. Heinrich Wilhelm. He redid me totally. Face, hair, eyes, the works."

"Fingerprints?"

"Fingerprints, too. He ran a small private hospital. I stayed there two weeks."

"And then?"

He waved his hand in boredom. "You're pretty smart. You've probably figured out the rest."

"We want you to tell us."

"I paid a forger to prepare Russian papers. Now I had a new identity as a resident of Moscow, and I slipped into Russia. My name was Anatola Ginzburg. I was a Jew, living in Moscow. From there it was easy. I applied for a visa to Israel. That was the time they were being freely given. To be safe, I paid a couple of hefty bribes, and my visa came through. So I joined the thousands of others immigrating to the promised land. I blended in."

His voice became more animated as he remembered the rest. "When the El Al plane landed at three A.M. at Ben Gurion one chilly March morning four and a half years ago, I came down the stairs clutching a battered suitcase in one hand and assisting a frail old woman in a babushka with the other. Behind us a young man took a violin out of his case and began to play. And when I reached the bottom of the stairs, and the old woman could walk herself, I cried for joy with the others. Then I joined them in falling down to kiss the ground with gratitude—even though my lips encountered only oily airplane tarmac instead of the land of Israel."

She looked angry. "Don't be such a cynical bastard. Those people were escaping persecution and realizing their lifelong dream."

He stared back at her harshly. "I'm not being cynical. I was thrilled to be here. General Chambers had mobilized the entire American military to find me."

"Yeah, that's right. You were just happy to save your neck." She yawned. "All right, one more subject. Yael Golan. When did you first meet her?"

He had known this was coming. "About four years ago in a café on Diezengoff in Tel Aviv. September the tenth, to be precise. I'll never forget that date. It was what we Americans call love at first sight."

"Why do I think you're hiding something?"

"Because you're the cynic. You don't believe in romance."

His comment stung her, which was what he'd intended, hoping she would drop the subject. "Why would I lie about this to you?" he said. "I've told you everything else you wanted to know."

Having been warned by Moshe that the subject of Yael was off limits, Sagit decided to back off though she was not persuaded that David was telling the truth. She was also tired from writing. She opened and closed her right hand to relax her fingers, while she leafed through her notes.

"It's late," he said, looking at the wall clock. "You want to sleep here tonight?"

She smiled. "You're a persistent fellow with a massive ego, aren't you?"

For once he didn't have to pretend. "I didn't mean that. I'll sleep in the living room on the couch. You can have the bed to yourself, if that's what you want." His voice and face were earnest. Waiting for her to respond, he compared her with Yael, which he didn't want to do; but he couldn't turn off his mind. She wasn't nearly as bold or headstrong. Probably more intelligent, though less physically beautiful. Despite the deliberately harsh manner she exhibited tonight, he had found on the plane and in Paris that she radiated a warmth. She . . .

Oh hell, what was the use of trying to articulate it? Love was chemistry, and they had a strong chemistry between them. He was convinced that she felt it as much as he did.

She closed her pad and gave a long sigh. "You don't get it, do you?"

"Get what?"

"What happened at the Bristol was business for me, and that's all."

He looked at her skeptically. "Who are you trying to convince? Me or yourself?"

He drove her to a point about twenty yards from the entrance to the kibbutz. From behind the wheel of the pickup, he watched her walk the rest of the way herself and climb into the back of an old battered Chevrolet Caprice. He sat in the moonlight to see if she waved or looked back at him, but she didn't.

After parking the pickup, he walked over to the dark, deserted High-Tech Center and went to his office in the back of the building. With only a tiny desk lamp for light, he booted up his computer.

In a matter of seconds, the marvelous machine was feeding him information about the French oil company PDF. It was one of the largest privately owned companies in

France. Madame Jacqueline Blanc was the owner of all of the stock. She was variously described as cunning, resourceful and as an industrial visionary. She was wealthy and eccentric. A Howard Hughes personality, but not a recluse. Through interlocking directorates she had slots on the boards of directors of a half dozen other important French companies, including Renault. PDF was involved in oil exploration and development around the world. It manufactured chemicals from petrochemical feed stocks at a number of facilities in France and scattered all over the globe. PDF didn't sell retail gasoline or other products. Rather, it sold only to other oil companies. PDF had had substantial contracts with Saddam Hussein before the Gulf War and with Libya before Quaddafi was ostracized. They had entered into several transactions to explore for oil in the former Soviet Union.

This is crazy, he thought. I don't even know whether PDF or Madame Blanc is involved. But all of his instincts told him both were. And those same instincts had kept him alive in some difficult situations over the years. He wasn't about to disregard them.

As he walked out of the High-Tech Center, he nearly stumbled on Gideon, sitting on the steps of the building. Startled, David said, "What are you doing here?"

"I could ask you the same thing."

"Working."

"The same for me."

He knew that he had to tell Gideon something. "The Mossad has asked me to cooperate with them on this Kourosh business. I'm working with Sagit, trying to obtain information for her."

Gideon stood up and looked at David in utter disbelief. He may have been just an old army vet and security guard, but he was smart enough not to believe a single word this hotshot spy posing as a computer expert told him. "I don't care about you, Mr. Super Spy. Daphna, your stepdaughter is a child of this kibbutz, and I don't want her to end up like Kourosh. You and Sagit should bring her home before something happens to her."

"We're working on it, Gideon. Believe me, Daphna's the first priority."

Madame Blanc puffed deeply on her Cohiba, blew the smoke out of the window of the Rolls Royce and studied the profile of Colonel Khalid seated next to her. In appearance, he reminded her of Anwar Sadat, especially the smile and the dark brown eyes. He was tall and thin, and he carried himself with great dignity. His skin was light brown and he had a very high forehead. Much of the hair was gone on top and he had a thin brown mustache, perfectly trimmed. His teeth were white and glistened when he smiled. He exuded confidence. He was someone whom others would follow.

The two of them were alone in the car. She had asked Claude, her driver, to take a walk. From their vantage point, parked on a bluff overlooking the airfield below, Khalid was peering intently through night-scope binoculars. He was studying loading operations conducted under the cover of darkness. Above, thick clouds in the Provence sky obliterated the moon.

Madame Blanc had no need to watch. She had been assured by the CEO of Granita Munitions that everything she had requested—the entire inventory on Colonel Khalid's list—all of the tanks, mortars, automatic rifles and ammunition—would be delivered to the airfield at midnight. The C130 cargo jet with Saudi markings had arrived a few minutes later.

"Four hours is all we'll need," she had assured the civilian who directed operations at this airfield—and who had been handsomely paid. Close friends of hers in the French military privately knew what she was doing tonight, but if they were asked about it, they would vociferously deny any knowledge. This was, after all, not a French governmental operation.

Looking at Khalid, she thought it was more than a little ironic that weapons were being shipped to a nation that had one of the largest stockpiles of unused weapons in the world. Khalid had explained to her the reason when he gave her the list. The core of his Democratic Front was comprised of air force officers, including the entire upper command. As yet they had only isolated support among the army, and access to the army's supplies was questionable. These weapons would be stored and concealed in air force hangars, where army supporters of the Democratic Front would gain rapid access to them at the time of the coup. Khalid's hope was that with this kindling, the whole army would catch fire.

Madame Blanc didn't question Khalid's knowledge of the Saudi military. From his dossier, she knew his father had been a much decorated air force pilot who died in an air battle with rebels over Yemen when Khalid was eight years old. As the only son, he had vowed to follow in his father's footsteps. Following an education at Oxford, at Saudi government expense, he joined the Saudi Air Force to become a pilot. His natural abilities were so strong that he never needed the influence of his father's colleagues to make it into officers school. When he was sent to Alabama for training on American fighters in a mixed Saudi-Israeli class, he was the only Saudi pilot to gain the grudging respect of the Israelis.

Satisfied, Khalid put his binoculars down on the thick leather seat of the Rolls and turned to Madame Blanc. "What happened with Greg Nielsen?" he asked.

"We're making progress. I'll know for sure in a few days. He's not an easy nut to crack." She paused and thought about what Victor had told her. "I'm making great efforts to enlist his help. Do you really think he adds that much?"

Khalid didn't hesitate. His tone was unyielding. "Absolutely. He's smart. He was committed to my cause. And he developed the defense systems for the king's palace. His participation means a great deal to me."

She tried to shake him. This David was proving to be trouble. It would be easier without him. "But you were planning to go forward before you accidentally happened to see him in Paris."

"I know that," he replied firmly. "But if we can get Nielsen on board, fewer lives will be lost."

"You have to crack eggs to make an omelet, my friend."

Her callous indifference annoyed him. The dead would all be Saudis, not French. "I want the minimum amount of bloodshed. For the long years that the House of Saud has ruled my country, as if it were their own private domain, their idea of justice was killing anybody and everybody who disagreed with their views. The bloodier their punishment, the more of a deterrent they thought it would be. Well, we won't operate that way.

"Their blatant corruption has produced a situation in which, if our group doesn't act now, and doesn't bring democracy to the country, the inevitable result will be a revolution staged by the fundamentalists, and Saudi Arabia will resemble Iran. This is the last chance to save my country. So you have to understand that our motives aren't selfish. We're patriots. Loyal citizens of the true nation of Arabia."

As Khalid continued with the lecture he had given her the first time they met, nearly two months ago, she stopped listening. She found the colonel to be tiresome. She didn't care what his motives were, and whether or not they were pure. For her, it was a matter of business—plain and simple.

If Khalid succeeded, PDF would become the dominant foreign oil presence in the country, and the American and British oil firms, which had so long been puppets of the Saudi regime, would be out. The deal she had cut with Khalid in return for her support was a five-year exclusive oil exploration and oil industry consulting contract to straighten out the inefficient and troubled Saudi oil industry. The new Saudi government would pay PDF a one percent commission during those five years on all oil exported from the country. At current market prices, that would be more than $500 million per year. But she wasn't prepared to stick with the current market prices. She intended to use the Saudi market power to work with other countries and drive the price higher, thereby increasing the amount of PDF's royalty.

"What precisely do you want from Nielsen?" she asked.

"I want him to analyze and to evaluate the defenses

being employed at the king's palace, and then I want him to develop a plan for overcoming those defenses." Khalid paused, looked at her thoughtfully and continued. "But I don't want him to know I'm involved."

Once they had been friends, but that was five years ago. Khalid didn't want to alarm Madame Blanc, but he had no idea what Nielsen had done since then. He couldn't be certain where the man's current loyalties lay.

Madame Blanc nodded her approval.

The plan was so good for PDF that she wanted it to succeed at all costs. If Khalid wanted help from Greg Nielsen or David Ben Aaron, or whoever the hell he was, then she would make it happen. Regardless of what had to be done.

An hour later, as the Rolls raced back to Paris on the deserted highway, Madame Blanc replayed in her mind the discussion with Khalid tonight. The good news was that he was solidly in favor of the coup. The wavering and uncertainty she had detected earlier were gone.

The bad news was that he was even more adamant about his desire to have Greg Nielsen participate. She didn't know what his reaction would be if she couldn't get Nielsen on board, but she didn't intend to find out.

Indifferent to the fact that it was almost three A.M., she picked up the car phone and dialed Victor's apartment in Paris. He didn't seem to fully appreciate the urgency of getting the job done. She decided to add her own pressure to the effort.

When he answered the phone, he showed none of the anger that someone usually expresses when they are awakened from a sound sleep. He had no doubt who was calling in the middle of the night.

"Hello, Jacqueline," he said before she said a word.

She wasted no time on greetings. "I'm going to make your job with Greg Nielsen easier."

"What's that mean?" he asked warily while he rubbed the sleep from his eyes.

"This is your client," she said brusquely. "And I'm giving

you a direct order, so pay attention. Before Nielsen walks into his meeting with you next Wednesday morning—and I mean, right before—I want his stepdaughter to be kidnapped, and I want her taken to the house outside Grasse. Is that clear?"

Her sharp tone had him fully awake. "Very clear."

The Rolls was moving at 120 miles per hour in the left lane of the Autoroute, and another driver was flashing his lights for the Rolls to pull over so he could pass. "I don't want her harmed at this point. Right now she's no good to us dead.

"Go faster, Claude," she barked from the backseat. "Don't let that lunatic pass us."

CHAPTER 9

David flew to Paris alone on Tuesday. He had persuaded
Sagit to cancel the Mossad tail, for the first day, telling her
that he didn't want Daphna to end up like Kourosh. Arriving at the Bristol, he took the first room he was shown,
to the surprise of the assistant manager, Gilles, who had
anticipated another trek around the hotel. He discreetly
handed David a sealed envelope. When the man left, David
opened it. There was a typed note that read:

> The car will pick you up at ten tomorrow morning. I
> hope you have a nice evening in Paris.
> —V

Also inside the envelope was a full frontal nude picture of
a voluptuous young woman, standing on a beach, with the
sea behind her. A Paris telephone number was written on
the bottom of the picture. The envelope also contained a
thick wad of French francs.

David put the money from Victor into his pocket. He
tore the picture into tiny pieces and flushed them down
the toilet.

Then he went to a pay phone in the hotel lobby and
called Taillevent. Three years ago, when he and Yael had
been in Paris, he had had the greatest meal of his life there,
thanks to Bruno's friendship with Monsieur Vrinat, the leg-
endary proprietor. But tonight he hadn't picked Taillevent
for the food. He wanted a place that the people following
Daphna couldn't possibly penetrate and listen in from a
nearby table.

Again Bruno Wolk's name worked wonders, and David was able to book a table for two at eight-thirty. Then he called Daphna and told her to meet him on the Champs Elysées in front of the United Airlines office.

The night was damp and rainy, and she huddled close to him under his black umbrella as they approached the restaurant's midnight blue awning. In the corner of his eye, David spotted Daphna's tail—a man in a green soldier's coat standing on the corner, pretending to be looking in the window of a wine shop. A car, also part of their team, pulled over to the curb near the corner.

After Monsieur Vrinat directed an assistant to take them to a corner table, well within the restaurant's wood-paneled inner sanctum, Daphna exclaimed, "Wow! I didn't know the kibbutz funded meals like this in Paris. Maybe I'll go back to Israel after all."

Ignoring her comment, David let his eyes roam back and forth across the rapidly filling restaurant. He hadn't used the phone in his room to make the reservation, for fear it was bugged, and he hadn't given Daphna the name of the restaurant on the phone. Logically, no one could have known where they were going in time to book a second table—even if that was possible in the completely sold-out restaurant—but he couldn't assume anything. Victor Foch was well connected in Paris. David didn't see anything suspicious. Still, he would make certain they kept their voices down. You could never be sure who understood Hebrew.

He had thought long and hard about the best way to explain the situation. Daphna was worldly, and yet she was young and fragile. He wasn't sure there was a good way.

After they each had a glass of champagne and ordered dinner, he began. "You were in the Israeli Air Force," he said awkwardly. "You flew helicopters. You learned to live with danger."

She cringed. "Please, I don't want to talk about that. Not now. Not ever."

He wanted to kick himself for beginning the discussion so poorly. So he decided to dive in, speaking softly, almost in a whisper. "Listen, Daphna, we were followed to the restaurant. We're in danger. Now. Both of us."

Stunned, she said, "What are you talking about, David?"

"Please keep your voice down. There are things in my past life that have caught up with me."

"You mean, when you lived in Moscow?"

"No, I mean when I was an American."

She nearly choked on her champagne. "But I thought . . . What do you mean? . . . You told me you came from Moscow. My mother said you were a Russian."

"Sometimes, things aren't the way they seem."

As they worked their way through first courses of salmon and mushrooms, and entrees of veal and quail, David told her about his job as CIA station chief in Saudi Arabia, about his hasty exodus from that country after his fight with General Chambers, his entry into Israel and the events of recent days.

Once the waiter had left them with large dessert menus and departed, David pursed his lips and looked at her. "They know that I care for you. So they're trying to use the threat to you to get me to comply. You see now why you're in danger?"

She nodded.

"So, I have to get you back to Israel for a couple of months, but you can't say a word to anyone until you're back home. Not even to your closest friends here in Paris. When you're safely back on the kibbutz, call the people at the Sorbonne and tell them that you had to rush home for a family emergency."

"But if these people are watching me, and they're even outside the restaurant tonight, won't they stop me from going home?"

"Oh, they'll try. You can be sure of that, but I'm working with the Mossad. We have a plan to deal with them."

"Tell me," she said anxiously.

"Tomorrow morning at exactly seven-thirty," he said, "I want you to go to a bakery called Bonte, located on rue Amelie, which is about six blocks from your apartment—"

She interrupted, "I know it well."

"As you know," he continued, "the bakery will be crowded then. I want you, quickly and unobtrusively, to go into the back of the bakery, where the ovens are, and ask for Guy. That's all you have to do. We'll take it from there."

She looked at him wide-eyed. She ran her fingers over the white linen tablecloth. "Why can't I stay here and help you?"

He wanted to be gentle with her. "Not now," he replied. "Trust me on that. Maybe later. The main thing now is to give me room to maneuver. I can't do that if they've got you at the end of a gun scope."

Reluctantly, she seemed persuaded. "How did you ever get into this spy business?" she asked.

"It's late," he said. "We've covered a lot of ground tonight. I'll tell you another time."

She refused to be put off. "I want to know. Besides, we still have dessert."

So as a decadent *dacquoise* sat untouched in front of Daphna, David began talking again.

"I was born in a place called Aliquippa, Pennsylvania, a small steel mill town in northwest Pennsylvania. My parents immigrated to the United States from Denmark when they were first married. My father operated a small restaurant across from a steel mill. They were good people, decent people. They went to church every Sunday. They taught me to love my country. I was a good athlete in high school, and I thought I could get an athletic scholarship to college because my parents didn't have much money. But I injured my leg in a game of American football in high school, and that was the end of my athletic career.

"Fortunately, I was also a good student, particularly in science and engineering. Carnegie Tech awarded me a scholarship in chemical engineering. But I almost didn't go."

"What happened?"

"My senior year in high school a couple of kids, a couple of punks from the next town, got drunk and robbed my dad's store. He was a man of principle, and he wouldn't give them the money in the cash register—the grand sum of twenty-one dollars." David swallowed hard. "They shot and killed him."

He paused to look at her. There were tears in the corners of her eyes. She was shaking her head in disbelief. "I'm so sorry. First your father and then last year my mother."

"Life can be unfair," he said sadly. His eyes were fixed on the wood-paneled wall across the room. She had lost him. His mind was back in Aliquippa, and the awful day he had heard about his father. She squeezed her hands together, waiting for him to continue.

Finally, he began again. "I didn't want to take that college scholarship, because I was the oldest of three children, two boys and a girl, but my mother insisted. She buried my father, and she did what she had to do. She went into that restaurant and ran it as well as my father had. She made me admire strong, self-reliant women."

Daphna thought of her mother. Yael had been a strong, self-reliant woman. "What did you do?"

"What she told me to do. I spent the next four years studying hard to be a chemical engineer at Carnegie Tech. Meantime, my younger brother refused to follow her orders and go to college. He left Aliquippa after high school graduation, went down to Oklahoma and made his first million in six months wildcatting for oil. So I didn't have to worry about my family's finances any longer.

"My senior year of college, I didn't know what I wanted to do. I figured I'd like to travel and see the world because I'd never been anywhere in my life, outside of western Pennsylvania. I wasn't tied to the area emotionally. I had a girlfriend from high school whom I'd outgrown. So when I saw a notice on the college placement bulletin board that said, 'Company engaged in international operations seeks chemical engineer for oil-related projects,' I signed up.

"The CIA recruiter snowed me, but he didn't have to try hard. I knew from my brother that defending America's sources of foreign oil was strongly in the country's interest, and we had already had the 1973 oil embargo. Besides, I wanted to serve my country in the worst way. I had volunteered for the Marines during the Vietnam War, when I was still in high school, before my dad was killed, but they wouldn't take me because of my bad leg. I cried about that. All through college I felt guilty that I was stuck in school while my friends had a chance to serve."

Daphna was on the edge of her seat, mesmerized by his story. "But I thought American kids of your generation hated the war in Vietnam."

David shook his head. He understood how Daphna had gotten that impression from the media. How could she understand the patriotism that so many first-generation Americans instilled in their children? "Not all of them. Just the vocal ones, and maybe in hindsight the smarter ones, but that's not how it looked then."

"So you signed up with the CIA and became a spy?"

"We don't like to use that word. I became a representative of the Company, as we called it. They sent me down to Texas to learn everything about the oil business, working for Spartan Oil, a large oil corporation. After that they gave me various postings through the Middle East, which gets us to five years ago and what happened in Saudi Arabia with General Chambers." David signaled to the waiter for the check. "And it's also time to get you home to sleep. We both have a busy day tomorrow."

As they left the restaurant, he handed her a package of matches that contained the Hotel Bristol telephone number. "Tuck it into your purse," he said. "If anything suspicious happens tonight, call me immediately."

Sagit was squatting down behind a second-floor window above the the Bonte bakery, with her eyes riveted on the street below, continually scanning from the right—in the direction she thought they would come—to the left, just in case she was wrong.

Last night, she had arranged to have a Parisian taxi driver sympathetic to the Israeli cause, who did jobs for the Mossad from time to time, wait on boulevard Haussmann as David waved for a cab after dinner, first to drop off Daphna and then to take him back to the Bristol. David had given the driver a report on the surveillance—one man on foot in a green soldier's coat, who had a large scar that ran the length of his right cheek, and another in a midnight blue Citroën sedan, license number PCG1095. As soon as he got home, the taxi driver had called Sagit with the information.

Suddenly, Sagit saw Daphna, dressed in a tan raincoat, rounding the corner. A man in a long green coat was about ten yards behind her. Sagit picked up the binoculars. It was Scarface, all right. A midnight blue Citroën then rounded the corner, following another ten yards behind.

Ready for action, Sagit felt a surge of adrenaline. She picked up the cell phone on the floor and called Avi in an old, battered green Renault parked on the rue Amelie beyond the bakery.

"It's time," she snapped into the phone.

"Position okay?" replied Avi.

"Precisely. Stay where you are until you hear from me."

As Daphna prepared to enter the bakery, Sagit scrambled down the staircase that led to a driveway running along one side of the building. A beige bakery van with BONTE printed on the side was parked in the back.

Scarface stood outside, but kept his eyes on the tall girl with blond hair as she walked into the bakery—mobbed with people as it was every morning. This wasn't London, and there was no orderly queue. Instead, there was lots of pushing and shoving as those in the rear tried to force their way to the front, where the clerks—all young women—tried to maintain their composure while frantically filling orders.

Scarface heard Robert in the Citroën call to him, and he looked away from the shop to see what Robert wanted. "Hey, get me a chocolate croissant."

"Not here," he replied. "It's too crowded."

Scarface looked back into the bakery. For a second he thought he had lost her, and he panicked. But then he spotted the back of a tall girl with blond hair and a tan raincoat almost up to the counter, ready to place her order. He breathed a sigh of relief.

His gaze remained on the girl as the clerk handed her a bag, and she placed several coins on the counter. When she turned around, though, he was horrified. She wasn't Daphna! As she walked toward the front door of the bakery, beads of sweat popped out on his forehead. There had to be another tall blond girl in a tan raincoat in the bakery. His eyes frantically searched the crowd.

She wasn't there!

"Oh, goddammit," he cursed. He'd lost her. Somehow, they had tricked him. They must have taken her out through the back. Suddenly he saw a beige bakery van move along the driveway, stop for an instant and turn to the left onto rue Amelie.

She had to be in that truck, he decided. He ran back to the Citroën, shouting, "Quick, Robert. Start the engine."

Daphna was lying flat on the floor of the bakery van, between trays of pastries and baskets of baguettes, just as Sagit had directed. In her hand she tightly clutched an Israeli passport that identified her as Leora Feldman and an El Al plane ticket for a flight this afternoon from Paris to Israel. The instructions that Sagit had barked to Daphna were still echoing in her head.

At the next corner, the van turned left and continued along for another minute. Suddenly the driver slammed on the brakes. From the front seat, Sagit shouted to Daphna in Hebrew, "Now move. Fast."

With that cue, Daphna sprang to her feet, opened the back door of the van and scrambled out, trying not to step on a tray of croissants in the process. Outside on the street, she saw a navy blue Opel sedan parked across the wide boulevard, facing the other way, just as Sagit had promised. The rear door of the Opel was ajar on the street side. Threading her way among fast-moving cars, Daphna ran across the street and threw herself into the back of the Opel and down on the floor, just as Sagit had directed. She felt a blanket descend over her body. The door slammed, and the car started moving.

*　　*　　*

Back on rue Amelie, there was pandemonium in front of the bakery. Scarface and Robert had gotten only about twenty yards in the Citroën when they encountered a battered old green Renault, stopped dead between two parked cars in the one-lane street. The Renault appeared to have engine trouble, and it was coughing and sputtering as the driver tried to start the engine, which was obviously flooded.

Scarface ran over to the driver, who was cursing in Arabic while repeatedly pressing down on the accelerator and feeding stiii more gasoline into the flooded engine.

"Fucking stupid Arab," Scarface shouted.

Pedestrians stopped to watch. Ignoring them, Scarface yanked the idiot driver out of the Renault and signaled to Robert in the Citroën. Together, they pushed the Renault down the street until there was an opening between cars. Then they ran back to their own car.

At the corner, they turned left just as they had seen the bakery van do. They drove fast down the boulevard, looking straight ahead for the beige vehicle, oblivious to the navy blue Opel that passed them in the other direction.

When they caught up with the van a few minutes later, it was parked in front of a brasserie. The driver was climbing out of the van and walking to the back. He opened the rear doors and pulled out a basket of baguettes.

The Citroën braked to a halt right behind the van. Scarface jumped out first. He pushed the driver aside and looked into the back of the van. There were only bread and pastries. He ran around to the seats in the front. Both were empty.

Frustrated, he shouted at the driver, "Where the fuck is she?"

The driver shook his head in bewilderment. "Who, monsieur, is she? You think I keep a tart in the back? Only fruit tarts, that's all." The driver laughed loudly at his own joke.

"Oh, go to hell," Scarface shouted and stormed away from the van.

At her seat in another brasserie across the boulevard, Sagit sipped an espresso and watched the scene unfold. Far from being relieved, Sagit was now tense and worried. The plan, up to this point, had been her own, and it had gone like clockwork. The rest of it, though, bothered her. She would have had the Opel drive Daphna north and east across the French border into Belgium, where she would get a plane from Brussels to Tel Aviv. But David had talked her out of it, arguing that a plane from Charles De Gaulle was better because they could get Daphna on it sooner—before Victor Foch and his people had a chance to react. The drive to the Belgium border would take hours, and border crossing guards could be alerted by then. In the end, she had yielded to him because he said it was his stepdaughter—Yael's child—involved; he should be able to make the decision. Now she was sorry.

Furious, Madame Blanc hung up the phone. He was smart, this Greg Nielsen, and he couldn't be underestimated. Their plan to get the girl out of the country had been very clever, but it wouldn't succeed. Madame Blanc had one more card to play.

The minister of transportation in the current government had been a protégé of Monsieur Claude Dissault, her mentor. Relationships like these had facilitated her rise to the top of the French business world, and she never hesitated to use them.

"Henri," she said to the busy minister when her call was put right through, "I need a small favor."

As the Opel approached Charles De Gaulle Airport, Daphna tried to calm her nerves. She was almost free. Within an hour she would be on a plane heading back to Israel.

Check-in at the El Al ticket counter went quickly. Leora Feldman's papers were in order, and a clerk handed her a business-class boarding pass.

Daphna knew the routine at Charles De Gaulle well. As she rode the motorized walkway up to the second level, she reminded herself that the only serious checkpoint occurred at passport control. Approaching the four lines that each led up to a heavy plate glass window, she glanced at the four clerks—all men—on the desks behind those windows. The bald-headed man second from the right appeared to be the most bored, and he was stamping passports with barely a glance. She picked his line.

Eight or ten people were ahead of her. Her knees were knocking, and she could feel perspiration forming under her arms. She trembled thinking how much international travelers were at the mercy of a government clerk who could detain them by simply lifting a phone.

Without appearing to do so, she glanced around the passport control waiting area. In the corner of her eye she could see two men dressed in dark suits with earphones in their ears, surveying the crowd. She could sense them boring in on her with beady black eyes. She looked away, hoping she was imagining their attention.

Only one person was ahead of her in line now, a gray-haired woman carrying a large straw bag. Daphna tightly clutched the Leora Feldman passport in her moist hand.

Suddenly, the telephone rang on the table in front of the bald man. He stopped processing passports to answer it, looking at his computer screen all the while. He glanced up, and in an awful instant, his eyes locked on Daphna. She looked away, but she knew they had targeted her. She considered running, but the two dark suits were watching her, moving in closer to her line.

Without any choice, she decided to press ahead. The woman in front of her was processed, and it was her turn now. As she placed her passport in front of the bald-headed man, the two blue suits closed in on her like bookends. "Please come with us, mademoiselle," one of them said.

David walked into Victor Foch's office with a great feeling of relief. Sagit had called him from the brasserie to say that Daphna's escape had gone according to plan. By now Daphna should be on a plane back to Israel.

His spirits were quickly deflated when Victor, with a surly expression on his face, handed David a fax of a Polaroid photo showing Daphna being led into a helicopter.

"You thought you were clever to involve the Mossad," Victor said. "Well, you've just made everything much more difficult for yourself and for the girl."

Stunned, David asked, "How did you get her?"

"I have no intention of telling you what happened."

Horrified, David studied the picture. "Bastard," he said. "Don't you have any honor at all?"

Victor's face was bright red. He shook his fist at David. "Don't worry about my honor. You'd better worry about the possibility that you and your stepdaughter will both end up like Kourosh."

David shook his head. "Not much chance of that, counselor. Your people want me too badly to kill me. Look at all the trouble you've gone to already, and you still haven't gotten a yes answer from me."

"You're pushing me to the limit."

David brushed aside Victor's words. The man was a mere messenger. He had no authority. "Then let me push a little more. I'm finished talking to you. I don't deal with lackeys or agents. Only principals."

"My principal can't be disclosed to you. It's out of the question."

David decided to press ahead. Since they had compiled a dossier on him, they had to know that Daphna was valuable to them as a guarantee that he would complete his assignment. Killing her now would never get him to acquiesce. What worried him was that they could torture her. He had to get to Victor's principal before events spiraled in that direction. The time had come to play his long shot.

"I already know who your principal is."

He was watching Victor now, looking for the involuntary twitch that would tell him he was right. "That's very funny."

"Actually, she's not a funny person at all. Madame Jacqueline Blanc is a damn serious woman."

Victor showed no visible reaction. For an instant David thought his gamble had failed, and he was in quicksand up to his shoulders. But the lawyer's next words gave it all away. "I've never even heard of a Madame Blanc," Victor replied.

David reached into his jacket pocket, pulled out a copy of the *Le Monde* article that showed Foch representing Madame Blanc's company, and handed it to the lawyer. "This time you did underestimate me," he said boldly. "While you were sitting in a law library, cracking books, some real players at Langley taught me how to do my work. They knew how to deal with Russians and East Germans. Dealing with you and Madame Blanc is like nursery school."

Now on the defensive, Victor protested, "But Madame Blanc has no involvement with—"

"Cut the crap, Victor, or to use your favorite expression, 'the time for playing games is over.' You're right. I did involve the Mossad in the escape plan for Daphna, but that's all so far. They don't know about you or Madame Blanc. However, I left a letter to be delivered to the director of the Mossad if I don't come back from this trip on schedule. It lays out your involvement and names Madame Blanc as the mastermind. I don't think either of you would like that letter to be delivered, because even if the French government didn't act, you can be sure the Mossad would. Am I getting through to you? Wouldn't that be enough to make your hair stand up—if you in fact had real hair?"

Instinctively, Victor touched his head to make sure his toupee was in place. Totally off guard now, he didn't know what to say. He was too worried about Madame Blanc's reaction to this development.

"It's very simple," David added. "I'll be waiting in front of the Bristol tomorrow morning at ten. Have your driver take me to a meeting with Madame Blanc."

"Or?"

"Or I go home, and you don't get the help you need from me."

Victor had recovered. He and Madame Blanc were still in command. He shook a finger menacingly at David. "You might go home in a wooden box. Not to mention what will happen to Daphna."

"That's certainly possible, but I'll take my chances," David replied with bravado. "When the letter gets delivered, you and Madame Blanc will pay for everything you've done to us."

Victor looked at him enigmatically. "Don't forget what happens when you wish for something," the French lawyer said.

"What's that?"

"You just might get what you want, and it may not be so great."

He said it in a way that troubled David.

"And if I have to reach you this afternoon?" Victor asked.

"I'll be at Renault for my meeting, as you well know. Which reminds me. I want to leave Paris this time with a signed contract from Renault for the kibbutz High-Tech Center. I want you to make it happen."

Before the lawyer could respond, David turned around and stalked out of the office.

At six the next morning, David went jogging in the Bois de Boulogne, and when he caught up with Sagit, also jogging at their predetermined location, they turned off into a deserted clump of trees.

"What the hell happened with Daphna?" he demanded.

"They grabbed her somewhere between the El Al ticket counter and the gate for the plane."

"Oh, shit." Furious at himself for having changed her plan, he shook his head. "You can say, 'I told you so.'"

She sighed and ran her hand through her hair in frustration over the situation. "That's not my style. Besides, it wouldn't help. Our ambassador in Paris called the French foreign office, demanding that they locate her and turn her over, and—"

"Don't tell me, let me guess. The French said that they're investigating, but so far they haven't been able to find out anything about her."

"Yeah, that's about right."

"Unfortunately, this Madame Blanc is well connected in

the upper levels of the French government, as I found out last night at dinner with a Renault executive. Meeting her should be a real treat."

Sagit reached into the pocket of her warm-up suit and extracted a tiny microphone at the end of a wire. "We want you to wear this when you meet with Madame Blanc."

"No way. Forget it. It's too risky with them holding Daphna. I won't endanger the girl by doing that."

She clenched her fists at her sides, losing patience with him and preparing to read him the riot act. Then she thought about what he had said. He did have a point. So she backed off. "Then how will we be able to keep track of you?"

"You won't. I'm a big boy. I'll take my chances."

"A loose tail, then. We insist."

Behind Sagit the sun was starting to break through the eastern sky. David studied her carefully. She would probably do what she wanted, regardless of what he said. "Very loose, then."

"Agreed."

"But if you want to do something constructive, have someone in the embassy's legal office check French land records, without disclosing their identity, to locate any property owned by Madame Blanc or PDF near Grasse in the south."

"Why Grasse?"

"Just a hunch, from something I heard last night."

Three hours later, David stood in front of the Bristol, waiting for Victor's driver. The black leather briefcase he clutched in his hand contained an executed contract between Renault and kibbutz Bet Mordechai for computer services to be supplied over the next year at a cost of three million francs. David had closed the deal with a handshake with Jean-Pierre Borchard, a Renault executive, at dinner last night at L'Ambroisie in Place de Vosges. The written contract was signed at breakfast this morning at the Bristol. Whether Victor was responsible, or whether Renault perceived the deal to be in its own interests, David didn't know.

He reviewed in his mind the information about Madame Blanc he had gotten from Jean-Pierre last night at midnight, when the two of them were finishing up dinner. After a round of champagne, two bottles of wine and a second Montral Armagnac, the executive was relaxed and loquacious. Always a believer in the maxim "You don't get apples if you don't throw rocks into a tree," David waded in slowly, asking Jean-Pierre if PDF might be a possible customer for Bet Mordechai's computer services.

After looking around the by now almost deserted restaurant, Jean-Pierre leaned forward, and said in a half conspiratorial, half locker room tone, "Not much chance of doing business there unless you've got an in with Madame Blanc. She's got gonads the size of melons, and she runs a tight ship."

"Then how do I get an in with this Madame Blanc?"

"Not with your cock. That's for sure."

"She doesn't like men?"

"Only young men. Twenty-five's Jacqueline's limit. She keeps them about six months and then tosses them aside. The current one's name is Michel. She figures that if we can keep twenty-something-year-old girls on the side, she can do the same. She's always trying to equal, or go one step better than, her male counterparts in this country's industrial complex."

Jean-Pierre paused to relight his cigar. "Even with these," he continued, smiling. "She smokes those long Cohibas. They put my little weenie Partagas here to shame. That's Jacqueline. She always has to have the biggest dick." Jean-Pierre laughed raucously, impressed with his own cleverness. "She can also be brutal and cruel. Literally, a killer, if she doesn't like someone, or if they cross her."

David paused to sip some Armagnac. "She sounds like a charming person."

"Charming she's not, but never underestimate Jacqueline's brains and her moxie. She's always one step ahead of the rest of the world. Early on, she decided that De Gaulle would sell us out in Algeria. People told her she was crazy, but she cashed out all of her substantial business interests in Algeria, while the rest of us were shouting 'Vive la France,' waving the tricolor with one hand, and with the other hand up our ass, to put it crudely."

"So is she part of the establishment now?"

"Oh, we finally let her join the Economic Club, all right," he said, slurring his words. "She was the first woman we took. In fact, she's the only one. She earned it," he admitted grudgingly. "Besides, we figured we might pick up some useful information, but that hasn't happened. She plays her cards too close to the chest."

"She ever been married?"

"Nope. Although there are rumors that she has a daughter somewhere down in Provence, near Grasse. That's where she's from, but nobody knows for sure."

"So you think I should find someone other than PDF to do business with in France?"

Jean-Pierre laughed. "It depends on how much you enjoy pain."

Less than ten hours later, David, his head throbbing from too much alcohol and too little sleep, thought about Victor's words that he might not be so thrilled to get his wish. If indeed Madame Blanc was the monster Jean-Pierre had described, that must have been what Victor meant.

David glanced over at the office building on the corner of rue St. Honore and avenue Matignon. Sagit was somewhere in that building, with binoculars trained on him. The Israeli embassy was only about three blocks away, and they had friends in the neighborhood. He had no doubt that she would keep the tail on him loose. She was damn smart, that woman, and she knew her business. He was just sorry he hadn't agreed to her escape plan for Daphna.

Waiting for the car, David was tense, and he squeezed the handle of his briefcase tightly. Stuffed inside was a box of the longest Cohibas he could find this morning at a shop on avenue Franklin D. Roosevelt. Suddenly, the familiar Mercedes, with Rolland at the wheel, ground to a halt in front of the Bristol. Without waiting for the driver to open the door, David climbed into the backseat.

Rolland eased the car into the heavy mid-morning traffic along rue St. Honore.

"Where are we going?" David asked.

Rolland didn't respond. Instead, he activated the automatic door lock, and the locks snapped down.

As the car moved, David kept his eyes riveted on the side window, trying to recall their route, in case he had to re-create it. They were heading north and west across Paris. Soon crowded streets gave way to suburbs and then open fields. David glanced quickly through the back window of the car. He imagined that Sagit's loose tail was somewhere on the highway back there. He just hoped that Rolland hadn't picked it up.

A few miles ahead, Rolland turned abruptly into the driveway of a small private landing field. A sleek Gulfstream jet was parked next to a brick building. The landing stairs were out and down.

David knew now he was on his own. Whatever he might have thought about Sagit's tail was irrelevant.

When David climbed the stairs, he was greeted by a good-looking flight attendant with long, flaming red hair, wearing a powder blue uniform with a miniskirt. "Where are we going?" he asked. She simply shrugged and replied, "We'll do our best to make you comfortable, monsieur."

They took off quickly to the north, into heavy clouds. David tried to keep his eyes off the redhead and on the scenery below, attempting to figure out where they were headed, but that wasn't easy. The two of them were alone in the cabin, and she sat provocatively in a seat facing him, her legs spread and the tiny skirt riding well up on her thighs; she wasn't wearing any panties. Well, she's a natural redhead, that's for sure, he thought. The pilot banked the plane to the left and finally straightened out.

When the redhead asked what she could get him, rolling her tongue over her lips, he refused to play Madame Blanc's game, whatever it was. "Black coffee, please."

Before heading off to the galley, she glared at him as if to suggest that he wasn't man enough for her. But he was busy studying the scene below. They were headed south, David decided. Soon clouds gave way to bright sunshine. After another half hour, David could see the deep blue

Mediterranean. Somewhere in this area was Grasse, where they might be holding Daphna.

The plane landed at a small airstrip outside of St. Tropez, where a car was waiting. The day was crisp and clear, and as they drove down the hill toward the city and the sea, David lowered the car window, hoping that the fresh air would revitalize his tired body. When he was with the CIA, he had been accustomed to heavy drinking sessions like last night, which went with the job; but they weren't a part of Israeli life. After five years he was out of practice, or at least his liver and the rest of his body were. By the time the car threaded its way along the narrow streets, filled with boutiques and small outdoor cafés, and reached the main harbor area, David was feeling better. They parked in front of the *Predator,* the largest yacht David had ever seen—complete with a helicopter on the upper deck.

On the sundeck in the rear, a woman dressed in a gray suit and striped silk blouse lounged on a stiff wooden chair, talking intently on a cell phone. Undoubtedly Madame Blanc, David decided. A pair of sunglasses were resting on her forehead. She was around sixty, he guessed. In her youth she must have been striking. Now her features were elegant, but she had hard edges. Her skin was tanned and leathery. Her hair was dyed black and tied up severely in the back. She had a self-confident air about her, as if she were the center of the universe. Her facial expressions, her hand movements, suggested posturing. She was an actress on stage, as if the world were watching her.

On a deck chair beside her, a handsome young man with sandy brown hair and wraparound sunglasses, wearing white slacks and a loose-fitting maroon shirt, sipped champagne and leafed through a glossy magazine. On the upper deck, four huge black men, dressed in khaki military uniforms, tightly gripped submachine guns and surveyed the scene around the boat in every direction.

David started walking toward the boat, but the driver from the car gripped his arm and stopped him. "We wait until we're called," he said. Beneath the man's jacket, the bulge of a gun was visible.

Squinting in the bright sunlight that sparkled off the
water, David studied Madame Blanc again. She had rolled
her right hand into a fist, obviously angry with whomever
was on the phone. He couldn't tell whether she was aware
of his presence.

A minute later, she finished the call and looked up. Then
she pointed a finger at the driver, the sign that David had
been summoned. With a nudge from the driver, he
started forward.

As he climbed onto the boat, she got up from her seat,
walked forward and shook his hand firmly. "The bold and
energetic David Ben Aaron," she said. "I've heard so much
about you."

He smiled broadly, exuding self-confidence, feigning
strength. "Compliments, I hope."

She smiled back. She would play his silly game for a
minute or two. "As you might imagine, Victor had nothing
but good words."

"I hope you'll form your own opinion."

"But I already have."

"And?"

All trace of her smile was gone. Her eyes had narrowed.
He'd better understand this was serious business. "You're
here, aren't you? Doesn't that tell you something?"

Out of the corner of his eye, David saw the young man
eyeing him suspiciously. Suddenly, Madame Blanc turned
to her young friend and said, "Do be a good boy, Michel,
and go back to the house. I have to take a ride with my
visitor." When Michel pouted, she added, "You know how
boring business talk can be."

Not trying to hide his displeasure, Michel got up and left
the boat. In a matter of minutes they were under way.

The table below, in a formal mahogany-paneled dining
salon, was set for lunch for two. It was quite a setting:
Limoges china, Christofe silver and Baccarat glassware.
Two olive-skinned women—Algerians, David guessed—in
starched white uniforms stood by the table, prepared to
serve. In one corner of the room a West African guard
stood at attention, gripping his machine gun. Before sitting

down, David reached into his briefcase and handed Madame Blanc the box of cigars wrapped in brown paper.

As she unwrapped the gift, she smiled. "I presume the Cohibas weren't a lucky guess. You're sending me a message. You're thorough, and you do your homework. Such men aren't to be trifled with."

He smiled again. He didn't want her to think he was intimidated by the situation. "Something like that."

"Today the message wasn't necessary. You see, David, I realized yesterday that I was underestimating you."

"Yesterday?"

"When you almost succeeded in executing your stepdaughter's escape from Paris."

He tensed, looking sternly at her. "I want Daphna released. She has nothing to do with this."

She waved her hand in the air, dismissing his words. "We'll talk about Daphna later. I have no reason to harm her. At this moment, she's quite comfortable and quite safe."

Madame Blanc signaled to the women waiting to serve. One spooned a cold Ligurian seafood salad, loaded with calamari, shrimp and mussels, from a blue china serving dish. Then she passed a basket of warm French bread. The other woman removed a bottle of white burgundy from an ice bucket, uncorked it and poured a little for Madame Blanc. She tasted it and smiled.

"It's Corton Charlemagne by Latour, 1989," she said. "I figured since I had a wine connoisseur coming for lunch, I should treat him well."

"A wine connoisseur?"

"But of course. Dick Holliday taught you well when you spent the year at Spartan Oil in Houston before the CIA decided to send you to the Middle East, and Bruno Wolk completed your education."

For several minutes they ate in silence. He tried not to appear too anxious. He would wait for her to take the initiative. For her part, she wanted him to absorb what he had heard so far.

Finally, she paused to sip some wine. Then she picked

up a blue folder resting at her feet and put it on the table.
"I'm amazed at what a colorful life you've had. I think I've
got it all now—from your football injury and father's death
in Aliquippa, Pennsylvania."

"Surely you can sympathize with a child having a bunch
of thugs kill a parent."

She continued without bothering to acknowledge him,
and he wondered if she'd buried those events from the Nazi
occupation long ago in the deepest recesses of her mind.

"I also know that you're near the top of the hit list in
Tehran for aiding the escape of the Shah."

"Just trying to do my job."

"For which, the Shah's great friend Bruno Wolk became
your eternal benefactor."

He maintained the same brittle smile. "Friendship is a
wonderful thing."

"The doctor he found to do the plastic surgery did a
magnificent job."

"I think so, too."

"It's too bad he didn't do anything about your teeth or
your limp."

"Not the province of a plastic surgeon, I'm afraid."

"True enough." She paused to study David. "Dr. Wilhelm did such a good job on you that I might even go to
see him myself. Maybe he can do something about these
lines," she said, pointing at her face.

He sat in silence waiting for her to continue.

She was staring at him, shaking her head up and down
with a tiny smile at the edge of her lips that showed amusement and some grudging admiration. He wasn't like anyone
she had ever met. "You're an interesting man, David Ben
Aaron or Greg Nielsen. Which do you prefer?"

"You can call me David."

"All right, David, but who owns you now?"

"Nobody," he said emphatically. "I'm my own person."

She didn't try to conceal the incredulity that showed on
her face. No one was his own person. "Victor is sure it's
the CIA as well as the Mossad. He thinks I'm crazy to have
anything to do with you."

"So why didn't you listen to your trusted adviser? Why did you agree to meet with me? What could I possibly contribute to someone so well connected throughout the world?"

"Now you want to talk about me? That's not such an interesting subject."

David was anxious for her to get to the point, already. "I'm tired of talking about myself. I want to know what you want with me."

She stood up. "For that discussion we'll have to go up on the deck and into the sun. It's turned quite warm today. I think I'll change into a bathing suit."

"I didn't bring one, I'm afraid."

She gave a bored smile. "No need to be unduly modest. I know what a man looks like. You all think your stuff is special, but no offense, if you've seen one, you've seen them all. However, the girls are shy. For their sake, I'll take them out while you undress here. You can just leave all of your clothes in this room," she said.

"I think I'll do without the sun and remain dressed."

She stared at him with eyes like lasers in a cold unemotional face, and spoke in a voice that exuded dominance and control. "Sorry, that's not an option, David. I want to be able to have a very thorough and frank discussion with you, and it's degrading to have someone search a luncheon guest to see if he's wearing a wire. Don't you think so?"

She was smart, just as Jean-Pierre had said. He had to give her that. If she wasn't such a monster, he might even admire her intelligence and cunning.

The guard would be watching him the whole time he undressed, and would afterward search David's clothes. If he was wearing a wire, he'd have no way of disposing of it or concealing it. A wire would mean Victor was right about him working for the CIA or the Mossad. He had no doubt about the result then. After an unpleasant afternoon of torture, they'd shoot him and toss him into the sea.

Madame Blanc rose from the table and started toward the ladder. "Oh, and leave your wristwatch down here as well," she added.

*   *   *

When he got up on the deck, buck naked, she was sitting in her straight back wooden chair, dressed in a skimpy violet Versace bikini, sipping an espresso and smoking a Cohiba.

"A great gift," she said. "Thanks."

She tossed him one. He picked up the sterling silver lighter on the table and lit it. Then he sat down across from her, in the deck chair next to the other cup of espresso, and crossed his legs. On the upper deck of the boat, he could see three guards. He guessed that the fourth was searching his clothes.

"I don't know why you insisted on seeing me," she said, staring at his crotch to intimidate him. "The deal Victor offered you was simple enough. You developed the defense system for the Saudi royal palace. We want you to describe it for us and tell us how it can be neutralized. If you had simply acquiesced when Victor first asked, we would have left you alone and we wouldn't have taken Daphna hostage." A bird of prey was circling overhead. She paused to finish her espresso while watching it plunge quickly into the water and catch a fish in its beak. Then she turned back to David. "If you don't agree to cooperate now, I've got a number of options. I can have Victor let the American government know where Greg Nielsen is. We can detain you in France and tell security officials in Tehran where you are. Or we can kill Daphna and you both."

David shifted in his chair, trying to cover himself as much as possible by clasping his hands in his lap. It was bizarre being naked for this discussion. "Why is the information so important to you? I assume you've got Saudi troops on your side. So what if they lose a few more people in the attack?"

"There are two answers to that question. First, I want to make sure the job gets done, and second, my Saudi partner wants your help to cut his losses."

David was alert. Now he was getting somewhere. "Who is he?" he asked warily.

"Sorry, I can't answer that. Now, do we have a deal, or . . ." She picked up the cell phone resting on the table.

"Or do I give an order to have someone kill Daphna, for openers?" She stared at him. "Well, what'll it be?"

David replied, "The issue's more complicated than you think."

"Tell me about it, then."

The sun was starting to drop in the sky. With the wind whipping off the water David felt chilly.

"Can I put some clothes on now?" he asked. "Are you finished with this macho nonsense game of yours? I'm literally freezing my dick off."

She raised her right foot and gently nudged his genitals. "It does look shriveled." She pulled a thick terry-cloth robe from a cabinet and tossed it to him. Then she put one on herself.

"Tell me about it," she repeated.

"First of all, it's true that I developed the defense system for the king's palace, and it was a sophisticated computerized system. But that was five years ago. It could easily have been changed since, or they could have tossed it out and installed a new one."

"I thought that, too, but when I asked, I was told it hasn't been changed. How can we determine that for sure?"

"I can tell you where in the palace we stored the computer disks describing the system. You'll need someone to get those disks and fly them to France for me to work with."

"How long will that take?"

"How long do I have?"

For a few moments she stared at him in silence, unwilling to answer.

"Look, Madame Blanc," he finally said. "I'm not stupid. I figured out that you're supporting a Saudi coup, obviously because of some kind of arrangement you'll have for Saudi oil if it succeeds. I just need to know when you're planning to strike."

"October 6," she said reluctantly. "About three weeks from now."

He shook his head, impressed with the answer. "A

month before the American presidential election. A good choice. Well, anyhow, the answer to your question is that if you get me the computer disks, and if you turn me loose with a sophisticated PC at one of your offices, I should be able to get what you want in a couple of days. However, I have to tell you that you're focusing on the wrong system. The palace defenses aren't your biggest problem."

"Really?" She sounded skeptical. "Then what is?"

If he was going to get Daphna and himself out of this alive and achieve something in the process, he had to gain her confidence by dangling in front of her, something she needed badly. He had only one card. He'd better play it now, while he still had the chance. "I also installed a high-tech system, computer-operated from either the royal palace or the Oil Ministry, which permits the Saudi king to set off explosions by remote control, which will cause major damage and fires at all of the most important oil fields in the country. The damage will be so widespread that it'll be years before the oil fields are up and running again. The idea is to deprive hostile attackers of the use of the country's oil for a very long time."

She put down her cigar and leaned forward in her chair, listening intently. It was obvious that he was telling her something new. "Are you bullshitting me?"

"I wish I was. I didn't want to install the system because of the environmental damage it would do, and because I couldn't stand the idea of destroying so much of a depletable resource. But in those days the White House jumped whenever the Saudi king made a request, and the king was certain that the fundamentalists would be carrying out a coup. He was determined to deny them the fruits of their victory."

"Do you think my Saudi partner knows about this?"

He wanted to get some information about her partner, so he asked, "Is he in the Saudi military?"

When she nodded, he continued, "Then probably not. The king never trusted the military. So he has his own forces, units of the National Guard, separate from the army and made up exclusively of Bedouins and desert people who defend him and the palace. They would be the only ones who might know about this second system."

She leaned forward and tapped her forefinger on his chest, straight at his heart. "You'd better not be lying to me about this system to blow up the oil fields," she said in a stone-cold voice.

Feeling as if he had leveled the playing field, he grabbed her finger. "I'm not lying. I spent a year of my life setting it up. Why would I lie about it?" He let her finger go.

"Could you deactivate it?"

"Sure, if I had access to this set of computer disks."

"And do you know where those are?"

"At least where they were five years ago."

"And you want me to bring those to you as well. So you could work with them?"

"If I wanted to."

She mulled over his words. "Here's the deal, then," she said. "You tell me how to deactivate both of these systems, and I won't tell either Washington or Tehran about you. Of course, I'll release the girl as well."

Without pausing to think, he shook his head. "Nope," he said. "That deal's not fair to me."

She laughed sardonically. "You don't exactly have much bargaining power."

Now he pointed his finger at her. "Oh, quite the contrary. You can kill me, but nobody else can help you prevent the destruction of the oil fields. Without that help, the coup won't give you the benefits that your Saudi partner promised. I'll bet he agreed to give you a percentage of all Saudi oil revenue for the next several years, as well as a management and consulting contract to help them straighten out their fucked-up oil business. Am I right?"

"You're close."

"So without me you've got squat! Nothing. A big goose egg."

A hint of dismay was visible on her face. She had underestimated him. She wasn't used to being put on the defensive, and she didn't like it. "And what is it you want in return for your help?"

David was improvising now. He suddenly saw the ultimate way to gain her confidence. "I want to be cut in. A piece of the action. I'm tired of running and hiding. Israel and the kibbutz are too small for me. I want some cash to build a house in Anguilla and live for myself while I still have a chance."

"How much is that?"

"Ten million U.S. dollars should do it." He gauged her reaction as he spoke. He didn't want to overdo it. So far nothing, just a cold, blank stare. "But in return for that I'll not only give you the information you need about the automated systems to defend the palace and to destroy the oil fields, I'll also re-create for you the CIA-developed plan to take over the Saudi oil fields. You can share it with your Saudi partner. It'll increase his chances of success. We were constantly developing plans like that in those days. Of course, we never used any of this. It was our form of war games."

She pondered his words for several moments. "If I were to agree to your proposal," she finally said, "I'd want you to go into Saudi Arabia right after the coup and stay about six months. Help my people get the oil business up and running."

David tried to restrain his excitement. This was what he wanted most—a chance to get back into the country, to kill Nasser. "That's okay with me," he said, "but we've still got one more big problem you're overlooking."

"What's that?"

"The good old U.S. of A." He said the words with contempt. "Washington will never sit back and let this coup happen."

"You don't have to worry about the United States," she replied firmly.

"With all due respect, Madame Blanc, there may be Saudi military officers leading the coup, but the Saudi king will tell Washington that they're fundamentalists, that it's Iran all over again, and they'll go berserk in Washington. They've got all those troops stationed in the country and on aircraft carriers in or near the Persian Gulf at all times.

Washington will order them to help the Saudi king put down the coup faster than you can say Charles De Gaulle. I know how it will go. I helped plan the potential response five years ago when we played out scenarios like this in Washington."

She lashed back. "But the American government will immediately be assured by the Saudi officers leading the coup that oil sales will continue uninterrupted after the change of government."

He paused to ponder her words. She wasn't naive or stupid. There was something she wasn't telling him. He pressed ahead, determined to find out what it was. "That won't be enough. That won't do it in Washington, when the Saudi king is screaming for help and yelling it's a fundamentalist revolution. You've got to understand how Washington—"

She cut him off. "I said you don't have to worry about Washington. It's been dealt with."

"How?" he demanded.

She scowled. "That's not your problem. I told you Washington won't intervene. I'm certain of it. So you can assume that."

"But it's not a reasonable assumption."

She was clearly annoyed at his persistence. "Drop it," she snapped. "Let's concentrate on your role. How do you want to proceed on your part of the deal?"

He decided to back off. He had gotten as much as he could from her. By continuing to press, he would jeopardize the deal he had made. "If you let me go downstairs, I'll get dressed and get access to my briefcase, which your people have no doubt finished searching by now. I'll make you a list of the computer disks for both systems that I need copied, and where they're maintained. If you have your Saudi partner get them to Paris, say one week from today, I'll show up at PDF headquarters. You give me a private room with access to a powerful PC, and I'll go to work."

"And you'll keep Victor informed about your progress?"

"I don't much like him."

She snarled. "The feeling's mutual."

"Why can't I report directly to you?"

"I'm out of town a great deal. He'll get me if you need me."

"What about my ten million?"

"You'll get two million up front, and two million at the beginning of each of the next five months."

He decided to push it, letting her know how much the deal meant to him. "I was thinking about five million up front."

"I'm sure you were, but two is all you're getting. Besides, you're not going to have time to spend a cent for the next six months, and if you stop performing . . ." she paused to toss her cigar butt into the darkening sea, "you can try to find the rest of my Cohiba at the bottom of the Mediterranean."

He reacted to her threat with a stony stare. He refused to be intimidated by her. "I figured as much. I'll give you a numbered Swiss bank account where you can deposit the money. At the Union Bank in Geneva."

She raised her eyebrows. "I don't like dealing with people who have numbered Swiss accounts."

"Yeah, well, I've been on the run from the CIA for five years, as you well know. American Express and Visa weren't exactly an option."

She accepted what he said. "I'll wire the two million before you leave the boat. For purposes of this project, you need a code name. We'll use 'Outlaw.' "

"Coming from you, I take that as a compliment. Now that we're partners of sorts," he added, "I want Daphna released right away."

She calmly grimaced. "Forget it. The girl's my insurance policy in case you don't perform. If you do, she'll be released unharmed on October 8, the date you go into Saudi Arabia. You can wait for assurance that she's back in Israel and safe before you board the plane that day. Those are my terms. Nothing else."

As he stared at her, he knew that she wouldn't budge. He didn't like it, but he could live with it. That gave the

Mossad a little more than two weeks to devise a way to get her out.

As if reading his mind, Madame Blanc added, "There is one other thing, now that we're partners of sorts, as you just put it."

"What's that?"

"You better have nothing else to do with the Mossad."

"That's understood."

She stood up, signaling the end of the conversation. "Well, it sure as hell better be. If I find that you're working with either the Mossad or the CIA from this point on, I'll get you and Daphna back on this boat, and while you're still alive I'll have my West African bodyguards rip the skin off both of your bodies with sharp knives." She pointed her finger at him again. "Her first. Then you. The bloody pulp of what's left of the two of you we'll feed to the sharks."

CHAPTER 10

"What success have you had locating Daphna?" Moshe asked Sagit across his desk when she finished an hour-long report about David's activities in France.

"David thinks they may be holding her somewhere near Grasse. We're searching quietly ourselves and with French people we can trust. We take seriously Madame Blanc's threat to kill Daphna if she finds out the Mossad's still in the act. To try to involve the French government with Blanc's political contacts would get us nowhere. When we locate Daphna, I'll put together a rescue plan for your approval. Is that okay?"

"Ach, what else can I do?" the black bear muttered in frustration, as he climbed out of his desk chair, cigarette in hand, and walked over to the broad window that faced the Knesset and the expanse of western Jerusalem, with the Hebrew University clustered among governmental buildings. He opened the window, letting the warm air strike him in the face.

Suddenly, Moshe wheeled around and said, "We have to call Washington and tell them everything that's happened. We also have to tell them not to go to the French government at this point under any circumstances, or the girl's dead."

She knew why Moshe wanted to call Washington, but she decided to order him to say it, hoping to talk him out of it. "You really think it's necessary to go to Washington?"

"I don't think it. I know it." He pointed to a manilla folder in the center of his desk. "When you were in Paris, I had our research people run current figures for me. Saudi

Arabia supplies almost twenty percent of all United States oil, and it's the single largest source for American oil imports. Suddenly America's interests in Madame Blanc's little caper are greater than our own."

She wasn't convinced. Why should Israel have to give priority to America's interests over its own? "We're vitally affected if another fundamentalist regime comes to power in the region. It's still our neighborhood."

"Agreed, but we're talking about a potentially crippling blow to the U.S. economy if Saudi oil falls into the wrong hands."

"At this point we don't know if it will be the wrong hands, because we don't know who Madame Blanc's Saudi partners are. And she told David that the oil flow to the U.S. would continue after the coup."

Moshe frowned and ran his hand through his uncombed mop of gray hair. "All of that's fine, but we've worked too hard to develop a close relationship with Washington and President Waltham to keep them out of the loop. Besides, this isn't only about oil. From what David said, it's very clear that Madame Blanc isn't worried about the risk of American intervention. Why not?"

"Because she has an American spy or a mole."

"Possibly, or because she has a key American official in the conspiracy. That's something Washington has to know about. I'll brief the prime minister later today, but I know where he'll come out on the issue. He puts close ties with Washington as a top priority. He'd never let me hold back something like this. It's not right. Besides, they'll make us pay for it later. We've got to reach a common plan of action."

Sagit protested. "But isn't the likely Washington reaction going to be to seek an immediate extradition of David, to toss him in jail and to strengthen security around the Saudi king? That may lead to Daphna's death as well?"

Moshe got a curious look in his eyes. Suddenly he understood the reason for her reluctance to tell Washington. She didn't want to put David at risk. He thought about those three condoms in the Paris hotel room. He had to get her thinking with her head again. "That's certainly possible. On the other hand, Washington could agree to give us a few days to find Daphna and get her out. They might even agree to let David stick with his infiltration of Madame Blanc in order to find out who in Saudi Arabia is being supported by her. Once he obtains that information, the Saudi king will be able to crush the insurgents. And unless the king has that information, the insurgents will be able to go back into the woodwork until the level of security falls again, in a couple of months or years."

"When you put it that way, the idea of letting David continue to operate with Madame Blanc makes a lot more sense for both of our governments."

"That's the way I would go, but I'm afraid your initial instinctive reaction will prove to be correct. That Chambers's personal animosity will preclude selection of the rational alternative, and they'll seek David's immediate extradition."

She raised her voice. "I can't believe that the United States government would behave so stupidly."

Moshe shrugged. "You may be right about what's smart and what's not, but it's still Washington's decision."

"Can we influence it?"

Puzzled, he looked at her. "What did you have in mind?"

"Well, I developed a pretty decent relationship last year with Margaret Joyner. Rather than simply call or send a written message to Washington, which will get the knee-jerk extradition reaction, I'd like to go over in person and talk to her one on one."

Moshe sighed deeply and considered her idea. "On a professional level, you've got my blessing," he said, "and I'm sure I'll be able to get the approval of the prime minister for your trip."

"And on a personal level?"

She held her breath as he looked at her sternly, like a concerned father. He had recruited her from the streets of Tel Aviv more than twenty years ago. Life had been cruel to her, and she had been at rock bottom, but he had seen something there—a spark that wouldn't die regardless of the winds, a desire to strike out at life's injustices, and an untutored but keen native intelligence—*sachel* in Yiddish, raw horse sense that you need to survive in the intelligence game. So he had taken her under his wing, and she had been his prized pupil, his star, through all these long years, as he gradually honed her skills. Now he could see all of these efforts going down the drain because of a man called David.

He could take her off the case, but he didn't have time for that. Besides, it was already too late. He knew she was in love with David, though he doubted if she knew it. In his typically enigmatic way, he said, "Don't lose yourself in the process of trying to save him."

"You better explain that, Moshe. I may be tired, but it was a little too elliptical and cryptic for me. To the extent I understood it, I didn't like it."

He hesitated, trying to formulate his words carefully. "I know you well, Sagit, I heard the nuances in your voice when you gave the long report of what happened in Paris. I think you're becoming personally involved with David Ben Aaron. Emotionally, I mean."

She blushed. "Take me off the case, then."

"There's no time for that. Unless you tell me that you can't do the job because—"

Now she was irritated at him, tired of constantly having to defend herself. "I can do the job," she said curtly.

"Good. Then let me tell you that I don't trust him. I think he has his own agenda. In France, he wouldn't cooperate enough so that you could track him to St. Tropez."

She fiddled with her hands in her lap and looked down at them. Moshe had no right to blame her for what happened in France. "None of us could foresee an airplane."

"I understand that, but it means that you have to take his word for everything he says happened in St. Tropez."

"That's true, but what specifically is worrying you?"

"Well, let me put it this way," he said slowly. "While being run by you, our CIA/Russian boychik managed to work things out so that he now has two million dollars in a Swiss bank account that he alone can access. That was never part of our plan."

She felt relieved that the money was the cause of his concern, rather than her personal involvement. "When I debriefed him, I pressed him hard on that point. He said that it was a sudden idea that popped into his head. He said that the ultimate objective was to find out who the Saudi coup leader is. He thought he had a better chance of getting inside Madame Blanc's group and gaining her confidence, in order to get that information, if she viewed him as a partner. She would believe that he was crossing the line from being someone who submitted to blackmail to being someone who was a co-conspirator, and she would be more open with him." Sagit gave him a seaching look. "You think he's conning us?"

"Well, let's put it this way. You're going out on a long limb for him. Maybe everything's just like he told you, and I'm being paranoid. It wouldn't be the first time with this job. Maybe he's planning to be an honorable kibbutz member and donate the two million dollars to Bet Mordechai, if all this ends well for him and us. Maybe he figures he bought a two-million-dollar insurance policy, in case all of this goes south on us and him, which is certainly possible." Moshe gave her a look of skepticism, signifying what he thought of that alternative. "Or maybe he's planning to get to Geneva ASAP, grab the two million, and take on still another new identity and disappear again. This time to Brazil or someplace like that."

His words saddened her. "And what about Daphna?" she said weakly.

"She's only a stepdaughter. He won't worry about what happens to her."

"But if that's the case, why did he tell me about the two million at all? I wasn't in St. Tropez. He could have kept it to himself."

"But if you later found out, you'd know he was conning us. This way he can say 'look how open and cooperative I'm being with you.' "

She was visibly shaken by his words. "My God, Moshe, do you really think . . . ?"

"I don't know what to think," he said sternly.

"If I persuade Margaret Joyner and the Americans to go along with us, and then he takes off with the two million and leaves us holding the bag, we'll look like a bunch of idiots."

"Unfortunately, that is an accurate characterization, and you would be destroyed in the process."

His words hung in the air. For several moments they sat and stared at each other, two people who had worked together so long, who knew one another so well and cared for each other.

"You have such a blunt way of expressing yourself, Moshe."

"So Sagit, my dear, do you still want to go to Washington?" She nodded. "Okay, when?"

"Right now," she said decisively. "If Margaret can see me tomorrow, I'll take the midnight plane."

"Good. I'll call her and set it up. Meantime, you go see Rachel in the library. She'll give you some books about Saudi Arabia to read on the long flight." He smiled at her. "I'd hate to see you waste your time sleeping."

Khalid stood alone at the fourth-floor window in the Defense Ministry building overlooking Justice Square in central Riyadh, the venue for beheading criminals, and stared at the deserted square below. It should be swarming with people on a Wednesday at noon, but today it was empty. This was no ordinary Wednesday. Utilizing air force intelligence sources, Khalid had learned two weeks ago that the reason was being referred to in clandestine whispers, in e-mails read and instantly deleted, and in hushed coded phone calls as "the women's march." The chief organizer, Misha'il, had been in Washington for the million women's march on Mother's Day in the year 2000. The organizers had selected a weekday, avoiding the Sabbath and further hostility from the clerics.

Khalid looked at the end of the square in front of the old clock tower. They were assembling—about two hundred women, he guessed, with their heads uncovered in defiance of law, and an equal number of young male students from the university who were supporting them. The exotically beautiful, dark-haired Princess Misha'il was in front of the crowd organizing them with a battery-powered bullhorn. They were not from the lower classes, but professional families. Some like Misha'il were from royalty. The signs they held explained their message: "The Koran doesn't bar women from driving." "Women should be free to eat in restaurants." "Women are people, not property."

The king hadn't trusted local police or even the army to deal with this protest. Instead, at the other end of the square, in front of the governor's office, crack units of the king's National Guard, fierce Bedouins from the desert, were assembling. Many of them were on horses. All were armed with wooden truncheons, in full battle dress with gas masks at their sides. There were no television cameras or press. No representatives of foreign governments. The king had assured that by cordoning off a one-mile area in all directions. The only ones permitted to enter were marchers, the guards and those like Khalid who had military credentials. An eerie calm had settled over the square below. The calm before a storm.

Khalid shook his head in dismay. The king could have prevented this march from ever occurring. All he had to do was keep the protesters out of the area, but that wasn't what he wanted. No, he wanted to teach these women and their sympathizers a lesson. Unless his strict rule was upheld, the entire state would unravel.

Khalid heard footsteps behind him, and he wheeled around quickly. It was Naif, an air force captain who was an aide and confidant of the colonel.

"Can I get you anything, sir?" the captain asked. "Water or anything else?"

"Nothing, thanks. Would you like to join me and watch?"

"I don't think so, sir. I'm afraid I know how it's going

to end. I'll stay here at the doorway and let you know if anyone's coming. Almost everyone has gone home.''

Ten minutes later, the protesters were ready. Khalid had learned that their plan was to get to the center of the square, where they would erect a temporary platform from wooden crates. There Princess Misha'il and others would speak. After that they would peacefully disband and go home.

Carrying their signs and chanting "Freedom for Saudi women," the group made it only about a quarter of the way across the square. That was when the National Guard units on horseback rode directly into the crowd of unarmed women and students, swinging their truncheons, smacking heads and arms, anything within range. Screams came from the crowd. Bloodcurdling screams of fear and pain. Screams of disbelief, Khalid thought, because in their naïveté these people never thought they would be treated this way. Khalid saw one soldier strike Princess Misha'il, and then blood flowing from her head and down her cheek. One eye was bloody and closed. Some of those who cowered on the ground were kicked and trampled by horses.

When the units on horseback had done their damage, the soldiers on foot wearing gas masks came through spraying tear gas. Then they, too, rushed into the crowd swinging their clubs. There were more loud anguished screams.

In a mere fifteen minutes it was over. The National Guard withdrew. No one was arrested. The king had decided that it was better to leave the bloody mess to set an example.

As best they could, the protesters cared for one another. They dragged their colleagues to hospitals—hoping that they would be treated, that Saudi doctors wouldn't be too intimidated to render help.

In despair, shame and anger, Khalid turned away from the window.

The captain drove him back to his base.

That evening in his house, Khalid didn't talk about what had happened. Not with his wife, Nura, not with his four children. His son was fourteen and his daughters seven, nine and eleven. He didn't talk at all; he was sullen and quiet. But they knew. They all knew, with varying degrees of comprehension, because the word had spread that afternoon through Riyadh, exactly as the king had intended. Even later in bed he didn't intend to talk about it with his wife. He didn't want her to know how sick he was inside, how he planned to change the situation in the country for his own daughters, who, had they been a few years older, might have been marching and been beaten to a bloody pulp.

After dinner, someone suddenly knocked on the door of Khalid's house. He glanced at his wife, who must have known what he was planning, because with the knock, she became white with terror. He got up to answer the door. It was Salmon, another colonel in the air force—one who had been unwilling to commit to Khalid's coup plans.

"We have to talk," Salmon said to Khalid.

Khalid put one finger to his ear and another to the walls. How could he be certain that the king's spies had not planted a listening device?

Outside in the rapidly cooling evening air, Salmon offered a cigarette to Khalid, who declined, then Salmon lit one up himself. "You know about today?" he asked.

"I saw the whole thing from a window in the Defense building."

"The son of a good friend of mine died from blows to his head."

Khalid was moved almost to tears—not just for this one boy, but for all of those who had died and were injured. "I'm sorry to hear that."

"He wasn't the only one, of course."

"I am ashamed. This is my country," Khalid said. "But we can do something about it."

Salmon paused to drag on his cigarette. He blew a smoke ring into the air. Finally he said, "That's why I came this evening. I'm ready to join you in the coup."

Khalid hugged Salmon. When they drew back, he looked him square in the eye. "We will succeed, my friend. We will succeed."

* * *

Sagit hoped that David would understand why she had to go to Washington. He didn't. He felt as if she had personally betrayed him.

"You might as well be signing Daphna's death warrant and mine," he said angrily, slitting his hand across his throat for emphasis. "Or sentencing me to life in prison. Besides, it's a totally stupid, naive idea. Are you the genius who thought of sacrificing me at the altar of American-Israel relations, or was that your boss?"

They were having dinner at a modern restaurant in Jerusalem called Taverna. She had thought it would be best to tell him about her trip in person before she went to the airport, but after hearing his reaction, she was no longer sure. At least, the hour was late, and the restaurant was deserted.

"Why not wait," he said, "before telling the Americans? I have a foot in the door with Madame Blanc. Let me get the whole story, including the identity of her Saudi partner, find out a way to engineer Daphna's rescue, and then you can go to Washington."

"We can't do it that way. We've worked too hard to develop a cooperative relationship with the American government at all levels. We can't break that commitment."

His face darkened. He was furious. "At least you're honest enough to admit that I'm the sacrificial lamb."

"That's not fair, and you know it."

"Just another week is all I'm asking you."

She bit down on her lip. Personally, she would have done what he wanted, but it was out of her hands. He was sophisticated enough in intelligence matters to realize that. "Sorry, David, we can't do it."

"Let me talk to Moshe, your boss."

"He's already signed off. We think going to Washington is the right thing to do."

In frustration, David pounded his fist on the table. "You don't understand how Washington works," he told her.

She responded stubbornly, "We think we can save you and still get what we want."

"And how exactly do you think *we* can pull that off?"

"Why don't you leave that up to us?"

He laughed contemptuously. "You're like a babe in the woods. They'll eat you alive in Washington, and laugh when they spit you out."

She knew very well that he might be right. Washington was a jungle, but she refused to share those doubts with him. "You underestimate me. I'm capable of playing what you Americans call hardball."

He laughed at her. "You'll never even get a chance at bat, to carry on with your stupid metaphor."

"But I think—"

"For God's sake, Sagit, I broke the jaw of a general who now happens to be the chairman of the Joint Chiefs, which makes him President Waltham's top military adviser. I'd like nothing better than to get even with that bastard who made me give up my life as Greg Nielsen." He leaned forward, his face close to hers, his expression grim and taut. "And his desire for revenge has to be every bit as great as mine. He's also a tough political animal and good at manipulating the media. What chance do you think I'll have on trial before a military court for the murder of those innocent Americans?"

"We don't think it has to happen that way."

"You're probably right." His voice was laced with disgust. "Once Tehran gets wind of the resurfacing of Greg Nielsen, they'll have a hit squad take me out. Is this my punishment for fucking and running in Paris?"

She turned red with anger, shouting at him through clenched teeth, "You're out of line, David."

He was equally loud. "Well, if you won't hold off going to Washington for my sake, at least do it for Daphna."

She lowered her voice, becoming professional again. "We'll work with Margaret Joyner on keeping our moves confidential. We won't endanger the girl."

"Go ahead. Have a nice trip. Kill both of us."

She had had enough of him tonight. The last comment did it.

It was already ten-thirty. The Mossad driver was waiting

for her in the front of the restaurant with her bag in the trunk. Without saying another word, she stood up, put some money on the table and walked quickly toward the door.

As she climbed into the back of the car, she replayed the conversation in her mind. She was trying to decide if maybe he was right about what would happen in Washington. However, what kept flickering in her mind was Moshe's suspicion concerning the two million dollars David had received from Madame Blanc.

Daphna tossed and turned, exhausted but unable to sleep. Suddenly anxious, she jumped up and ran over to the door, checking that she had remembered to turn the dead bolt. Then she sat down in the chair in the corner and pulled her knees up close to her chest, rocking her whole body while she whimpered softly.

Every day of her captivity had left her more depressed. The women inside the house, Mary and the others, were all nice enough to her. The food was good. The house was comfortable, and she could roam around it at will. No one followed her when she was inside. Outside, it was a different matter. There was a swimming pool in the fortresslike mansion that was perched alone on top of a hill, encircled by a high stone wall. Once she stepped outside to use the pool or just to get some air, she knew very well that she was in a deluxe prison. Four armed men stood guard on the inside perimeter of the wall, and they all watched her closely.

It was the idea of being a captive that was wearing her down, the idea that she was so helpless, at the mercy of her captors if they turned on her.

After what David had told her, she knew why they were holding her. So he would help them with whatever they wanted to do in Saudi Arabia. But what if he couldn't help them? What would happen to her then?

And even if he could, then what? He wasn't her real father. Why should he care what happened to her? Why should anybody care? Why should anybody come?

She thought about her mother and the bomb on the bus. What does the world want from Israelis? Why don't they leave us alone? We want to enjoy our lives and families like everybody else. Why do we always have to be the targets for lunatics and madmen? The whipping boys for pompous, supposedly high-minded world politicians?

She had loved her mother, though they had never spoken about emotions or love. Yael was too tough for that, too hardened, too self-reliant. All those years she lived alone, she never complained because Daphna's father had been killed in the Yom Kippur War.

Just then it occurred to her that she had only herself to depend upon, now and for the rest of her life. She had to stop feeling sorry for herself and take action. She would begin here in this house. Tomorrow, she would start finding a way to escape.

Yet she thought about the four armed guards, and she was filled with terror.

Then she stiffened. She had more backbone than that. As an eighteen-year-old, she had gained admission to the Israeli Air Force—the most difficult and prestigious branch of the Israeli military. She had come through basic training with distinction and was selected as part of an elite group to fly helicopters. She had learned plenty about survival and escape. Now was the time to begin applying some of those lessons.

She walked over to the window of her third-floor bedroom and looked out. All was silence under a full moon. An armed guard leaned against the wall and smoked a cigarette, his gun on the ground. She tried to raise the window, but it didn't budge. She quickly realized it had been nailed shut. That was enough for tonight, she decided. Tomorrow, she promised herself, she would begin trying to find a way out of this prison.

David sat at the table in Taverna and slowly sipped a double espresso. The conversation with Sagit had left him drained. Now that he had cooled down, he was convinced that she had good intentions in making the trip to Washington, and that she honestly believed she could somehow save him and Daphna. The difficulty was that her mission was doomed from the start.

David could see the outcome as clearly as the palm of his hand. Last year he had followed in *The New York Times* General Chambers's selection by President Waltham and his confirmation by the Senate as chairman of the Joint Chiefs, the highest-ranking military officer in the country. It had been a smooth process. The issue of Chambers's culpability for the Dhahran attack five years ago—or at least David's view that Chambers was at fault for not heeding the CIA's information and beefing up defenses at the facility—was never even raised. On the other hand, the general's broken nose and jaw, inflicted by a renegade, crazed CIA agent, had been discussed in a way that evoked sympathy for Chambers. It was a classic example of the military closing ranks behind one of its own. Chambers would no doubt blow sky-high when he found out David was in Israel. Outraged beyond belief, Chambers would demand David's immediate extradition and trial. How could Sagit hope to stand in the way of the pressure he would mount? To David, the outcome was certain. He would have to develop a plan for himself based on that premise.

As soon as he returned to his house at the kibbutz, he took a large map of Israel and its neighbors out of a desk drawer, unfolded it and spread it across the kitchen table. The country was so small. It was a sliver of land, the size of New Jersey. But right now for David that small country represented a virtual prison.

Escape by air was impossible. He was certain that Sagit wasn't bluffing when she told him that Passport Control would pick him up if he used either his Israeli or earlier Russian passport. He had destroyed the passports the CIA had given him in Saudi Arabia, not only because they would trigger an alarm, but because he had known that upon entering Russia, where he was constantly subject to search, he had to be totally clean.

He focused on the border crossing points by car. There was the one into Jordan at the Allenby Bridge and another into Egypt in the Sinai, but the results there would be the same, because passports were subject to careful scrutiny. His eyes ran over the broad expanse of the Judean desert. He could wander in it, like Bishop Pike, but to what end? Physically, the Jordan River was easily crossable, but that wasn't the problem. Because of Israel's diligence in trying to keep out terrorists, the entire border was carefully monitored with sophisticated electronic devices. If he attempted an illegal crossing, even from west to east, he would likely be shot.

Thinking, David put his head into his hands and closed his eyes. There had to be an answer.

Suddenly, he had it.

Fishing boats went out from towns along the coast south of Haifa. He could buy his way on one of those boats and pay the fisherman to get him to a small port in Lebanon that wasn't carefully guarded.

The U.S. currency he had brought back from a trip to Geneva two years ago and hidden away for an emergency like this would enable him to bribe an Arab truck driver to take him to Tyre or Beirut, where he could hire a boat to take him to one of the remote Greek islands. From there, he could make contact with Bruno and lie low until Bruno found a way to rescue him. As soon as Bruno got him to Geneva, David would tell Bruno about Daphna. Bruno's contacts in France were like tentacles reaching throughout the country. He would find a way to win Daphna's release. Guards could always be bribed for money. Then he would withdraw Madame Blanc's two million dollars from the bank, take on a new identity and disappear again, this time to Venezuela, where there was a thriving oil business that could use his services. He raised his head and smiled. It was all falling into place for him now.

Within a half hour David had filled a small knapsack he had hidden with clothes, toiletries and cash from Europe, while Tchaikovsky's *Pathetique* was playing on the stereo in the living room. He slipped into the knapsack a picture of Yael and him that had been taken a year before her death. They were at the kibbutz swimming pool having lunch. He rummaged through several drawers until he found a picture of Daphna in uniform standing next to an Apache helicopter, and he packed that as well. Taking the pictures might prove to be a problem, but that was a risk he was willing to take.

At seven o'clock the next morning, he set off for the coast, driving one of the cars of the kibbutz. As he drove, a strange melancholy began to grip him. He felt badly knowing that he would never return to Israel. He wasn't Jewish. He was Lutheran by birth, an atheist by choice. Yet he had come to love this peculiar, stubborn, idealistic country, thrust into a sea of hostile neighbors.

Then reality abruptly struck him like a blow to the face. Suddenly, in the light of the morning, the plan he had developed last night didn't make much sense. How could Bruno win Daphna's release? Even if he could, resettlement in Venezuela wouldn't be an answer. Two governments with powerful intelligence networks, not to mention Madame Blanc and her thugs, would be scouring the world for them. Besides, that wouldn't be a life for Daphna, running and hiding with him.

And what about for himself? He was sick and tired of running and hiding. Five years of it was enough. Perhaps it was the lack of sleep, but he felt weak and tired. He didn't have the energy or the desire to start over from scratch one more time. Anything would be better than that—even facing the music in Washington, if that's what he had to do.

He pushed down on the brake, turned the car around and headed back to the kibbutz. He'd just have to wait and see what Sagit could pull off for him in Washington.

CHAPTER 11

"CIA headquarters in Langley," Sagit said to the driver as she climbed into a cab at National Airport.

Riding past the Potomac River on the right, Sagit wondered what emissaries of small nations must have felt when they came to Rome at the time of Julius Caesar. This was her sixth trip to the United States—all on Mossad business. Each time visiting the monolith in its seat of power was a sobering experience. The emissary didn't have much leverage.

On the long flight from Israel, Sagit had slept little. When she wasn't reading the books about Saudi Arabia that Rachel had given her, or rehearsing what she would tell Margaret Joyner, she thought about her most recent visit to Washington, last year. Following three days of intensive discussions with CIA and DIA people, Joyner had arranged a two-day working session with Sagit and three CIA antiterrorist specialists at a lodge in central California.

Sagit was thrilled by the trip. She had never been to California before. Raising her eyes high among the giant redwoods in Muir Woods and standing below the cliffs in Yosemite blew her away. The incredible vastness and beauty of America were mind-numbing to the Israeli, whose idea of a forest was a grove of pine trees planted by pioneers fifty or sixty years ago. Sagit tried to capture as much of it as possible on film with her Nikon.

In addition to the humbling vastness of the country, that two-day session gave Sagit a chance to get to know the CIA chief. Margaret Joyner was the first woman to hold the post of CIA director. A petite woman with short gray hair and a small pair of black-framed reading glasses that typically rested halfway down her nose, with a brilliant analytical mind and independent judgment, Joyner was from San Francisco, where her two married daughters lived. Her husband, a high school English teacher, had been killed in a car crash in Potomac, Maryland. While driving home from a high school prom he had been chaperoning, he was struck by a drunk driver.

At the time of her husband's death, Joyner had been in her second term in the U.S. Senate, where she had risen to chairman of the Senate Intelligence Committee, which oversees CIA activities. Under her leadership, the committee shifted from critic to careful supporter of a revamped CIA, which finally rid itself of the last of the Cold War warriors in senior positions.

Two terms in the Senate were enough for her amid the tortoise-like pace of action and the frustrations of the world's most deliberative body. As she was winding down, she threw her support early and forcefully behind then Pennsylvania governor Harry Waltham because he was basically a decent and honorable man even if he wasn't the most brilliant presidential candidate of all time. As a result of Joyner's support and hard work, Waltham carried California, which was the difference between victory and defeat. A grateful president-elect offered her any post in his administration, and she picked director of the CIA, because of her intelligence background in the Congress. The good old boys at Langley almost went berserk at the idea of a woman in the job, but Waltham considered Harry Truman his role model. So he said, "To hell with them."

Sagit had learned from Joyner that in American governmental decisions, personal friendships and relationships often carry the day in complex matters of policy. Sagit was hoping that she had forged enough of a relationship with Joyner to influence her now. As the cab stopped at the guardhouse at the end of the CIA driveway, she mentally ran through her planned pitch one more time.

Margaret Joyner was waiting for Sagit in her huge seventh-floor corner office, which faced toward the Potomac and

Washington. All the CIA chief knew from Moshe's call yesterday was that Sagit was coming on a matter of the utmost importance, and it was essential that no one else be present at their initial meeting. Intrigued by the seriousness in Moshe's tone, Joyner had acceded to that request.

As a secretary ushered her into Joyner's office, Sagit was pleased to see on the wall a photograph she had taken of Joyner in front of a giant redwood. Joyner's ubiquitous silver thermos of coffee and two china cups rested on the round table in one corner.

"I'm flattered that you framed and hung the picture I sent you," Sagit said.

"And it's here every day, I assure you." Sagit looked puzzled. "Meaning that I don't hang in its place a picture a Japanese took before a meeting with Japanese intelligence representatives, and so forth."

The two women laughed together easily.

Joyner walked over to the table, poured two cups of coffee and handed one to Sagit. "Just what I need after flying all night," the Israeli said.

Joyner smiled at the comment. The two women had hit it off the first time they met. "How's Moshe doing these days?"

"Like an old battleship, he keeps on going."

"Yeah. Well, the old battleship sounded worn out yesterday on the phone."

"He's constantly under pressure from the Knesset."

At the mention of the legislature, the smile left Joyner's face. "Tell me about it. I must waste two days a week placating members of Congress. The curse of democracy." Joyner paused to sip some coffee. "I think we better get started. I'm due at the White House in two hours."

She's only got an hour and a half for me, Sagit thought. I'd better be succinct. But if I get her on board, she could get the support we need today. "Before I begin," Sagit said, "let me ask you: does the name Greg Nielsen mean anything to you?"

Joyner was so startled her coffee nearly sloshed out of her cup. "Are you kidding? The fugitive agent? I was chairman of the Senate Intelligence Committee at the time of the Dhahran incident, five years ago. We've been trying to get our hands on Greg Nielsen ever since, but he's managed to elude us. It's as if he vanished into thin air." Her eyes sparkled with intensity. "Don't tell me he's shown up in the promised land claiming that his Lutheran parents were really Jewish."

"You're close, but it's a lot more complicated than that."

"My God, if he managed to get out of Saudi Arabia and make it to Israel, then we did train him well." Her voice disclosed grudging admiration. "Is he up to some new mischief now?" She was very anxious to hear what Sagit had to say.

"Actually, someone else is, and they've pulled him in."

"Okay, tell me about it."

For the next half hour Sagit talked, uninterrupted, explaining to Joyner what had happened, starting with the break-in by Kourosh at the dentist's office in Haifa. She spoke as fast as she could, occasionally struggling with English, but covering everything of importance, including David's trips to Paris, his reports of a planned Saudi coup and Daphna's kidnapping, but omitting her own personal involvement with him. As Sagit spoke, Joyner took off her glasses, fiddled with them, and shook her head from time to time, impressed by Nielsen's resourcefulness and nerve.

When Sagit finished talking and stopped to catch her breath, Joyner asked, "So what's the bottom line?"

Sagit spoke slowly, wanting to recall precisely the English words she had framed so carefully on the plane. "Greg Nielsen, or David Ben Aaron, as we call him, is giving both of our governments a choice. He'll continue with Madame Blanc, pretending he's in with her, in order to find out who in Saudi Arabia is behind the coup, if, and only if"—she glanced up at Joyner—"the American government is prepared to give him immunity from all criminal charges growing out of the Dhahran incident, and the Israeli government is prepared to do the same with respect to violations of immigration law. And he wants it in writing from both of us."

Incredulous, Joyner tossed her glasses down on the desk. "A total immunity from prosecution? No way. He's got to be kidding." She looked offended by the rogue agent's gall. "I'll call Ed Simpson, the AG. He'll have somebody at Justice draw up extradition papers within the hour. Who does Nielsen think he is? He's not exactly in the driver's seat."

Joyner reached for the phone.

"Hold off for a minute, will you, Margaret?"

There was an anxiety in Sagit's voice that made Joyner stop. The CIA director linked the fingers of both of her hands together, put them under her chin, and studied her Israeli visitor.

"Your initial reaction was identical to ours," Sagit said, "but then we thought about it some more. Sure, prosecuting Greg Nielsen's important, but in the larger scheme of things, we care more about the possibility of a radical regime coming to power in Saudi Arabia. It would have a devastating effect on the stability of the entire region, not to mention the fact that the Saudis can easily reach Israel with their advanced weapons. Their American-made weapons."

Joyner leaned back in her chair and closed her eyes, thinking. As Sagit watched, she decided to stop talking and let the CIA chief ponder what she had said.

Finally Joyner opened her eyes. "I'm stunned by what you've told me, Sagit. I'm not trying to minimize the impact on Israel of a radical regime coming to power in Saudi Arabia, and the effect on the U.S. economy of disrupting the flow of Saudi oil would be absolutely devastating. On the other hand, I'm not sure I can justify giving Nielsen immunity under any circumstances after what he did."

Sagit continued smoothly, "Well, we look at it this way: If we toss Nielsen in jail and alert the Saudi government, chances are that Madame Blanc and her Saudi partners will abort their planned coup. We'll feel good about that, but the Saudi government will never know who was planning the coup, and those people will go underground for some period of time."

Joyner finished Sagit's thought. "While the Saudi government cracks down and kills every political dissident they can get their hands on, the people who should be the target of this crackdown will slip away. Then they'll rise to pull off their coup in the future when the Saudis least expect it."

"Exactly. The only way we can be sure that the real people planning the coup are arrested and executed is if we can get some independent information about who the perpetrators are. David Ben Aaron, or Greg Nielsen, as you call him, might be able to get that information for us. At least he's our best shot."

"Based upon what you've told me, I'd have to say he's our only shot."

For several minutes they sat in gloomy silence, while Joyner tried to evaluate her alternatives. Finally she sighed. "Giving Nielsen immunity would be a tough call for the President to make, and it would be his call. However, there is one fact in your account that makes a big difference for me."

"What's that?"

"According to Nielsen, Madame Blanc told him that there was no need to worry about the possibility of American intervention on the side of the Saudi king when the coup takes place. But I need to know, why not? This is absolutely critical for me. Does she own one of our people over there, or what?"

Sagit seemed impressed with Joyner's deduction. In fact, this was playing out precisely as the Israeli had hoped. Joyner's desire to know about a possible American traitor was the only thing that could give Sagit what she wanted in Washington. "You think that's a possibility?"

"I don't know. Our current station chief is a guy by the name of Bill Fox, who was Nielsen's assistant. About six months ago his wife, who would never move to Saudi Arabia, divorced him, and Fox didn't ask for time off to try for a reconciliation or to be with his kids, which is what usually happens in these situations. When I heard about it, I wondered if he had something going on over there. Maybe he's gotten sucked in through a personal relationship with the group that's planning the coup. At any rate, before I would recommend a deal on immunity, Nielsen would have to agree to find out why Madame Blanc is so confident that there won't be American intervention, as well as finding out the name of the Saudi ringleader."

"With that addition, do you think the President will accept this approach?"

Joyner picked up a pen and tapped the table. "I don't know, Sagit, I honestly don't know. Everything you and your government have learned firsthand, I can accept—the killing of Kourosh and all of that—but when we get into conversations Nielsen had with Victor Foch or Madame Blanc, I just don't know if I can believe him. It's not like Greg Nielsen has the greatest credibility around here. How do I know he hasn't made some of this up to get the immunity he wants?"

Sagit closed her tired eyes and massaged her forehead. Joyner's question cut to the heart of the matter. She needed a few moments to frame her answer properly in English, with which she never felt completely comfortable.

"That's certainly a possibility, and Moshe and I have repeatedly agonized over the same question. But at the end of the day, we always come out with the same conclusion: with what's at stake, can we afford not to believe Nielsen?"

"Meaning that he has us over a barrel."

"Over a barrel?"

"Sorry. American slang. It means, I'm reluctantly coming around to the conclusion that the deal with Nielsen is the right move for my government because of the importance of Saudi oil to us, and because I damn well want to know whether Madame Blanc owns Fox or one of my other people over there, but it'll still be a hard sell to the President." She paused for a moment. "What's going to make it even harder is General Chambers."

Sagit was more cautious on this subject. Suppose a Mossad agent had broken the jaw of one of the highest Israeli Army officers. What would be his fate? "David believes that he was justified in what he did five years ago. That

Chambers was trying to set him up to take the fall for a breach of security that was Chambers's responsibility."

Each time Sagit had mentioned Chambers's name, Joyner scowled. She didn't like the man. She didn't trust him. "I was never able to resolve that issue either way. What I do know is that General Bradley Chambers hates Nielsen. He's constantly after me on the subject. He finds it incomprehensible that we haven't been able to find Nielsen. He's convinced that the CIA is protecting Nielsen because he's one of our own. The desire for revenge has become an obsession for Chambers."

"But you said that it's the President's decision."

"It is, but the distinguished General Chambers," she said derisively, "knows how to play the Washington game. Since getting his appointment as chairman of the Joint Chiefs, thanks to friends on the Hill, he's managed to ingratiate himself with Harry. Personally, I don't see how. I think the man's hubris, arrogance and desire for power are unlimited, and I've tried to point that out to Harry, very gingerly, of course, but he's not buying. They've become big golfing buddies, and he likes to regale Harry, who spent the Vietnam War safely at a JAG post in the Pentagon, with stories about his military exploits in Vietnam, which, to be fair, were formidable. So I'll have to contend with this male bonding."

"Anything I can do to help?"

"If you're politely asking whether you should make an appearance at my meeting with the President, the answer is no. This is a battle I'll have to fight myself. The best thing you can do is get some sleep this afternoon."

Sagit nodded.

"Where are you staying?"

"They booked me into the Hilton up on Connecticut Avenue."

"Meet me at the Cosmos Club for dinner at eight. I'll give you a report on what happened."

The two women rose and Joyner walked Sagit to the door.

As soon as Sagit left, Joyner called the President's secretary.

"Say, Kathy, are we still on schedule for the noon meeting with the Mexican ambassador and Langston from DEA?"

"He hasn't started his presentation to the Girl Scouts yet. As usual, we're running a little behind."

"Hold Langston and the Mexican ambassador outside somewhere. I need ten minutes with him first about another subject."

Finally, the last Girl Scout had left the Oval Office, and Joyner was alone with the President.

"Those little girls in their uniforms are so eager and innocent," he said. "They give me a good feeling about the future of the country." Harry Waltham leaned back in his black leather chair and put his feet up on the empty green leather-topped antique desk. "Were you a Girl Scout when you were a kid, Margaret?"

"That's a sad story. I desperately wanted to be, but my Nob Hill mother didn't think it was classy enough for her precious daughter. I cried my eyes out about it one night, but Father took her side, as always, so that's the story of me and the Girl Scouts."

The President chuckled. "You've undoubtedly gotten over it. Right?"

Joyner laughed. She loved bantering with the President. "I have not, Harry. It scarred me for life."

"Well, if you feel that strongly, I invited them back next year. I'll have them make you an honorary member."

"It's not the same thing, but thanks anyhow."

He chuckled again. "Poor little Margaret."

Her expression turned serious. "Listen, Harry, I hate to ruin your good mood, but I've got some news you're not going to like."

He groaned. "Just what I need. I've already heard this morning that the tax-cut proposal I staked my whole economic program on is in trouble in the Senate, and Illinois, which I thought was solidly in our camp for

November, is now up for grabs. I'm not sure what else
could happen."

The President didn't like beating around the bush. So
Joyner decided to toss her news on the table like a live
grenade.

"There's a chance of a coup in Saudi Arabia. They could
cut off our flow of Saudi oil."

Waltham yanked his feet off the desk and bolted to an
upright sitting position. "Come again, Margaret?"

She repeated what she'd said.

"Jesus, that's the last thing I need less than two months
before the election. A crisis about our supply of oil."

Harry had been fortunate. So far, he hadn't had a major
foreign policy crisis in his presidency. She was uncertain
how he would behave when faced with life-and-death decisions, and she worried that he would unduly defer to the
military, which meant General Chambers. "You're right. It
would be a disaster politically."

"How good's your information?"

"The Mossad picked it up. I just met with one of their
top people this morning. They think the information's solid.
I've heard what they have, and I'm prepared to go along
with them, though I've still got some doubts."

"Who's planning the coup?" He was racking his brains,
thinking what he knew about internal Saudi politics, which
wasn't much. "Fundamentalists?"

"We don't know yet. I'm working with them on a plan
to get the answer to that question."

"Do anything it takes to find out. Then we'll get together
with the Saudis to stop it."

"What if it means giving immunity from prosecution to
Greg Nielsen?"

At first the President didn't respond. She obviously
thought he knew who this Greg Nielsen was, and the name
sounded vaguely familiar, but for the life of him, he
couldn't recall where or when he'd heard it before. "Who
the hell is he?"

"The former CIA agent who broke General Chambers's
nose and jaw five years ago in Saudi Arabia."

"Oh, Christ. I remember reading about that guy. I was governor of Pennsylvania at the time." He looked at her with concern. "Brad's never going to buy the idea of giving immunity to this Nelson."

"His name's Nielsen."

"Yeah, Nielsen. Whatever."

Joyner wanted to shout out, "Look, Harry, you're the President. You can't possibly let someone's personal vendetta stand in the way of protecting the country's supply of oil even if he is your golfing buddy," but that wasn't the way to get what she wanted with Harry Waltham. So Joyner kept her emotions in check and said, "Iran and Iraq are already in the hands of loonies. If it looks like Saudi Arabia's going the same way, the price of gasoline will quickly shoot to three or four bucks a gallon and you and I will both be looking for other work after November."

He sucked in his breath. "So what do you want to do about Brad?"

"Let me try to bring General Chambers around on this through the NSG. We're meeting today at five."

The President was relieved that she had offered to handle it. He knew Chambers well enough to know this would be one ugly mess. Once on the golf course, he had asked the general about his jaw, which he was rubbing, obviously feeling some discomfort, and Chambers practically went beserk, as he recounted his side of the Dhahran events five years ago. "All right. You try it that way. If you can't get a consensus, then pull me out of anything I'm doing and call me into the meeting. I'll make the decision."

"One other thing, Harry. I don't think we should say anything at all to the Saudis until we know exactly who's involved. Otherwise, they'll go on a witch hunt, and the real perps will slip away, to try it another day."

"Agreed. Tell Frostie at State and the others on the NSG that I want absolute secrecy until we have a better handle on the whole thing."

Joyner left the Oval Office feeling satisfied. She had gotten as much as she could possibly have hoped for. She would be very busy for the next several hours, until the five o'clock meeting of the National Security Group, or NSG, as it was called, which consisted of Charles Frost, the secretary of state, Bill Hayes, the secretary of defense, Ralph Laurence, the President's national security adviser, General Chambers and Joyner. She was able to set up one-on-one meetings with Hayes and Laurence, and she won each of them over to the immunity deal for Nielsen. She knew that they both resented the way in which Chambers had become a confidant of the President on defense and military affairs, and she used that resentment to bring them around to the view that no one's personal animosity, no matter how justified, should stand in the way of the best interests of the country.

Unfortunately, she couldn't get on Frost's calendar before the meeting, and she'd have to present the matter cold to him and Chambers.

The NSG met in a conference room just down the hall from the Oval Office. As Joyner approached the door, she saw General Chambers and Frost huddling in a corner, whispering about something. She wasn't surprised. Lately, Chambers had been spending a great deal of time with the former Princeton history professor. Joyner's analysis was that Chambers shrewdly felt that if he had Frost with him, he could carry the day with Waltham on most issues, notwithstanding opposition from the others on the NSG. To ingratiate himself with Frost, Chambers would frequently make a point of soliciting his views as "a renowned historian" in a group meeting.

Ralph Laurence chaired the NSG, and he put Joyner at the top of the agenda. As she reported on her meeting with Sagit and gave her recommendation for immunity for Greg Nielsen, she watched General Chambers, seated at the other end of the polished wooden table, in his immaculate, heavily starched and metal-laden brown uniform. The general was listening to every word and tapping his fingers on the table.

She glanced over at Frost. The secretary of state wasn't hard to read. He was looking at Chambers, prepared to take his cue from the general.

When she was finished, she said, "Well, what do you think, gentlemen?"

Chambers spoke first. His tone was even, cold and analytical. "With all due respect, Margaret, I don't think we should reward this renegade with immunity. My own recommendation is that we get Ed Simpson at Justice on the phone right now. Tell him to prepare extradition papers for Nielsen ASAP. And if the Israelis don't cough him up, we suspend all aid until they do."

"I'm on board with that as well," Frost said.

She turned to Laurence and Hayes. "What do you two think?"

One at a time they fell in behind Joyner's proposal while Chambers scowled. He realized she had lined them up ahead of time. He and Frost were outnumbered three to two. More important, he couldn't be sure how Harry Waltham would decide the question in this face-off between him and Joyner. He knew that Joyner enjoyed a close relationship with Harry as well, and the President particularly listened to her on political matters. With the election so close, if she inserted political considerations, he might very well lose.

So, he decided to resort to a strategy he had used effectively in Vietnam. If you're not certain you can win a battle, withdraw. Let the enemy think that you're vanquished, when in fact you're regrouping at another locale where the terrain is more favorable, and you'll have the element of surprise. He'd set a trap to catch Nielsen on another day. Chambers would beat him, even playing by Joyner's rules. He rubbed his right hand over his jawline. It was five years since Nielsen had broken it, and he could still feel it every day of his life. Well, now he would have a chance for revenge.

"My dear Margaret," he said in a patronizing voice, "in the spirit of harmony, I'm prepared to go along with the majority here. However, I think that when Ed Simpson has his people at Justice draw up the immunity papers for Nielsen, they should make it explicit that if Nielsen's not fully cooperating, and I mean fully and openly at all times, in this business, then the immunity is off, and we'll move immediately to arrest him."

Hayes added, "It's what we lawyers call a condition subsequent."

"Call it whatever you want," Chambers said. "It becomes a critical part of the deal. And everyone in this room should agree in writing that Ed Simpson will be the judge as to whether or not Nielsen is giving us that full and open cooperation."

"Your conditions are fair enough," Joyner replied, happy she didn't need the President to resolve a bitter dispute. After all, she had to work with General Chambers on lots of other matters.

For his part, the general was satisfied as well. He was confident that they had just given Nielsen the rope with which to hang himself.

The Cosmos Club had a rule against papers in the dining room. So when Sagit entered the marble-floored foyer, with the grand sweeping staircase that went to the second floor, Margaret led her along a corridor lined with pictures of club members, who had been Nobel and Pulitzer Prize winners, to a deserted reading room at the end.

When they were seated, the CIA chief reached into her briefcase and handed Sagit the immunity paper Attorney General Simpson had prepared. Then she recounted her battle with General Chambers. "I just hope Greg Nielsen doesn't let us down. For his own sake as well as ours."

"Well, now he has the incentive to work with us."

"I hope so. I went out on a very long limb for this deal."

Joyner's words sent a chill down Sagit's spine. Moshe had used exactly the same phrase, telling Sagit she had gone out on a long limb for David. The stakes had just increased. She hoped she wouldn't look like a fool. Sagit asked, "What do we do about communicating as this goes forward?"

"You and I will be the sole contacts between our governments. This matter gets the top security clearance. 'Need

to know' only. Copies of documents are to be numbered
and tracked. Nobody goes to the French government or
Saudis unless President Waltham gives the order."

Sagit could barely conceal the relief she felt at hearing
Joyner's report.

"Now let's go eat," Joyner said, "I'm starving."

In the dining room, after Joyner wrote out their dinner
order for a waiter, who had just deposited a basket of hot
popovers, Sagit said, "You told me this morning that you
were chairman of the Senate committee that investigated
the Dhahran incident five years ago?" Joyner nodded.
"What do you think really happened, Margaret?"

Joyner closed her eyes, and fiddled with her glasses, trying
to remember what she had decided five years ago. "Well, it
was a little ambiguous, but I had two primary conclusions.
And, as I recall, most of the other committee members
agreed with me. First, the moderates Nielsen was working
with, led by Air Force Colonel Azziz, had nothing to do
with the attack on the American housing complex. It was
the work of radical fundamentalists, planned and executed
by a Hezbollah cell organized by Iran. If Nielsen hadn't
struck Chambers and run away, I doubt if he would ever
have been charged with responsibility for the attack. The
American government never washes its intelligence linen in
public if it can avoid it. But even if he had been charged,
my guess is that Nielsen would have been exonerated."

"But would he have gotten a fair trial?"

Sagit's comment rankled Joyner. "My committee would
have seen to it, and the CIA director at the time had
enough clout with the White House to ensure it. Besides,
Nielsen actually warned Chambers about the likelihood of
an attack a week earlier, and Chambers didn't do anything
to beef up security. So Chambers would have had egg on
his face if Nielsen had gone to trial. As it was, with his jaw
broken and Nielsen on the run like a guilty man and renegade agent, the Pentagon was able to get away with a
whitewash report clearing Chambers of any blame."

"So, in retrospect, Nielsen was foolish to have struck
Chambers?"

"That's how it looked to me at the time of my committee's investigation, but of course hindsight's always twenty-twenty."

Sagit looked at her glumly. "So having acted rashly, Nielsen took on the mark of Cain and became a pariah, even though he was right. And Chambers became the sympathetic injured war hero."

Joyner thought that summary was biased toward Nielsen, but she decided not to argue with Sagit. She was beginning to understand that there was a personal factor involved. "That's about it."

"That doesn't seem fair."

"So what else is new?"

Joyner paused while the waiter deposited their salads. Then she asked, "You care for this guy on a personal level, don't you?"

Sagit blushed. "How do you know?"

"From the way you sound."

Sagit clasped her hands together and moved them nervously. "I guess you're going to tell me that's unprofessional under the circumstances."

"I'm not going to tell you anything of the sort. I'm not your mother, and you're a big girl. Besides, people always do what they want to where matters of the heart are involved." She paused, narrowed her eyes and gave Sagit a sharp look. "What I will tell you is to advise Nielsen or David, or whatever you call him, to watch his step. Chambers gave in too quickly today. My guess is that he's going to set a trap."

David finished reading the two conditional immunity papers—one from each government—that Sagit had handed him. They were alone in his office in the High-Tech Center at the kibbutz, and the door was closed. When he had first seen her walk into the building, from his window, he was certain that she had come with state security people, waiting at the kibbutz entrance to arrest him. Now a smile of relief appeared on his face.

He put the documents down on his computer table, looked squarely at her and uttered in a soft voice, "Thank you. I underestimated you. I feel as if I've gotten my life back, and I won't forget this. I promise you that."

"Before you're overcome with joy and gratitude, let's go over the deal one more time, so there's no misunderstanding. We want two items of information from you. We want to know who the Saudi ringleader of the coup is, and we want to know why Madame Blanc's not worried about the possibility of American intervention on the side of the king. Do you understand that?" she asked, sounding like a schoolteacher.

He nodded.

"Second, you'd better reread the condition requiring full cooperation."

"I know what it says."

"Read it again," she snapped, irritable and tired from two very long plane rides in less than three days. As he reread the document, she said, "It means working with us fully and openly. No more Lone Ranger stuff, as you Americans say."

"I wouldn't think of it," he said blithely.

"We're not kidding, David. General Chambers can't wait for you to slip up so you'll lose your immunity, and Margaret told me that their attorney general, this Ed Simpson, is a stickler for compliance."

His voice took on a tougher edge. "You're coming through loud and clear. I'll think about it on the flight to Paris tomorrow."

She was startled. "Paris?"

David reached into his desk drawer and handed her a fax that had arrived hours earlier.

Monsieur David Ben Aaron.

Your customer's computer parts will be in Paris on Monday. Plan to start work Tuesday morning. A room has been reserved for you at the Bristol Monday evening.

—V

Sagit said, "Victor came through with what you wanted."

"You sound surprised."

His self-confidence, bordering on arrogance, annoyed her. "Pretty smug, aren't you?"

"He had to do it. Madame Blanc gave him an order."

"I'm going with you to Paris."

He shook his head from side to side. "Uh-uh. A very bad idea. It could get me killed and wipe out all of your good work getting me the immunity."

"We'll take our chances on that."

"Thanks a lot."

"Look, David, these people are serious professionals. You can't operate solo. We'll be very careful. You won't even know that we're there, and we won't set up any surveillance. I'll be holed up in a small hotel on rue Cambon. From Paris I'll be in a better position to direct our efforts to find Daphna."

"What have you learned so far?"

"Zero. We still haven't located the property near Grasse."

"You've got to do better," David said, raising his voice. "We have to get Daphna out of there."

Sagit thumped the desk with her fist. "Don't tell me how to do my job. You worry about your own assignments. I'll give you the number of my cell phone. Call me in Paris if you need anything."

The next morning, when Sagit drove west from Jerusalem to make the plane to Paris, Moshe's lecture from last night was still ringing in her ears: "I don't want a repetition of the Marseilles affair, when we accidentally killed two bystanders in that ridiculous shoot-out on the docks, or France will cut off diplomatic relations. Is that clear?"

"Very clear, Moshe."

"That means you don't use a gun under any circumstances, and you don't get arrested. Even if you find Daphna. Is that understood?"

She nodded.

"Say 'Understood.' "

"Understood."

CHAPTER 12

"I'm honored by your personal presence," David said to Victor as Rolland eased the car into the heavy morning rush-hour traffic along rue St. Honore. Before responding, Victor pushed a button and a thick glass partition slid up behind the front seat, isolating the driver from their conversation.

"Since you managed to ingratiate yourself so well with Madame Blanc, she wanted me to provide a little extra service."

"I tried to be as charming as possible on the boat at St. Tropez. I'm happy to hear that I succeeded."

"The truth is that she found you an awful bore personally. It's what you told her about the Saudi royal family's capability to blow up their own oil fields that got her attention."

"No doubt she checked with your friends in Saudi Arabia, and she found out I was right."

"And that's damn lucky for you."

David could barely restrain the smile that wanted to break out on his face. Now that Madame Blanc had gotten an independent verification of what he had told her, he must have gained a substantial measure of her trust, which had to be pissing off Victor to no end. He decided to push Victor for more information.

"I'll bet she raised hell with your Saudi partner about why he withheld that information."

"Frankly, they didn't know about it. They had to dig to confirm what you said. So anyhow, I'm supposed to be nice to you."

"Now that we have to be together, maybe we'll be like Tevye and his wife in *Fiddler on the Roof*. We'll learn to love each other."

Victor gave David a stony stare. He found nothing amusing or clever about David's remark. "I doubt that. What's your game? I'll find out sooner or later. You know that, and then I'll break you."

David cracked a smile, feigning amusement at the Frenchman's paranoia. "There's nothing to find out."

"Bullshit. The CIA's pulling your strings. Maybe the Mossad as well. Eventually, the truth will come out."

"And here I thought you were so hostile to me because you didn't like Jews."

Victor sneered. "I don't, but you're not a Jew. The fact is that I'll enjoy giving the order for your execution when you make a slip and blow your cover."

"You don't believe in mincing words, do you?"

"Why should I? We had a good thing going here before you came along. I don't like the idea of your screwing it up."

David sneered. "Oh, you had a wonderful thing. You had the right to pump oil out of oil fields that would be on fire for months and damaged for years. You're the one who's lucky that didn't happen. Madame Blanc strikes me as the type who lashes out at her subordinates when there's a royal fuck-up. You'd have been at the top of her list. Not to mention your Saudi connection. And who was that again?"

The lawyer grunted, "Sorry, you're not that much of a partner."

"Eventually I'll have to know who it is."

Victor stared out of the window, while self-consciously touching his toupee to make certain it was in place, and trying to decide how much information he should give David. "You'll find out on October 8 along with the rest of the world. That's the day we're putting you on a plane to Saudi Arabia to help us straighten out their oil industry, assuming that you haven't blown your cover before then, which I think is damn unlikely."

They were leaving Paris and heading north on the A1. David straightened his jacket to conceal the holstered Beretta he'd picked up last evening at the Hotel Gironde. With Madame Blanc's report on him in the blue folder, quite a few people now knew about his assistance to the Shah. Any one of them could leak that information to Iranian security agents, who regularly worked the major European capitals.

David said, "Can I ask where we're going?"

"PDF headquarters. Madame Blanc thought it safer if you worked there."

"Did they get everything I need?"

Victor shot David a nasty look. "Not they. I had to deliver it myself."

"Well, I sure appreciate that."

"Yeah, I've got nothing better to do than fly off to London to run errands for you."

David wanted to ask, "Why London?" but he didn't want to encourage Victor in his suspicions by asking too many questions. Besides, he had a pretty good idea of the answer. Madame Blanc was trying to minimize French contacts whenever possible. Kourosh had been flown to Rome initially. No doubt a Saudi emissary had personally flown the computer discs to London, where they had been handed off to Victor.

Having concluded he had gotten as much information as he could from the French lawyer, David turned away and looked at the French countryside. As far as he was concerned, they could ride in silence the rest of the way.

Dora, the director of the children's program at kibbutz Bet Mordechai, happened to be in the administration office when a telephone call came in for David Ben Aaron. Nobody had told her that he had gone to Paris. So she transferred the call to the High-Tech Center, thinking that he would be at work there.

Batya answered it on the front desk, as she did all outside calls.

"Hello," she snapped, annoyed that she had been disturbed in the midst of cramming for an exam she would be taking at the Technion next week, for a degree in advanced mathematics.

"I want to speak with David Ben Aaron," a man's voice said in French.

Batya had studied French in school and spent a summer as a teenager in Dijon as an exchange student. "Who's calling, please?"

"I'm calling from Paris, from a large French steel company. We've heard about your computer developments, and we want to talk to David Ben Aaron as soon as possible. This could be a very large order for your kibbutz."

Batya perked up. With one more large order, they could get both a new swimming pool and a new dining hall.

"I'm sorry, he's not here right now."

"Do you know how I can reach him? This is an important contract."

"It's fortunate for you that he's in Paris right now."

"Oh, that is fortunate. Do you have his hotel? I could call him there."

Batya looked at the note David had left her. In case of an emergency and "only an extreme emergency," she could reach him at the Hotel le Bristol. This certainly qualified as an emergency.

"Le Bristol," she said eagerly.

She hung up the phone and went back to her linear algebra book. Minutes later, something began to bother her. The caller's French had been perfect in terms of grammar, but he had an accent that she had rarely heard. Middle Eastern. Maybe Arabic or Iranian. And none of those people could ever get a top job at a French steel company. A jolt of fear shot through her body. She had made a mistake. A horrible mistake.

She ran out of the High-Tech Center to find Gideon.

After driving for fifty minutes, they arrived in Chantilly, dotted with thoroughbred racing farms. The black Mercedes turned off the road at a sign that read PDF WORLD-WIDE HEADQUARTERS. A hundred yards down the way, they came to a stop at a shiny metal guardhouse with two uniformed men inside. David watched as one of the guards emerged with a clipboard in his hand. The other, with a pistol holstered at his waist, carefully studied the car through a bulletproof glass window.

As soon as the man with the clipboard recognized Victor, he nodded and waved them through. The long driveway was lined with pine trees. The grass on both sides was thick and manicured. All of the grounds were well tended, David noticed.

They pulled up to the front of an ornate marble and glass four-story structure with the company's logo in gold above the front entrance. It was obvious that Madame Blanc had no desire to hide her company's profitability.

As Victor leaned across the seat and opened the door on David's side, he said, "You're on your own, monsieur super spy. This is as far as I go. Work as late as you want today. Then ask whoever's on the reception desk to call you a cab. I'll pick you up tomorrow morning at the Bristol. Same time. You can give me a status report then. Any questions?"

Good riddance, David thought. He was sick of the French lawyer. "Nope, I'm all set."

Victor reached into his jacket pocket and pulled out a card, which he handed to David.

"This has all of my phone numbers—office, home, cell phone and pager—to reach me any time. Call if you need me, but I trust that you won't."

Walking into the building, David thought about Sagit and their conversation yesterday. Minutes before he had boarded the plane for Paris, she had sternly lectured him in a small office at Ben Gurion Airport that the Mossad maintained. "Remember, David, you need to get two items of information for us and only two: the name of the Saudi ringleader of the coup, and why Madame Blanc isn't worried about the Americans. You get those items, and you get out. We want you back here alive. We don't want to have to rescue two hostages."

He had responded, "Don't forget that Madame Blanc

offered me a lot of money to stick with her program for six months. I don't hear you or your Washington friends coming close to matching that. But then again, maybe you're hoping I'll ask you to retire with me to Anguilla, where we can live happily ever after with Madame Blanc's money."

Her face had screwed up in anger. "That's not funny. That bank account of yours in Geneva doesn't do much for the comfort level in Jerusalem or Washington."

"That's precisely why it helped me establish credibility with Madame Blanc."

The floor of the reception area was all shiny black marble except in the center, where the letters PDF were inset in white. David crossed them as he walked to the teak reception desk. A young woman with wire-framed glasses, dressed in a smartly tailored blue and gray plaid suit, sat behind the desk. DANIELLA was the name on the brass plate. Behind her on the wall hung an oil portrait of Madame Blanc, made about ten years earlier, David guessed. In two corners of the room stood armed guards watching him carefully.

Daniella asked for an ID, and when he showed her his Israeli passport, she asked him to sign the visitors log. As he did, she pointed to a sign on her desk that said CHECK ALL WEAPONS, TAPE RECORDERS, COMPUTERS OR SIMILAR HARDWARE.

"Would you open your briefcase please?"

One of the guards moved in to help with the inspection. David saw that he would have to pass through a metal detector at the other end of the reception area, so he took the Beretta out of its holster and laid it on the reception desk. Neither the guard nor the receptionist showed any surprise.

"It'll be returned to you when you leave," Daniella said as she put it in a desk drawer.

"Do I get a claim check?" he asked.

Without cracking a smile, she replied, "I doubt we'll get any other guns today."

Minutes later, accompanied by an armed guard, he was

in a richly wood-paneled elevator riding to the top floor. The guard accompanied him along a marble corridor lined with oriental carpets until they reached a closed steel door.

With a small remote-control device, the guard opened the door. Another armed guard stood on the other side, and he now became David's escort.

He deposited David in a small office where a matronly woman, in her late fifties David estimated, with neatly coifed gray hair, wearing a navy skirt and cream-colored blouse, was typing on a computer. The walls were adorned with prints of two Monet flower paintings. On her desk there was a picture of her family—including two grandchildren about three and five years old. There was also, curiously enough, a wooden model of a guillotine.

When she heard the footsteps, she turned off her computer and swiveled around in her chair. "Welcome to the Task Force, Mr. Ben Aaron," she said. "I'm Colette Martique, the chief administrator."

And chief baby-sitter, he thought.

She stood up and stuck out her hand.

"Pleased to meet you, Colette," he said, shaking it.

Colette deposited him in an adjacent windowless office, equipped with a PC. The walls were bare. She pointed at the gray metal box on the desk. "It has everything you ordered," she said, and quickly departed.

David booted up the computer and selected the top disc from the box. It had the system for defense of the royal palace in Riyadh, which looked precisely the same as the one he had installed seven years ago. As he evaluated the data and descriptions on the computer screen, he kept thinking about the two items of information Sagit told him he needed. They might be stored somewhere in the information system for what Colette had called "the Task Force." Somehow, he would have to gain access to the computer system for the Task Force, but as long as Colette was next door, he couldn't risk trying. He wasn't at all fooled by her grandmotherly look. Given the rest of the security in the building, he had to assume that she had been instructed to keep tabs on him. His only chance would be to work late into the evening, and hope she left before then. In the meantime, he would work on developing a plan for the attack.

Two hours into his work, Colette walked into the office without knocking. "The Task Force eats lunch together in the company restaurant, but I was told you're supposed to be isolated. So I'll take you myself."

"Aren't you wondering what I did to deserve such treatment?"

She looked at him with a cold, dour expression. "Not particularly. I'm happy to follow instructions."

Accompanied by an armed guard, she led him to the restaurant downstairs. An isolated table in the corner must have been set aside for them because she went directly to it. They were served salad, grilled filet of sole and crème brûlée. "What do you do for the Task Force?" he asked her.

She looked around nervously. "It's probably best if we don't discuss business at lunch."

"How did I know you were going to say that?" She didn't respond. "Okay, Colette, can you talk about yourself?"

She was from Bordeaux, in the south. Her husband, a petroleum engineer and a longtime employee of PDF, was presently in Russia, where PDF had exploration contracts. She eagerly talked about her family, while gracefully deflecting his repeated efforts to slip in questions about the Task Force. Now he decided, she was friendly, but she was no fool.

Back upstairs, David went to work again with intensity, continually looking at the clock on the wall, hoping Colette would leave. At six o'clock, she popped into his office, wearing a blue raincoat and carrying an umbrella.

"I'm going home," she told him. "They said you can work as late as you want. Tell one of the guards in the hall when you've finished for the day, or if you need to use the rest room. He'll escort you."

The implication was clear: Don't leave this office by yourself.

"Will you be back tomorrow?" she asked.

"I'll need at least one more day."

He waited a full thirty minutes after she left before trying to gain access to the Task Force computer system. He needed a password, and he tried every possibility he could think of: Saudi Arabia, Middle East, Arabs, Saudis, Task Force, oil, Saudi oil, Paris, Riyadh, and on and on, but nothing worked. "Dammit," he cursed, and slapped the side of the machine, but nothing happened. After an hour he gave up. He was totally shut out.

Recalling what Sagit had said after her return from Washington, he began to worry. If he couldn't obtain either of the items the Americans and Israelis wanted, would General Chambers be able to convince Ed Simpson that he had failed to cooperate, and would he be extradited to the United States? Suddenly, the availability of Madame Blanc's money in a Swiss bank account began to look good as an insurance policy.

The armed guard took him back to the reception area, where a hard-looking young man, with a pugilist's nose that had been broken and poorly set, was on duty. He called David a cab. When it came, he returned David's Beretta before being asked. "You'd better be careful with that thing," he said.

As soon as she had gotten Moshe's call passing on Gideon's information about the mysterious phone call to the kibbutz, Sagit had telephoned the Bristol and asked for David's room. There was no answer. When she went outside, she found it was raining lightly. Mindful of Moshe's admonition, "Don't use a gun and don't get arrested," she stopped at nearby shops and bought an umbrella and a can of pepper spray. "It's not a gun, Moshe," she said to herself, "but I have to find a way to protect him." Then she took a cab to the Bristol and walked up and down rue St. Honore, close to the hotel, pretending to window-shop, but watching for anything suspicious, and making certain she wasn't being followed.

About eight in the evening, she saw two men approach the hotel on foot. They took positions flanking the front entrance. One man was tall and thin; the other short and stocky. Both were wearing black leather jackets and were bare headed. Their faces were olive-skinned and swarthy.

They could be waiting for David to come back to the hotel, she decided. Each man had a hand in his jacket pocket, clutching a weapon, she guessed. They would set a trap. Now she was certain of it. She had to decide where to position herself, but she didn't know if David would arrive on foot, and if so, from which direction? Or whether he'd be in a taxi or other vehicle. At least the street was one-way for vehicular traffic. That helped a little.

The rain had turned to a raw and chilly fine mist. There were very few people on the sidewalk. Even the hotel doorman waited inside until someone approached the Bristol.

Sagit decided to walk across the street from the hotel, still pretending to be window-shopping. Immediately across from the Bristol was the prestigious fashion house of Christian La Croix, composed of two boutiques separated by a narrow path that ran back to a courtyard and then to the gray stone building that housed the company's headquarters and haute couture collection.

With her umbrella up, she turned unobtrusively into the narrow path toward the courtyard, pretending to look at the shoes in the side window.

Quietly she slipped around a corner of the building, where the two men could no longer see her. From that vantage point, she could still peek out and watch the scene in front of the hotel.

She waited like that for a half hour. To avoid being seen by the two men, she closed up her umbrella. The rain began coming down harder, and it was cold as well as damp, soaking her through her clothes. Several cabs pulled up in front of the Bristol, but there was no sign of David in a car or on foot.

Another cab approached from her left. As it slowed to a stop, she recognized David's face through the half-open rear window. Instinctively, she ran from the courtyard onto the sidewalk and shouted in Hebrew, "David, careful. They're trying to kill you."

As soon as she got the words out, the tall man raced toward the cab, with a gun in his hand.

David yanked the Beretta out of its shoulder holster and kicked open the back door of the cab, on the hotel side. When he spotted the tall figure rushing at him, David ducked. The attacker shot through the back of the cab, shattering the window on the other side. The cabbie screamed, while David aimed and fired. He thought he struck his assailant, but he didn't wait to find out. He sprang out of the door of the cab, hitting the ground and rolling along the cold hard cement and cobblestones in the direction of the back of the cab. The sharp edges of the stones cut into his legs and arms, but he disregarded the pain and continued to roll. He heard bullets ricochet off the street, as his assailant, wailing in pain, with blood gushing from his right eye where David had shot him, couldn't get a clear shot. Suddenly, David stopped rolling. In an abrupt motion he raised his head and steadied his gun hand, aiming at the heart of the tall man coming toward him. He fired. It was a direct hit, and the man went down.

Sagit yelled, "There's another one!"

With that, the short stocky man, clutching a knife in his left hand and a gun in his right, ran across the street toward Sagit. David, his arms and legs bloodied from the cobblestones, jumped up and chased them.

She raced back into the Christian La Croix courtyard, clutching the can of pepper spray in her hand. Around the corner of the building, she crouched down in a dirt patch that held a small tree and some bushes. When the attacker entered the courtyard, he ground to a sudden halt, looking around for her. Once he saw her, he cut sharply toward the dirt patch. That was when she sprung to her feet and pushed down on the spray can. The cloud of pepper spray struck the man in the face. He cried out in pain, then dropped his knife and fell to his knees on the muddy ground in a corner of the courtyard, screaming and holding his face with his hand.

Sagit kicked the gun out of his other hand, then shouted to David, "Let's go before the police come."

"I have to find out who sent them."

"Don't be a fool, David. We'll be arrested."

"You go, then. You're Mossad. I'm private. I can take the heat." She hesitated. "Please, Sagit, I'll call you on your cell phone."

Remembering Moshe's instructions, she reluctantly acceded, running out of the courtyard and along the sidewalk until she hit the avenue Matignon, where she turned left. From there it was only a short distance to the Champs Elysées, where there was always a crowd to blend into, no matter how bad the weather.

Back in the courtyard, David knelt and tried to push the stocky assailant down on his back, but the man thrashed wildly, scratching David's face with sharp, clawlike fingernails and narrowly missing his eyes. David could taste his own blood in his mouth. He punched the man hard in the stomach again and again, and finally the thrashing stopped.

David pushed him back flat on the ground and straddled the man, using his knees to pin the man's thick arms to the ground. David gripped his assailant's throat with both of his hands and shouted, "Who sent you?"

"God is great!" was the response. David picked up the man's head, then slammed it hard against the muddy ground.

The assailant strained with all of his might to throw David off. David could feel his control weaken, but he pushed down hard and barely kept the man tight against the ground. The man raised his knees and tried to kick, but David tightened his grip on the man's throat, draining his strength.

"Who sent you, you bastard?"

"God is great."

With his hands tight against the man's throat, David pounded the man's head mercilessly against the wet ground.

"Talk, or I'll kill you . . . Talk or I'll kill you."

Suddenly, light burst in the courtyard. A busload of the security forces routinely stationed at the nearby Palais de l' Elysées had arrived at the scene. Two of them ran into the courtyard with their pistols drawn. Immediately, they went for David.

"Get him," someone called. "Get that man."

Powerful hands pulled David off, yanking his arms back until he had to release his grip on the man's throat. A hard rubber club smashed into the side of his head and, semiconscious, he lost the will to resist.

Roughly, they slapped handcuffs on him and dragged him back to their bus.

For Victor, it had been a perfect evening thus far. The kind of evening that dreams are made of. His wife was out of town, visiting her ill mother in Avignon. He had taken Françoise, the newest French film blond bombshell, to Verdi's *La Traviata*, where her low-cut, sequined magenta dress turned every set of male eyes in the grandiose opera hall. They dined at the Crillon after the opera, and she invited him back to her apartment for a nightcap. Lest he have any doubt about her intentions, she disappeared for a couple of minutes and returned carrying two snifters of cognac, dressed only in a white terry-cloth robe that she made no effort to tie in the front. He was bursting with excitement. For months he had been dying to get inside that gorgeous golden bush, and he was almost there. He hadn't touched her yet, and already he had a giant erection.

Then the pager in his jacket pocket began beeping. Oh Christ, not now, he thought. He pulled out the pager and looked at the phone number from which the call had been made. It wasn't one of Madame Blanc's numbers, and only one other person had the pager number. Not even his wife had it. I'll kill that damn Israeli, he thought.

Quizzically, he studied the number on the pager.

As he did, Françoise looked at him in irritation. She wasn't accustomed to having a man's business interfere with her getting sex when she wanted it, and she wanted it right now.

Victor got up from the sofa and walked across the room.

"Where are you going?" Françoise demanded.

"To use the phone. Just for thirty seconds, I promise, *ma chérie*."

She pouted. "I'm looking at the clock. If it passes thirty seconds, I go into the bedroom and lock the door. You go home. Is that clear?"

He knew she meant it. His erection was already withering.

The phone was answered by a man who said, "Philippe, National Security Police."

Oh shit, Victor thought. "My name is Victor Foch. Someone called me from your number."

"I'll get the prisoner now," he said. There was a delay while Philippe put the phone down to get David.

Victor didn't even bother looking at the clock. There was no need for that. He sighed in resignation when he heard the bedroom door slam loudly and a dead bolt snap into place.

An hour later, Victor and David were seated at a table in a small brasserie that stayed open all night. The lawyer was still in the double-breasted charcoal Brioni suit, starched white shirt and Hermes tie he had worn to the opera. David was in the wet and dirty clothes he had been wearing when the police pulled him off the stocky assailant. His pants were mud-stained and torn at the knees. His scratched face was streaked with mud and caked with dried blood, as were his arms and legs. His whole body ached from the blows the police had inflicted with hard rubber clubs in the van on the way to jail.

They were the only customers in the brasserie. A surly waiter deposited two cups of double espresso and quickly departed, hoping that David wouldn't get too much mud on his chair.

"Well, your name certainly carries influence," David

said. "All I had to do was mention it, and the police stopped smacking me around. And then you sprang me in record time."

"Goddamm it, Nielsen! Cut the bullshit and tell me what happened."

"You've got it ass backwards. You damn well better tell me what happened," David replied angrily.

"What the hell's that mean?"

David leaned forward and grabbed the lapels of Victor's jacket. "My analysis, while waiting around for you to come, was that you told the Iranians about me, and where I was staying. The rest was up to them, but they botched the job."

"You really believe that?"

"Just as sure as God made little green apples." Victor looked at him in bewilderment. David added, "That's an expression they use in Texas when they're positive something happened."

Victor pushed David's hands away. "I don't care about your stupid Texas slang. I just can't believe that you think I had anything to do with this."

"Well, you sure as hell don't like me. You haven't made any secret of that."

"Absolutely true. But you're overlooking something."

"What's that?"

"You've managed to con Madame Blanc, who's my most important client and who believes that you're valuable to her project." Victor scoffed. "She's told me that I'm personally responsible for your safety. What's more, she's a person I wouldn't cross under any circumstances. With her intelligence network, she'd find out in hours that I was responsible for your death." Victor gave David a sly smile, letting him know how attractive the prospect of killing David was for him. "Much as I'd like to get rid of you, I might as well be signing my own death warrant, and I'm afraid you're not worth paying that price."

David paused to sip his espresso, thinking about what Victor had just said. He had to admit that the French lawyer's argument sounded persuasive. But if Victor hadn't called in the Iranian hit squad, then who did? Was it the same people who had tried to kill him in Green Park in London?

David said, "Did the police give you any information about the two who attacked me?"

"You killed both of them."

David looked at him in disbelief. "I only killed the one. The other one was still alive when the police came."

Victor looked David squarely in the eye. "Not by much. The pounding on his head caused a cerebral hemorrhage. He was dead before they got him to jail."

"Are you sure?"

"Quite sure. The time of death was recorded as nine-thirty P.M."

David knew there was something wrong here, but he was too weary and battered to put his finger on it. "Could the police identify them?"

"Negative. They both had Iranian passports in their pockets. Their names and fingerprints didn't come up on French police records or on Interpol, but the names could have been phonies."

David looked at the natty lawyer anxiously. "Will I be charged? What happens now with the police?"

"Not a damn thing. You're off the hook. I've fixed it all."

Grudgingly, David said, "Thank you. I appreciate that."

The lawyer gave him a surly look. "I didn't do it for you. I did it for Madame Blanc. But even so, I had to use up a lot of chits that meant a great deal to me. We're talking double homicide on your part, one with an unlicensed gun, among other crimes. Don't do it again. I won't have such an easy time if you stage a repeat performance."

"Understood."

Victor finished his espresso. "I'll take you back to the Bristol for a couple of hours of sleep. Remember, tomorrow's a working day for you."

David frowned. "Forget the Bristol."

"What's that mean?"

"The Bristol's too hot for me. They know about it. I've got another place to stay."

"Wherever you want. I'll drive you."

"Nope, I can't take a chance of us being followed. I'll get there myself."

David handed Victor his room key at the Bristol. "If you want to do something useful, then pack up my things at the hotel. Deliver them to me at eleven tomorrow morning, when your car takes me back to PDF."

Victor found the idea of cleaning up after David distasteful, but he decided that he had no choice. Madame Blanc's orders had been clear. He had to keep David safe at all costs. "Where shall I meet you?"

"There's a brasserie where avenue George V hits the river. I'll meet you there at eleven o'clock."

"Why there?"

"It's a busy commercial area. I think I'll be safer in a crowd. Besides, I have to go shopping for clothes in the morning."

Even though he was exhausted and beaten, he made sure to follow his routine of changing Metro trains to make certain he wasn't being followed. At the second station he used a call box and dialed Sagit's cell phone.

"Can you meet me at the Hotel Gironde near the place des Invalides?" he asked.

"I'll be there in thirty minutes."

"Tell the man at the reception desk that you want Micky Mantle's room. Oh, and bring some alcohol or something to treat cuts, would you?"

Half an hour later, she was still gripping the can of pepper spray when she knocked on the door to his hotel room. David had arrived only a few minutes earlier himself. She took one look at him and pulled back with apprehension.

"I better get you to a doctor," she said. "We have some people we use in Paris."

"Nah, I'll survive. It's only superficial."

"I was worried when I didn't hear from you. I sent one of our people from the embassy to talk casually with the doorman at the Bristol. He said the police arrested two men. One sounded like you."

"Yeah, well, the police did more to me than either of those guys." He lifted up his shirt and showed her the bruises on his chest and back.

She swallowed hard, upset by what had happened to him. "Can I help clean you up?"

"That I could use."

She washed the cuts and bruises on his face with warm, soapy water and then helped him into a hot tub. He winced from pain when the hot water stung his wounds. As she scrubbed and washed his cuts with alcohol, he bit down hard on his lip. Afterward, she draped around him a thin cotton robe the hotel provided.

From her purse she pulled a flask with cognac and handed it to him. David took a long gulp, then raised the flask to her. "You saved my life tonight. I won't forget that."

His gratitude was so genuine that it lit up her face with pride. "Well, having worked out that great deal for you in Washington, I didn't want all my hard work to be for nothing. Now, tell me what happened after we separated."

He described the rest of the night for her, including his discussion with Victor. When he was finished, he said, "I'm convinced that snake, Victor, didn't send the two Iranians to kill me, but I sure as hell want to find out who did. Got any ideas?"

"I have a friend in the French secret police, somebody who worked with us back in '56. He's close to retirement, but he still has warm feelings toward Israel from those days. I'm meeting with him tomorrow to enlist his help with Daphna. I'll ask him to find out if there's any more information on the ID of the men who attacked you. That could give us a start."

"Use any sources you can. If we don't find and stop the bastards, they'll try again."

"I'll do that." She looked worried. "In the meantime, why don't you get some sleep? I'll stand guard."

He pointed at the canister on the bed. "With your trusty can of pepper spray?"

* * *

Daphna watched the first rays of sunlight slip through the narrow gap between the heavy gray curtains. It was morning already, and she hadn't slept a minute. She had spent the night tossing and turning in her bed. All night long she had relived in her mind, over and over, her last mission in the Israeli Air Force. She cursed at herself. She would need all of her wits if she was going to pull off the planned escape that she had developed in her mind yesterday.

In theory, it should be easy. On each of the last three mornings, exactly at nine o'clock, an Aerospatiale Alouette III helicopter had landed on a small concrete pad just beyond the swimming pool. That was when Daphna swam laps, making sure to keep up her strength.

When she swam, only a single armed guard watched her, and most of the time he looked bored and stared off into space. The helicopter had one pilot, and he left the chopper alone when he disappeared into the house with supplies.

All she had to do was suddenly leap out of the pool, overpower the guard and get to the chopper. She should easily be able to fly it over the walls of the château, to the nearest large town, before the kidnappers got her.

That was the way it went in theory. It was a good plan. It had a strong chance of succeeding because she had been such a good prisoner, acting frightened and intimidated, that the level of surveillance had dropped. They weren't expecting her to try to escape. She would have a strong element of surprise.

But her plan had one more major problem—besides all of the obvious ones. She wasn't certain that she'd be able to force herself into that helicopter and actually put her hands on the controls. Until last night, she had buried the tragedy of her last mission so deeply in her subconscious that she never spoke of it and never even thought about it.

It had been a rainy, foggy morning in mid-January. All night long terrorists from southern Lebanon had been firing rockets at an Israeli town on the border. Most of the residents had spent the night in bomb shelters, and that's where they were in the morning, repeatedly calling Jerusalem and demanding that the government stop the attack. In view of the weather, putting Israeli jets in the air wasn't an option. So the air force commander decided to use four Boeing Apache helicopters equipped with hellfire laser-guided missiles, which were stationed at a nearby base, to conduct a surgical strike against the terrorists' position. Each had a crew of two, and Daphna was the pilot of one of those Apaches. In front of her sat Yuri, her copilot/gunner.

The four choppers were still in Israeli airspace, flying north, when the terrorists suddenly let loose with a barrage of rockets. One of them struck the front of Daphna's helicopter, and Yuri was wounded by flying shrapnel. A second struck the rear, knocking off the tail rotor. The chopper veered sharply out of control, spinning wildly. Desperately, Daphna tried to call the base on her radio, but all she could get was static. She was on her own.

The only chance she had was a guided crash landing. Below, she spotted a cluster of fruit trees on an Israeli kibbutz, and she decided that was the best she was going to do. She tried to stay calm, not panicking as she struggled to get control of the chopper. Meanwhile, anguished cries of pain came from Yuri. She could see the blood flowing down the side of his head.

"Hold on," she called out through clenched teeth. "We're going down."

The trees softened their landing, as Daphna hoped, and the Apache had a unique fire-control system that prevented it from exploding. But on impact Daphna struck her head hard on a side panel and lost consciousness.

She came to hours later. She was in a hospital. She'd suffered a concussion, a broken collarbone, a broken arm and three broken ribs. Yuri wasn't so lucky. Her commanding officer told her that Yuri had died from wounds incurred in the air. Daphna didn't believe him, though. She was sure that he had died in the crash. That she had killed him. The three other choppers had returned safely to base after knocking out the terrorist position. The guilt she felt was horrible.

Despite psychiatric counseling, Daphna refused to get into a helicopter ever again. She was so traumatized that she refused to discuss the incident with anyone, not even with her mother. Her broken bones healed, and she served out the rest of her military duty in a desk job processing paperwork for air force purchases. She vowed that she would never go up in a helicopter again—a vow that she had never even contemplated breaking until now.

She put on the one-piece black bathing suit Mary had provided, her palms wet with perspiration, her knees knocking and her teeth chattering, despite the warmth of a beautiful fall day in Provence. As she walked downstairs toward the pool, she told herself, Just get to the chopper first. Don't think about flying it.

When she approached the pool, the helicopter pad was empty. But it was still early. Based on the schedule of the last few days, it shouldn't be here for another ten or fifteen minutes.

As she swam, she saw Yuri's face, the blood flowing down it, in her mind. I'm never going to be able to do it, a part of her said. Another voice responded, Don't be a fool. It's your only chance for escape.

Each time she turned at one end of the pool, she glanced up to survey the scene. The guard was playing a small hand-held video game. Overpowering him shouldn't be a problem. Yet the chopper still hadn't come. It was late.

When she was too exhausted to swim any longer and the helicopter hadn't come, she pulled her weary body from the pool.

Then she heard Mary telling the guard that once the prisoner went back into the house, he was to drive into Grasse for supplies.

"But where's the helicopter?" he said. "It's good weather, no?"

"I got a call. They need it for something more important. They're not going to use it to bring us supplies for a few days."

Listening in, Daphna didn't know whether she felt sorry or relieved.

* * *

"Nice suit," Colette Martique said to David when the armed guard deposited him in her office late the next morning. "I believe that blue pinstripe is becoming on you."

"I can't tell you how happy that makes me feel."

He looked at her and smiled. Victor must have told her something about what happened, because she didn't comment on the bruises and scratches on his face.

"Just trying to help the local economy," he added.

She was astounded that he could jest after what had happened. "Well, Paris is after all the fashion capital of the world."

"Don't let a Milanese hear you say that."

It was time to get down to business, she decided. "Another long day today?"

"Probably."

At the moment the wooden guillotine on her desk caught his eye again. It was a beautiful reproduction, about six inches high. It even had a metal blade in the raised position.

He walked over to her desk and studied it carefully. "What a great model," he said. "Where did you get it?"

She grew flustered. "It's nothing, really. Just a child's playtoy."

He touched his finger against the blade. It was sharp. "Pretty rough toy for a child. How long have you had it?"

"I said it's nothing," she replied sharply. "Now, I think you should get to work."

An hour later, she took him to lunch, the same as yesterday.

Afterward, back in his office, he took a pad of paper from his briefcase and drew a rough map of the Ras Tannarah oil fields along the Persian Gulf. With his eyes focused on the computer screen, he marked the approximate locations at which explosions would occur in the oil fields if the system was activated from the royal palace. Then he began marking a series of X's to represent major oil installations and O's to represent key Saudi military defensive positions. Suddenly, he became aware of the scent of cigar smoke in the doorway behind him. He bolted upright and wheeled around in his chair.

It was Madame Blanc, watching him carefully. She was puffing on a Cohiba.

"I hope I didn't disturb you," she said. "But I like to pop in unannounced on all my employees from time to time. I find that it keeps everyone on their toes."

This woman has got to be hated by everyone in this building, he thought. "I'm sure they love it."

"Victor told me what happened to you last night. You want one of the medical people here to take a look at you?"

"It's nothing. It looks worse than it is."

"I'd be happy to give you a bodyguard when you're in Paris."

"I'll be okay. Don't worry about it."

She flicked cigar ash into the wastebasket in his office. "I've got a significant investment in you. I have to worry."

"And here I thought you just liked me."

She smiled. "At least you haven't lost your sense of humor."

"That'll never happen. But I would like to know who sent those two Iranians to kill me."

She scowled. "I'm working on it, but so far no luck."

"I figure you have a leak somewhere in your organization."

"That thought has occurred to me as well, and it doesn't make me happy." She paused to puff on her cigar. "You want to tell me what you're doing now?"

He explained to her about the system of explosions and also what each of the X's and O's represented.

"This map of yours," she said, pointing at the paper on the desk, "is so crude. Aren't you going to need something more specific?"

Well, isn't that nice, he thought. I put the bait out there, and she snapped it up. "You bet, but I'll need detailed maps to do that. They'll be in the next shipment I'll need from Saudi Arabia."

She looked concerned. "It's already September 16. There's not much time."

"Don't worry. I'll do what it takes to meet your deadline. Victor will have my wish list tomorrow."

She seemed satisfied. "I hate to admit this," she said, "but if you weren't involved, I'd have nothing at all after the coup if the Saudi king gave the order to blow up those oil fields."

He gave her a knowing smile. "Unfortunately, that's true."

She puffed deeply on her cigar and blew the smoke over his head. "If Victor gives you a problem tomorrow about the new materials you want, ask to see me. We'll work it out."

"I appreciate that."

She turned around and left the office with a cloud of smoke trailing behind her.

For several minutes David sat staring at his rough map, wondering, What the hell am I doing? Am I helping her succeed? Have I in fact become a part of this conspiracy?

It's not that simple, he told himself. If the coup takes place, I can't let the Saudi king blow up those oil fields under any circumstances. To destroy that much precious fossil fuel and to do that much environmental damage would be criminal under any circumstances.

Satisfied that what he was doing could be morally justified, he returned to his crude map. He worked on into the afternoon, making progress, but biding his time until Colette left, which occurred at six o'clock. Again, he waited a full thirty minutes before trying to enter the Task Force computer system. Then he punched in his new guess at a password—"guillotine"—and held his breath.

Presto, it worked. He was in the system.

Nervously, he glanced over his shoulder, half-expecting Madame Blanc to make another surprise visit, but no one was there. He began with the concept the Company had pounded into his head in his initial training sessions. "Follow the money."

He pulled up the financials for Operation Guillotine.

Madame Blanc's accounts were professional and precise. Expenditures were arranged in a long column. There were payments for weapons, to Granita Munitions, a French company, with each purchase separately listed with date and amount. There were payments for air transport for the weapons; payments for shipping permits and related expenditures, which he assumed meant bribes to French officials; payments for communication systems; payments for PDF overhead attributed to the project; payments for investigators' expenses. He kept looking for a payment to a Saudi officer or officers, but there wasn't a single Saudi name on the payment list. All the payees seemed to be French.

Then his eyes focused on the payment to him last week of $2 million deposited into the Union Bank of Switzerland. It even showed the number of his Swiss bank account. The payee was identified as Greg Nielsen/David Ben Aaron. She didn't use his code name of Outlaw. With this computer record, how could he ever persuade someone that he wasn't a coconspirator? No doubt, that's what she intended. He decided to scan back over the names of the French payees. Suddenly a name popped out at him. Two payments of $15 million each had been made to a Henri Napoleon. The amounts had been deposited into a Credit Swiss account on the Bahnhoffstrasse in Zurich. The account number was 55XQ3. David committed the entries to memory.

Then it all fell into place for him. Henri Napoleon must be the code name for the Saudi military officer who would be leading the coup. These deposits were Madame Blanc's payoff to him.

All of that was fine, but it still left him with the question: who was the Saudi represented by the code name Henri Napoleon?

He looked at the calendar on his wristwatch. October 6 was less than three weeks away. Having the name Henri Napoleon didn't tell him a damn thing about the Saudi heading up the coup.

He heard the sound of approaching footsteps in the corridor. David quickly turned off the computer and tensed, pretending to be studying the map he had made this afternoon.

It was one of the security guards. Gripping his gun, the guard paused in the doorway and eyed David suspiciously.

"I'm authorized by Madame Blanc to be working here this evening," David said.

The guard grunted and moved on.

David waited five minutes before he started up the computer again. Working as swiftly as possible, but pausing frequently to glance over his shoulder, he searched through the rest of the files of Operation Guillotine. They laid out in detail the developing and marketing program that PDF had for Saudi oil following the coup. They projected price increases and PDF profits, by reducing output. Madame Blanc had a carefully developed plan to reassemble the oil cartel of the seventies and to drive up the market price of crude, thereby maximizing PDF's profits. If she managed to pull it off, the U.S. economy would be hurt the most, because America had never done anything other than talk about energy conservation.

David continued searching the file. There was nothing about the Saudi ringleader.

Satisfied that he had gotten everything he could from the file, he turned off the computer. Then he closed his eyes, put his weary head in his hands, and rested it on the desk, thinking. There had to be a way to get at Henri Napoleon.

On the way back to the hotel, an idea began taking shape in his mind. At first it was fuzzy, but by the time the taxi dropped him at the Metro so he could take his two subway rides back to the Hotel Gironde, the idea was becoming a plan. It was raining again tonight, not hard, just a light drizzle. David was impervious to it. From the Metro exit he walked to a small brasserie a few blocks from the hotel. He ordered steak et frites and a bottle of Côtes-du-Rhône. As he ate and sipped the wine, he fleshed out the idea with more and more details. It was coming alive. It might even work.

He spotted a pay phone near the lavatory in the back of the brasserie. When he finished eating, he called Victor at home. "I'm not in trouble tonight," he said.

Recalling how David had wrecked his plans last evening,

Victor sounded derisive when he replied, "Glad to hear that."

"I want to meet you tomorrow morning at eight to give you a status report."

"My office."

David had expected Victor to suggest that location. He was ready with his response. "No, I'm still worried about another attack by the Iranians. They may have a stakeout there. Let's use the same brasserie we did today, at the end of avenue George V. I'll get a table in the back. We'll have coffee together, then walk along the river and talk. No risk of being overheard."

Victor groaned. He had an early meeting with another client. He'd have to reschedule that. "I'll be there," the lawyer said reluctantly.

Next, David called Sagit on her cell phone.

"Can you meet me at the Louvre, near the I. M. Pei entrance?"

"I'll be there in twenty minutes."

Sagit was glad he had picked the meeting place in front of the Louvre. The grassy area was deserted. The rain had stopped. She could easily spot him there, standing alone. She didn't see anyone else.

They fell in stride together, like a couple out for an evening stroll, heading toward the Tuileries.

He told her what he had in mind. Then he said, "I think we should fly from here to London."

"It's too risky," she replied. "They may be watching you leave the country."

"Good point."

"Let's go back to Israel first. It'll take a little longer, but we should still make it in time. Besides, I'll need to get authorization and make arrangements. It's easier for me to do all of that in Israel."

"You'll need a picture of Victor. The others won't know what he looks like. Maybe the French Lawyers Association has pictures of its members."

"I've got a better idea. Where are you meeting him in the morning?"

"At the brasserie where avenue George V meets the river, at eight o'clock."

"Make sure you come out of the brasserie with him, and stop to tie your shoe for a second. When he stops, I'll take some pictures."

He looked alarmed. "Won't he see you?"

"Telephoto lens. Don't worry, I'll set up somewhere he won't see me. Taking his picture is easy." Their eyes met. "What's worrying me is whether this great idea of yours will work."

"I admit it's a bit of a long shot." He looked ambivalent about it himself.

"I can't think of anything better right now."

"What about Daphna? Will your friend from the French secret police do anything for us?"

"He's willing to help. I asked him to get me a printout from the phone company of all of the phone calls made in and out of Victor Foch's office in the last month and the addresses of the parties to those calls."

"You figure that Victor was in touch with the place where they're holding Daphna?"

"That's what I'm hoping."

On the rue de Rivoli, adjoining the park, two police cars were approaching with their sirens blaring. David paused for a minute preparing to cut and run if they were coming after him, but they sped by without stopping.

"What did your friend tell you about the men who tried to kill me last night?"

They were passing under a light, and he saw her grimace. "First of all, Victor lied to you. You only killed the one you shot. The other one was alive when he was taken to jail. When Victor came down to the jail, he was in a rage. He wanted to know who sent these people. He told the police to use every means at their disposal to find out."

"Which is consistent with what he said. I mean, with the idea he didn't send them."

"Well that's one possibility. But, anyhow, they tried to beat the information out of the one you had been pounding in the courtyard across from the Bristol. They weren't as gentle with him as you were. Eventually, he died. Score another one for the French police."

"Are you certain of this?"

"The time of death was originally recorded as six-thirty A.M. It was later changed to nine-thirty P.M., before the suspect got to the jail."

He wasn't surprised by what the police had done. Only that it had been done so crudely. Obviously, they didn't think anyone would check the records. "What did the police learn from this gentle interrogation?"

"All they could find out was that the two men were in fact Iranians, and the order came from Tehran to kill you. Despite Victor's insistence, the prisoner either didn't know or wouldn't say who sent him."

The next morning, in the brasserie, as David and Victor sipped coffee, they discussed opera. The two men shared a love for Giuseppe Verdi, the musical genius born in a small farming village, who had little formal training as a young man and was then rejected by the Milan Conservatory as being too old when he applied. David's favorite opera was the refined *La Traviata,* while Victor preferred the brutality of *Rigoletto*. Anyone who overheard their conversation would have thought they were two friends who met for a few minutes before work.

It was a bright sunny morning, and as they left the brasserie, David stopped, bent down and tied his shoelace. He never looked up. He assumed that Sagit was in place, that she was focused on Victor and snapping away. They walked at a leisurely pace along the river. On the other side, the Eiffel Tower cast an imposing shadow over them.

"What have you accomplished in the last two days?" Victor demanded. "Madame Blanc is anxious to know."

"I figured as much. The answer is that I've done everything I can with the information I have."

Victor shot David a skeptical glance. "Meaning what?"

"I'm about three-fourths of the way finished."

"What do to you mean by finished?"

Looking Victor squarely in the eye, David answered without a trace of hesitation. "I mean, having a plan to neutralize both systems—the palace defenses and the oil field explosions."

"So how do you finish the job?"

"I need some additional information and materials."

The Frenchman was suspicious. "Like what?"

He gave Victor a handwritten piece of paper. "It's all there. It includes detailed maps of the oil fields. Approximate numbers and types of Saudi military personnel that will be available for the attackers. Precisely what equipment they'll have as well. Not names of individuals, because I know that's sensitive, but numbers and types." David paused and waited until Victor looked up from the paper before continuing. "Don't use fax or telephone lines to get the information. That's too dangerous. I want you to have documents with the information brought to me from Saudi Arabia to Paris—just as you brought the computer discs."

The lawyer was still convinced that David had some other agenda. They walked in silence for several minutes while Victor thought about David's request.

"You're asking for quite a bit."

David shrugged his shoulders. He already knew how Madame Blanc would respond. He didn't have to appear anxious. He was in the driver's seat. "If you're afraid the messenger will be shot, then I'll ask Madame Blanc myself. But she said you were to be the intermediary."

Victor gloated, believing that David had overplayed his hand. "The point is that Madame Blanc won't like this new development. She expected you to be done by now."

"Look, what I'm asking is fairly simple and straightforward," David said. "Talk to her. I'll stick around Paris until I get an answer. In case she wants to talk to me."

"And after that?"

"I'm going back to Israel until the new stuff comes from Saudi Arabia. I don't want to raise any suspicions by being gone too long. When you have what I need, you fax me in

Israel, the way you did the last time, and I'll be back in
Paris the next day."

Victor stared into the muddy Seine, weighing David's words.

"Be back in two hours at that brasserie at the intersection of George V," the lawyer finally said, "where we met
this morning. I'll get a message to you."

"I don't like it at all," Victor said to Madame Blanc after
reporting on his conversation with David.

They were seated in her vast corner office at the PDF
headquarters. Outside, the sun was struggling to shine between heavy clouds.

She was wearing a burgundy Valentino wool pantsuit. As
she took off the jacket that covered a cream-colored silk
blouse and hung it over the back of her desk chair, she
said, "What don't you like about it?"

"I don't trust him."

"You never have."

"Don't you understand my concern? Why does he need
so much additional information? Why won't he stay in Paris
until it arrives?" He looked sharply at her. "He's got his
own agenda, and it worries me."

She paused to puff on her cigar. "Look, if it weren't for
Greg Nielsen, we would never have known about the system to blow up the oil fields, and we'd have ended up
with nothing."

"Our Saudi friends should have known about it."

She was getting irritated with him. "They should have,
but they didn't. That's precisely my point."

"So he gave us something useful to gain our confidence.
And, by the way, he was paid a lot of money for that. I
still think . . ."

She laughed. "You know what I think?"

He waited, not wanting to hear the answer.

"It's the green-eyed monster raising its ugly head. I think
you're jealous of his relationship with me."

The truth stung, but he denied it, "Nothing could be
further from the truth."

"Don't give it another thought." She pointed her forefinger at him. "Be patient, Victor. I'll get what I need from him, and then I'll dispose of him." She squashed out her cigar in an ashtray and tossed the butt in the wastebasket. "About like that."

Victor wasn't content to be patient. Knowing that Madame Blanc would be furious if she ever found out, he arranged to have two private detectives follow David once he left the brasserie. They were both in place before Victor's driver parked a block away and delivered the envelope with the simple message inside: "We accept your proposal. Have a nice trip home."

Then Victor waited by the phone. Airport, my ass, he thought. He's not flying home. He's meeting somebody in Paris, from the Mossad or the CIA, to brief them.

David waited to open the envelope and read the message until the driver left. He smiled softly, thinking that Madame Blanc must have taken his side in an argument with Victor. He took his time finishing his espresso.

No sense rushing, he thought. He guessed that Victor had arranged a tail. He wanted to make certain Victor's people actually saw him board the El Al plane at Charles De Gaulle. So they could let Victor know, and he could grind his teeth. The thought made David smile. He enjoyed staying one step ahead of the French lawyer.

David boarded the plane early. He took his aisle seat in the second row of first class, and accepted a copy of *Ha'aretz* from the flight attendant. He pretended to be reading, but in fact he was studying every passenger who boarded the plane, trying to see if the men following him in Paris had boarded the plane.

They were about to close the door, he noticed. Nothing at all had looked suspicious. He breathed a sigh of relief.

Then he saw her come through the door. It was Sagit, wearing a large black hat. She passed without acknowledging him, and then she sat down five rows back—in the last row of first class.

An hour into the flight, she went to the lavatory in front of the plane. He followed her and was standing in front of the door when she opened it from the inside.

He whispered, "How did you know what plane I was on?"

"We tapped into El Al's computer. We can get access to all the carriers' passenger lists that way."

"And you boarded the plane to make sure I went directly home?"

She glared at him. "You have been known to disappear. Look for me in the baggage claim area at Ben Gurion and follow me out of the terminal."

She led him to a small cubicle that had been constructed underground at one end of the terminal building. The walls were a faded gray and appeared to be soundproof. Inside was a simple wooden table and two chairs. He guessed that security agents used the room for interrogating suspicious individuals who flew into Israel.

Having spent so much time in rooms like this interrogating suspects himself, he felt a little uncomfortable at first. Quickly, he shrugged it off.

"How are the pictures?" he asked.

She reached into her bag and produced half a dozen black-and-white five-by-sevens of Victor Foch.

He studied them. The clarity reminded him of her other pictures, the ones he'd had developed in Paris. "You do good work," he said.

"Thanks," she said enthusiastically. "It's more than a hobby. It's a passion with me."

"And you are a passionate woman. I know that."

"Look, wiseguy . . ."

"No, really, they're quite good. I mean it." He met her eyes. "You could always quit the Mossad and become a professional photographer."

"Sorry. I want more from life than doing weddings and bar mitzvahs." As far as she was concerned, the personal talk was over. It was time to deal with Moshe.

CHAPTER 13

They made the last plane that night from Tel Aviv to London. Actually, the plane left an hour late as a result of Moshe's phone call to the president of El Al. When the airline executive initially refused to accede to his request, Moshe cajoled, shouted, cursed and ultimately threatened to call the prime minister before the executive gave in. The other passengers grumbled and chafed at the unexplained delay, despite the complimentary drinks being served, while a courier rushed a phony Israeli passport to the airport for David, and a digital cell phone that he could use for secure direct communications with Sagit's phone.

At Heathrow, they ignored each other and took their own cabs to the west end of London. Sagit checked into the Hyde Park Hotel, still using her Gina Martin passport, while David's cab dropped him a short distance away at the Four Seasons. As he checked in, using the phony name on the Israeli passport, he kept glancing over his shoulder, across the lobby, expecting another Iranian or one of Madame Blanc's West African guards to burst through the front entrance.

In the elevator, a different thought took hold. He was playing a powerful hunch in coming to London with Sagit. What if he proved to be wrong? What if they didn't use Victor or London this time? He grew worried thinking about it.

A long, hot shower relaxed him. He picked up the phone and called Sagit's cell phone. "Listen, Gina Martin," he said when she answered. "We haven't seen each other since Paris, and I heard you were in London. I was wondering if you might like to drop by the Four Seasons for a nightcap?"

"Did something happen?" she asked nervously.

"No," he said playfully. "I just can't stand working so closely with you, and not being with you at night. It's killing me."

She hit the off button on her phone.

Well, no harm in trying, he thought. He climbed into bed naked, thinking about her. The cool sheets felt good against his weary body, but he still couldn't sleep.

Half an hour later, his cell phone rang. It was Sagit. "Your theory was right," she said, a little breathless. "I just got a call from a friend back home."

"You want to come over and tell me about it in person?"

"I don't know," she said hesitantly.

"I mean just to talk business."

She was still reluctant. Where would it lead with him this time? "Only for a few minutes."

"That's all. I promise."

He put on a heavy terry-cloth bath robe and waited for her.

Her face was aglow with excitement when she arrived. "My friend at El Al just called. They tapped into the computers of all the carriers with Paris-to-London service."

"And?"

"Victor Foch is on a four P.M. Air France flight tomorrow into Heathrow."

"Home run," he said. She looked at him puzzled. "It's an American expression. Baseball. It means we scored big."

"It also means that we have a lot to do to get ready for his arrival."

"And a whole day to do it," he said mischievously. He walked over and kissed her softly on the lips.

She pulled away from him and backed up to the wall. "C'mon, David, this is really crazy."

He moved toward her, letting his robe open in the front. He kissed her again, while unbuttoning her beige silk blouse.

She could feel his penis, already erect, pressing against

her cotton skirt. "We should wait," she protested weakly, "until this is all over."

He unzipped her skirt in the back, pushed it down to the floor and slipped his right hand into her already wet panties. "I've learned that in this life you can never afford to put off wonderful things. Who knows about tomorrow."

With his left hand, he unsnapped her bra, and then began to stroke her breasts gently while kissing her. All of her better judgment melted way. She surrendered herself entirely to him.

After making love, they fell asleep in each other's arms. A couple of hours later, she awoke. Quietly, she dressed and slipped out of the room.

On the bureau she left him a note that read: "At eleven o'clock, be at the northwest corner of St. James Park."

By the time Victor's plane lifted off at Orley Airport, Sagit and David had everything in place in London. Mindful of the slip-up in Daphna's escape from the bakery in Paris, Sagit had three teams of agents armed with sophisticated telecommunications equipment to follow Victor's cab. They each had a copy of one of Sagit's photographs of Victor, who had been code-named Vicky.

Meantime, David paced anxiously in his room at the Four Seasons, eyeing the cell phone on the desk.

When it rang, he got it on the first ring.

"Vicky just walked into the Dorchester," Sagit said.

Her voice was all business. He had a fleeting thought about last night. Then he answered her in kind. "It figures. That's the Saudis' club in London. I'm on my way."

"Don't forget to hook up the two-way radio I gave you."

He touched the center of his white shirt, behind the tie, and felt the wireless microphone that was taped to his chest. Inside his right ear he had a small hearing device that resembled a tiny white button. Attached to his belt was what looked like an ordinary pager. The entire system was wireless—and connected with an identical one Sagit and the other members of her team were wearing.

"It's already in place."

"Just don't get too close until I tell you Vicky's gone."

"I'm not an idiot, and I'm not that rusty."

Waiting in a car parked on Curzon Street, a block from the Dorchester, Sagit tapped her foot nervously against the rubber floor mat in the front passenger seat. She was wearing a beige fur coat over a black velvet miniskirt and a snug white cashmere sweater. Heavy makeup was caked on her face. On her head, she had a blond wig. Outside, the night air was clear and chilly. Rain and fog were expected to move in later.

"What's going on in there?" she asked impatiently.

"It's only been three minutes and twenty seconds since Vicky went inside," Gadi, the driver, answered her in Hebrew.

"It seems like an hour."

"Nothing's happened yet. Ariel will let you know. He's . . ."

Suddenly, she heard Ariel's voice in her earphone.

"Vicky's in the bar off the lobby on the right. He sat down at a table with an Arab."

"Civilian or military?"

"Saudi Air Force uniform. A captain, I think. No name plate on his uniform."

"What are they doing?"

"They ordered drinks. They're talking."

"What about?"

"Give me a break, Sagit. I'm at the newsstand across the lobby."

Gadi didn't want to run the heater in the car while they were parked. Her fingers were numb from the cold. She rubbed them togther and said, "what's happening now?" There was a long pause. "Well, Ariel? Tonight?"

"Drinks came. Champagne for Vicky. Whoops, there it goes."

She was alarmed. "There goes what?"

"The Saudi had a brown folder on the floor at his feet. He just kicked it under the table. It's now resting at Vicky's feet."

"Home run," she said.

"What's that mean?"

"Forget it. What are they doing?"

"Talking."

There were several minutes of silence. Then Ariel said, "Vicky's getting up and leaving the table. He's heading toward the front door of the hotel."

"And the Saudi captain?"

"Still sipping his drink."

"Good boy. It's show time."

She adjusted her blond wig reached for the car door and said to the driver, "How do I look, Gadi?"

"Like a London tart."

"An expensive one?"

"More than I can afford."

She threw him a kiss and opened the door.

"Be careful. Some of those guys play rough."

Gadi's comment made her smile. He was just a kid, twenty-one years old. She had been turning tricks before he was born—a fact she never let herself forget. It's good to remember whence you came, she thought. It helps you to evaluate where you are.

She turned the corner and sauntered along Park Lane toward the main entrance of the Dorchester. On the way she passed Victor, waiting for a cab. He looked her over, and she gave him a soft smile. For an instant she thought he might proposition her, but he remembered the folder in his hand, gripped it hard and climbed into a cab.

Inside the hotel, she strolled into the bar just off the lobby and sat down at a table about ten yards away from the Saudi. When she took off her coat, she watched him watch her as her short skirt rode halfway up on her thighs.

There were only a couple of other patrons in the bar. In one corner, two emaciated elderly men, their skin dotted with liver spots and each wearing the same school tie, sipped martinis and discussed life in India when it was still a British colony. In another corner a pianist, a middle-aged man from the West Indies, with sad, tired eyes, tapped out an old Frank Sinatra tune. She ordered a glass of white wine and waited for the captain to make his move.

It took him less than five minutes to cross over to her table. "Would you like some company?" he asked awkwardly.

"How could I turn down a good-looking army officer?" she replied, and pointed at the chair across from her.

"I'm an air force captain," he said in heavily accented English as he sat down. "My name is Naif."

"You mean, you fly those big jet airplanes?"

"The F-15 is the finest plane in the world," he said, gleaming with pride, "and I'm the best. Nobody can catch me when I open it up."

She gave him a thumbs-up sign. "I always wanted to ride in one of those babies, but it must be scary."

"I've got nerves of steel. Danger doesn't bother me," he boasted. "Maybe I'll take you for a ride some time."

"God, I'd love that."

When it comes to impressing women, she thought, men can be so stupid. Suddenly there was a commotion in the lobby. Two bellmen were wheeling a huge cart filled with packages from Chanel, Valentino, Tiffany, Escada, Gucci and other Bond Street shops. Behind the cart, a Saudi princess, her face unveiled, was barking at the bellmen to be careful because there were china and glass in some of those packages.

"A little shopping spree," Sagit said.

Her Saudi officer looked down at the table. The disgust was visible in his eyes, but he didn't say a word.

When the caravan had finally disappeared into the elevators, he looked down at Sagit and asked: "What do you do?"

She rolled her tongue over her lips. "Oh, a little of this and a little of that."

"Are you from London?"

"From Holland. I've only lived here two years."

He was watching her tongue and fantasizing. "I've never been to Holland. What's it like?"

"Looser than here. The British are an uptight bunch. At least on the surface. In private, some of them can be pretty wild. If you know what I mean."

He smiled. "Can I buy you another drink?"

"If you'd like to, but not here. This place is boring."

He was delighted that she wanted to go with him. If he played his cards right, she might end up in his bed tonight. "Where would you like to go?"

"There's a private gambling club not far from here. The White Elephant. We can have dinner, too. I'm starving."

"I'd like to do that."

She hugged herself. "It's chilly outside. You want to go up and get a coat?"

"Actually," he said, "I think I'll go up and change into civilian clothes, if you don't mind waiting."

"I've got nothing but time tonight, honey."

He glanced at the check resting on the table. Then he reached into his pocket and produced a hotel room key attached to a heavy brass ring on which the number 417 was carved in dark letters. With a flourish, he signed his name and room number on the check and stood up. "You won't run away while I'm gone, will you?"

"I'm just going to powder my nose in the ladies' room." She touched his cheek and let her hand linger there for an instant. "Promise to be here when you get back."

She watched him enter the elevator before she went into the ladies' room. When she was inside a toilet stall, she unbuttoned her blouse and whispered directly into the microphone taped between the two cups of her bra.

"David, how much of that did you hear?"

He was in a car outside of the hotel. "The whole thing," he replied dryly. "You played the part well. Very convincing."

His voice was so strained. Was he thinking about how she had seduced him in Paris, that first time? "Thanks."

"When he comes down, I'll be near the desk and spot his room number when he drops off the key."

"No need to do that. His room number is 417. I saw the key."

"Our plan was brilliant. That was easy."

"It was too easy," Sagit said ruefully.

"You're never happy. What's worrying you now?"

"We better be careful. Somebody could be setting us up."

"You worry too much."

"He practically handed me his room key. That smells bad. We could be in for a rough evening."

"Then make sure Ariel and Murray stick close to you."

"Why don't you take one of them for backup on the fourth floor?"

"Never used backup in my life. I'm too old to start now."

David entered the hotel and took a seat at the bar. He ordered a glass of tonic and waited patiently. Glancing over his shoulder, he saw the Saudi captain, now dressed in a business suit, and Sagit leave the hotel. That was his signal. Trying to appear nonchalant, he walked along the bank of elevators and slipped into an open door. Quickly, he pressed for the fourth floor and the elevator began to move.

Room 417 was in a corner at the far end of the hall. David trod softly down the plush royal blue carpet. If he was being set up, as Sagit had said, then what? Would Madame Blanc be sitting in the room waiting for him with a couple of her West African guards? Or would it be Victor with a couple of his goons? And what would David say? "Gee, sorry, I must have the wrong room." Or, "Just checking the minibar."

To make matters worse, he realized that he wasn't armed—not even a simple pocket knife. His plan had been brilliant, all right, a brilliant way to put himself in a noose.

In the old days he would never have been in a situation like this. I'm just too old for this business, he thought sadly. It's a young man's game.

Walking softly, he managed to shrug off those thoughts. The risks tonight were worth taking, he told himself. Inside the room, the Saudi captain might have left behind papers that would provide David with a lead as to who was heading up the coup in his country. At the very least, he would learn the captain's name, and most likely his air force unit. That would be a powerful lead.

The corridor was deathly still as he stopped in front of

the door to 417 and listened carefully. Not a sound came from the other side of the dark wooden door.

With moist hands he reached into his jacket pocket and pulled out a set of the narrow pieces of metal, joined to a ring, the standard burglar's tool that he had been taught by the Company to use in picking locks. While his fingers worked slowly and methodically, his ears were listening for any sound. In less than a minute, he felt the lock roll over. He put the metal ring back in his pocket and slowly opened the door a crack. The room was pitch dark. Cautiously, he opened the door all the way and stepped inside.

Suddenly, the lights went on. Startled, David looked up. A man dressed in a Saudi Air Force uniform was sitting in a high-backed chair directly across what was the living room of a suite, and watching David's every movement.

"My God, Khalid, it's you!" David blurted out. "I should have guessed."

Four powerful hands grabbed David. Khalid's two bodyguards had been waiting in ambush on either side of the door. Like bookends, they collapsed on David.

Roughly, they searched him. The burglar's tools and the pagerlike device on his waist were tossed onto a nearby table. As one of the guards frisked David, he felt the small microphone beneath David's shirt. He pulled up the shirt and ripped the microphone from David's chest. That, too, went onto the table.

"That's enough," Khalid said in Arabic. The guards moved away.

"Whom are you working for?" Khalid demanded to know.

David could tell from his uniform that Khalid was now a full colonel. Except for a thin mustache that had been added, Khalid looked the same as he had five years ago.

"I could say no one."

"But I wouldn't believe that, and my men here would be effective at obtaining the real answer."

"I'm afraid it's too late for that, Khalid. I shouted out your name before they took away my microphone. That's all we wanted to know. Who was behind the coup. My colleagues will come for me now."

"Tell them you're okay. Tell them to go away."

David picked up the microphone and in Hebrew said, "It's all right. Don't worry about me anymore tonight. I'm with an old friend. Keep your captain for an hour, ditch him and meet me back at your hotel."

Annoyed, Khalid said, "Repeat it in Arabic and then English."

David complied with the order, which satisfied Khalid, who directed one of his men to stand in the corridor outside the room. Then he placed the microphone on the floor at his feet, stood up and crushed it into a useless pulpy mess.

"Now tell me who you're working for, or we'll force the answer out of you." The colonel's eyes were cold and menacing.

"But I thought we were good friends, Khalid."

"Once we were, but that was a long time ago. Things are different now."

"What happened to the old Chinese proverb that if you save someone's life you're responsible for him forever?"

"And I saved your life by flying you out of Saudi Arabia after the Dhahran bombing five years ago?"

"Precisely."

"We're not in China, Greg. Now tell me whom you're working for."

"The Mossad, of course. They recruited me right after I came to Israel five years ago."

"What about the CIA? How do I know you're not working for them?"

"You heard me talking into the microphone. The language I picked was Hebrew. Have you ever heard a CIA agent speaking Hebrew?"

Khalid's cold, hostile look softened. "I guess not."

The momentum was shifting, David thought. "Now I want to ask you something. What are you doing here?"

"You forget, Greg, I'm no fool. Your second request for information raised alarms in my mind. You wanted too much information. Asking for troop strength and so forth. It just didn't seem right given your limited role for Madame Blanc. I figured that you have your own game going on behind Madame Blanc's back. And I have to know what it is," Khalid said, smiling slyly. "So I decided to set a little trap for you tonight, even having the captain flash the room number on the key to your colleague to make it easier. You took the bait."

David was impressed. Khalid had outfoxed him. "And here I thought I was so clever in trying to find out who was behind the coup."

"Remember, you taught me a lot about intelligence work that last year you were in my country."

"I hope you didn't share your suspicions about me with Madame Blanc."

Khalid smiled and rubbed his hand over his mustache. "If I had, you'd probably be at the bottom of the Thames right now."

"Yeah, that's about what she'd do."

The colonel was staring hard at David, trying to decide what his next move should be.

Watching and waiting, David felt as if he were in a chess game with Khalid. Behind that smile and genial manner, he knew the man could be as tough and cruel as the circumstances warranted. Now with his own life, those of his wife and children, and scores of other officers, at stake, he would kill David—old friend or not—in an instant if he thought it was necessary.

David decided to take the offensive. "Killing me won't help you, Khalid. As of a few minutes ago, the Mossad knows you're behind the coup. Telling Madame Blanc about me won't do you any good either, because she'll be furious that you came to London tonight on your own. She might even decide to call off her participation, and you certainly don't want that, this late in the game."

"What are you getting at?" the colonel asked suspiciously.

"I've got a proposition for you to save your coup. I may even be able to get you Israeli and American support."

"I'm listening."

"Not tonight. Not here," David said. He didn't like playing his cards while Sagit was still with the Saudi captain. From what had just happened, Khalid couldn't be underestimated. He might have a plan to hold her hostage. David also didn't want to run the risk of their conversation being taped.

"When?"

"Tomorrow morning at nine o'clock. The Four Seasons Hotel has a steam room in the health club on the lower level. That way neither of us will have to worry about the other one wearing a wire. I'll make sure they let you in, and no one else will be there."

Khalid was mulling over David's offer.

"You've got no choice," David said, revving up the pressure. "Unless I turn off the Mossad tonight, their agents here will file a report with Jerusalem that will be sent immediately to Washington. You'll be arrested as soon as you land back in your country. As to what happens after that," David shrugged, "I'll leave that to your imagination."

Khalid hesitated, looking very unhappy. David had managed to turn the tables on him. "And if I agree to meet with you tomorrow morning, you'll stop the Mossad people from reporting to Washington at least until after our meeting?"

"I'll do that, Khalid. I promise. Well, what'll it be?"

The Saudi looked unhappy. "As you just said, what choice do I have?"

It was close to midnight when David and Sagit met back at the Hyde Park Hotel.

"Let's walk in the park," he said. "I'll tell you what happened tonight."

It was raining lightly and dense fog covered the city. David grabbed one of the large hotel umbrellas, and they crossed the road to Hyde Park.

Huddled under a single umbrella, it was easy to talk. David kept looking around, but no one was on foot nearby.

It was too damp and miserable for the tourists who normally wandered through the park at night.

Without interrupting, she listened to his recounting of the evening. When he finished, she said, "You like this Colonel Khalid, don't you?"

"We were friends when I was in Saudi Arabia. As close as we could be under the circumstances. He invited me to his home for wonderful dinners with his wife, Nura, a lovely woman, and their four children. A boy and three girls." David paused, remembering those evenings. "And he saved my life at great risk to himself. But it's more than that."

"What do you mean?"

"I respect him. He's a decent man. With integrity. Somebody who's not in it just for the power, but genuinely wants to help his country. Now, what about you? What did you do tonight?"

She gave him a devilish glance. "I won twenty pounds at roulette, and I had a good dinner."

"And the captain?"

"You don't have to worry. He was a perfect gentleman, even though he lost about ten thousand pounds." She turned around and beagn walking swiftly back to the hotel. "We better get back. I have to get a cab to our embassy."

"Now? This late? What for?"

"I want to use the secure embassy phone line to call Moshe. Then I want to call Margaret Joyner in Washington. We have to report to her."

"Report on what?"

"Everything that happened tonight."

Alarmed, he said, "You can't do that, Sagit."

"Why not?"

"You weren't listening. I promised Khalid we wouldn't do that."

She was furious. "You weren't authorized to promise that."

"I did what I had to do. I gave Khalid my word. You've got to honor it."

"I don't see why."

He kicked the muddy ground in frustration. He couldn't

believe she was taking such a ridiculous position. "Besides, spilling your guts about what we have so far is stupid."

She bristled. "You have such a nice way of expressing yourself. Tell me why what I want to do is stupid."

From the sound of her voice, David knew he had gone too far. He softened his tone. "Because I'm not finished with Khalid yet. You've got to let me talk to him tomorrow. Then we'll decide what to do."

"What are you so worried about?"

"People in Washington often act impulsively. Suppose the President picks up the phone and calls the Saudi king. Khalid's family will be beheaded about an hour after he makes that call. These are real people. People I know." He could see that she was skeptical. "Trust me. You know the Saudis don't believe in due process. So we can't tell Washington until we have the whole story, and until we have a plan for dealing with all the facts." He was pleading with her. "You've got to believe me."

She relented partially. She would only tell Moshe for now. A report to Margaret Joyner would wait until they had the complete story. Sagit was certain that Moshe would go along with that. As for Joyner, Sagit didn't like holding out the information from her. She was worried that her personal involvement with David was clouding her judgment. Tonight she vowed to sleep alone. "I'll wait until tomorrow morning," she said.

With a towel wrapped around his neck, David sat on a wooden bench in the steam room and glanced at his watch. It was five minutes past nine. What if Khalid didn't show? What if the Saudi colonel found some new way to outsmart him? Khalid was smart. He couldn't be underestimated. Particularly now when his life was on the line.

No, he'll be here, David thought. He glanced down at his wrist. Through billowing clouds of steam, he followed the black sweep second hand of his watch.

Suddenly, the frosted glass door opened. It was Khalid with a white towel draped around his waist. His dark-skinned body was tight and lean. He obviously still worked

out extensively. He looked young for forty. A long scar
ran across his abdomen, the result of a knife battle with a
hotheaded young officer in training, David remembered.

In each of his hands, Khalid carried a cup of ice water.
He handed one to David and sat down.

"Thanks for coming," David said.

"You didn't leave me much choice, but I wanted to. We
were such good friends when you were in my country, and
I treated you so rough last evening. I wanted to apologize."

"You don't have to. You had a lot at stake. Besides, five
years is a long time. People change. How are Nura and
the children?"

"Everyone's fine. Thank you."

"Your son, Hisham, must be quite a young man now,
and I'll bet he's still a good soccer player."

"He is," Khalid said with pride. "The captain of his
school team. And a good student."

The memories were rolling back in now. "Does he still
want to be an air force pilot?"

"He's not sure. Perhaps he wants to work with computers. The king's done his best to shut out the Internet, but
as always the forbidden fruit is the best. What about you?"

"I had an Israeli wife. Yael was her name. She died a
year ago."

David decided to leave it go at that.

"I'm sorry," Khalid replied. He paused for a moment,
startled by David's news. He wanted to ask about Yael,
but he didn't think this was the time or place. "Now the
question is, where do you and I go from here?"

David looked him squarely in the eye. "You'll be pleased
to know that I kept my end of the bargain. Nobody from
Israel reported to Washington."

"I wasn't worried," Khalid responded, very relieved.
"You always kept your word with me. In a way, you're
responsible for all of this. You realize that?"

"What do you mean?"

"Six years ago we had the grim choice of continued rule
by the House of Saud or turning the clock back eight centu-
ries and having rule by the fundamentalists, as they do in

Iran. You encouraged me and some of my fellow air force officers, including Colonel Azziz, to think that we could create a democratic alternative. So I decided that the time was right now to organize a group of officers myself to stage a coup."

"What's taken you so long to get to this point?" David asked. It was a question he'd had last night.

"Conditions in the country had to get even worse, which they have. The economy is in shambles because of corruption and mismanagement. Despite our massive oil revenues, our foreign reserves are nearly exhausted. The middle class has a reduced standard of living, and per capita income has plunged in the last five years. Meanwhile, key positions in the oil industry are awarded to friends of the royal family, and they're running it into the ground."

Becoming agitated, Khalid struck the side of his hand against the hot wooden bench. "You can forget about personal freedoms. A newspaper editor wrote an article raising questions about a system of justice that still has decrees by regional princes, and they cut off both of his hands. A married woman whose husband fled the country four years ago slept with an unmarried German construction worker, and they stoned her to death. There are fewer Saudis in college now than ten years ago."

Khalid's eyes were blazing with aminosity. "While all this is happening, the fundamentalists are getting stronger and stronger. They're totally wired in with the rulers in Iran, and Mohammed Nasser is planning to launch his own coup on January 1 by assassinating the Saudi king."

At the mention of Nasser's name an intense loathing showed on David's face. It was so strong that Khalid pulled back and paused for a moment before continuing. "So, unless some intermediate democratic alternative is found soon, Saudi Arabia will become like Iran. That's certainly not in Israel's or America's best interest. The Israelis should understand that I and my air force colleagues are a preferred democratic alternative. They shouldn't do anything to stop my coup from succeeding. You have to make those Zionist hotheads in Jerusalem understand that."

"How hard is your information that Nasser will move on January 1?" Khalid hesitated. "I need to know. It will help me persuade Israel not to act."

"Very hard. You taught me a great deal about the value of intelligence. I have a mole buried deep at the top of Nasser's organization."

Here was a way, David thought, to test the information Bill Fox had given him at their meeting in Green Park. He asked Khalid, "Which terrorist acts has Nasser been responsible for, according to your mole?"

"This year the assassination of a number of Saudi princes and some of their families. Always in a brutal way. Six months ago, an attack on the U.S. embassy in Kuwait. Then August a year ago, a bomb on a bus in Jerusalem—"

That was it. "You're sure he was responsible for the bus bomb?"

"I'm positive. And there's one more."

"What's that?"

Khalid smiled with satisfaction, knowing that he was about to drop one more bit of significant information on David that his old friend never expected. "The attack on the Khobar housing complex five years ago that you know so well. He planned the entire operation. With it he established himself as the undisputed leader of what had previously been a handful of splinter groups. Money and arms began flowing from Iran to Nasser, and he built an organization."

Khalid saw the stunned look on David's face.

"What will you do about Nasser and his people once you launch your coup?" David asked.

"We haven't been able to decide that. To put it mildly, there are serious disagreements at the top of my own group. Believe it or not, some of my colleagues want to bring him into our tent."

David was incredulous. "That's insane. You either crush him, or he'll destroy you."

"Personally, I couldn't agree with you more, but I'm trying to run a somewhat democratic organization."

David finished his ice water and moved to a lower bench

where it wouldn't be so hot. Khalid dropped down beside him.

"With all of these lofty ideals of yours, how did you get mixed up with Madame Blanc?" David asked.

"Through a friend who directs security for the national oil company. I sought Madame Blanc out when I learned that Nasser planned to move on January 1." Khalid frowned. "But she's a devil. That woman. She wants too much control. I wish I'd never met her."

"But she's given you military equipment."

"True. That'll make the battle easier."

"And when I finish my work, you'll have a blueprint for your attack, which will save lives."

"That's my doing." Khalid looked guilty. "A couple months ago, when I saw you by chance in Paris, and recognized you by your distinctive walk going into a Left Bank hotel, I insisted that she find a way to get your help."

"So you're the one? Thanks a lot for ruining what was left of my life."

Khalid smiled. "You have too much energy to take early retirement. Besides, you owe me for that airplane ride five years ago."

"So you turned that French devil on me?"

Looking at David somberly, Khalid said, "I'd take help from any source to free my country from the ironclad rule of the royal family."

"But very conveniently, the French devil's paying you money, too. Lots of money to lead this coup."

Khalid looked indignant. "I've accepted arms from her and money to pay operational expenses. Plus there were certain officials who had to be paid to look the other way or to grant permits when we brought arms into the country. But not a cent of her money has or ever will land in my own pocket. Doing what's best for my country is my sole motive." He wiped beads of perspiration from his forehead and then continued earnestly, "You have to persuade the Israelis not to endanger my cause by reporting what you know to the Americans or doing anything else. They should sit on the sidelines and let events unfold."

"As long as you mentioned the Americans, I've got something to ask you."

"Go ahead."

"The first time I heard about your coup, I thought that the Americans were your real problem. Not the Israelis. I still think that the minute you fire your first shot, the king will call Washington and claim it's the fundamentalists mounting an attack. The entire U.S. military will come to his aid—soldiers on the ground in Saudi Arabia, aircraft carriers, the whole works. Washington's lost Iran and Iraq as reliable sources of oil, and they're not about to repeat that mistake with the largest prize of all. Why are you so worried about the Israelis? Why not worry about the Americans?"

Khalid responded hesitantly. "Madame Blanc has taken care of the risk of American intervention."

David mopped his face with a towel. "That's what she told me, but how in the hell has she done that?"

Before answering, the colonel sprang off the wooden bench, walked over to the door and opened it. He looked around, making certain it was deserted in the corridor. Then he returned to the bench next to David and said, "I'll tell you all I know about the Americans if you promise that the Israelis won't get involved once the coup starts."

"Why are you so worried about the Israelis?"

"Be serious, Greg. Next to the Americans, the Israelis are the most powerful military force in the region. They could decide to back their own puppet for Saudi ruler like they did with Bashir Gemayal in Lebanon."

"I'll do my best to make sure that doesn't happen. I promise you that." David had said those words easily, making himself sound like a player in Jerusalem. What he was figuring was that Israel would be happy to be rid of the House of Saud—its avowed enemy—and would never do a thing unless the fundamentalists tried to seize control. "Now tell me what you know about the Americans."

Khalid was satisfied. He leaned toward David and whispered, "General Chambers."

With a start, David pulled his head back at the mention of the name. "General Chambers what?"

"She's told him all about the coup. She's gotten him to agree that there won't be any American military intervention."

Does Khalid really believe this? David wondered, looking hard at the colonel. If Khalid had any doubts, David couldn't see them. So David pressed on. "Be serious. Chambers is only the chairman of the Joint Chiefs. He's not the President. He doesn't have the authority to decide whether or not the United States will intervene."

"But he's persuaded her that he'll be able to convince the President not to intervene."

"Why would he do something like that?"

Khalid shrugged. "I don't know. Maybe now that he's back in Washington, he's taking a broader view of things. He's come to realize that U.S. interests in Saudi Arabia are doomed in the long run by an alliance with the House of Saud. Perhaps he now believes that the best way to assure the continued flow of Saudi oil is to let us work out our political problems ourselves."

David threw his hands up in the air, waving off this absurd proposition. "You're talking nonsense. Fools don't become wise men when they get to Washington. In fact, the opposite usually happens."

Khalid chuckled.

David wasn't laughing. "None of this makes any sense," he said.

"Maybe Chambers has already spoken to the President, and he has the President's agreement that there won't be any intervention. Perhaps the American government has already decided on its policy in advance of the coup."

"I don't believe it," David said, but he couldn't tell Khalid why without giving away his own involvement with the Americans through Sagit's trip to Washington and her discussions with Margaret Joyner. If the President and the other top officials in Washington were onboard, they would never have authorized his mission and his immunity from prosecution. And, in fact, Margaret Joyner had specifically wanted him to find out why Madame Blanc was so confident that there wouldn't be American intervention. No, Chambers was off on some venture of his own.

That thought touched off a surge of adrenaline. If Chambers was exceeding his authority, out on a limb on his own, then dammit, David would make sure to cut it off. He'd get even with that bastard once and for all. He'd pay for everything that happened in Dhahran and for making David a fugitive for five years of his life.

Totally deadpan, in a matter-of-fact voice, not wanting to make Khalid suspicious about what he was thinking, David asked, "Have you ever discussed the coup with General Chambers yourself? I mean apart from Madame Blanc."

"We've had two meetings so far. We have a final one set for next week on the 14th in Riyadh. I'm going to review with him where preparations stand for the attack."

A plan was forming in David's mind. He said, "When Chambers visits next week, ask him directly about the possibility that the President will order military intervention on the side of the king, and see what he says."

When Khalid didn't respond, David added, "Just to satisfy yourself that he really has this base covered."

Khalid paused to mull over David's words. "That's probably a good idea. Now tell me what you'll do for me with the Israeli government."

"I promise you, Khalid, that I'll do my best to get the Israelis to stay totally out of it, and I think I'll be able to succeed. Intervention's not in their own best interest, and it appears not to be where Washington's headed either. So I don't think there should be a problem."

Suddenly, David had another thought. Perhaps his desire for revenge against Chambers was clouding his mind. "What about Bill Fox?" he asked. "My former assistant. I understand that he's still the CIA station chief in Saudi Arabia."

"He is, but he has some personal problems."

"What's happening?" David asked, feigning ignorance. He wanted to know how much had slipped out about Fox's problem.

"I don't know all the details. I hear rumors that his personal life is messed up."

"What are the rumors?"

"I better not say."

"Oh, come on, Khalid."

"His wife divorced him, and he's getting it on with a Saudi princess."

"Jesus," David said, acting shocked, "that's like holding a loaded gun to his own head. Has he flipped out?"

His ruse had worked. Khalid believed him. "It's possible," Khalid replied.

"It is also possible that he's in Madame Blanc's pocket." David's words startled Khalid. He hadn't figured on that. "Suppose she bought him somehow, maybe with a promise that he gets to keep his Saudi princess and receives a bundle of cash, millions of dollars, if he files misinformation reports once the coup starts. That would help deter American intervention, and Fox would need the money to keep his Saudi princess in style, maybe take her to live abroad after the coup. What do you think?"

As Khalid pondered the question, David became more convinced that the Henri Napoleon payments had gone to Fox.

Finally, Khalid shrugged. "Anything's possible with Fox these days. Do you still have that remarkable memory for numbers?"

"I sure do."

Khalid recited his private telephone number at home and his cell phone number. "Use these if you ever have to call me in an emergency." He stood up. "Now that we're finished, can we leave this room before I melt?"

David replied, "As quickly as possible. I think I'm going to die from the heat. I just wanted you to be the first to say it."

"You look like a soggy noodle," Sagit said to David.

They were in his hotel room at the Four Seasons. He had combed it for bugs and was satisfied it was clean. The curtains were drawn tight in case someone outside had a telephoto lens aimed at the room.

"Thanks, that's how I feel. Do you know how long I was in that steam room with him?"

"As a matter of fact, I do. I was getting ready to send in Murray." She tossed him a large plastic bottle of Evian. "Drink up before I lose you."

He chugged down the whole bottle of water. Beads of perspiration still dotted his forehead, and he wiped them away with his hand.

"Was it worth it?" she asked.

"You bet."

He described the conversation for her, but left out his supposition that Fox was Henri Napoleon, because he wanted to bore in on General Chambers as Madame Blanc's Washington card. As he spoke, Sagit listened, amazed, with eyes wide open.

"It doesn't make sense," she said at the end. "We're missing something."

"That's what I keep thinking."

"If President Waltham and his top people were tuned in, then they would never have been so interested in what I had to say and in wanting you to find out the details of the coup in return for immunity."

David loved talking with her. She was smart, and they were usually on the same wavelength. "Precisely, Dr. Watson."

"Which means that—"

He completed the sentence for her: "General Chambers is flying solo on this."

"But why?"

"That's the question I can't answer."

With a quizzical expression on her face, she pondered the question of what General Chambers's game was. She, too, was stumped. "But somehow we have to find the answer. If I take what we have now back to Margaret Joyner in Washington, I suspect that General Chambers will deny everything, and she'll be powerless to stop your extradition."

"I agree with you. What we need is concrete evidence against Chambers, and then we can nail him." An eager glint came into his eyes, which she immediately caught.

"I don't want this to turn into a personal vendetta of yours against Chambers," she said sharply. "There's a lot more at stake here."

He was annoyed by her comment, but he decided he'd better conceal his reaction or he'd never get her to go along with what he wanted to do. "I wouldn't think of it. But back in the steam room, I had this idea that we should try to tape Chambers's conversation with Colonel Khalid next week. That would give us the evidence we need. The trouble is, we would need Bill Fox's help to do that, and as you heard, he's not the most reliable. He never was, even in his good days, five years ago."

"Nothing you've told me about Fox inspires any confidence."

David walked over to the window and stared out, as if the answer could be discerned twelve stories below in Hyde Park. Finally, he turned around and said, "My feeling is that we have to go with Fox. He's all we've got. What do you think, Sagit?"

She gave a long sigh. "Bugging the chairman of the Joint Chiefs is a high-risk move. We could get hurt if this blows up on us. Israel would end up in a diplomatic nightmare with Washington, particularly if the press picked it up."

"That thought's been running through my mind. For you, the price would be terrible. For me, it would mean extradition and a jail sentence. But I just don't see anything else we can do."

Unhappily, she weighed the options. Finally, she said, "Okay, we'll go for it. I think I can get Moshe on board, and hopefully he'll persuade the prime minister."

Suddenly, David remembered the fax in his pocket, which he'd picked up from the concierge in the lobby on his way up to the room. "It's from Batya at the kibbutz," he said, bringing it over to her. "Victor faxed me. The information your Saudi captain friend passed to Victor at the Dorchester is now at PDF. They want me in Paris tomorrow. I've got to go there and finish up. I figure it'll take me two days."

"Suppose Madame Blanc doesn't let you leave Paris?"

He hadn't thought of that possibility. He stopped to ponder it for a few moments. "I'll have to take my chances. If I don't go now, that would set off alarms. All our work would go down the tubes, and they would probably kill Daphna. We have to get her out." He looked at her accusingly. "Isn't there anything else you can do?"

"We've got plenty of people working on it."

"But where the hell are they?"

"You don't have to curse at me."

"I'm sorry. It's just frustrating."

"Well, it is for me, too. About an hour ago, my contact in the French secret police delivered a list of the phone calls in and out of Victor's office during the month of September. It has phone numbers and addresses. We're systematically plowing through that list."

David looked at her anxiously. "Just tell your people to work quietly. If Madame Blanc thinks I'm involved with the Mossad, she won't hesitate to kill Daphna."

From Charles De Gaulle Airport, David took a cab directly to the PDF headquarters. Colette Martique had the new information that Victor had brought from London waiting in the office he had used before. When he tried to banter with her, she looked away. He could feel the tension in the air. Maybe it was because October 6 was a little more than two weeks away. Or had something else happened? Had Madame Blanc learned about his meeting with Khalid in London? Were they planning to kill him and Daphna after he completed his present project?

He worked until midnight at the PC, until his tired eyes began blurring over. Then he went back to the Gironde for five hours of sleep. He started again at eight the next morning, absorbing all of the details and then typing a report with his plan of attack and information about the automated systems for the royal palace and the oil fields. He finished at noon and read each page carefully as the computer spat out his unsigned report. He felt as if he were back at the CIA. This was the coup he wanted to develop five years ago. Which side was he on now? He was preparing it, but he would also help to defeat it. He had lost any sense of perspective. He decided to turn off his mind and continue reading.

Suddenly, Colette poked her head into his office. "Madame Blanc would like to know when you'll be ready to meet with her."

He checked his watch. "Tell her two o'clock this afternoon."

He passed up lunch and continued refining what he'd written.

When he was ushered into Madame Blanc's office promptly at two, he handed her his report. Victor was sitting in a corner of the room. She leafed through the document and the maps in the back.

"How many copies did you make?" she demanded to know.

He stared at her calmly, unwilling to be intimidated, determined not to raise any apprehensions in her mind. "You have the only one."

From the corner of his eye he saw Victor looking at him suspiciously. He tossed his thin briefcase to the lawyer.

"You're welcome to search my bag," he volunteered.

Victor blushed.

"That won't be necessary," she said. "What about the computer disc you used to prepare the report?"

His face was set in stone. "Erased. No other record exists."

"Good. Give me an oral summary, then."

He preceded to explain to her the most efficient way for her Saudi ally to seize control of the palace and the oil fields. He told her where the king's strongest defenses were focused and how those could be overcome. He gave her specific numbers and types of military forces.

Then he continued: "Now let's talk about the automated systems I installed and how they can be neutralized." He saw he had her on the edge of her chair.

"Around the Saudi Royal Palace, land mines have been planted three feet deep into the ground, twenty yards away from the walls, at four-foot intervals. When a five-digit code is entered on a control pad located behind a picture of the Al Aksa Mosque in the king's bedroom, the mines will rise in metal casings to the surface, where they can be individually or collectively detonated by remote control. A system of automated heat-seeking rockets has been built into the palace walls and roof. When activated by a second five-digit code on a panel in the same location, they will strike any attackers shooting at the palace from the ground or from planes overhead. This automated hardware is in addition to fifty of the most experienced crack troops of the National Guard, composed of members of Bedouin tribes, whose loyalty to the king is strongest and who are housed at all times in the palace. They are billeted in the west palace wing, but are constantly in a state of readiness. Both of the automated systems can be deactivated by entering a different five-digit code on a control pad behind a painting in the office of the minister of defense in Riyadh."

She was impressed with what she had heard. He was good, this fugitive CIA agent. "What about the system to blow up the oil fields?"

"At the back of my report is a map of the Saudi oil fields. I've marked the appropriate locations at which underground bombs are planted that can be exploded by a remote control device that the Saudi king carries with him at all times."

She unfolded the map and studied it for a few minutes.

"Assuming these are substantial bombs, which I imagine they are, the oil fields would be out of action for a long time."

"That's precisely the point." He was getting to the punch line. Watching her, he could see that she was engrossed in his presentation.

"So how do we deactivate the system?" she asked impatiently.

"The Saudi Oil Ministry has a regional headquarters building in Ras Tannarah. In the director's office on the third floor, there's a control pad with nine numbers. Again, punching in a five-digit code will deactivate the system of explosives for the oil fields. The Saudi king doesn't know we installed the means to deactivate these three systems. It was my idea. The only one who knew about it was the top CIA brass in Washington."

"And you've provided me with those five numbers as well as the codes to deactivate the defensive system in the royal palace?"

David took a deep breath. The moment of truth had come.

"Well?" she demanded.

"No. I haven't."

She pounded her fist on the desk. "That was our deal."

"I've had second thoughts. I might never see my money if I give you the codes now. Instead, I'll fly to Saudi Arabia forty-eight hours before the attack with your people. I'll give you the three codes then, assuming that Daphna has been released."

As she stared at him, astonished by his unmitigated nerve, Victor chimed in. "Leave me alone with him and a couple of your bodyguards for an hour. I promise you, he'll tell you everything you want to know."

"And I promise you I won't. The CIA taught me how to deal with torture." He shrugged. "Besides, you know my story as well as I do. Since my wife's death last year, I have nothing to live for. Except now you'd be giving me a purpose. To deprive your people of the prize you want so dearly. That's worth dying for."

"Well, why don't we test that thesis?" Victor said, rising to his feet. "Or why don't we bring Daphna here, and you can watch her be tortured?"

Madame Blanc waved him down.

"I've read enough profiles of our friend here to know that we won't break him, and the girl's just his stepdaughter." What she didn't add was that, despite twenty-four hours of torture at the hands of the Nazis and a young daughter's screams, her own mother had never divulged a single bit of information. In view of that experience, she had read a great deal about torture. With some people it just didn't work. David had all of the characteristics of someone who wouldn't crack.

She looked at him coldly. "You'd better be in front of the Bristol at ten P.M. on October 4. We'll fly you out to Saudi Arabia then."

"I'll be there."

Victor broke in. "Why not have him stay in Paris until then? We'll be able to watch him."

David had an answer ready. "It's the Jewish New Year next week. Businesspeople who are abroad come home for the holidays. I had enough hard questions to answer when I returned with my face all scratched and bruised the last time. If I don't make it home, they'll get suspicious. The kibbutz security director will make calls to the Mossad." He paused and looked at Madame Blanc. "You know I'm right. Don't you?" When she didn't respond, he continued, "Besides, I've already proven my value as a partner. If it weren't for me, your people would never have known about the system to blow up the oil fields."

"Don't try to change the subject," Victor snapped. "I want you to remain in Paris because I want to make sure you're here on the 4th."

"You're forgetting that I have a huge financial incentive. Try eight million dollars."

"But you already have . . ."

Madame Blanc had heard enough. "Leave him alone, Victor. He's done what I wanted so far. Let him do it his way."

She turned to David. "Be in front of the Bristol at ten P.M. on October 4. Victor's driver, Rolland, will pick you up then. You'll fly out to Saudi Arabia with my people that night. We'll keep you there as long as we need you."

He was tempted to ask, And then what? But he knew the answer, which she would never tell him: Then we'll kill you, of course.

Sagit was waiting for David at Charles De Gaulle Airport in the boarding area for El Al flight 016 from Paris to Tel

Aviv. As soon as she saw David, she pulled him off into a deserted corner.

"I heard from the embassy in Paris. One of the phone numbers that appears frequently on the calls in and out of Victor Foch's office is a house outside of Grasse. It's a property owned by a company that's a sub of a sub of PDF. A large house surrounded by a high stone wall."

David felt a surge of excitement. "Great, let's get her out."

She knew this would be his reaction. She had been dreading the battle with him that was coming. But calmly and professionally she responded, "We have two people in the area watching the house. Even with binoculars, because of the wall they can't tell whether anybody's occupying it."

"Daphna has to be there," he said. "They should storm the house and get her out."

"We don't even know if she's there," she said, raising her voice and sharpening her tone.

"Then we'll apologize to the owners and go away."

"That's not an option."

"What are you saying?" He sounded exasperated.

She moved in close to him, standing toe to toe. "I spoke to Moshe in Jerusalem. He was very explicit, to put it mildly. His command is that we don't do anything illegal on French territory. He's already called his counterpart in the French secret service to get their help."

"Oh, for Christ sake," David said. "That won't do us a bit of good."

"Don't shout at me," she snapped back. "You're not the director. From you, I don't have to take it. Besides, we already formulated a plan to go in and get Daphna out before I spoke to Moshe. We even had one of our people, Shimon in Marseilles, preparing a disguise and false papers to get her out of the country. But Moshe is the boss, and I can understand where he's coming from. Let's wait and see what happens."

David was red in the face. The veins were pulsing, in his neck. "Not on your life. I'm going down to Grasse. I'll go in myself and get her out."

"You can't. You don't know where the house is."

He stared hard at her. "You're going to tell me."

"Yeah," she said, locking eyes with him, refusing to bend, "so you can get yourself killed and Daphna as well? No, David, I did it your way after the bakery in Paris. This time we're doing it my way. You're getting on this plane to Tel Aviv. I'm staying in France to direct our operations."

He clenched his teeth and slowly shook his head. "You can do whatever you want, but no way am I leaving France until I know she's safe."

She sucked in her breath, trying to decide how to respond. At that moment, her cell phone rang. David watched her face freeze with tension as she listened carefully.

"I understand," she said grimly. ". . . KMB310 . . . Yes . . . You're both okay, then? Get another car as soon as you can and comb the area."

She turned off the phone and looked at him anxiously. "They're moving her. Our people tried to follow, but a truck blocked the road and then smashed into their car to take them out of the game."

David pounded his right fist into the palm of his other hand. "Big surprise. After Moshe's call, somebody in the French government tipped off Madame Blanc. The rest was predictable. So what are you doing now?"

"We have a license plate number for the car they're using to move Daphna. I have to call Moshe and report to him. Then I'll stay right here until we get some more information."

Daphna was sandwiched in the back of a gray turbo diesel Mercedes—license plate number KMB310—between a tall, thin man with a scar on his cheek and the matronly Mary, who had been in charge of Daphna's confinement at the house in Grasse. Up front there was only the driver, who pushed the car fast across roads still illuminated by the rapidly setting sun. Daphna tried to take stock of her situation.

Before they had left the house, she had overheard much

of Mary's end of a phone conversation through a crack in
her bedroom door. They had decided hastily to move her
to a boat that was docked in St. Tropez, and from there to
get on to the open sea. Mary had rejected the idea of drug-
ging Daphna for fear that would draw greater attention
when they moved her to the boat, and because she was
confident they could keep "the girl, who's been a mouse,
under control during the move."

As the car raced down the steep, winding road from the
hills to St. Tropez, Daphna knew that she had to find a
way to escape before they got her on that boat. Once she
was on the boat, she was as good as dead.

It was twilight as they made their way slowly in the heavy
traffic toward the dock in the heart of St. Tropez. Pedestrians, many of them carrying shopping bags from the smart
boutiques, crowded the narrow cobblestone streets as the
gray Mercedes wove its way through. At the dock area, it
could have been noon. Hundreds of bright lights, glistening
off the water, illuminated the area. The cafés that faced the
water were filled with tourists, and half a dozen huge yachts
sat in their berths.

Daphna saw a policeman directing traffic and looked at
him hopefully. As if reading her mind, Scarface said,
"When we park, we're going to walk about fifty meters to
the boat. You'll walk between me and Mary. I'll have my
left arm around your shoulder, as if we're lovers. In my
right hand I'll have a gun with a silencer in my jacket
pocket pointed at your side. If you try to scream or do
anything to cause a commotion, I'll shoot, and you'll be
dead. Is that clear?"

Daphna nodded, looking frightened, but her brain was
churning. In her air force training they had covered scenarios like this. What to do when enemy soldiers or terrorists
capture an unarmed pilot. It was long ago, so long ago. She
forced her mind to think, to remember.

The car ground to a halt.

"Okay, bitch, out!" Scarface barked as he opened the
door.

Mary came around the car and, like a couple of bookends, they moved close to Daphna. They began walking directly toward a huge yacht about fifty yards away. Daphna could feel Scarface's arm around her shoulder and his awful garlicky breath as he kept his face close to hers. He held the gun in tight against her rib cage. No one on the street was paying any attention to them.

In training, she suddenly recalled, they had said, "Never believe you don't have a weapon. Your body has powerful weapons. Use them."

One chance is all I'll get, she thought. I better not waste it. Carefully she moved her right arm in close to her body. Then with all the force she could muster, she drove her elbow into his ribs. She could feel bone cracking, and she jabbed deeper to bruise his spleen.

A jolt of excruciating pain shot through Scarface's body. He let go of the gun and dropped to his knees. Mary had no time to react, for Daphna had already bolted toward the old stone citadel. She saw a narrow cobblestone street on the right running up the hill, and she dashed up the street, threading her way among tourists wandering along. She glanced over her shoulder. Scarface had recovered. He was running with a limp, in obvious pain, followed by Mary and the driver of the gray Mercedes. Daphna turned left, then right and then left again, hoping to lose them, but she quickly realized the folly of that. There were so few streets in the old city, and with three of them following her, sooner or later they would track her down.

Up ahead, she saw a small four-story hotel called the Yacca. She darted inside the front door and toward the bar in back. The clerk behind the reception desk was too busy on his computer to notice her. Just before the bar, she spotted a sign that said TOILETTE and pointed up one flight of stairs. She took refuge in the rest room and caught her breath. This was safer than being out on the streets, but how long could she stay here? Scarface would undoubtedly try all the public facilities in the few hotels in the area.

She walked out of the rest room and snuck up the stairs, glancing down the corridor on each floor for an open room in which she could hide. On the top floor she saw a chambermaid come out of one room and go into the adjacent room midway down the deserted corridor. Between the two rooms the chambermaid had parked a cart of supplies with a pass key dangling from a hook on the cart. Daphna tiptoed down the corridor, grabbed the pass key and unlocked Room 404, where the maid had just been. In an instant she returned the key to the cart and slipped into Room 404. It was dark, and she stood at the door and held her breath, hoping the room was empty. When she didn't hear any sounds, no people asleep and breathing, she turned on a light and looked around. The room was obviously occupied, but the people were out—no doubt for dinner. It was still early evening. They might not be back for a while.

She snatched the phone from the cradle and dialed Sagit's cell phone, hoping she could get her. Miraculously, Sagit answered on the first ring.

"It's Daphna," she stammered with relief.

"Where are you?"

"I escaped."

"Wonderful." Sagit wanted to conceal the incredible stress she had been feeling for the last couple of hours, to avoid alarming Daphna any more than necessary. But her voice was still cracking with tension. "Where are you?"

"In a small hotel in St. Tropez called Yacca. They're searching for me outside. I managed to get into the room of one of the hotel guests. They're not here right now."

Sagit had gained control of her emotions. "That's great," she said, sounding steady and reassuring.

"But I don't know what to do now."

There was a pause while Sagit's mind raced quickly, formulating a plan.

"Are you still there?" Daphna asked nervously.

"I'm thinking."

On the verge of panic, Daphna said, "Please tell me what to do. Please."

"Okay, what's the room number?"

"404."

"Whose room is it?"

"I don't know."

"Look around. You'll find something that tells you."

Daphna saw a copy of the American edition of *Time* magazine on a table. A subscription label read "Mr. and Mrs. Benjamin V. Cohen," with a New York City address.

She told that to Sagit, who said, "Listen carefully. I'm going to arrange for somebody to come and get you as soon as possible. His name's Shimon, and the pass code will be 'water.' He'll have a man's disguise for you and false papers. He'll get you out of the country, but you have to do exactly what he says. Is that clear?"

"Yes. Yes," she said anxiously, "but how soon will he be here?"

"Two hours, depending on traffic," Sagit said, sounding confident and in control. She desperately wanted to allay the young woman's anxiety. "He has to come from Marseilles. You must stay in Room 404 until he calls you."

Daphna's spirits, which had rose, now collapsed. "That's a long time. What if the Cohens come back before Shimon gets here? What do I do then?"

"You're smart and resourceful, Daphna. You managed to escape your abductors. I think you'll figure how to handle a couple of tourists from New York. Just don't leave the room."

As Daphna put the phone down, she fought off a tide of despair and terror. Sagit was right. She had been smart and resourceful. If she could handle Scarface, she could handle the Cohens. She began searching their suitcases, half-unpacked, and the dresser drawers, looking for a weapon and some rope to tie them up if they returned before Shimon came. In one of the suitcases, she found a hair dryer that she could use as a weapon. She decided that Mr. Cohen's shirts with long sleeves would suffice to tie them up. As she searched the bureau drawer for shirts, she came across the couple's American passports. Suddenly, a different idea began taking shape in her mind. She leafed through Mr. Cohen's passport first. It had been issued eight years ago. In those eight years, he had made seven trips to Israel. Mrs. Cohen had been with him on five of those trips. With her plan formulated, she turned off the room lights and sat down on the floor of the closet. In her hand, she held the handle of the hair dryer, but she hoped she wouldn't have to use it.

About an hour later, she heard the sound of a key being turned. She held her breath and gripped the hair dryer hard. Through a crack in the closet door, she saw the outside hall light first. Then the room light went on. Mr. and Mrs. Cohen were in their late sixties, Daphna guessed. She was a large rotund woman with freshly coifed gray hair piled high on her head. He was portly, with wire-framed glasses, and slightly shorter than his wife. She doubted that either of them ever did any exercise. If she had to deal with them physically, it would be no problem.

She waited until they had closed the door and were well inside the room before she jumped out of the closet and confronted them with the hair dryer in her hand. She suddenly realized how frightening she must look. She was filthy from running, her blond hair was wild, and she had a desperate look in her eyes. The Cohens were frightened half to death and too scared to scream. The first words out of her mouth were crucial, she realized. So she stared at them and said, "I want you to do something to help the government of Israel."

By now the Cohens had recovered from their initial fright, and Mrs. Cohen screamed, "You get out of our room right now, or I'm calling the front desk."

"Wait a minute, Evelyn," her husband said. "Let's hear what she has to say."

"Are you crazy, Ben? She's here to rob and kill us."

Ben Cohen was looking at the hair dryer in Daphna's hand. "Go over to the bed next to the phone," he said to his wife, "but don't pick it up. We'll listen to what she has to say. If we don't like it, you call the front desk."

Daphna didn't like the arrangement, but she was willing to gamble on persuading Ben Cohen. Meantime, he moved himself between Daphna and his wife.

"Okay, young lady," he said, "now tell me what you want us to do for the government of Israel."

"Do you understand Hebrew?" she asked.

"Only a few words."

"Okay, I'll talk in English. But it's complicated and very difficult for me to explain. I'm an Israeli student at school in Paris. I was kidnapped by terrorists, but I escaped before they got me on a boat. Now they're looking for me on the streets outside. But I hid in your room. Soon an Israeli will come here to take me home."

Dumbfounded, Ben Cohen asked, "Do you have any identification?"

"Nothing. The terrorists took it all. I live in kibbutz Bet Mordechai north of Haifa. Ask me about Israel. I'll tell you."

Evelyn Cohen said, "This is all preposterous. There are plenty of Israeli criminals. I'm calling the front desk, Ben."

"Please, Mrs. Cohen," Daphna said. "If I wanted to rob and beat you, I would have done it when you walked into the room. Yes?"

That made Evelyn Cohen stop and think.

"Why don't you go to the French police?" Ben Cohen asked Daphna.

"I'm afraid they'll help the terrorists." He nodded slowly, weighing what she said. "Please, Mr. Cohen, you remember the bomb on bus number eighteen in Jerusalem last year?"

"Evelyn and I were in Jerusalem on that same street one week earlier."

"Well, my mother was on bus number eighteen. She was killed in the explosion."

With those words, Daphna had won over Mrs. Cohen. "What do you want us to do to help you?"

"Please let me hide until the Israeli comes for me."

"We'll do that," she said. "In the meantime, do you want something to eat? We can order from room service."

Daphna suddenly realized how long it had been since she had last eaten. "Yes, please," she said. "But I have no money. When I'm home, I'll mail you money."

Ben Cohen laughed. "I don't think that'll be necessary."

For the next hour, while she ate, Evelyn and Ben Cohen peppered Daphna with questions about her kibbutz, her mother and her air force duty. They sought her views about the political situation, the Palestinians and Syria. She quickly concluded that, while they were critical of the Israeli government in some respects, still they cared deeply about the Jewish state, where a number of their relatives lived. Their questions pushed her English to its limit, and Daphna found the session exhausted her already weary body.

Finally, the telephone rang, and Daphna was relieved, hoping it was Shimon.

"I'll get it," Ben said.

She watched him apprehensively as he picked up the phone and listened for several long seconds. Then he cupped his hand over the speaker part of the phone. "It's someone named Shimon. He says the word is 'water,' and he wants to speak to a young woman friend of his."

Daphna was ecstatic. She ran across the room and eagerly picked up the phone.

"It's Daphna," she said in Hebrew.

"Are you okay?"

"Right now I'm great."

"Good, I'm on the way up."

When he got to the room, Shimon entered carrying a shopping bag. In Hebrew, he asked Daphna, "Do they speak Hebrew?"

"No," she replied.

"Good, then we can talk. Go in the bathroom and change fast," he said, handing her the shopping bag. "There's a black wig, a ski cap and men's clothes inside."

While she was in the bathroom, he whispered to her through an opening in the door. "The people who grabbed you are very well connected. St. Tropez is swarming with cops, and there are roadblocks leading out of the city."

"Where are we going?" she asked.

"East by car. We have Italian plates and Italian ID. Even fake Italian passports. My job is to get you safely to Genoa."

"You think we'll be okay?"

"Well, they're looking for a young blond Israeli woman. So use the charcoal to give yourself a beard."

When she emerged from the bathroom, even the Cohens barely recognized her. Shimon checked to make sure the corridor was deserted. Then he turned to the Cohens and said in a matter-of-fact tone, "If you tell anyone about us, I'll personally come to New York and kill both of you."

Daphna winced. When they left the room, she whispered to Shimon, "You didn't have to say that. They're nice people. We can trust them."

"They had to know it's not a game. Our lives are on the line, and we're still a long way from safety. If police or the kidnappers come to their room, what would they do without my threat?"

Their flight from Paris to Genoa had been uneventful. Now Sagit and David waited for Daphna and Shimon in a coffee shop, deserted because of the late hour, in the terminal building of Genoa airport. Their eyes were riveted on the front door of the building, visible through the open door of the coffee shop. Out on the airfield, a small unmarked jet waited on the runway to whisk Daphna, Sagit and David back to Israel.

The problem was that there was no sign of Daphna.

David took a sip of lukewarm coffee, glanced at the clock on the wall for the thousandth time and said, "They should have been here by now. Something happened."

Sagit was tired of providing him with possible explanations. He had been in the business. He knew what it was like waiting for people you were trying to get out of enemy hands. "They could have hit traffic. You know what those roads are like."

"Well, why didn't he call?"

"I know Shimon. He'd play it safe. He wouldn't run the risk of having the call picked up."

Grimly David shook his head. "Your plan was too obvious. All Madame Blanc had to do was get her friends to cover the border crossing point where the road from Nice runs into Italy. That's the first thing she would have done. It was a no-brainer. And they probably never even made it that far. There are so few roads out of St. Tropez. A couple of well-placed roadblocks in the town would have done it."

He got up from the table and paced the room nervously like a caged animal. An olive-skinned woman mopping the floor looked at him apprehensively.

"For God's sake," Sagit said to him, "can't you stop pacing? You're driving me crazy. What's wrong with you?"

"Nothing's wrong with me," he snarled. "I want to get Daphna out of France."

"So do I. You were a professional. You know what these situations are like. I can't believe you behaved so emotionally when you were with the CIA. They would have bounced you out of the Agency in a minute."

David came back to the table and sat down. "You're right," he replied. "I didn't behave like this. But this situation is different."

"You mean because it's Yael's daughter?"

"That's some of it."

"And the rest?"

He took a deep breath and sighed. "There was one part of the story I didn't tell you that Friday night back at the kibbutz."

"Why is it that I'm not surprised?" Feeling the tension as much as he was, she fished around in her purse, hoping that she had left a pack of cigarettes there when she had quit smoking, but her hand came up empty. "Since we have nothing to do here but wait, you want to tell me now?"

He hesitated.

She looked at him angrily. "I think you owe me that much after the deal I got for you in Washington."

"I'm sorry. You're right." He stopped talking while two policemen on patrol passed by their table and nodded. "That Friday night I told you what happened in Saudi Arabia. But before that Greg Nielsen was a young CIA agent working in Iran, when the Shah of Iran was still in power. Let me tell you what happened."

Greg had become convinced that the Shah was seriously at risk because of the Moslem fundamentalists. He was certain that the supporters of Ayatollah Khomeini were being grossly underestimated by the American government, as well as by SAVAK, the Shah's secret police. His difficulty was that his information came from sources, that couldn't be identified, and was often uncorroborated. He needed a smoking gun—a tape recording or copies of critical documents that would be persuasive to the Shah and to CIA headquarters in Langley.

One night, following a meeting of supporters of the Ayatollah in a rural area about a hundred miles north of Tehran, he broke into their headquarters and stole the documents he needed. As he was running through the woods to get back to the closest large village, about five miles away, where he had left his car, he suddenly heard footsteps and people chasing him. He ran as fast as he could, but his lame right leg slowed him down. Then he heard the unmistakable sound of a gun firing, and a bullet whizzed over his head. He had a Beretta holstered to his chest. So he stopped, hid behind a tree and took out a pair of nightscope glasses. Then he began firing.

He couldn't tell how many were pursuing him. He kept still and waited. A couple of minutes later one of them made a frontal assault on Greg. He waited until the man was twenty yards away before firing into his chest. The man screamed and fell to the ground. Greg heard a movement on his left. Before he could fire, a bullet tore into his left shoulder. His assailant was screaming as he ran at Greg. Meantime, Greg knew he had only one bullet left, and he caught the man right in his heart. Now he was in trouble. From the shouts, he knew there were two more, but he had no chance of stopping them without ammunition. He dropped his gun and, with blood oozing from his shoulder, he began running again.

They were gaining on him, and he thought his situation was hopeless. Suddenly, to the right, he heard more gunshots, and the last two pursuers screamed as they were hit.

Weak and dazed, he looked around to see his savior. He thought he had died or was dreaming when, like an apparition, a beautiful tall blond woman approached with a gun in each hand.

Without even bothering to introduce herself, she ripped off his shirt and tied it tightly around his left shoulder to halt the flow of blood. Then she said in English, "Let's get the hell out of here before they send backup."

Together, they jogged toward the village, but after a mile he was too weak from the loss of blood. He was on the verge of passing out. She half carried and half supported him the rest of the way, while he still clutched his briefcase.

It was nearly midnight, and the village was dark and quiet. The blond woman knew the village, and she headed straight to the house of a Jewish doctor who supported the Shah. Without asking any questions, he treated Greg's wound and then hid the couple behind boxes of medical supplies in a supply shed in the back.

For the next two days, the couple hid in the shed, with the doctor bringing in food while the Ayatollah's people combed the countryside for them. During those two days Greg learned that the blonde was an Israeli and a member of the Mossad. From her own intelligence sources, she, too, had learned about the meeting of the Ayatollah's supporters, and she had been conducting her own surveillance. Greg, of course, agreed to share the documents in the brief-case with her. But something else happened in those days and nights alone in the doctor's shed. Contrary to the regulations of both of their employers, the two of them fell in love.

David stopped talking and looked up. Sagit shook her head slowly.

"So Daphna's your child as well as Yael's. I should have guessed. That's the reason Moshe refused to tell me why Yael left the Mossad. He must have forced her out when he learned that one of his protégées had become pregnant with the child of an agent of another country's intelligence service. It still pains him to talk about it."

David's eyes narrowed. "She told me that she had had enough of life in the Mossad, and she was quitting. She wanted to have our child and a normal life back in Israel."

"So you didn't see her again until you came to Israel from Russia five years ago?"

"We were too much in love for that." She looked sharply at him. "Over the years we developed a way of corresponding. We would arrange clandestine meetings in Europe about twice a year when she was on a fur-buying trip. In fact, that was the reason she started the kibbutz fur business. Anyone who picked up one of my letters would have thought I was Danish. I was a fur trader, and we were discussing a transaction. Once Yael even brought Daphna to Copenhagen, when she was three. The rest of the time I had to settle for pictures."

"Does Daphna know that you're her father?"

Sadly, he shook his head. "I should have told her, but I was afraid it would put her too much at risk. Obviously, I'll tell her as soon as I see her again—if I see her again."

Sagit didn't respond. The hour was growing late. She was beginning to worry herself.

She decided to keep talking to him to pass the time. "What happened to you in Iran after Yael left?"

"I stayed in the country, serving the United States, as I had been trained. Repeatedly, I tried to warn my government about the threat posed by Ayatollah Khomeini and his fundamentalist crowd, but they wouldn't listen to me in Washington. After that I became CIA station chief in Saudi Arabia."

"Can I ask you one more question?"

"Sure, go ahead."

"It's kind of personal."

"C'mon, Sagit, I've already told you things no one else knows. At this point, you've fully opened me up. I have no more secrets from you. Ask whatever you want."

"Did you ever consider quitting the CIA and starting a normal life with Yael once you knew she was pregnant?"

He gave a long, low sigh of resignation—the sigh of a man who had made a serious mistake long ago in his life and would regret it for the rest of his days. "I constantly thought about it," he said ruefully. "But I was a professional soldier. My top priority was serving my country.

Other things had to find their place. In essence, I kept saying, I'll quit next year. I'll quit next year. I'll join Yael in Israel. Or I'll go to the United States with her, and we'll live there! But things always kept coming up. First, the situation got really dicey with the Shah. And after that I became the station chief in Saudi Arabia. I could never pull myself away from the job. I thought I loved my country more than I loved Yael, and more than I loved Daphna."

He looked melancholy. "I would have had twenty years with her instead of five—or a lifetime, because if we had been together she would never have started the fur business, and she would never have been on bus eighteen that day." He took a deep breath. "Amazing that I could have been so stupid, isn't it?"

As Sagit thought about his words, she remembered two relationships she'd had with perfectly wonderful men, whose offers of marriage she had rejected because married life wouldn't have been compatible with her Mossad career. She and David were more alike than she cared to admit. "Sadly, it's the old spy dance," Sagit reflected. "You go round and round in circles, sometimes you change partners, but the music never stops."

He brought his hand up to his chin and nodded in agreement. "You feel that way, too? I mean about your own life."

"When I'm honest with myself."

"So how'd you get into this business and why'd you stick with it so long?"

Sagit never had a chance to respond. There was a commotion at the entrance of the terminal building as a burly, unshaven man burst inside followed by what looked like an effeminate man wearing a ski cap.

"Quick," Sagit shouted to Shimon, "follow us."

With David in tow, she raced toward the airfield and the waiting Israeli jet. Shimon and Daphna were only a few steps behind.

In a matter of seconds, the airplane door slammed shut, the engines were revved up, and the sleek jet headed for the runway. Only then did Daphna rip off the ski cap and black wig, letting her long blond hair cascade down to her shoulders.

As Sagit took Shimon to the front of the plane for a debriefing, David led Daphna to the rear cabin, where they could be alone. There in the dim cabin light over northern Italy, he told Daphna that he was her biological father, and he described the long-term relationship he and Yael had. Initially she was angry that he hadn't told her before. "We could have been a family. Now it's too late."

"Please, Daphna, you have to understand I was an exile and a fugitive. People were trying to kill me. If you knew, you'd be at risk. Your mother and I talked about it. We decided we had to protect you."

Gradually, his words sank in, and her anger softened. Finally, when the shock of what she had learned passed, all that she could think about was that she now had a father. After all of these years she had a father. She hugged him tightly. Tears ran down her cheeks. They were tears of joy.

There was no joy in Paris as Victor finally got up the courage to make the phone call that he had been dreading.

"Well?" a furious Madame Blanc demanded when she answered.

Victor's voice was quavering. "They haven't been able to find her."

"And you never will. By now she's no doubt in hiding and in touch with her embassy."

"I'm not . . . not sure," he stammered.

"Well, I am. Why did you hire a bunch of fucking incompetents?"

"Jean has always been efficient in the past. I've never had a problem with him before," he said, thinking about the man with the scar on his face. "These people are very good."

"Oh, horse shit! First the bakery. Now this. After two mistakes, he belongs on the bottom of the Mediterranean."

"But . . ."

"No buts." Her sentence had been passed. Her firm voice

communicated that there could be no chance for reconsideration. The message would not be lost on Victor. "I want you to make it happen. I want people to know that I won't tolerate failure."

Victor paused to wipe the perspiration from his forehead. "What about the operation in Saudi Arabia?" he asked.

"We continue as planned," she replied emphatically.

"Shouldn't we reconsider after what David did?"

"From the story you told me earlier, she escaped on her own." She paused to think about David, and Victor's animosity toward the former CIA agent. "The information he's given me so far has panned out. He's been more helpful than some other people I thought were dependable."

Victor's hand was trembling so badly he almost dropped the phone. Still he responded, "But with the girl gone, he'll never show up in Paris before the attack. We'll never get those codes from him."

"It's irrelevant. With the information I've gotten from him, I can have Khalid make adjustments in his attack. Besides, the money in Nielsen's bank account makes him vulnerable as a co-conspirator and will keep him silent. I'll have the bank tip me off if he tries to show for the money. After the attack, I know how to deal with him. I've got connections with some high-ranking people at BMW. We'll use them to lure him out of Israel to Germany to discuss his automotive computer system. We'll kill him there."

Moshe had a red phone in his office that was a secure line to the director of the CIA in Langley. With little fanfare, the line had been installed several years ago to assist the two governments in dealing with international terrorism.

Sagit used that phone to call Margaret Joyner, while Moshe sat across the room and listened. "We managed to get the hostage out of France," Sagit said, "and we're making good progress in getting the answers to both of your questions."

"Good progress isn't enough. I need something specific."

Sagit gulped hard. "We know that there are Saudi Air Force officers involved," she said. "Right now I can't be more specific, and please, Margaret, keep even that information to yourself."

"For God's sake, Sagit, look at a calendar. It's already September 22. People at State and Defense are getting antsy over here. To put it mildly. Frantic is more accurate. They're all over me. You can't believe the pressure I'm under. They want me to have our people get involved directly. Ralph Laurence, God bless him, wants to fly to Riyadh and talk to the Saudi foreign minister."

What a stupid idea, Sagit thought. She was beginning to understand why David didn't want to involve the Americans, apart from his own personal situation. "If he does that, he would destroy everything we've set in place."

"I figured as much. That's why I've been putting them off. But I can't do it forever."

"We need just a little more time."

"How much is a little more?"

"One week. I'll come to Washington in one week with the results of our investigation. If you're not satisfied, that still gives you another week to do whatever you want."

"You've got to tighten that schedule. I can't live with another week's delay."

While Sagit was thinking about the schedule David had given her for General Chambers's visit to Saudi Arabia, Joyner said, "Sagit, you can have three more days and that's all."

Sagit remembered her grandfather, the rug merchant in Baghdad. "The whole world's one big souk," he used to tell her. "So always bargain hard."

"I can be in Washington, on the 27th, five days from now, but that's the absolute best we can do."

"How about the 26th?"

"It's just not possible, honest. We both want accurate information. I can't cut it any closer."

She heard Joyner sigh deeply at the other end of the phone.

"All right," Joyner finally replied. "Fortunately, the President's heavily occupied with his tax-cut bill, and he'll be out west for the next couple of days for campaign appearances. Surprisingly, General Chambers hasn't been on my case about Saudi Arabia. As far as the other wolves are concerned, I'll keep them at bay for another five days. Anything I can do to assist you?"

Sagit was delighted to hear Joyner's question. She had been wondering how she could steer the conversation around to the help they needed. "There is one thing. I could use a couple of American passports. No matter what cover we create, arriving in an Arab country with an Israeli passport guarantees lots of official attention."

"How many do you need?"

"Two. One for me, and one for our Russian immigrant."

"That's easy enough to do. Take a couple of photographs to the American embassy in Tel Aviv. Ask for Mary Pegnataro. She'll have passports for you within an hour, along with credit cards, and bios if anybody should ask."

Sagit hung up the phone and repeated the conversation to Moshe. "And you think you're going to get everything in the next five days?" he asked.

Uncertain how to respond, she left the question hanging in the air.

CHAPTER 14

Alexandra and Carl Holt from Bloomington, Indiana, buckled their seat belts when the captain of Lufthansa flight 820 from Frankfurt to Dubai announced that they were crossing the border from Saudi Arabia into United Arab Emirates, and the plane would be landing in a few minutes. Directly ahead, the sparkling blue waters of the Persian Gulf suggested a quiet calm totally at odds with the violent regimes in Iran and Iraq that abutted its waters. The plane was crowded with a combination of Germans in search of sun and good beaches, wealthy residents of UAE returning from western Europe, their bags stuffed with luxury items, and businessmen in search of the riches that flowed in a neverending stream of black gold.

When the flight attendant, a pretty dark-skinned woman with an Arab name tag, had asked if they had ever been to the UAE before, Alexandra explained that it was their first visit, and they were quite excited. "My husband," she said, pointing at the man next to her staring intently out of the window, "is a professor of world history at Indiana University. He's on sabbatical and anxious to study the history of the region." She herself, Alexandra said, was an amateur photographer and thought "the clear blue skies will be superb for taking good pictures. Besides that, we thought we'd have a perfect vacation. We heard the beaches are great."

The flight attendant nodded in approval. She had been born in neighboring Sharja, and the beaches in the area were wonderful.

Sagit smiled. She presumed that the authorities in Dubai

wouldn't raise any questions when the flight attendant reported on her American passengers in seats 2A and B.

The spanking new terminal was fitting for oil-rich Dubai—with one of the highest per capita incomes anywhere in the world. With their American passports, the Holts moved quickly through passport control. When the agent asked if they had ever visited Israel, Professor Holt quickly answered in an indignant voice, "That place has no interest for us."

In response, the agent nodded and stamped their passports. The customs agent made no effort to look inside Sagit's camera bag.

On David's recommendation, they had reserved a room at the Jebel Ali, a 270-room beachfront resort, with riding stables and a golf course, on 128 lushly landscaped acres about twenty-five miles south of Dubai along the Arabian Gulf. David thought that it would be sparsely occupied because it was out of season. That, coupled with its out-of-the-way location, made it perfect.

He drove carefully along the highway that paralleled the beach, keeping his distance from some of the speeding maniacs on the road. It was a harsh, forbidding terrain with dusty light shrubs and sandy desert. They passed a camel racetrack.

"I never saw one of those before," Sagit said.

"Let's go tonight," David replied.

"You can. Not me."

Their king-size room, facing the Gulf, was huge, and when the bellman had gone, David turned the radio on and checked the room thoroughly for bugs. Satisfied, he took a coin out of his pocket. "Before I order the cot, let's flip to see who gets it tonight."

"Listen, wiseguy. With the kind of hotels you pick, you blew my budget long ago."

"Hey, you forgot, Uncle Sam's paying for this one. We use the credit cards Margaret Joyner supplied."

"From what CIA records must show about your expense reports in the past, I'm surprised that she agreed to do that."

"Ah, but she wants to keep track of where we are. What better way to do that than credit card receipts?"

Sagit was dismayed that she hadn't thought of that. "How'd you figure that out?"

"It's SOP with the Company," David said in a condescending voice, displaying a touch of superiority that CIA officials displayed toward the intelligence agents of other countries. "In the U.S., we have a large budget. We can toss money around."

"We?"

"Sorry. They. Old habits die hard." He looked chagrined. How could he sound like that? He'd never be a part of the Company again, not in a million years. "But we'll fool her. We won't use her credit cards until we check out. By then the information on our location that they disclose won't do her any good."

The sun was setting behind the hotel. Through the glass doors that led to a patio, David could see that dusk had settled over the water. A hotel employee was gathering up the few remaining chairs and umbrellas from the deserted beach.

To avoid having the call traced to the hotel, David picked up Sagit's cell phone. From memory, he dialed his old office number. He got a recording: "You have reached the office of the United States Agricultural Mission. No one is here right now to take your call. Please leave a message, and we will call you back."

He hung up and called Bill Fox at home. Not expecting to reach Fox this early in the evening, he planned to leave a sufficiently enigmatic message so Fox would return the call to the cell phone.

To his surprise, Fox answered. "Bill Fox here, who's calling?"

"It's your old friend, Gunther from Portland, Oregon, Bill." He knew that Fox would recognize his voice; and "Portland, Oregon" was the code they had agreed to use at their London meeting in Green Park. He just hoped that his former aide would have enough wits not to announce his real name. The Saudis might have bugged Fox's house, or someone might be listening in on the unsecured line.

"Good grief, Gunther, I haven't spoken to you since Helen's funeral in Portland. How long has that been?"

"About five years."

"God, how awful. Helen and all those people dying in that gas explosion. I still get the willies thinking about it."

C'mon, Bill, David thought. People may be listening. Don't overdo it.

David continued, "Well anyhow, I'm over in Dubai for a few days on business, trying to sell computer software to the Conoco people. I've got a good connection in Houston. I figure I might be able to parlay it into some business here."

"So how the hell are you?"

"Pretty good overall, I'd say, though I'm not getting any younger." Sagit looked at David apprehensively. Shouldn't he cut this banter and get to the point already? He raised his forefinger, asking her for a little patience. He knew how to play Fox.

"How the hell is old Jack?"

"About the same . . . Say, any chance of getting you to come over here for lunch or dinner? We could catch up on old times."

"You tell me when."

"Tomorrow for lunch. One o'clock at the Jebel Ali. I'll meet you in the lobby."

"I'll be there, pardner."

As they sat down at an isolated table in the luxurious hotel dining room that evening, Sagit said to David, "I don't like the idea of our depending so much on Fox. We can't count on him."

"C'mon, Sagit. We've been through this a dozen times. It's the only chance we have."

She took a deep breath. "I know that, but I still don't like it."

"I've got an idea. Let's forget about Fox and this whole business until noon tomorrow. We've been through so much in the last few days. Tonight and tomorrow morning should be a break for us. We owe it to ourselves. Let's compartmentalize. Please, Sagit."

She hesitated for a moment. "It's hard to turn off."

"Will you try?"

"I'll try. I promise."

"Great."

He signaled the waiter for a bottle of Dom Perignon.

After two glasses of champagne, the rest of the world began to fade into the distance. For the first time, no one and nothing else existed. Just the two of them.

He told her about himself as a young man growing up in Aliquippa, Pennsylvania. He talked about his father's death and how he had felt. He told her about his anguish during the Vietnam War because his leg prevented him from serving his country, and he was relegated to being with draft dodgers and druggies who had no respect for the wonderful country in which they lived.

"I'm no right-wing fascist," he said, "and I can even understand the case against the war, but nobody should burn or piss on the flag, for God's sake."

Wonderful fish courses came. He ordered a bottle of 1985 DRC La Tache, proving that with enough money anything can be brought to anywhere on the globe. He told her about his first sexual experience when he was sixteen, with his cheerleader girlfriend in the backseat of an old Plymouth Valiant after a football game in which he had scored two touchdowns against Ambridge.

The lamb and rice arrived, and he asked her to talk about when she was young. She was startled. For an instant, she hesitated, looking chagrined. She had never spoken about her childhood before with anybody, not Moshe, and none of the men she had dated. With David, though, her inhibitions gave way, and the words came rolling out. She told of her grandfather, the rug merchant, the patriarch who had led the family's exodus from Iraq to Israel when the Iraqis drove out virtually all of the Jews, sending them to the despised Zionist state.

"The Israeli government wanted to help us, but there

were too many of us, all coming at the same time from all of the Arab countries, and the Israeli economy wasn't strong then, like it is now, when the Russian immigrants came. It was so hard. My family settled in the Hatikvah section of Tel Aviv. What a joke. Hatikvah. Hope. We had no hope. It was a slum. Like the Lower East Side of New York a hundred years ago. We were too poor to hope. All we could do was worry about food for the family.

"As long as Grandfather lived, we had some dignity. When he died, that went, too. I was twelve at the time, and I had been his favorite. My mother died a year later. I was the oldest of five children. I had two brothers and two sisters. We all slept in the same room."

He listened to her mesmerized. It was a part of the Israeli saga he had never heard.

"The Israeli economy started to take off then, fueled by money from Jews in the United States, and my father was healthy. He could have worked in construction, but he was lazy. He thought it was beneath him. In truth, it wouldn't have mattered if he had earned money. He wouldn't have gotten food for us, anyway. He would have just lost it playing cards. That gambling of his . . ."

For an instant tears welled up in her eyes. She quickly wiped them away with a napkin.

"What's wrong?" he asked.

"You talked about losing your virginity with a cheerleader in the backseat of a car. Mine wasn't quite as romantic as that. My father gambled it away."

He was nonplussed. "What do you mean he gambled it away?"

"Once when he ran out of money playing cards, he offered sex with me to keep playing, and he lost."

"You're kidding."

She shook her head. "I wish I was. Ach, with such a fat, dirty, smelly old man. I threw up for a full day afterward."

"Why did you do it?"

"Because I was a fool. He was my father, and he told me to go with that man. I listened to him. It was the last time I ever listened to him.

"After that night I decided to take charge of the family, but I needed to earn money. I was only fourteen then, but I was well developed. I looked a lot older and—"

He interrupted her. "With what you'd gone through, it's no wonder."

"So anyhow, I talked to a couple of other girls in the neighborhood, who always seemed to have money. They took me with them down to Ha'Yarkon Street along the beach in Tel Aviv. They told me what to do. I hated it, but I had five mouths to feed. So I did what I had to do. At least most of the customers were clean. Not like the old man. They were American soldiers or American tourists whose wives were out shopping."

A look of disgust covered her face. She was relieved finally to be telling the story, but sickened as she thought about what she had done in those days. Her eyes looked sad, her skin pale. "Then Moshe from the Mossad found me one day. He wanted girls to train and to send into Iraq as Mossad agents. He recruited three of us about the same time. 'Moshe's girls,' they called us. Yael, myself and a girl by the name of Leora, whose family had been upper class in Alexandria, Egypt, until the Jews were expelled in '56."

Past the prostitution part of her story, the color returned to her face. Her voice became animated. "Anyhow, he gave me an apartment in a better area of Tel Aviv and money every month. One day I moved my two brothers and two sisters to that apartment without telling my father. I never saw him again. Moshe sent over a woman—a Holocaust survivor—to live with the children when I went away to Iraq. Sara was her name, from Poland. A wonderful woman. She had lost her whole family in Auschwitz. After I heard about the boxcars and the camps, I didn't feel sorry for myself. As much as the Arabs hated us, even in '48, they never did anything like that."

"You never married?"

She shook her head. "I've had relationships over the years, but I've always broken them off because of my job. I told myself that I was married to the Mossad." She paused, then slowly she added, "That's all rationalization. The truth is, you're the first man . . ."

She stopped in mid-sentence.

"What?" he asked.

She blushed. "I don't want to tell you."

"C'mon." He smiled at her. "No secrets tonight. I'm being honest with you."

She swallowed hard. "You're the first man I've ever really been in love with."

Once the words were out of her mouth, she was relieved. She was in love with him, and she refused to fight that fact any longer.

They didn't order dessert or coffee. Alone, inside the gold-encased elevator, they kissed passionately as the elevator climbed three floors. Inside their room, they kissed the entire time they removed their clothes. Naked, he picked her up and carried her out to the plush white-pillowed chaise on the balcony. There they made love slowly and tenderly in the glow of the moonlight.

For an hour afterward, they lay in each other's arms on the chaise. When she fell asleep, he picked her up and carried her inside.

As he placed her down on the bed, she clutched his arm and said, "And you'll be here in the morning, won't you?"

He kissed her gently. "I promise I will. I love you, too, Sagit."

The next morning they made love on the balcony before breakfast and again afterward. They went downstairs, and he insisted on buying her a bathing suit, an orange string bikini that she said she was too embarrassed to wear, but he convinced her to do it anyhow. They swam and sunned on the beach until the alarm on his wristwatch went off. It was eleven-thirty.

"Time to go to work," he said glumly.

They showered and dressed. Then, pretending she wanted to take pictures, she climbed to the deserted roof of the hotel, with him holding her camera bag. The noon sun was beating down on them as they found a position near an air-conditioning vent to avoid being too obvious. Their backs were to the sea. In front of them were only sand and desert. It was two hundred miles to the Saudi Arabian border.

After she set up her camera, with a powerful telephoto lens on a tripod, David focused on the long road from the highway to the hotel. They had to make sure Fox wasn't being followed.

He studied the passengers in each car or taxi approaching the hotel. About half an hour later, he spotted Fox in the back of a taxi, wearing a tan suit, flowered tie and brown straw hat. There weren't any other cars on the road behind the taxi. Even when Fox's cab pulled up in front of the hotel, the road was empty.

"He's alone," David said.

"Good. Let's get out of here."

She began to disassemble the tripod and camera.

"Wait in our hotel room," she said. "I'll check the lobby to make sure there's no one who came ahead to watch him."

"Good idea. I'll take the camera gear back. Call me if he's by himself."

As Sagit emerged from the elevator on the lobby floor, she looked in vain for Fox for several minutes. Finally, she found him, sitting alone at the hotel bar. From the doorway, she watched him sipping a Perrier, obviously preoccupied, deep in thought. She didn't have a good feeling about him.

Back in the room, she told David: "My instincts say that we shouldn't use Fox. We've got to find another way. Using him will come back and bite us. I've seen it happen again and again in intelligence work, and I'm sure you have, too, when you deal with a guy who's consumed with personal problems."

David grimaced and thought carefully about what she said. Finally he replied, "I can't argue with you about the risks, but I don't see another way, and time's running out on us."

"So what? Let it run out. Suppose you don't get your

revenge on Chambers for forcing you to abandon your former life? So what?"

He took a deep breath, trying to calm himself. He was so close to nailing Chambers, but he needed her support. That meant appealing to her rationally. "It's not that. I want to establish the answer to Margaret Joyner's two questions."

"C'mon, David, it's me. You answered one of them with Khalid. They won't be able to argue you didn't cooperate. Your desire for revenge will ruin us."

"I've got to do it. Please, Sagit, try to understand."

She sighed. "As long as you understand the risks, I guess it's your call."

"Where'll you be?"

"Up here in the room, watching from the patio. Take him out on the beach and then to the poolside restaurant, so I can see you."

David sat down on a bar stool beside Fox. Before the CIA station chief had a chance to look at him, David whispered, "Remember it's Gunther, from Portland, Oregon." Then he slapped Fox on his back and raised his voice, "Bill Fox, how the hell are you?"

"Real good," Fox said, blaring out the words. "Even better since you decided to come to the region and visit." He called to the bartender. "Get my friend from home here a drink."

"Just tonic for me," David said.

They faked a reunion conversation for a few more minutes in case anyone was listening. Then David said, "The beach here is great. Let's take a look before lunch."

There was a jetty built of rocks that reached out into the gulf. It was deserted and would let them talk in total privacy. David led the way.

"Who the hell tried to kill us in London?" Fox asked.

"I think I was the target. At least the first one, but I haven't been able to find out a damn thing. What about you?"

"Zero as well. Of course, I didn't want to tell anybody

I was there. I've kept totally quiet about our meeting. When I got the call from you yesterday, I was ecstatic. I figured that you might have a way of helping me do something about the fundamentalists in Saudi Arabia, or getting me out of the country and into hiding with Jameelah."

Nothing's changed about Fox, David thought. He's still thinking of himself. "I'm afraid it's not that simple. I've learned a lot about what's happening in Saudi Arabia since our London meeting, and we're going to have to solve your problem in stages."

Fox was sweating profusely. He took off his straw hat and mopped the perspiration from his forehead and face with a handkerchief. Then he began fanning himself with the hat. In the meantime, David was studying Fox's face carefully. He wanted to know if Fox would answer the next question truthfully.

"Do you know anything about an October 6 coup in Saudi Arabia?"

"What?" Fox asked incredulously. "What are you talking about?"

"Then you haven't heard anything?"

"Not a word. Is something being planned, and I don't know about it?"

"It's very possible."

"Oh shit. How'd I miss it?"

Because you're a moron and sex has taken over your mind, but he concealed those thoughts and responded as if they were colleagues and partners. "I'm trying to get solid confirming information. If I get that information, I plan to take it back to Washington where I can trade it for immunity from prosecution for myself. At the same time I'll be able to persuade Margaret Joyner to accept your information about Nasser and the fundamentalists and get the Saudi king to crack down on them, which is what you want. So we'll both come out of it winners."

"And you want me to help you get that confirming information? That's why you wanted to see me today?"

David snapped his fingers. "You're still as sharp as ever, Bill."

Fox laughed. "And you're still as full of crap as ever."

"Yeah, that's probably true. But anyhow, I've learned since our London meeting that there's a coup being planned for October 6, and General Chambers is right in the middle of it—on his own and without any authorization from Washington."

Fox's eyes popped wide open. "You're bullshitting me."

"Wish I were."

"Who's working with him from the Saudis? Some of their military people?" Fox resumed, fanning himself with his hat.

"I'm trying to find out."

"I guess I don't look too good as the Company's station chief if I didn't know about any of this."

"That's only half your problem." David sounded concerned and sympathetic. He was Fox's friend, confidant and supporter. "I came to warn you, Bill, that if this thing goes down, Chambers is going to get your ass thrown out of Saudi Arabia and fired from the agency. You'll never be allowed in the country again, and you'll never see Jameelah again."

"He can't do that. Why, Margaret Joyner would never . . ."

"C'mon, Bill. Your personal life has hardly been a model of propriety."

Fox was crestfallen. "And unfortunately Chambers knows about that."

David nodded. "You know these things always get out."

"But Chambers has been so friendly to me on his last two visits. He's brought me a case of Johnny Walker each time. We've had one-on-one private briefings. He's treating me with respect."

A cigarette boat shot by in the Gulf. David paused to watch a couple of oil-rich Gulf playboys push the speed higher and higher. He was waiting for the engine to explode, but instead it just died. As they floated with the current, they waved for help.

David turned back to Fox. "He's conning you, Bill. He's

always been a wily bastard. You know that. What's he want from you in return?''

Fox hesitated. David held up for a minute, not wanting to appear too anxious. C'mon Bill, he thought. Grab the hook. When Fox didn't respond, David continued, "Look, Bill, I'm trying to save your ass. If you don't want my help, that's all right.''

Feeling defensive, Fox tried to rationalize. "He wants all my reports to Washington to be blindly routed through his office. He'll read them and immediately pass them on.''

"And you agreed to do that?"

"He promised to make me deputy director of the DIA, the first of the year. He wants to evaluate my work till then."

"And the coup's scheduled for October 6." David was losing patience with this fool. His tone was scornful. "What's that tell you?"

"That he'll kill the messages he doesn't want anyone to see. That he's playing me for a fool and a sucker.''

"You got it."

"And what do you think I should do about the bastard?"

Relieved that he now had Fox precisely where he wanted him, David was ready to move on. "I've got an idea that will help both of us.''

Fox looked at him warily. "Yeah, what?"

"Chambers is arriving in Saudi Arabia tomorrow.''

"I know that."

"When he's there, he's going to have a meeting with an air force colonel by the name of Khalid.''

"Your old friend Khalid?"

"Exactly. My hunch is that they'll be discussing the coup in that meeting, and—"

Fox interrupted. "Sorry, Greg, I doubt if I'll be invited.''

"I'm sure you won't be, but I want a tape of that meeting.''

Fox took his handkerchief out of his pocket and wiped his face again. "How do you propose I do that?"

"You used to be very good at that sort of thing, as I

remember," David said, trying to make it sound simple, "and you have all of the Company's toys at your disposal."

Fox was suspicious. "And what'll you do with the tape if I can pull it off?"

"Take it to Washington and destroy General Chambers—the one big obstacle in the path of both of our future pursuits of happiness."

Fox curled up his lips pensively. His hand with the hat trembled. "I don't know, Greg, bugging the chairman of the Joint Chiefs. You're asking for a lot."

David put his arm around Fox's back and turned them toward the hotel. "Well, you and I are going to have lunch now. You think about it while we eat."

David led the way back to the outdoor restaurant alongside the pool. It was late now. They were the only patrons for lunch. That suited David. When their cold seafood salads came, he said to Fox, "I assume that you're still seeing your Saudi princess?"

"Jameelah. Yeah."

"It's a risky business."

Fox was defiant. "Some things are worth running risks for."

Not wanting to unnerve Fox at this critical juncture, David backed off. "You're the only one who can judge that."

"It's really all Alice's fault," Fox finally said. "She wouldn't move over here. Neither of us could live like that, seeing each other every couple of months, year in and year out. And when we were together, things didn't go so well even then. Sexually, I mean. I guess, you use it or lose it. Now with Jameelah, I feel like a young man again."

What an idiot, David thought, but I'll play your silly game. "And if you help me and do what I asked, you'll be able to continue on in your relationship with Jameelah for a very long time."

"That's what I want. To live with her in the lake region of northern Italy, where nobody'll bother us."

"Takes big money to do that," David said gingerly, not wanting to confront Fox directly with his suspicions of the

Henri Napoleon payoff from Madame Blanc, for fear that Fox would panic and refuse to make the Chambers tape.

"Money's not a problem," Fox replied quickly, adding further fuel to David's suspicions.

For several minutes, they ate in silence. Finally, Fox put his fork down and said, "I'll make the tape you want of Chambers's conversation under one condition."

David was elated, but he kept his reaction in check, wanting to hear what Fox wanted. "What's that?"

"You won't tell anyone how you got it."

"Agreed."

"How do you want me to deliver it to you?"

Under the table, David rolled his hands into fists and squeezed them in a sign of victory. "Chambers's meeting with Khalid is tomorrow. Have a courier dressed in a business suit come to the lobby of this hotel the following morning at eleven A.M. Tell him to put a white flower in his lapel. He should turn the package over to the man who identifies himself as Gunther."

Back in Riyadh, Fox went to work making calls to the various high-ranking military people who would have knowledge about the general's plans for the next day. The general's recent open closeness with Fox, along with his position as CIA station chief, gave him easy access to information.

He learned that Chambers's plane was scheduled to arrive at 0800 in Riyadh. The meeting with Colonel Khalid was set for 1400 in the office of General Foreman, whose office Chambers regularly used when he visited Riyadh, holding court and having his visitors come as if he were a foreign potentate. Fox's last meeting with Chambers had occurred in that office.

Armed with that information, Fox opened the combination lock to the Company's storage room that housed the "toys," as Greg had described them. In a matter of minutes, he found exactly what he was looking for, a tiny microcassette recording machine that could be taped to the bottom of the conference table in Foreman's office, and was sensitive enough to pick up any conversation in the room. He programmed it to turn on at 1400 and operate for two hours.

With the recording device in his briefcase, he drove to the four-story building that housed General Foreman's office. It was almost midnight. All of the lights in the building were off except for those in the front entrance hall. A Sergeant Prescott was on duty, just inside the front door.

Fox flashed his ID, but it was unnecessary. Prescott knew that Fox was the CIA station chief and a confidant of General Chambers.

"Can I help you, sir?" the sergeant asked.

"Just here on a routine security check of the building before the general's visit tomorrow."

Prescott was surprised. "I thought DIA already did that."

"Redundancy on security checks is never a bad idea. We can't be too careful with a chairman of Joint Chiefs coming."

"I agree with that, sir," Prescott said as he waved Fox through. Once he reached the top floor of the building, where Foreman's office was located, he turned on a single light in the far end of the corridor, away from the office. In semi-darkness, he advanced down the corridor. Inside Foreman's office it was almost pitch dark. Fox extracted a small flashlight from his briefcase, and he crawled along the carpet and under the oak table. With trembling and perspiring hands, Fox fixed the recording device to the bottom of the table.

At ten minutes before eleven, David stationed himself in front of the newsstand in the lobby of the hotel, appearing to glance at the periodicals in half a dozen languages. He spotted the thin, slight young man with the white carnation in his lapel as soon as he walked through the automatic sliding glass doors. In his right hand, the man held a dark brown knapsack.

As David moved across the lobby to meet the man, he said softly, "Gunther."

The courier reached into the knapsack and extracted a cardboard box wrapped extensively with heavy tape, which he handed to David. Trying to conceal his excitement, David walked slowly to the elevator and went back to their room, where Sagit was waiting.

Quickly, they cut off the wrapping tape.

Inside, there was a microcassette and a small machine for playing it. David searched for a note from Fox, but there wasn't one. That was smart, he decided. Fox was using his brain again.

First, they listened to the entire tape once. The key segment was twenty-two minutes into the tape. They played that portion again:

GENERAL CHAMBERS: You're doing a good job, Colonel Khalid. I'm certain that your effort will succeed. In eleven days it'll be the end of the House of Saud, and the beginning of your rule in Saudi Arabia.

COLONEL KHALID: I don't want a bloodbath here.

GENERAL CHAMBERS: You won't have one. Not the way you've planned it.

COLONEL KHALID: Unless the American government intervenes militarily on the side of the Saudi king.

GENERAL CHAMBERS: You worry too much. I told you in our first meeting that won't happen. The American government won't send a single soldier to the aid of the king.

COLONEL KHALID: But have you told your president about the coup? Has he agreed not to intervene? Or is this just your prediction or hope?

GENERAL CHAMBERS *(irritably)*: Your carping on this point is beginning to annoy me. I speak for my government. That's all you need to know."

David clicked off the machine and said gleefully, "We've got the bastard. He's mine."

Sagit didn't share his enthusiasm. "Don't get too confident," she told David somberly. "Everything we have depends upon Bill Fox. With that guy's personal problems, it could all prove to be a house of cards."

*   *   *

That afternoon Carl and Alexandra Holt stopped at the desk of a travel agent in the hotel lobby and booked a flight to Indianapolis, Indiana, with connections in Frankfurt and Washington.

As the travel agent repeated the word "Washington," David felt apprehensive. What would be waiting for him in the American capital after these long five years? Sagit told the hotel clerk that a family emergency had developed at home, and unfortunately they had to leave early, but they hoped to return to Dubai soon and "to your beautiful and exotic country." That seemed acceptable to the clerk. Sagit doubted that he would report anything suspicious to the police about his American visitors. They had hidden the microcassette inside one of Sagit's cameras. She disposed of the machine in an airport trash bin in the women's rest room, immediately before clearing customs.

At Frankfurt Airport, she called Moshe from a public phone. "Dubai worked out the way we had hoped," she said. "I took a lot of good pictures."

"Where are you off to now?"

"We're headed back home, to the good old U.S.A."

"I'll bet you can't wait to get there."

"You can say that again."

"How's Carl?"

"You know the professor. He's always eager to get to the next thing."

CHAPTER 15

"Play that damn tape one more time," Margaret Joyner said to Sagit and David in a voice trembling with anger. "I want to hear the entire forty-five minutes that General Chambers was with Colonel Khalid."

The three of them were alone in Joyner's office at CIA headquarters in Langley.

As the tape started to play a second time, Margaret leaned back in her burgundy leather high-backed chair, with her glasses up on her head and her eyes closed, listening carefully to each word and intonation. Her hands were joined together, with her fingers interlocking, and pulled up under her chin. Deep creases lined her forehead. She was stunned by the tape. How could Chambers do this? she thought. The answer came to her in an instant. Because he was an arrogant egomaniac who thought he knew more than anybody else in Washington—a self-anointed demigod who was divinely designated to make national security decisions. She was trying to piece together Chambers's motivation for backing Khalid. Did he believe that military rule in Saudi Arabia would be preferable for the United States to a fundamentalist regime, allied to Iran, which was the other alternative as the House of Saud crumbled? Or was he worried about the possibility of the United States becoming bogged down in a protracted land war in the Middle East, as it had in Vietnam? Regardless of his motives, this was still wrong. He was usurping the power of the President, and he should be discharged from the military.

When the tape was finished, she took off her glasses and

fiddled with them. Sagit and David sat silently, letting her think, waiting for the verdict.

Finally, she said, "Well, you answered the two questions that I asked. The Saudi ringleader is Colonel Khalid. And Madame Blanc's not worried about the possibility of American intervention on the side of the king because Khalid's assured her that he's gained the support of General Chambers. So I guess you've carried out your end of the bargain. You're entitled to immunity from prosecution."

While relieved to hear her words, David had no intention of stopping. "But this is only the beginning," he said. "How do we proceed now against Chambers?"

"*We* don't do anything," Joyner said curtly. "I'm going to install you two in a little country inn, the Hilltop, about half an hour from here in the Virginia countryside. We sometimes use it as a safe house. The question is what do *I* do now, and right now I'm not sure." She tossed her glasses on the desk. "This is so damned explosive," she continued. "If I go to the President first, he'll ask me if I've played the tape for General Chambers, and what does the good general have to say about it? And if I go to Chambers first, he'll scream bloody murder and go on the attack."

"But what can Chambers possibly do?" David asked. "I'd give anything to be there when that pompous jerk hears the tape. The evidence is so clear and convincing. It nails him to the wall."

The CIA director gave a short, nervous laugh. "You of all people shouldn't underestimate General Chambers. Besides, he hates you so much that he'll do anything to destroy you."

"And I feel the same way about him." David's tone was hostile and belligerent. "As far as I'm concerned, it's payback time, and I'll shout for joy when the President strips those medals off his jacket and tosses him out of the military."

Joyner was irritated. "You two boys can play your games of macho revenge if you want to, but I won't let President Waltham or our government get caught up in the cross fire.

We've got an important question to face right now: do we go to the Saudi king and tell him about Colonel Khalid?"

"You can't do that," David protested. "You'd be signing Khalid's death warrant."

Joyner brushed a few strands of gray hair out of her eyes. "Of course, you don't want us to tell the Saudi king about Khalid. You want Khalid and his military buddies to succeed. That's where you were five years ago."

"Khalid's a good man. Saudi Arabia would be a lot better with him in charge, rather than the corrupt and repressive House of Saud."

"At least you're consistent."

"Really, Margaret." David said, raising his voice, while he leaned across the desk, close to her. "Khalid's the only chance for that country, which means he's the only chance for assuring the continued flow of Saudi oil to the United States in the long run."

"Don't you shout at me."

David pulled back. "Sorry. I got a little carried away."

Furious, she stared at him. "No offense, Mr. Nielsen, but you forfeited your right to participate in the American government's decision on this issue when you decided to turn tail and run five years ago. Now that the exile's returned, he doesn't get to pick up where he left off."

"I had no choice," he replied sharply.

Sagit squirmed in her chair, unhappy that the discussion with Joyner had taken this confrontational tone, but not knowing what to do about it.

Joyner was ready with a harsh retort to David. "I know that's what you thought at the time, but have you ever considered that you may have been wrong?"

"Hindsight's always twenty-twenty. I would still have done it the same way, but I'm not the issue now, General Chambers is."

Sagit saw her opportunity. "Yes, unfortunately, General Chambers is the issue," she interjected.

"I'm afraid you're right, Sagit," Joyner responded in a softer voice. Then she chuckled sardonically. "Here's the irony, Greg."

"David, please. I've gotten used to it."

"Here's the irony. You agree with what General Chambers is trying to do, namely keep the U.S. on the sidelines and let Khalid bring down the House of Saud."

"Yes."

"At the same time, you want to destroy Chambers to get even with him for what he did to you five years ago. You're walking quite an intellectual tightrope there."

"I realize that, but he hung himself. He's crossed the line. He's usurped the power of the President. When I used to live here, that violated something called the Constitution. I presume it still does. I just think President Waltham should be the one to make the decision of what action the United States takes in response to Khalid's coup."

She pointed to the bruises on David's face that were now healing. "What happened to you?" she asked.

"Someone tried to kill me in Paris. A couple of Iranians. For the help I gave the Shah at the end, they put me near the top of their hit list. Even higher than Salman Rushdie."

"Who tipped off Tehran about you?"

"That's what I want to know. At the time, I included you on my list of possibilities, Margaret."

Sagit cringed at his words. Not too tactful, David, she thought.

"Are you crazy?" the CIA director fired back.

"Why not? I was a renegade agent. The Paris attack happened right after Sagit came to Washington."

Outraged, Joyner shot to her feet. Her face was bright red. She raised her right arm, poised to throw him out of the office. "The hot desert sun must have fried your brain. You sound like a paranoid fool. I wouldn't have been fighting for your immunity at the same time I was arranging for your execution."

"Forgive me. I shouldn't have said that." He thought about his conversation with Victor Foch at the French café after the attack. "It's just that everybody seems to have a good excuse, but sooner or later, I'm going to find out who did it."

Joyner glanced out of the window, trying to make up her mind how to proceed.

They watched her in silence. Finally, she turned back to her desk and gathered into a neat pile the notes she had made this morning.

Sagit asked, "Well, Margaret, what did you decide? Whom do you go to first, President Waltham, or General Chambers?"

"Neither. First I go to the techies downstairs. I want a written statement from a sound expert that it's really General Chambers's voice on that tape."

Sagit looked horrified. "You don't think that I—"

"No, of course not, but at least I want to take that argument away from General Chambers. After that, my next stop will be the Oval Office. The boss was anxious to get his tax cut bill through the Congress before they recess for the election, but it's not going to happen. So he's cranky and unpredictable these days. I don't want to risk Chambers getting in there before I do."

Joyner buzzed her secretary and told her to arrange transportation for Sagit and David to Hilltop. Then she turned back to her visitors.

"One question that's going to come up is how you two happened to get this tape of General Chambers's conversation."

Sagit looked at David, who responded without hesitating. "I'm afraid I can't tell you that."

Joyner was astounded. "C'mon. You've got to do better than that."

"I'm sorry, Margaret. The tape will have to speak for itself."

"That won't make my job any easier." She paused. "We can start that way for now, but don't be surprised if I come back to you on this point."

"I can't believe Brad would do this," an incredulous President Waltham said to Joyner.

They were alone in the Oval Office. On the other side

of the thick bulletproof windows, half a dozen gardeners in gray overalls raked leaves.

"There's got to be a mistake. Are you sure the tape's accurate?"

"I ran it through the Agency's voice lab before coming over, and I personally spoke to Yoshi Ueno, our top sound expert. She says that it's clearly General Chambers's voice. That's good enough for me."

Waltham's face showed the anguish of betrayal. "But if it's accurate," the President said, "then that means Brad thinks he's the President of the United States, because he sure as hell never talked to me about any of this. Right?"

"I think that's a reasonable conclusion."

"Do you remember anybody electing my supposed friend, General Chambers, to be President of the United States?" he asked in a voice dripping with sarcasm.

"Not that I recall."

He waved his hands in disgust. "Christ, this whole thing makes me madder'n hell. I should fire the bastard like Truman did with MacArthur. What do you think?"

Instead of waiting for her answer, he hit the intercom and picked up the phone, "Kathy, get the attorney general on the horn."

Seconds later, Ed Simpson was on the phone.

"I've got an emergency that needs your immediate attention," the President said. "Drop whatever you're doing and get over here right now."

"I'm on my way, Harry."

Joyner sketched in the background for a flabbergasted attorney general. Then she played the tape again. As she listened to it for what was now the fourth time, Joyner practically had Chambers's words memorized.

When it was finished, the President turned to Simpson and said, "That fucker Chambers is out of line. Plain and simple. And as commander-in-chief, I should fire him ASAP. Don't you agree, Ed?"

The attorney general glanced at Joyner, paused to

straighten the blue polka-dot bow tie that he was wearing with matching suspenders, and looked over at the President. "I'll reserve my judgment until I hear what General Chambers has to say."

The President snorted. "Typical waffling lawyer answer."

"No, I'm serious, Harry. I know that wasn't the answer you were looking for, but I told you when I took this job that I wouldn't be a yes man. I wouldn't be one of those attorney generals who is in the President's pocket. I'd give you my honest independent judgment on legal issues. It hasn't been easy. But I think I've done it, and you've been the better for it."

"All right, Mr. Integrity. Since we know from the CIA sound people that it's General Chambers's voice, you tell me what Chambers could possibly say that would justify his words on the tape."

Simpson shrugged. "I don't know the answer to that question, but I do know that I learned long ago, as both a prosecutor and a defense lawyer, never to reach a conclusion about guilt until the accused gets his chance to respond."

The President scowled. "I guess that's what I deserve for taking you off the bench and making you AG."

"No, I'm serious, Harry. Personally, I've never been fond of General Chambers. He's slick and manipulative with the press and with other top officials in the government."

"With me, too?"

Simpson gulped hard. "Well, let's just say he's worked mightily to ingratiate himself with you. So I've got no brief for Chambers, but he's still entitled to his day in court . . . so to speak."

"Okay, Ed, I want you to undertake an investigation. You be the judge, but for God's sake, conduct your inquiry with speed, in real time. Not lawyers' time. I'm talking hours, not days and weeks. This thing's unfolding too fast. If this tape's accurate, we're talking about a coup in ten days in the world's richest source of oil. And make sure it stays out of the press."

*   *   *

Following the President's order, the AG moved on the inquiry that afternoon. He summoned General Chambers to his office on the fifth floor of Main Justice—the gray stone structure that occupies a whole block between Ninth and Tenth on Pennsylvania Avenue. With Chambers and Joyner seated on opposite sides of a rectangular conference table, and Simpson at one end, he directed his secretary to play the tape. Being an experienced trial lawyer, he kept his eyes trained on the general as the tape played. Chambers looked down at the table, listening with a cold, detached expression, stroking his jaw and shaking his head.

When it was over, Chambers shot to his feet in righteous indignation. "Who made this goddamned slanderous phony tape?" he shouted.

Simpson replied, "There's no need to raise your voice like that." Then he turned to Joyner.

"I don't know the answer to that," she replied.

"But Greg Nielsen delivered it to you. Didn't he?"

"That's correct."

Chambers charged around the room with his hands behind his back and a surly expression on his face. "The bastard's trying to ruin me. He's still carryin' on our battle from five years ago. Where the hell is he? I want him to explain how he got that fuckin' tape."

Simpson interjected. "You can sit down and lower your voice, General Chambers."

"I'm sorry, Ed." Chambers said, sounding abashed. Then he continued in a soft, pleasant voice, trying to persuade the AG that he was the reasonable one in this imbroglio. "This whole thing's so outrageous. I lost it for a minute." Watching the general return to his chair, Simpson was beginning to doubt the accuracy of the tape. Could Chambers be that good an actor?

"Now, tell me, General Chambers, what difference does it make how Nielsen got the tape?"

"All the difference in the world, Ed." His voice was smooth and self-confident. He was ready for a man-to-man chat with Simpson, whom he was now looking at exclusively, as if they were a couple of good old boys getting together in the locker room after a round of golf. "Because the whole thing's a damned lie. The tape's a fabrication. A creation of modern technology."

"Do you deny that you participated in the conversation with Colonel Khalid portrayed on this tape?"

"Of course I deny it. I had a meeting on September 24 with Colonel Khalid in Riyadh. That much is true. But we discussed expanded cooperation between the Saudi and American air forces, and that was all. This tape's a phony. I'll tell you what happened, very candidly. Nielsen must have had somebody bug my meeting with Khalid and then take a tape of that meeting, put it together with recorded public speeches of mine, and use sophisticated sound equipment to make up this phony tape." He paused and looked pointedly at Joyner. "Since he pulled crap like this, he's obviously not carryin' out his end of the bargain we made. In my opinion, he just blew the deal for the immunity we gave him. He should go straight to jail to await trial for what he did to me and the Americans who died at Dhahran five years ago. And if you hand me a Bible, I'll swear to every word I just told you."

"How about a polygraph?" Joyner asked.

Without hesitating, Chambers replied, "Absolutely."

The AG weighed Chambers's words and then turned to Joyner: "Could Nielsen have prepared a phony tape the way General Chambers just said?"

"I don't know for sure. I'll have to ask our sound people."

"But what do you think? Is it possible?"

Chambers was nodding his head.

The AG added, "Talk to the your technical people in Langley this afternoon, Margaret. Ask them whether it would be possible to prepare this tape using an individual's recorded statements. General Chambers, you can do the same with DIA. Then both of you meet me back here tomorrow morning at ten." Simpson paused. "General Chambers, I'll listen to anything else you have tomorrow morning as well. After that, I'll file my report with the President. I'm doing this according to the book."

Chambers looked very pleased to hear that. In a relaxed, complimentary voice, he replied, "I don't doubt that, Ed. You've always played fair, and I appreciate that."

It was the height of the afternoon rush hour when General Chambers's limousine pulled away from the entrance to the Department of Justice on Pennsylvania Avenue and began the slow trek back toward the Pentagon. The Fourteenth Street Bridge resembled a parking lot, and the black Lincoln Town Car inched along in traffic. In the backseat, the general was on the car phone with Major Corbin, the head of internal security at American military command headquarters in Saudi Arabia, whom he had just woken out of a sound sleep.

"I have reason to believe," he told the major, selecting his words carefully, "that there was a breach of security on my recent visit on September 24 in Riyadh. Someone may have planted a listening device in General Foreman's office. I want you to find out who it was."

"Yes sir," the major snapped. "When do you need the information?"

"An hour ago. And I want you to regard all of this as highly confidential. Nobody, including General Foreman, is to be told anything unless I personally authorize it. Is that understood?"

"Yes, sir."

Two hours later, General Chambers was back in his office, standing at the window, staring at the nearly empty Pentagon parking lot, and thinking about who the traitor could have been. He quickly rejected General Foreman, who had only recently been transferred from Germany. His focus turned to General Mac McCallister, the base commander at Dhahran. McCallister had been in Saudi Arabia five years ago, and Chambers always believed Mac had sided with Greg Nielsen, although Mac never had the guts to come out and say it to his face. More recently, Chambers felt Mac was part of a cabal of generals who were resentful of the power he had as chairman of the Joint Chiefs. Mac could easily have gotten access to General Foreman's office and planted the bug.

Suddenly, General Chambers's telephone rang. It was Major Corbin. "I have one thing to report, sir."

"What's that?" Chambers asked, holding his breath.

"I just learned from Sergeant Prescott, who was on duty the night before your visit, that at approximately 2345, William Fox, the CIA section chief, entered the building through the front door to do a security check that was never authorized by me. I don't know if—"

Chambers interrupted him. "Thank you for your help, Major. Now it seems as if I was given incorrect information. Apparently, there was not a breach of security."

"I'm happy to hear that, sir."

"And I trust that you'll keep our little discussion today to yourself?"

"Absolutely, sir."

When he hung up the phone, Chambers mused aloud, "Fox. That little prick Fox did it." Fox had been close with Nielsen five years ago. He was vulnerable personally right now. Nielsen could have used him.

Chambers was relieved. McCallister would have been difficult to deal with. On the other hand, he could easily crush that little turd Fox, and in an instant he knew exactly how to do it.

Chambers's next call was to Fox.

It was almost five in the morning in Riyadh when the phone rang, and Fox stopped tossing and turning in bed to answer it. "Fox here," he said in a groggy voice.

Then Chambers replied in a voice as cold as steel: "This is General Chambers. Now, you listen up, mister. You're going to do what I order you to do right now, or else I'll tell the Saudi authorities about you and your loving princess, Jameelah."

Wanting to have as much information as possible for the next day's showdown with General Chambers, Margaret Joyner rode out to the Hilltop to have dinner with David and Sagit and to brief them about what had happened this afternoon. As the driver of her car focused hard on the narrow, winding country roads, Joyner closed her eyes in the backseat, trying to guess what Chambers would do. Then it struck her. Bill Fox!

She had forgotten that Fox had been Greg Nielsen's assistant. He must have helped Nielsen get the tape. That conclusion sent a chill up her spine. Damn, she thought, suddenly feeling a personal measure of responsibility for the drama that was unfolding. She had heard unconfirmed reports that Fox's personal life was in a shambles with the breakup of his marriage, but she hadn't authorized a confidential investigation of Fox because she believed that loyal longtime CIA agents were entitled to a measure of privacy. That viewpoint of hers had been sneered at by top Company officials, and now she was beginning to realize that however good her motivation, she shouldn't have left an agent in the field whose personal situation might have made him vulnerable to manipulation by someone like Greg Nielsen. But it would make Fox subject to manipulation by General Chambers as well. She wasn't getting a good feeling about where this was headed. Using Bill Fox wasn't your best move of all time, David, she thought somberly.

Margaret Joyner waited until dinner was over, after David had drunk some wine, to tell him the result of her deduction. The three of them were seated in front of a roaring fire. While Joyner and David were drinking cognac, Sagit sipped her third cup of coffee. She figured that after the report Joyner had given her and David of her meetings with the President, the attorney general and Chambers, she would never sleep tonight in any event.

The CIA director looked squarely at David and said, "I'm not asking you to confirm that it was Bill Fox who helped you. If you promised him confidentiality, then you can keep it. But I want you to know that I figured it out. I don't care what you say."

"So why are you telling me this?" David responded testily.

"Because if I figured it out, I suspect General Chambers has as well. And because Fox has some personal problems, which you may or may not know about, he may prove to be an undependable ally."

"I know all about Fox's personal problems," David

snapped back, "but desperate times require desperate measures. He was the only game in town. And as for Chambers figuring out it was Fox, so what? The tape is the evidence. It speaks for itself. What difference does it make who planted the bug?"

"I think you're underestimating General Chambers. I hope to hell I'm wrong, but Chambers plays to win, regardless of the consequences."

"I know that all too well."

The CIA chief and David were staring at each other. Neither of them saw Sagit purse her lips, look down at her hands and shake her head sadly.

General Chambers arrived ten minutes late for the meeting with Simpson and Joyner. In his hand he held a thin brown briefcase. His entire demeanor manifested righteousness. He was aggrieved. He wanted vindication.

"Coffee?" Attorney General Simpson asked.

"I prefer to get down to business, Ed. Serious accusations have been leveled against me. I want to clear my name."

Simpson put down his china cup, moved over a yellow legal pad and picked up a pen. "Very well then, we'll begin," he said in his inquiring jurist's voice. "Margaret, have you asked CIA technical officials whether the tape could be a fabrication?"

"Their answer is that it's possible but extremely unlikely." She sounded tentative and uncertain.

Simpson turned to General Chambers, "What about the DIA experts?"

"Ditto. They tell me that it's technically possible." There was nothing tentative or uncertain in the general's voice. He sounded victorious, while trying not to gloat because that would put off the AG.

"So where's that leave us?"

"Fortunately, you don't have to resolve that issue," Chambers said self-confidently. "We know for certain that this tape's a phony."

They both looked at him with startled expressions.

"Why do you say that?" Simpson asked.

Instead of responding, Chambers reached into his briefcase and pulled out a document. As he handed copies to Simpson and Joyner, he had the look of a blackjack player holding an ace and a king.

"This affidavit was faxed to me this morning," Chambers said.

While they read, he sat in silence, watching with a smug expression on his face.

> I, William Fox, do hereby swear that the following statement is true and accurate:
>
> 1. On September 22, Greg Nielsen called me from Dubai and asked me to meet him at the Hotel Jebel Ali in Dubai on the following day. I agreed to do so.
> 2. When we met in Dubai, Nielsen told me that he wanted to repay General Chambers for what had happened five years ago. He had learned that I had committed an indiscretion with a young married Saudi princess, whom I love, and he threatened to disclose this relationship to the husband of the princess unless I helped him in his effort to gain revenge against General Chambers.
> 3. Specifically, he asked me to create a taped conversation between General Chambers and Colonel Khalid following a script which he handed to me. Then I was told to destroy the script. Reluctantly, I did exactly what he asked, and the tape I created is the one he brought to Washington. The taped conversation is a complete phony.
> 4. I regret my role in this matter. I am prepared to resign from the CIA and to accept my punishment. Mrs. Joyner, I beg your forgiveness.
>
> Signed and sworn before me this 26th day of September. Gladys Keller, Notary.

Joyner finished reading and shook her head in disbelief. Dammit, she should have ordered an investigation of Fox's life when she heard about his marital problems. She would have learned about the Saudi princess and pulled him out of there. But she was fairly certain that the affidavit was the phony, not the tape. How could she ever prove it?

Grasping at straws, she said, "Let's get Bill Fox on the speaker phone."

Simpson was leaning back in his chair, tugging on his blue polka-dot suspenders and trying to decide what to do about this legal and political quagmire. He was quick to jump on Joyner's suggestion. "An excellent idea, Margaret."

It was the end of the afternoon in Saudi Arabia. In his office, Fox was waiting for the call that General Chambers had told him would almost certainly come from Attorney General Simpson once Chambers turned over the affidavit.

Fox first heard Mrs. Joyner's voice, "Bill, this is Margaret Joyner. I'm on a speaker phone in Washington with Attorney General Simpson and General Chambers."

Simpson broke in. It was his investigation, and he would question the witness. "Mr. Fox, this is the attorney general of the United States. Are you alone there?"

"Yes, sir, I am."

"I want to know, did you prepare and fax an affidavit to General Chambers this morning?" the AG asked crisply.

There was a long pause.

"Well, Mr. Fox, did you hear the question?"

"Yes, sir, I did," Fox responded in a trembling voice.

"You did what?"

"What you said . . . I typed up an affidavit."

"And you signed it in front of a notary?"

"Yes, sir."

"Her name was Gladys Keller?"

"Yes, sir."

"Are you aware that it's a crime of perjury if any statement in that affidavit is false?"

"Yes, sir."

"I'm going to ask my secretary to read a document to you. Then I'm going to ask you whether that's the affidavit you prepared and signed. Do you understand?"

"Yes, sir, I do."

When his secretary finished reading the affidavit, Simpson asked Fox if that was the affidavit he prepared. In response, there was a barely audible grunt.

"You'll have to speak up, Mr. Fox," Simpson said.

"Yes, sir, that's my affidavit," he replied in a halting voice.

"And you admit to preparing a fabricated tape of a conversation between General Chambers and a Colonel Khalid of the Saudi Arabia Air Force?"

"Yes, sir. I did that."

"Why did you prepare the tape, Mr. Fox?"

"Like I said in the affidavit, Greg Nielsen blackmailed me on account of this Saudi princess."

"Then why did you admit preparing the tape in the affidavit?"

"Because when I spoke to General Chambers, I realized that preparing this tape was wrong. I'm willing to accept my punishment."

"Where did you do the work preparing the tape?"

"Mrs. Joyner, am I allowed to answer?"

"Yes. Please."

"The CIA has a sophisticated lab here in Saudi Arabia. As Mrs. Joyner knows, I've worked a lot with sound and other technical equipment. I've gotten training from people in Langley. It's not that difficult if you have a sample of the recorded voices of each of the participants. It's not like you splice words together anymore. That's how we used to do it in the old days. Now we have this fantastic new machine that Voice Com, a company in Silicon Valley, built for the Agency. It's called a Scrambler. All you have to do is enter a sample of the voice of each speaker into a computer, with a numerical code, and then you type in the text that you want, designating each speaker by number in a script format. The machine does the rest."

"How did you get a sample of each speaker's voice?"

"I had a meeting with General Chambers before his meeting with Colonel Khalid on September 24. I wore a wristwatch which is also a recording device. Then when I met with Colonel Khalid later that day, I did the same thing."

Fox's voice sounded pitiful and pathetic, but also credible. As Margaret Joyner listened to him, something strange happened. She suddenly found herself becoming confused. Was Fox now telling the truth? Had Greg Nielsen tried to dupe her with a phony tape he had asked Fox to prepare? Had he persuaded Sagit to go along with him? Or maybe the Israelis had their own reasons for wanting to destroy Chambers, or for wanting to influence U.S. policy in Saudi Arabia.

The attorney general said: "You realize, Mr. Fox, that what you did is cause for dismissal from the Agency, and that you could be charged with a crime."

"Yes, sir, I know that. I was hoping that by being honest now you wouldn't be so hard on me."

"That's not a decision for me to make. That's something that will have to be decided by Tom Roche, the general counsel of the CIA. I imagine you'll be hearing from him."

"Yes, sir."

The AG looked at Joyner and Chambers. "You two have anything to add?"

"Nothing," they replied in unison.

"Thank you, Mr. Fox," Simpson said and clicked off the phone.

He turned to Joyner. "Does the Agency have that kind of voice Scrambler machine in Saudi Arabia from Voice Com, and does it work as Fox said?"

"I don't know. I'll have to make a call to Langley."

"Why don't you do that? You can use a phone in the outer office."

When Joyner called Yoshi Ueno, in the agency's lab at Langley, the sound expert confirmed everything Fox had said about the Scrambler. By now Joyner found herself becoming convinced of the truth of what Fox had just said. On the other hand, she couldn't believe that Sagit was a part of this scheme. If she was, Joyner would raise hell with Moshe, no matter how much she liked Sagit, and she'd make sure the President personally called the Israeli prime minister.

She dialed the number of Sagit's cell phone.

"Are you alone?" Joyner asked curtly.

"David's out running. I'm at the Hilltop drinking coffee."

"What happened when David met with Bill Fox in Dubai?"

Sagit was alarmed. Margaret's question could only mean that her dire prediction about General Chambers last night after dinner had come true. "I don't know. He wanted to have the meeting himself. Just the two of them. I didn't argue. I thought that made the most sense. So they were outside, on the beach, and then in the patio dining room." She paused for an instant, trying to frame her answer carefully, trying to select the right words in English. She wanted to do everything she could to help David, and yet she still had her responsibilities to Moshe and the Mossad. "I stayed in the room or in the lobby of the hotel, watching them and the surrounding area for anything suspicious. But I never heard what they said. And I never spoke to Bill Fox. I saw him only briefly before and after his conversation with David."

"Afterwards, what did David tell you about his discussion with Fox?"

Sagit flinched. Joyner's tone was sharp, sounding like a prosecuting attorney. No longer like a personal friend.

"David said that Fox agreed to tape the conversation between Chambers and Khalid, which would take place on the following day."

"Did you believe him?"

Sagit hesitated. "Absolutely. I had no reason not to. But why is this significant?"

"I don't know yet. Ed Simpson is still conducting his inquiry. Things are moving slowly, as they always do in Washington. I hope to have this wrapped up by the end of the afternoon. There's no need for worry on your part."

Joyner hung up the phone and stared at it for several moments. She believed Sagit, whom she had gotten to know and like. David was a different matter. Last night, after dinner at the Hilltop, she had returned to Langley and read everything in the Greg Nielsen personnel file. In many ways it wasn't flattering. On the one hand, he was described as hardworking, dedicated, a real patriot, deeply concerned about the welfare of the country, and often having brilliant insights as an intelligence agent. On the other hand, he had never been a team player. In Iran, he had acted alone in an unsuccessful effort to influence the Shah to deal with the fundamentalists, contrary to agency policy. In Saudi Arabia, again contrary to Agency policy, he had encouraged Colonel Azziz and his supporters who were opposed to the royal family. "Impulsive," "hotheaded" and "stubborn" were terms that cropped up repeatedly in his annual personnel reviews.

Still, Bill Fox had to be an emotional wreck, without any sense of judgment, if he was actually having an affair with a married Saudi princess, as he admitted in the affidavit. As soon as she spoke to her deputy in charge of personnel, Fox would be brought home on the first plane out unless he refused to leave, which was possible at this point, because anything was possible with Fox. A married Saudi princess? Oh, c'mon. Nobody could be that stupid. So she asked herself again, Who was telling the truth? David? Or Bill Fox?

Deeply troubled, she walked slowly back into the AG's office and sat down at the conference room table, pondering that question all the way.

"We have that sound equipment," she reported somberly to Simpson and Chambers, "the Scrambler that Fox described."

"And you didn't know about his affair with the Saudi princess?"

"I knew that he was having marital problems."

"Well, I'm not telling you how to run your agency, but shouldn't somebody have investigated this man's personal life once you knew about his marital problems?"

She winced. Ed had gotten right to the point, as she'd expected. Squirming in her chair, she made no effort to shift the blame. "In retrospect, of course the answer's yes. We'll bring him home now."

"Nothing like closing the barn door when the horse is out," Simpson grumbled.

They all sat in silence, waiting for the AG. Finally, he buzzed his secretary. "Call Kathy at the White House. Get me on the President's calendar today as soon as possible. Tell her there will be three of us. I'm bringing Margaret Joyner and General Chambers with me."

Chambers could barely contain his feeling of triumph. It had been a long road to gain this sweet revenge. After Fox's meeting with Joyner and Chambers in Washington, the general had instinctively felt Fox would lead him to Greg Nielsen, and putting a tail on Fox had done just that. He couldn't believe the assassin he had hired had missed Nielsen in Green Park. Then there had been Paris. Rather than hiring someone himself, he had simply leaked to an Iranian unit operating in Europe the information that their old nemesis, the Shah's friend, was staying at the Hotel Bristol. Again, the Houdini-like Nielsen had gotten away. Not this time, Chambers thought joyfully. Your luck has run out. You'll be a very old man when they finally release you from a federal penitentiary.

From the back porch of the Hilltop, Sagit watched David trudging wearily back to the inn. He had started out running, but out of shape, he returned walking. Deep in thought, he didn't even notice her. But she saw the clearly defined ridges in the forehead of his ruddy face—much deeper and longer than ever before. Heavy clouds were forming in the western sky. A squirrel cut quickly across the path in front of him, then disappeared into the woods. She cared for him so much, the way she had never thought it was possible to love. She was blaming herself for getting him into this quagmire in Washington.

It wasn't what Margaret had said but how she'd said it. The usual warmth had been missing in her voice. She was cold, professional, bureaucratic, as she had been when Sagit first met her last year, before California. Sagit thought she had broken down that barrier. Now it was back up again. She blamed herself for believing—naively, she realized—

that she could control what happened in this monster of a city that regularly destroyed people's lives and their dreams.

She walked down the steps and met him on the dirt path. "You look like you just lost your best friend," he said.

"Margaret called."

"And?" he asked apprehensively. She reported the entire conversation to him, almost verbatim. "Shit, he beat me," he said, sighing.

She didn't respond. She knew he was right.

He continued, "Last evening Margaret told me I was underestimating General Chambers."

"Yeah, but look at history. There are lots of generals like Chambers who thought they were omnipotent, and eventually they got their due. Look at Caesar . . . and Napoleon . . . and MacArthur . . . and even Saddam Hussein, who got devastated when he sent his troops into Kuwait, why . . ."

Suddenly David's eyes came to life. "What did you say?"

"I said that even Saddam Hussein . . ."

"No, I mean before that."

"Look at Caesar and Napoleon and . . ."

"That's it. Napoleon."

"What's Napoleon have to do with this?"

"Everything. When I was in Paris devising the plan for Madame Blanc to give to Khalid, I broke into the computer at PDF. The password was 'guillotine' for this Saudi operation. Well, anyhow, I got a look at the finances for the operation. I learned that Madame Blanc had made two payments of fifteen million dollars each into an account at the Credit Suisse Bank on the Bahnoffstrasse in Zurich. The payee was someone whose name or code name was Henri Napoleon."

She put her forehead into her hand, closed her eyes and shook her head in dismay. When she opened her eyes, she looked at him accusingly. "And you never told me?"

He glanced down at the ground, feeling defensive. As their relationship had evolved, he should have dealt with her an as equal partner, but old habits die hard. "Look, I guess I'm not much of a team player. I'm sorry. Besides, I just assumed at the time that Henri Napoleon was the code name for the Saudi military officer in charge of the coup. Since we still had to find out who the Saudi officer was, I didn't bother telling you about the code name."

"So once you found out that Khalid was the Saudi officer, you assumed that Napoleon was his code name?"

"Yeah. Except that Khalid denied ever getting any money for himself from Madame Blanc, and I believed him. Then I concluded that Bill Fox was Henri Napoleon, but as I think about it some more, Madame Blanc would never make payments that large to somebody at such a low level. It has to be Chambers. It fits with everything else we know. She would also think it clever to give Chambers a general's name for a code name."

Listening to him, she thought, My God, if you had told me what you knew earlier, I might have helped you avoid the quicksand you're in now. There was no use chastising him. They had to go on from here. "So Madame Blanc had paid off Chambers to the tune of thirty million dollars to that point."

His face lit up with excitement, and he was gesticulating as he began speaking rapidly, his mouth trying to keep up with his thoughts. "Absolutely. That money, and perhaps more, has got to be the payoff for Chambers persuading the President not to intervene militarily when Khalid launches his attack. That's why she told me the first time I met her that I shouldn't worry about the American government intervening militarily. Chambers is in her pocket. She figures that she has Washington neutralized."

"Do you think General Chambers could ever deliver on a commitment like that?"

He paused for a moment and squeezed his hands together, trying to think about what Chambers would do to follow through on his commitment to Madame Blanc. "As chairman of the Joint Chiefs, he's the President's top military adviser. General Chambers is also someone who spent time in Saudi Arabia. And he has a close personal relationship with President Waltham. If he were to advise the President in the strongest terms that thousands of American lives would be lost in a bitter Saudi civil war, I don't think that this President would intervene one month before he's up for reelection." He paused for a minute. "No, I think Madame Blanc had the right idea."

Sagit never heard David's last sentence. Her mind was churning, trying to come up with a way to use this information, to turn the tables on Chambers. "Then all we need are copies of the records from this Swiss bank account she set up for him."

"Be realistic, Sagit, you're not going to get access to Chambers's Swiss bank account. Swiss banks zealously guard information about their accounts. That's why I opened one myself when I was on the run five years ago."

Now she was excited, confident that she was on the right track. She brushed aside his qualms. "What I need from you is to use that great memory of yours. Did you see an account number for Henri Napoleon at Credit Suisse in Zurich?"

He closed his eyes, racking his brain. Finally, he said, "55XQ3. That's the number."

"Fantastic." She hugged him tightly. "Yes!"

David brightened up, now beginning to share her enthusiasm. "Okay, you and I are going to get on the first plane to Zurich this evening."

"We can't," she said.

"Why not?"

"Your deal was immunity for full cooperation. Chambers has probably convinced the attorney general to order your arrest. If you're not here, they'll cover the airports. If we're together, they'll stop me as well. I've got to go to Zurich myself."

"We'll be able to get out in time. They'd never move that fast."

"You're wrong. With Chambers driving the response, everything will move on a fast track."

"I will admit it's a gamble."

"One that you can't afford to lose. The safer bet's for me to go alone."

He nodded, thinking about what she'd said, before he reluctantly agreed. "But I won't stay here and let them take me. I had a good friend when I was with the Company. Tim Donnelly, who was deputy director. Tim had a house in St. Michaels on the eastern shore of Maryland. I'll lay low at Tim's house, and that'll give me flexibility."

She handed him her cell phone, and he punched in Donnelly's number from memory. When the recording began, "You have reached the Donnelly's. No one is here . . . ," he hung up.

"Tim had a guest house in back that I used a couple of times when I was in Washington for consultations. 'Key's in the can in back,' he always said. 'No need to call. Just come.' All I need is an hour's lead time to avoid the manhunt they'll set up. So you should wait one hour. Then call Margaret and tell her I've disappeared into the woods. You've looked everywhere, and you can't find me. You're afraid I may have taken off again. Just like five years ago."

She nodded. "And then I go to Zurich to get the evidence we need."

"Wait until tomorrow evening. Give it a day to settle down. But don't let Margaret know what you're up to in Zurich until you get the evidence and you've hidden a copy. I don't trust anyone except you."

He recited Donnelly's number and said, "Call me when you have the evidence, and I'll come running."

"What if I don't get it?"

"There are thousands of boats in St. Michaels. From the Chesapeake Bay, I could go anywhere in the world."

She was annoyed. All he was thinking about was himself. The Solo Runner was off again. "And what do you want me to do? Take over your kibbutz fur business and sneak off to meet you in Europe twice a year?"

"That's not funny."

"It wasn't meant to be."

Five minutes later, he packed some clothes in a small black duffel bag. He held her tight and kissed her. "Listen, Sagit," he said. "One thing I want you to know, regardless of what happens, I don't blame you for going to Washing-

ton in the first place. You got the immunity for me. I
screwed up. It's my fault for using that jerk Bill Fox."

Then he was gone.

Within fifteen minutes of Sagit's phone call to Margaret,
half a dozen unmarked navy blue cars descended on the
Hilltop, their red bubble lights on the dashboards flashing,
their sirens blasting. They used dogs to help search the
woods, vicious dogs that tried to pick up the scent they had
gotten from some of the clothes David left behind.

Sagit was convinced that Margaret believed she was in
on some plan with David, but Margaret didn't press hard.
The CIA director knew that they would never find David
until he wanted to be found. Still not persuaded that the
Fox affidavit was true, she was content to let events unfold.

Half a world away, Bill Fox had developed a plan to
jump-start the rest of his life. Prince Faisel, Jameelah's husband, was at home for five days before a trip to Beirut to
gamble and to frolic in the reestablished fleshpot of the
Middle East. Fox couldn't see her during those five days
and nights.

By the time the prince left for Beirut, Fox would present
Jameelah with a plan for her escape with him to Europe.
His idea was to put her in a wooden crate with air holes,
containing a battery-driven heater, and arrange for the
crate to fly in the storage compartment of a C-130 cargo
jet that the U.S. Air Force was flying to Frankfurt.

There they would start their lives over. They'd go to the
lake country of Italy—the most marvelous place in the
world for lovers. And from there, all things were possible.

The prince shouldn't miss her. He had three other wives,
two of whom were even younger than her twenty-three
years. But that was five days from now.

In the meantime, he had to think about that awful sixty-
two-year-old fat husband of hers, sodomizing his wonderful
Jameelah, because that's the way the prince liked it—
tearing that precious sensitive skin. God, it drove him crazy
just thinking about her pain. Several times in the past he

had been tempted to go to their mansion with a gun and shoot the bastard, but that would only lead to a death sentence for her and him. Better to wait the five days.

He glanced at the phone, expecting it to ring any minute with Margaret Joyner or one of her assistants calling to summon him back to Washington. He was betting that the bureaucracy wouldn't move that fast, but if it did, he'd find a place to hide in the Saudi desert for five days. He already had a couple of possibilities.

As far as Greg Nielsen was concerned, Fox was sorry that he had to do in his old buddy, but General Chambers left him no alternative. It was a choice between Nielsen and Jameelah, and that was no choice at all.

In self-justification, he asked himself, What did Nielsen ever do for me? He left me holding the bag five years ago to explain what happened with Azziz, while he hightailed it to God only knows where.

Suddenly, Fox heard a knock at his front door. Surprised, he looked at the clock. It was almost midnight.

"Who's there?" he called through the closed door.

"It's Abdullah," a familiar man's voice replied. He was Jameelah's servant, whom she had enlisted to assist in her clandestine liaison.

Fox quickly opened the door. "What's wrong?" he asked.

"Prince Faisel went to Beirut this evening. She wants you to come now, to see her."

It took Fox less than a minute to put on a white cotton *thobe* over his own clothes, and the standard red-and-white cotton headdress that he wore whenever he went to see her.

He drove himself, following Abdullah. In the car, he turned on a CD of Sinatra singing "My Way." He was trembling with excitement at the prospect of seeing Jameelah so soon. It had been a great bit of luck for him that the prince had left earlier—before the CIA could summon him back to Washington. He had a whole plan for the evening. He'd tell her about the plane for Frankfurt. They were leaving almost daily this week, as military supplies were being shuttled between Frankfurt and Saudi Arabia.

But before they discussed that, he'd make love to her—

long and slow, just the way she liked it. He could feel his penis stiffen in his pants as he thought about it. God, it was never like that for him with Alice. Not even when she was twenty-three.

The prince's palatial house had a long driveway. As Fox followed Abdullah, he turned off his headlights and the music. The house was dark and still.

After parking his car in front of Abdullah's, where it couldn't be seen from the road, he took off his shoes. Outside, it was cool and pleasant. Treading softly, he followed Abdullah up to the front door. Without glancing back, the servant opened it and let himself in. Fox followed two steps behind.

As soon as he was in the pink marble entrance hall, Fox looked around, trying to get his eyes accustomed to the dark.

Suddenly from behind him, a heavy object crashed down on his head. He felt himself losing consciousness.

Sometime later, and he had no idea how long, someone placed an awful-smelling substance under his nose to wake him up.

A piece of heavy duct tape was wrapped across his mouth. His hands were tied tightly behind his back, and his feet were bound with rope around the ankles. Then he was dragged by powerful arms to the back of the house.

Outside, the swimming pool was bathed in floodlights.

To his horror, he saw his princess, his beloved Jameelah, bound and gagged the same way, standing on the concrete pool deck near the shallow end. Two men held her tightly. All of the other members of the household except the prince—wives, children and servants—stood around the pool. They marched Fox past her, while the household members jeered. He saw that her eyes were red from crying. Her face was bruised and caked with blood where she had been beaten.

He tried to move, to fight his way free, but the ropes were too tight, the arms pulling him were too strong. There was no possibility of resistance as they led him around to the deep end of the pool.

To his horror, he watched as her oldest brother came forward, holding a heavy stone in his hand. That was the cue for all of the others standing by the pool to go over to the pile of stones that had been deposited in a corner and pick one up. Her brother fired the first stone at Jameelah with all the force he could muster. This would avenge the disgrace that she had brought on his family. It struck her in the center of the forehead, knocking her down. In rapid fire, the others unleashed their stones at the prone Jameelah.

Fox couldn't bear to look. He knew that they would continue throwing until she was dead. As he closed his eyes, someone fastened black waterproof plastic bags containing large rocks to his feet. Then he was roughly dragged to the edge of the pool and tossed into the water.

As Fox felt himself sink, the face of General Chambers popped into his mind. Chambers was responsible for Jameelah's husband, the prince, finding out tonight. He was certain of it. God, what a fool he had been.

With the small black duffel in his hand and dressed in slacks and a shirt, David walked along the road ten minutes from the Hilltop to a main highway. At the intersection was a combination diner/truck stop on the side of the road heading west from Washington. He walked over to one of the diesel pumps, eyed the truckers who were filling up and settled on a big burly African-American whose company, Royal Trucking, was headquartered in Roanoke, according to the printing on the side of the truck.

David said to the trucker, "My car just conked out on me. I have to get to Roanoke. I'm supposed to get married down there. If I don't make it, she'll never understand. Please, I'll play you two hundred dollars in cash for a ride."

The driver, who looked like he'd played football in high school, stared at David. He didn't believe a word of the bullshit story David had just told him. But he didn't care. Hell, he could easily handle this city dude if he tried anything funny. "Three hundred," the trucker said. "Payment up front."

"But no radio," David replied. "All they play around here is country music."

The trucker laughed. "I don't like that shit either."

David reached into his wallet and extracted three hundred-dollar bills, part of the emergency cash he had brought back from Switzerland to hide in the kibbutz, then carried with him whenever he left the country. He handed the money to the trucker.

"All right. Get in."

As they drove south and west—exactly the opposite of his ultimate destination—David embellished his wedding story, but the trucker still wasn't buying, so they talked about high school football days. They talked about growing up in a small town. Finally, they talked about oil and how the price of gasoline was already killing trucking companies like Royal, which the driver's brother-in-law owned.

In Roanoke, David thanked the trucker and jumped out. It was late afternoon. He walked through a rundown area near the business center until he found what he was looking for—a seedy-looking used-car dealer. There was a fifteen-year-old Ford Tempo for sale on the lot, with a purchase price of six hundred dollars. For a thousand dollars in cash, the man never even asked David's name, and he installed a set of plates that he had been keeping for a situation like this.

The clunker drove better than David had thought from the test ride. He drove it across the state of Virginia, avoiding Richmond, until he got to the Tidewater area. Then he crossed the Chesapeake Bay Bridge and tunnel to the eastern shore. Near Crisfield, Maryland, he abandoned the car in a wooded area where no one paid attention to cars left that way.

It was one in the morning, and he checked into a Days Inn for a few hours' sleep. At four A.M. he was up, walking toward the waterfront with the chilly, salty smell of the bay awakening all of his senses. Overhead, Canada geese were flying in formation, searching for a place to hunker down for the winter.

He went into a small café and nursed a cup of coffee—

listening to watermen talk about their recent catches of oysters—now that crab season was winding down. One man, in a black waterproof jacket, clearly a longtime waterman, was particularly down on his luck. He was paying off a new boat, his wife was pregnant with their third child, and he hadn't even gathered enough oysters last month to make a mortgage payment. David waited until the man headed out to the dock, then followed him.

It was still dark. At his boat slip, David approached the waterman. "How about running me up to Oxford? I'll pay you three hundred dollars in cash."

The man eagerly took David on board.

It was just the two of them, swilling hot strong coffee to keep warm on the Chesapeake Bay. It was all so pure and clean that it made David glad to be alive and free, and he vowed to stay that way, regardless of what it took.

At Oxford, David hopped the ferryboat across to St. Michaels. He was now confident that no one could trail his steps. He was also relieved to find that no one was at the Donnellys' house, which was on the water and totally isolated in the woods. It didn't look like anyone had been there for days, maybe even weeks. Tim and Linda must be off traveling somewhere.

Tim's boat was still tied up at the dock in back. David made certain it was ready to go on short notice, if he had to borrow it. Satisfied that he could be on the water in five minutes if necessary, he let himself into the guest house.

Exhausted, he collapsed on the bed, and into a deep sleep, with the telephone right next to him in case Sagit called.

CHAPTER 16

Trying not to look too smug, General Chambers walked into the Oval Office just in time for the noon meeting. The President was on the phone, seated behind his large green leather-topped desk. In front of him sat Joyner, Charles Frost, Ralph Laurence, Bill Hayes and Ed Simpson.

Speaking into the phone, the President sounded angry and shrill. "C'mon, Chip, you told me yesterday we had your vote on the tax cut package. You put me over the top in the Senate. Now you're waffling. You can't do that . . . If you force me to I'll play hardball . . . I'll close Thompson Air Force Base. You know how many jobs that'll cost your state . . . Atta boy . . . I knew we could do business." He slammed the phone down. "That prick better not change his mind again." He looked at Hayes. "When we're done here, you get hold of that *Post* reporter who covers the Pentagon—what the hell's his name?"

"Jonathan Wilson."

"Yeah, Wilson, and you leak to him that we're considering closing Thompson Air Force Base. Tell him to run it tomorrow morning, quoting an unnamed Pentagon source. That'll keep the pressure on Chip Parker. I don't want to lose his vote."

Now President Waltham was ready to shift gears mentally. He looked around the room. "Why this meeting of the Sanhedrin?" he asked quizzically.

"I called the meeting," Margaret Joyner said. "A possible coup in Saudi Arabia is the subject."

She hated raising the topic in such a large group without giving the President a private briefing first, but the tax cut

bill and the reelection campaign had taken every minute of
his time this morning, and he had made it clear to all of
his aides that nothing short of an attack on the United
States came ahead of these two items until twelve o'clock.

The President looked at Joyner quizzically. "I thought
that Saudi Arabia coup business was all a fabrication by
that fellow . . . what's his name?"

"Greg Nielsen."

"Yeah, Nielsen. Incidentally, have you caught him yet?"

The AG responded: "The FBI is leading the search. A
picture of what he looks like now, the new Greg Nielsen,
after plastic surgery, has been given to agents at every international airport. Jack Doyle's directing the operation
himself, but so far nothing."

"So why are we meeting?"

Frost broke in before Joyner could respond. "Mr. President, what Ed's report shows is that Nielsen fabricated this
whole notion of an attack on the Saudi king and palace to
frame General Chambers and to settle a personal score
with him. Nielsen's the only source of information about
this so-called Saudi coup. So we've got nothing left to worry
about. There is no reason for us to meet."

"That's not exactly what happened, Charles," Joyner
said.

"It's pretty darn close. So why are we here?"

"Because my station chief in Saudi Arabia, who happened to be the key witness against Nielsen, also happened
to have been killed in Saudi Arabia in a mysterious way a
few hours after we received his affidavit and heard his testimony on the phone."

Frost had lost countless battles to Joyner before the President in the past. He was delighted to be waging one he
was confident he could win. "It wasn't mysterious at all.
Bill Fox was in an adulterous relationship with a Saudi
princess. The prince caught them in bed and bumped them
both off. What's that have to do with a coup against the
Saudi government?"

Joyner had been racking her brain to come up with an
answer to this question, ever since she heard about Fox's

death. While she hadn't been able to hit on a plausible answer, she knew deep down there had to be a connection. "The coincidence is too much for me. It's like the same number popping up three times in a row on a roulette wheel. It could be coincidence, but personally I'd put my money on a crooked wheel." She paused and looked at the President. The crooked-wheel analogy was one he had used himself a year ago, with her. By trotting it out now, she hoped to garner a little more sympathy with him for her position. "I think we should talk to the Saudi king and warn him that there may be something coming down the road. At the same time, let's follow up with the French government on the activities of PDF and its chairman, Madame Blanc. I think we can do those things quietly."

Frost shot back, "Oh, c'mon, Margaret, if we do what you want, we might as well be putting the story on the front page of *The New York Times*. It'll divert attention from the tax bill, where the President wants all of the focus to be."

Joyner glanced around the room. No one else raised a voice in her support. Ed Simpson was looking concerned, staring hard at General Chambers. She turned hopefully to the President, but from his expression, she knew that his mind was on other matters. She was beaten.

"What was the date for this so-called coup?" the President asked, suddenly cutting back into the discussion.

"October 6," Joyner responded.

"We'll still have time after the Senate vote on the tax cut," he decided. "Let's leave it alone for now."

"I think that makes sense," Joyner responded, concluding that the promise of a fresh look in a couple of days was all that she could possibly come away with under the circumstances.

As the meeting broke up, she led Ed Simpson into a small empty office across the hall and closed the door softly. The AG locked his thumbs behind his blue polka-dot suspenders, deep in thought.

"You looked worried about something in the meeting with our leader," Joyner said to the AG.

"Yeah, back in the days when I was the U.S. attorney in New York, before I went on the bench, I never liked it when one of my witnesses died right after he testified. I didn't care what the cause of death was. I didn't like it one bit. And Chambers was awfully quiet in there. He never keeps quiet in a meeting like this."

"He didn't have to talk. He gave Frostie the script."

Troubled, Simpson thought about the meeting some more and what had happened to Bill Fox. "The whole thing doesn't sit well in my gut, which has become sensitized to these things over the years. Then there's the new development of Greg Nielsen's disappearance. Where do you suppose he's gone?"

"I've got no idea."

"I bet that Israeli woman knows where he is."

"I'm with you on that a hundred percent. I've already got twenty-four-hour surveillance on her with my own people."

"Jack won't be happy that you're using CIA people for domestic work."

"I unilaterally decided to make an exception here. Greg Nielsen used to be one of our own."

He frowned. "You can have him. That guy's trouble."

Margaret Joyner wasn't the only one who had set up surveillance on Sagit, hoping to find Nielsen. Once General Chambers learned from Jack Doyle, the FBI director, that Sagit had checked into the Hilton Hotel on Connecticut Avenue, General Chambers called Captain Peter Carlton, who worked for the Defense Intelligence Agency, or DIA, as it was known in the Washington alphabet soup. DIA was the Pentagon's counterpart to the CIA. One major difference was that there was no civilian control of the DIA.

Three years ago, when Chambers had begun an affair with the wife of a freshman congressman from Oregon, he needed a driver who was totally discreet and could conduct effective surveillance in front of the Four Seasons in Georgetown. Carlton had done the job perfectly.

To Chambers's disappointment, the congressman wasn't

reelected and the affair ended after a year and a half, but he never forgot what Carlton had done. Now he summoned the captain to his office at the Pentagon. Carlton had a closely cropped light brown crew cut and a nose that had been broken and set poorly when he played football at Texas A&M.

"This is top secret," Chambers said, in a soft voice, just above a whisper.

"Yes, sir."

"I want constant surveillance on an Israeli woman now in Washington, with frequent reports directly to me. She's part of an intelligence operation of theirs to acquire information about American weapons programs that we don't want to share with them. Am I making myself clear, Captain?"

"Absolutely, sir."

"Change into civilian clothes. I don't want you to stand out, and I don't want her to pick up the tail. So keep it as loose as you can."

"We've gotten more sophisticated these days. We have electronic tracking devices that key to a person's unique body odors. Even if she's good, she'll never know I'm there."

Chambers picked up a cell phone on his desk and handed it to Carlton. "Keep it with you and power on at all times. Anywhere in the world she goes, I want you to follow her."

When Carlton left the office, Chambers gave a large sigh of relief. There was no way that he would let Nielsen and this Israeli woman disrupt his plans.

From the time she had left the Hilltop yesterday, Sagit knew that she was being followed. There were two men and a woman—all CIA, she guessed—who kept switching off on the surveillance. So she went to the Mazza Galleria Mall on upper Wisconsin Avenue, wandering in and out of stores, pretending to be shopping, moving up and down stairs and finally ducking into a boiler room and hiding there until she lost them. Then she took a cab to the Israeli embassy on International Drive. The Mossad's designated contact in the tan brick three-story building was an assistant cultural attaché by the name of Uri Baruch.

Without asking any questions, Uri placed Sagit in a room with a phone, hooked up to a secure line to Jerusalem. Moshe listened without a word to her report of what David had told her yesterday about the Zurich bank account.

"You still there?" she asked when she was finished.

"Of course I'm still here."

"You're so quiet."

"I'm thinking and looking at airplane schedules because I figure you're about to ask me to authorize a trip for you to Zurich."

"The trip's not the problem. I'll need some help at the bank."

"And here I thought you were planning to break in yourself."

"So what do I do?"

"Tell Uri to get you a reservation on Swissair flight 129 tonight out of Dulles, to Zurich. It's the last flight, and it leaves at seven forty-five. So you better get moving. They'll give you a ticket at the embassy, and they'll take you to the airport. Rivka from the embassy in Switzerland will meet your plane tomorrow morning. She'll tell you everything then."

Sagit climbed into the back of the embassy car with a first-class ticket in her purse, because Uri said that's all he could get for a flight over tonight and back tomorrow. "It'll break Moshe's budget," Uri had told her, "but I had no choice."

She smiled, thinking about all the traveling she had done with David, and said, "I broke Moshe's budget long ago."

It had started raining and a curtain of fog was settling over Washington. As the driver was struggling to make time in heavy traffic and poor visibility, Peter Carlton, too far back to be noticed, continued his relentless pursuit. Exhausted from a sleepless night and a tension-filled day, Sagit wanted to doze, but she was worrying about Margaret Joyner and what she had done to her relationship with the CIA chief. It wasn't just the professional relationship between the Mossad and the CIA that were at issue. The CIA chief had done so much for her and David. Regardless of what David thought, she had to trust Margaret. She couldn't leave town, seeming to vanish into thin air, without telling the CIA chief.

She waited to call until she was at the gate.

"Where are you?" Margaret asked. "I've been worried sick about you. I was getting ready to send out a search party."

Sagit was glad she had called. "I'm at Dulles Airport."

"Going home for consultation?"

Sagit hesitated. It would be so easy to say yes and to end it there, but Sagit couldn't do that. Not to Margaret. She didn't care what David had said.

"No, actually I'm going to Zurich."

"Why Zurich?"

"I'm afraid to explain it on the phone. Besides, it's a real long shot."

There was a pregnant pause. Finally Joyner said, "What about your friend, David? Where is he?"

Sagit answered truthfully: "I haven't heard a word from him since he took off and ran."

From the same gate area, Peter Carlton called General Chambers. "I'm at Dulles Airport. Target subject and I are on Swissair flight 129. She's in first class and so am I, to stay close to her, but I couldn't get the name she's using." Carlton was apologetic. "I was behind her in line at check in, and she was speaking softly. I do know that her final destination is Zurich."

When Chambers heard the word "Zurich," he cringed. There could only be one reason for Sagit to go there. Calmly Chambers said, "Call me from the plane in two hours with her seat number."

"Yes, sir."

As Chambers put the phone down, he decided that Greg Nielsen was even smarter than he had thought. But it still wouldn't do him any good. Once Chambers had her seat number, DIA could get her full name from the passenger manifest, and if she was traveling on a U.S. passport, the passport office could fax over her picture. There was no way that the Israeli woman would leave Switzerland alive with the information Nielsen needed.

Chambers picked up the phone and dialed Paris, waking Victor Foch in the middle of the night.

"This is Henri Napoleon," he said. "We have a problem." Victor rubbed the sleep from his eyes as the general continued. "But I think I know how we can solve it."

While Chambers and Victor made their plans, Peter Carlton glanced around the plane to observe that the target subject was in seat 6B. He set the alarm on his watch for the time to call General Chambers. Then he proceeded to enjoy dinner and the movie. Regrettably, he couldn't drink; he was working. Still the caviar and rack of lamb were pretty good, even with club soda.

When he called Chambers, he whispered into the air phone, "Subject is in 6B."

"Listen carefully, Captain. You did a great job, but as of now you're off duty. I've got somebody else, who knows Zurich, to pick up surveillance when the plane lands. Why don't you take a couple of days off? Go sight-seeing in the Alps. Enjoy yourself. Submit all of the bills to me personally."

Peter Carlton bounded off the plane at Kloten Airport in Zurich. Without any bags and a U.S. government passport, he whizzed through passport control and customs. As he emerged from the arrival hall into the terminal, he was surprised to see the familiar face of Hal Vernon, a former colleague and friend from the DIA, who had transferred to the CIA when his military duty had ended. He knew that the Company had stationed Vernon in Switzerland to focus on economic espionage.

"Hey, Hal, I didn't realize that I rated a receiving party."

"You don't. So don't get excited."

"Then what are you doin' here, little buddy?"

Carlton's nickname for Vernon grew out of the latter's height, which was just an inch over five feet.

"Surveillance and baby-sitting. Trying to keep tabs on a little girl and make sure she stays safe while she's in Zurich. It's very top-level stuff. Mrs. Joyner called me herself."

"Who's the baby?"

"Name's Alexandra Holt. They faxed me a picture. Dark hair. A pretty good looker."

"Let me see."

While continuing to keep his eye on passengers emerging from the arrival hall, Hal reached into the pocket of his black leather jacket and handed Peter the fax.

"Holy shit," Peter said. He rubbed the sleep out of his eyes from the night on the plane and looked at the picture a second time.

"You like her that much?"

"No, it's just that . . ."

"Here comes our little girl, Alexandra Holt," Hal said, nodding in Sagit's direction as she walked through the exit.

"That's her, okay. You can bet it."

"You know her?"

"Take me with you. I'll tell you in the car."

Sagit spotted Rivka, and the two of them cut quickly across the terminal toward the exit for the parking lot. So intent were Peter and Hal to follow the fast-moving Israeli women that they never saw the two Frenchmen who fell in behind them.

Once they were in the car, and following the green Opel with Alexandra Holt inside, Peter said to Hal, "This doesn't compute. First General Chambers told me that this lady is an Israeli spy who's trying to make off with top-secret information. Now Ms. Joyner wants you to make sure she stays safe."

Hal shrugged. "I've met the other one before. Rivka's her name. She's definitely Mossad. Has a phony position on their embassy staff for cover. As far as what's going on . . ." He snickered. "At our level, we just follow orders. Ours is not to reason why. Ours is just to . . ."

"Yeah, I know. Do or die."

"Well, didn't you learn that long ago? They're mostly morons in Washington, anyhow. We have to assume they changed their minds between the time you received your orders and when I received my call. Nothing else makes sense. Now, the most recent order is to keep Ms. Holt safe. So that's the way we play it."

Peter wasn't fully convinced, but he didn't argue. "I guess so. I'll even help you if you'll travel around with me for a few days after Alexandra Holt, or whatever her name is, leaves your turf. General Chambers told me to have a good time at the government's expense."

Hal's eyes lit up. "You've got a deal. Let's go to St. Moritz, where the high rollers hang out."

"Any action there?"

"You can gamble to your heart's content."

Peter laughed lasciviously and poked Hal playfully on the shoulder. "No, I mean pussy."

"Don't be such a damn provincial, Peter. With European women there's always plenty of pussy around."

"Now, don't you go taking on pseudo-sophisticated European airs with me, little buddy. You and I both are Texans."

Hal was glancing nervously in the rearview mirror. Outside, it was a gloomy morning, but even so he'd noticed that they were being followed by a black Mercedes as they headed toward the center of Zurich. Or maybe they weren't being followed. Maybe it was Alexandra Holt and the other woman in the green Opel who were being followed. When the green Opel cut into the left passing lane, Hal held back. Sure enough, the Mercedes surged forward, moving up behind the Opel. Hal kept his eye on the Mercedes. It had French plates. There were two men in the front, and they seemed intent on following the women. He doubted if they knew he and Peter were there.

"Ms. Holt and friend have company," Hal told Peter. "Two men in a black Mercedes with frog plates."

Peter leaned forward, straining to see the two cars in the gray morning mist. Then he turned to Hal. "Life's suddenly gotten very interesting. You got a piece?"

"Are you kidding? This is Switzerland. People don't carry guns."

Peter was nonplussed and dismayed. "Really?"

"Yeah, really." Hal chuckled and pointed at the holster at his hip.

"What about for me?"

When the three cars stopped for a red light, Hal reached down to his ankle holster and tossed a Beretta to Peter.

"Now we're just a couple of Texas boys out for a little morning's entertainment."

In the green Opel, Sagit said to Rivka, "We're being followed by two men in a black Mercedes with French license plates F1625."

"You want me to try and lose them?"

"No, don't bother. I have a feeling they know where I'm going an hour from now. Do what you planned to do. I doubt if they know we've spotted them. We'll have the element of surprise this way."

They passed the train station and turned down the Bahnoffstrasse. At the far end, without any warning, the green Opel made a sharp turn into the parking garage just behind the Bar du Lac Hotel. The Mercedes remained on the street.

When Rivka had parked on the second level and they were getting out of the car, Sagit said, "Pop the trunk."

She rummaged inside, checking the contents of the trunk. Then she extracted a tire iron, which she concealed under her coat. As they crossed from the garage into the hotel via the bridge on the second level, she and Rivka looked around warily, but no one was lurking in the hall.

In the hotel dining room, Sagit told the waiter: the table against the wall, as far as possible from the door or any window. She placed her coat on the floor, next to her chair, with the tire iron still concealed.

"Now we'll have breakfast," she said. She asked a tuxedo-clad waiter to bring hot chocolate for Rivka, coffee for her, and a plate of pastries.

When the food arrived, Rivka took a bite of a croissant and a sip of chocolate before she began talking. "Moshe called me last night. Actually, this morning might be more accurate."

"Did he tell you what this is all about?"

"You know Moshe. He just gave me the essential facts. I'm supposed to tell you that you have an eleven o'clock appointment with a vice president of Credit Suisse about four blocks down the Bahnhofstrasse. His name is Helmut Gauber. He's from a long line of Swiss bankers. A real Zurich establishment family. The good news is that in the early 1960s, while he was in college, our friend Helmut happened to meet and fall in love with a Jewish girl named Anna.

"Her parents had both been born in Milan. Like many other Italian Jews, they did okay during the war, when it was Mussolini. Once the Germans moved into northern Italy at the end of '43, they rounded up all of the Jews to send them off to the death camps. Somehow Anna's father managed to smuggle his wife and two-year-old Anna across the border. Moshe thinks he paid somebody to row them across the lake from Stresa at night. The rower would only take the mother and baby. Anna's father died with the rest of the family."

Rivka had to stop talking and take deep breaths. Her own grandparents were survivors of Treblinka. Most of her family had perished in the Holocaust.

"Helmut was only three or four years old when the war ended. So he grows up, marries Anna, and goes into the banking business like everybody else in his family. He starts to learn about the world's best-kept dirty secret, how the Swiss banks not only took and kept for all those years money deposited by Jews who were being killed by the Germans, but how they helped finance the German war effort. What particularly outraged him was that the Swiss banks accepted gold the Nazis looted from Jews, including dental fillings, wedding rings and watches that had been smelted into gold bars, and provided the Nazis with hard currency in return for the gold to buy equipment. Anyhow, Anna wanted to go to Israel to visit as a tourist. So Helmut goes along with her for a vacation. Together they go to Yad Vashem. They see the names of her father and other family members whom the Nazis killed. For the first time,

Anna tells Helmut that her father had a successful leather factory in Milan, a big house and lots of art. He can guess where their money and property went. Right into his hometown, maybe even his bank. He's beside himself with guilt and anger. Not just for how his countrymen behaved during the war, but how they responded once their dirty little secret came out. In Israel, he also visits with Israeli bankers, to see how the banking business is run in Tel Aviv, and somebody tells Moshe about him. They meet over coffee. He tells Moshe, 'If I can ever do anything to help you, please let me know.' "

"So I'm to be the beneficiary of Helmut's guilt," Sagit said sarcastically.

"You could put it that way."

Sagit pulled her hands up from her lap and held them out to Rivka. "How else would you put it?"

Rivka took a deep breath and swallowed hard. Since she had been stationed in Switzerland, she had gotten used to hearing expressions of cynicism from her fellow Israelis about the Swiss. Some were justified; others were not. "I would say that you're the beneficiary of Helmut's decency. His father and grandfather may have been villains, but Helmut's a good man. He risks losing his job, going to jail and never working again in his country, if he gives you what you want."

Sagit was still skeptical. "Did he tell Moshe he'll give it to me?"

"Moshe called him last night. Helmut agreed to talk to you. That's all. So he has no idea what you want."

Sagit groaned. "Oh, great. Helmut's back home now. The enthusiasm he felt in Israel is over, I'll bet."

"Maybe yes and maybe no. You'll have to convince him yourself."

"Are you supposed to come with me to the meeting with Helmut?"

Rivka glanced around the room, studying the diners—mostly businessmen having a breakfast meeting, a few tourists, dressed more casually, no one who looked suspicious. Neither of the men from the Mercedes were anywhere in sight. Not surprisingly, they didn't want to make their move in the crowded restaurant. She turned back to Sagit. "Moshe thought one-on-one was better. I'm just the chauffeur. I'll drop you off and wait for you in front of the bank. Assuming we make it that far."

"You mean because of our friends in the Mercedes waiting outside?" Rivka nodded. "Oh, we'll make it all right," Sagit said.

Before they left the restaurant, Sagit asked the waiter for an empty wine bottle, and she slipped a pack of matches from the table into her pocket.

She peeked out of a side window off the hotel lobby and saw that the Mercedes was still parked, alone, on the street, with the two men inside keeping warm with the engine running.

She and Rivka retraced their route back to the green Opel—up to the second floor of the hotel and across the bridge. While Rivka kept her eye on the entrance to the garage, Sagit checked their car to make certain no one had planted a bomb when they were in the restaurant. Then she opened the trunk and filled the wine bottle with gasoline from the can Rivka kept in case she ran out of fuel. She tore off a piece of a rag in the trunk, saturated it with gasoline and stuffed it into the top of the bottle to serve as a wick.

"Wait ten minutes," Sagit told Rivka. "Then you start the car and drive slowly down toward the exit, but not close enough that those men can get a direct line with their gun."

Meantime, Sagit scrambled back across the bridge and down the stairs in the hotel. She exited the hotel through a side entrance and snuck up on the Mercedes from the rear, in a low crouch, trying to avoid detection through the car's mirrors, with the tire iron gripped hard in her right hand and the bottle of gasoline in her left.

When she was twenty feet from the Mercedes, she put down the tire iron and held a lit match to the wick on the bottle. Then she rolled the bottle toward the car. At that instant, the man on the passenger side spotted her and jumped out of the car with an AK-47 in his hand. She ducked behind a building, but he saw her and gave chase, spraying bullets as he ran. Meantime, the car exploded with the driver still inside.

She ran down an alley that was a dead end. Boxed in by brick walls on all sides, she thought she was doomed. Still, she ran from side to side in a zigzag pattern, dodging bullets.

Suddenly from nowhere, a shot rang out, and her assailant crumpled to the ground. Standing next to him was a man with a closely cropped light brown crew cut, whom she had noticed in line behind her at Dulles Airport and on the airplane.

Rivka, who had left the Opel in the garage, ran up to Sagit.

"Quick," the man with the crew cut said. "Come with me. Both of you."

While pedestrians shrieked, Peter led the women to Hal's car, waiting with the engine running. Hal kicked it into gear and roared away.

As Sagit tried to catch her breath in the backseat, Hal said to her, "Margaret Joyner sent me. She wanted to make sure you stayed safe."

"You're CIA, then."

Rivka interjected. "He's Hal Vernon, their Zurich branch chief."

Hal was pleased that she remembered him from their one previous encounter at a gathering of U.S. and Israeli intelligence agents in Europe, related to the spread of Soviet weapons. "And this is my friend Peter," he added.

Sagit let her breath out in a large whoosh. She was so relieved that she had told Margaret she was going to Zurich.

"You saved my life," she said to Peter. "I can't thank you enough."

"Yeah, well, I'm not real fond of people who try to blow somebody away with an AK-47."

"Where are you taking us?" she asked.

Hal responded, "Tell me where you want to go."

Rivka gave him the address of Credit Suisse on the Bahnoffstrasse.

He made a sharp turn and headed toward the bank.

"Peter and I will wait in the car for you in front. After you're done there, we'll take you anywhere else you want to go."

Victor Foch hung up the phone and paced his office angrily. *"Merde,"* he cursed aloud.

He still couldn't believe the report he had gotten from his Zurich contact. Both men were dead, two experienced assassins, and the Israeli woman didn't even have a scratch. He knew the Mossad was good, but how in the world did this woman ever pull it off?

He wanted to shout aloud with frustration, but he got himself under control. "Think," he told himself. "Think."

She was going into the bank now. She seemed to have three bodyguards—two men and a woman. They must be Mossad agents. Let's assume, Victor thought, that she comes out of the bank with the evidence that would be devastating if it got to Washington. What can I do to stop her?

Doing anything else in Zurich was hopeless now, but . . . there was another way . . . a better way to block her from taking that evidence to Washington. He didn't have much time. He had to move quickly to get everything in place. He couldn't fail, or . . . He didn't even want to imagine what Madame Blanc would do to him. Not to mention the fact that the millions and millions of dollars he planned to make on this Saudi deal would disappear into thin air. It can't happen, he thought with renewed determination. I won't let it happen.

Sagit tried to shake off her fright from her perilously close escape. After identifying herself to a receptionist inside the bank, and while waiting for Helmut Gauber or his secretary to come for her, she went to the ladies' room to make herself presentable.

When she returned to the reception area, Helmut, tall and thin, smartly dressed in a gray pinstripe three-button suit and black wing-tipped shoes, was waiting for her.

Across his vest he wore a gold chain that undoubtedly held a watch in the pocket at one end. He greeted her formally and coldly, as any banker would greet a potential client. Then he led her into the elevator and up to his office on the third floor. Alone in the elevator, as they rode in silence, she studied him carefully for body language. Looking proud and defiant, he didn't seem like a man who was afraid of violating the law. On the other hand, he seemed so cold and aloof that she couldn't imagine him being moved emotionally, even by what he had seen at Yad Vashem.

When they reached his office, he offered her coffee and waited until his secretary had deposited two cups of espresso and departed behind the closed door before beginning in a clear, bold tone, "I want to help. Tell me what you want."

She breathed a huge sigh of relief. This was a good start, but what would he say when he heard her request? She cleared her throat and said, "I have an account number. I need copies of the signature card opening the account and copies of all documents showing any deposits or withdrawals from the account."

Without batting an eye, Helmut swiveled around in his chair to face an IBM PC.

"What's the account number?"

"55XQ3."

Swiftly, he punched a number of computer buttons and waited until the printer spit out several pages. Helmut studied them carefully and handed them to her.

Yes, she thought, elated. Yes! David was right.

General Chambers had opened the account on the 31st of August, this year. Among the papers Helmut handed her was a copy of the signature card and other documents, confirming that transfers in the amount of fifteen million dollars each, from an account at this bank in the name of Alpha Corp., had been made into General Chambers's account on August 31 and September 20 of this year. Then on September 21, he had withdrawn all of the money in the form of a cashier's check payable to Bradley Chambers.

She looked up at Gauber, who said, "You're probably wondering what happened to the cashier's check."

She nodded.

"That, unfortunately, I can't get from the computer. It would require following official procedures, which I don't think either of us would want to do."

"Agreed."

"However, let me see what I can find out about Alpha Corp." He went back to the computer. This time he produced a document showing that Petroleum de France (PDF) had transferred into the Alpha Corp. account the sums paid to General Chambers. She had everything she could have hoped for. A clear paper trail.

She wanted to rush across the desk and kiss Helmut Gauber.

Instead, she rose calmly, thanked Gauber for all of his help and shook his hand. He said nothing else and showed no emotion.

She didn't have the faintest idea what he was thinking. With the information in hand, she departed quickly, hoping to leave before they sent someone else to replace the two who had been in the Mercedes. She thought about faxing the documents to Joyner, but remembering how General Chambers had managed to distort the tape of his conversation with Khalid, she rejected that possibility. The additional ten hours or so didn't matter. She wanted to be there in person to explain and defend the documents to Joyner.

Hal, Peter and Rivka not only drove Sagit to Kloten Airport, they also walked her up to passport control in order to make certain she was safely on her way back to Washington.

"Now you guys can go home," Sagit said. "And thank you so much."

"Wrong," Hal replied. "Now we go up to the tower and watch the airfield. We don't leave Kloten until your plane is in the air."

"But don't you think . . ."

"Forget it," Rivka replied. "I'm with them on this."

The three of them stood and watched until Sagit waved from the other side of the glass partition. In her hand she was tightly clutching her black leather purse, which contained the papers Helmut Gauber had given her.

In Paris, Madame Blanc picked up the phone and called General Chambers. In several staccato-like sentences, she reviewed what had happened, while the general listened in stony silence.

"So the bottom line is," she said, "we have to assume that she got copies of the records of your account at Credit Suisse. I doubt if she found out that you moved the money to the Alliance Bank on the Jardin Brunswick in Geneva. However, the American government will easily get that information and follow the money once they have Sagit's report. As I recall, you now have three million in cash in a vault at Alliance in Geneva. The remainder is in a numbered account at Alliance."

He was flabbergasted. "How did you know?"

"Never underestimate me," she said, wanting to retain his confidence after everything that had happened. "Knowledge is power. I always know."

"If you're so powerful, why can't you prevent her from delivering those bank records to the people in Washington?"

"I may be able to do that, but she's very good, and I think you should take out an insurance policy in case we fail."

"An insurance policy? I don't understand."

The general was pacing back and forth with the phone against his ear, eager to hear how she thought he could elude the freight train that he saw barreling down on him.

"What you need to do," she said, "is get that money out of Switzerland. Keep some cash for yourself, the three million, for instance, and bury the rest in a couple of different banks in places in the world where the U.S. government will never be able to find it. At the same time, you have to get yourself to a country that doesn't have an extradition treaty with the United States."

Her words startled Chambers, confirming his worst fears of what might happen to him. He was stunned that his victory had been converted into a doomsday nightmare scenario in such a short period of time. "That's a great suggestion," he replied, trying desperately to keep his composure, "but I've only got a window of about twenty-four hours to do all of that before that Israeli woman manages to get the attention of the right people in Washington. I'm a military man, not an international financier."

"That's true, but I am, and I could help you."

Her offer made him suspicious. "Why the generosity?" he asked in a dubious voice. "You didn't strike me as the type."

"Let's say I take care of my partners. I reward loyalty."

That struck him as funny, and an involuntary laugh forced its way from his mouth. "Why not say that the reason you're doing this is because you don't want to take the chance that I'll seek immunity and testify against you?"

She tried to sound positive and encouraging, wanting him to view her as the safe haven in this storm. "That possibility has crossed my mind. So you might view my offer as a win-win scenario."

Win-win, my ass, Chambers thought. Lady, you don't give a shit about me. All you care about is yourself and your money. Still, what were his other options? This wasn't the type of decision he was used to making on the spot. He needed time to sort it all out. "Can I think about it?"

"We don't have time. The only way it'll work is if you get on one of your Air Force jets ASAP before the Israeli woman arrives. Then meet me in the bank vault area at the Alliance Bank in Geneva when it opens at nine tomorrow."

"You've got it all worked out, don't you?"

"Yes." She gave a short, smug laugh. "That's how I always do things." Then she continued in a voice exuding confidence and control. "Oh, and one other thing. We can't be seen together. So I'll come in disguise, but I'm sure you'll recognize me, unless of course I didn't make much of an impression on you."

With those words, she hung up the phone. Chambers

stood for several moments with the dead phone in his hand, contemplating what she had told him to do.

From his standpoint, she was right, of course. If the Israeli woman made it back with those documents, he was finished. Going to Geneva was the safe course. If he found out the Israeli woman had been stopped, then he could return to Washington and resume his life as if nothing had happened. He could come back to Washington and tell that asshole, Harry Waltham, how to deal with the Saudi coup. Just what the country needed was some political hack, he thought bitterly, some fool in the White House like Harry Waltham, who didn't have the faintest idea of military considerations or tactics, committing the American military to intervene in a protracted bloody Saudi civil war.

He refused to stand around and be crucified in the press, before Congress and in the courts. As for the money in the Swiss bank, he deserved every cent of it. He had spent thirty years serving his country, putting his life on the line. Why the hell should he have to retire next year with a piss-ass pension while hundreds of thousands of assholes his age were awash in money that they made during those same thirty years? He was every bit as smart as they were. Hell, he graduated first in his class at West Point. He could have been as successful in their fields as they were. But they made their fortunes only because people like him made this great country strong enough so the economy could grow.

Being chairman of the Joint Chiefs still had certain perks. Chambers picked up the phone and called the commander at Andrews Air Force Base. "I need my plane," he barked. "Put on maximum fuel and have it ready to go in thirty minutes. This is a classified national security mission. I'll advise the pilot of the destination immediately prior to flight."

Then he placed his briefcase on the desk and emptied it. He'd need lots of room for the three million dollars in cash. As he started toward the door with his empty briefcase in hand, he suddenly stopped. The whole situation had gotten so dicey that he better be prepared for anything. He reached into his pocket, took out his key ring and walked over to the cabinet at the bottom of a built-in bookcase. After unlocking the door, he extracted a .380 Walther PPK automatic pistol with Sionics suppressor that had been popular among American commandos in Vietnam—just in case events went south on him.

As the plane took off, Sagit felt wired, strung tight from the morning's harrowing experience. Only when they leveled off at cruising altitude did she begin to relax. It's over, she thought to herself. At last it's finally over. She couldn't wait to see David and to tell him how fortunate it was that he had remembered Henri Napoleon and his account number, and that he was forgiven for not telling her earlier.

The seat next to her in first class was empty, and Sagit was grateful she wouldn't have to talk to anyone. With her purse on her lap gripped tightly with both hands, she dozed. The two sleepless nights and all of the day's activities had taken their toll.

Two hours out of Washington, still clutching her purse, she walked up to the front of the cabin to use the lavatory. The other passengers were watching a movie, reading or sleeping. Behind a curtain at the far end of the cabin, the flight attendants were yakking away. As she locked the door behind her, she thought, these bathrooms in first class are huge compared to what I'm used to, or maybe it's Swissair or this plane. Splashing cold water on her face refreshed her. She considered what would happen when she returned to Washington. Hal had said he would call Margaret and have CIA people meet her at Dulles, but it suddenly occurred to her that the Blanc-Chambers people might make one final try to get the documents from her in the terminal. Just to be safe, she took the bank papers out of her purse, stuffed them into her blouse and buttoned her jacket over it. When she walked through the Dulles terminal, she would still grip the purse tightly, hoping that an assailant would grab it and run.

As she unlocked the lavatory door and started out of the compartment, she suddenly felt the door push hard against her. Instinctively, she back-pedaled to avoid being trapped in the door. She called out, "Hey, there's somebody in here."

A ruddy pockmarked face appeared around the door. He was a big and powerful man, and he forced his way into the lavatory shoving her back against the wall and locking the door behind him. Before she could scream, he cupped a hand over her mouth.

"Give me the bank papers," he said to her in a French-accented English, "and I won't hurt you."

When she didn't respond, he grabbed her purse. While using his body to pin her against the wall, he searched the purse with his other hand, to no avail.

"Bitch," he shouted. "Where are they?"

She could hear the roar of the airplane engines, and she knew that they would drown out any sounds coming from the lavatory.

She struggled to get free, but he was too strong. She tried to raise her knee, to jam it into his groin, but he was pressing her too tightly against the wall. He reached into his pocket and extracted a garrote with a noose at one end. Quickly, he slipped it over her neck and began to tighten it. As he worked, she shifted her weight, trying to free her hand.

She could feel the noose tightening. She had to free her hand. Maneuvering in such a confined space was difficult. She heard the engine of the airplane humming through the lavatory wall.

"Where is it bitch?" he demanded. She felt the noose tightening. Finally her hand slipped free. "Tell me now, or you die."

In a single motion, her arm shot up. With the side of her hand she viciously chopped at the pressure point on his neck. She knew that she had scored a direct hit when she felt the noose relax.

Then she took her fist and slammed it hard into his stomach and groin, again and again, mercilessly. He grunted helplessly, unable to recover. Finally he collapsed onto the toilet.

With cold fury, venting all of the anger and frustration

at the injustices that had been done to her and David, she punched him repeatedly on the side of the head until he passed out. Then she sat him down on the toilet, bracing his back against the raised top of the seat. Struggling with little room to work, she took off his pants and white Jockey undershorts.

After kicking him hard in his genitals with the toe of her shoe, she pulled the belt out of his pants and used it to bind his ankles together. With his garrote, she tied his hands together. Next, she ripped his undershorts apart and stuffed the several pieces into his mouth. She rolled up his pants and jammed them under her skirt. Then she left the lavatory.

Nearby there was a flight attendant carrying a glass of water to a passenger.

"This toilet is broken," Sagit told her, sounding like an irritated passenger.

The woman locked the door from the outside and hung up a sign that said DO NOT USE.

Sagit went back to her seat, feeling better than she had in days. She smiled to herself thinking how surprised the cleaning crew at Dulles Airport would be when they found her Frenchman.

CHAPTER 17

Margaret Joyner moved quickly once Sagit handed her the documents from the Zurich bank. Within an hour she had persuaded the attorney general to obtain a warrant to search General Chambers's house at Fort Myer.

Surprisingly, they found information about the account at Credit Suisse, including a copy of the signature card and copies of the deposit slips. There were also records of phone calls to Credit Suisse from Chambers on the dates the deposits were made. They even found a leather journal in which General Chambers recorded for posterity, à la Richard Nixon, his involvement in Madame Blanc's conspiracy.

From Fort Myer, Joyner and Ed Simpson went to the White House. It was almost seven-thirty, and the President was upstairs in the living quarters putting on his tuxedo for a state dinner in honor of the Japanese prime minister.

In stunned silence, he listened to Simpson present the case against General Chambers. When the AG was finished, the President was seething with anger.

"That dirty bastard," he shouted, "arrest him right now."

Joyner responded, "We don't know where he is."

"Then find him."

"We're trying, Harry. It's not easy. So far we've established that he took off this morning on the Air Force jet he regularly uses. He must have leaned on the pilot to file a phony flight plan because it says: 'Destination: Tokyo. Purpose of flight: national security matters.' We can't make radio contact with the plane. We've tried every airport or base in or around Tokyo. Nobody has any idea that General Chambers is coming."

"So he could be . . ."

"Still in the air, or anywhere that's near an airport," she said, finishing his thought.

"That certainly narrows the field. What about Zurich? Suppose he moved his money to another Swiss bank?"

"We've alerted the Swiss government. They're watching every Swiss airport. I've got a couple of my own men at Kloten in Zurich."

The first lady tapped gently on the door. "We're running late, Harry," she said.

"Then we'll be late. This is too damn important."

He paused to get his breath.

"I'll call the Swiss president. They can arrest him if his plane lands at a Swiss airport."

Joyner and Simpson nodded their acquiescence, then listened in silence while President Waltham conveyed his bizarre request to a stunned Swiss president. As soon as he hung up, Joyner said, "I agree that General Chambers is important, but we still have to deal with the Saudi coup in light of this new development. That's even more important."

He nodded. "You're right, Margaret. Arrange a meeting in my office tomorrow morning at ten. You two be there. Get Frost and Bill Hayes and Laurence. We'll decide then what to do about Saudi Arabia."

The President grabbed his tuxedo jacket and started toward the door. "Oh, and bring that guy who started all this. The one who took off and ran. What the hell's his name . . . ?"

"His real name is Greg Nielsen." Margaret said.

"Yeah, Nielsen. Bring him to the meeting tomorrow morning as well."

An hour and a half away, at St. Michaels on Maryland's eastern shore, Sagit and David were lying naked in the king-size bed in Donnelly's guest house. She had called him as soon as she knew he was in the clear. He had given her directions, and she rented a car to race into his waiting arms. That was an hour ago. Now their clothes were scattered across the floor, and half-empty glasses of champagne were on the end table.

Suddenly, her cell phone rang. "Don't answer it," he said.

She pulled away from him. "I have to."

He watched her nodding. Saying, "Uh-uh . . . Yes. I'll tell him . . . Certainly. I'm sure he'll be there."

"What was that all about?" he asked.

"You're invited to the White House at ten A.M. tomorrow to participate in a major review of American policy in Saudi Arabia."

He shook his fist in the air in a sign of victory. "Yes," he shouted. "Yes. The fugitive agent is invited back."

At Andrews Air Force Base, General Chambers told his pilot, who had flown for him for the last three years, that this flight involved serious national security considerations. As a result, the pilot should file a Tokyo flight plan but head in the direction of western Europe. Once they were over the Atlantic, Chambers ordered him to cut off all radio communications. Anticipating that the U.S. government would be watching Swiss airports, General Chambers decided that the better bet would be to land at Lyon in southeastern France and drive to Geneva.

Meantime, the general, taking a cue from Madame Blanc's remark about being disguised, went into the lavatory on the plane and changed into civilian clothes. In a suit and tie, with a black leather briefcase at his side, he looked like a typical American businessman.

Then he went into the cockpit and gave the pilot a final set of instructions: "I want you to land at Lyon and rent a car in your name, which I'll use. Then I want you to go back to the plane, refuel and take off without me for Tokyo. Is that clear?"

"Yes, sir," the pilot said, mystified but pleased to be part of a national security matter that involved cloak-and-dagger activities of this magnitude.

At five minutes past nine in the morning, when General Chambers reached the lobby of the vault area of Alliance Bank on the Jardin Brunswick in Geneva, a woman dressed in a nun's habit was waiting for him with a burgundy leather briefcase at her side. At first he didn't recognize her, but then she nodded to him and gave him her uniquely pernicious smile.

Once Chambers identified himself, an attendant—a heavy-set brunette in a smartly starched navy blue uniform, went with him to retrieve his safe deposit box, then led the general, followed by Madame Blanc, to a windowless cubicle with a small table in the center and a chair on each side. The attendant left the box on the table and closed the door behind her.

"That's a helluva choice for an outfit for you," Chambers remarked.

"Meaning that you don't think godliness is one of my virtues?"

"That's one way of putting it."

She replied, "Maybe that woman in the blue suit thinks you're going to give a contribution to my convent." Then she laughed.

"Look, can we get on with this?" he said testily. "I'm afraid I don't have much of a sense of humor today. First of all, did you stop that Israeli woman before she got back to Washington with the documents from the Zurich bank?"

"I'm afraid not," she said, screwing up her face in anger as she thought about how incompetently Victor had handled Sagit's visit to Zurich.

Chambers took a deep breath. "I didn't think you would."

She pretended to be embarrassed. "But everything else is taken care of."

"Okay. Tell me."

As they sat down across from each other, she said, "One of my private planes is standing by at Geneva Airport waiting to fly you to Bali."

Her words blew General Chambers away. Nonplussed, he shook his head in disbelief. "Bali?"

"*Oui*, Bali. It's part of Indonesia, which doesn't have an extradition treaty with the U.S.," she explained patiently. "The other two options I considered for you were Lebanon and South Korea. Legally, you would be all right in both of those places as well, but I figured you'd live a lot better in a paradise like Bali. If I'm wrong, I can easily change the destination."

The picture of a huge house on a hill overlooking the sea, and a scantily clad dark-skinned young woman to share it with, popped into his mind. Maybe this wouldn't be so bad after all. It was certainly a helluva lot better than Lebanon or South Korea. "No, Bali's the right choice."

"Now, let's talk about your money." She pointed at the box. "I assume you have the three million U.S. dollars in there." He nodded. "Which leaves you twenty-seven million in your account here at Alliance. Correct?"

"Exactly. And another two payments of fifteen million each I have coming from you."

He expected her to object, but instead she said, "Of course. My recommendation is that you divide the twenty-seven million and the other thirty, as it comes in, equally among banks in Andorra, Beirut and Bali."

At first he wondered why she had selected these places. Then he decided that U.S. authorities probably couldn't touch money in their banks. Not wanting to show his ignorance, he went along with her. "That sounds good."

"To expedite the process, I brought with me all of the forms you'll need to set up the numbered accounts and to transfer the money by wire." She unzipped her briefcase resting on the floor, reached inside, extracted several bank forms and placed them on the table.

"Very efficient," he said. "Thanks."

"It's the least I could do. You gave up a lot for me."

He sighed, thinking about how close he had been to succeeding. His aching jaw reminded him very well why he had failed. There was one reason and only one. "And it all would have worked if it weren't for that damn Greg Nielsen." As he said the name, a wave of intense anger surged through his body.

She frowned. It was a bloody miracle that the animosity of those two hadn't destroyed her as well. Somehow she had survived being in a ring with two pit bulls. Well, now the fight's over, boys. She decided not to share any of those thoughts with the general. She simply said, "Life's sometimes like that. We have to roll with the punches."

He glanced at the documents, and she saw his hesitation. "Take your time and read them," she said. "Our planes don't have a schedule."

Chambers wasn't familiar with bank forms, but they all seemed to be what she had represented: withdrawals from Alliance and deposits into three new accounts identified by number at banks in Andorra, Beirut and Bali.

"Where do I sign?"

"I've placed an X at each line that needs your signature."

She watched him carefully as he took a pen out of his pocket, leaned over the documents and began signing. When he was fully engrossed in signing the papers, she reached back into her briefcase. Stealthily, she pulled out a syringe. With a single swift motion, she brought it up and stuck it into his prominently visible jugular vein.

Caught in the midst of writing, he was slow to react. By the time he did, it was too late. The potassium chloride solution had done its work. He fell back into his chair. His entire body convulsed. His eyes bulged. Then his heart stopped beating.

Coldly, she sat in her chair and watched him die, muttering to herself, "So sorry, General Chambers, you were no longer of any use to me. Only a liability."

Methodically, she put the syringe back into her briefcase. She extracted the three million dollars from the vault box and put that in there as well. Then she used his pen to complete his signature on the documents he hadn't signed, copying his scrawl from the ones already signed. The three new numbered accounts were in her name. She had now recovered the entire thirty million dollars. With the bank forms in her briefcase as well, she exited the room and closed the door behind her.

The blue-suited attendant looked up from her desk.

"Monsieur will need at least another hour," Madame Blanc said. "He asked that no one disturb him."

She proceeded to take the elevator up to the main floor. Walking slowly and deliberately to avoid drawing any attention to herself, she left the bank and stepped into a waiting limousine. The windows were one-way glass, and she soon had changed back into her business clothes. When they stopped for a traffic light, she spotted a green trash can on the corner. She handed a shopping bag with the nun's habit to the driver and asked him to place it in the green can. Meantime, she used an alcohol-based solution to take off her excessive makeup.

"Take me to the airport," she said to the driver.

They assembled at ten in the morning around the conference table on one side of the Oval Office.

David couldn't believe that he was back in this room. His last visit had been in January 1979, when Jimmy Carter was President and David had been asked to explore for him what the fall of the Shah of Iran would mean to American interests in the Middle East. He had been instructed by the CIA director at the time, Stafford Turner, to moderate his predictions of the dismal developments that would occur in Iran as the Ayatollah would, in his view, "turn the clock back to the tenth century" and "American interests would suffer a powerful and long-term political blow." David refused to heed the director's instruction. It was a stormy session, and Jimmy Carter became furious at him for being "such a Cassandra." Yet time had proven him prophetic.

He leaned forward in his chair, and stared at President Waltham at the other end of the table. The head of the world's only superpower was looking tense and concerned. The prospect of a major military intervention coupled with the risk of losing Saudi oil was not something that he wanted to deal with so close to the vote on his reelection. Not to mention the disappearance of the man he had selected to be chairman of the Joint Chiefs.

Just as the meeting was about to begin, Kathy, his secre-

tary, came in and handed him a small piece of pink paper.
He read it quickly and shook his head. "Oh, boy!" he exclaimed. "General Chambers is dead. He was found in a
bank vault in Geneva, Switzerland. According to Swiss
medical authorities, he died of a massive heart attack. He
was DOA at a local hospital."

Reactions around the table were mixed. Laurence and
Hayes were delighted that they wouldn't have to deal with
the issue of Chambers's disappearance. Frost was stunned,
and his lower lip began quivering. Joyner was thinking to
herself, Harry, Christmas just came early for you this year.
And David didn't believe the story of the heart attack at
all. He knew exactly what had happened. Chambers was
no longer any use to Madame Blanc, and was disposed of.
But David kept his views to himself.

The President said, "I want some spin control on the
Chambers story. I'll call the Swiss president right now and
tell him we want to keep the part about the Swiss bank
out of the press. He'll readily agree to that. It doesn't do
them any good. I'll tell him we want the body shipped
home quietly via military transport. We'll get him back to
Walter Reed at night, and then we'll release the official
version that General Chambers suffered a heart attack
when he was home in bed. That's it. Nothing else. And we
don't release anything to the media until we're all set up
at Walter Reed. Anyone here have any trouble with that?"

When no one responded, Waltham placed the call to the
Swiss president. Returning to the conference table, he said,
"General Chambers gets a hero's funeral and burial at Ar-
lington. I won't let those sharks from the press have a feeding frenzy like they did with Vince Foster. Now, let's get
down to business. Who wants to tell me what to do about
this Saudi mess?"

Ralph Laurence picked up the ball. He pointed to David
and said, "Since your credibility has been established, we
can now start with the premise that a coup is planned for
October 6, which is five days from now. We know that a
Colonel Khalid is planning the coup and that it's financed

and organized in part by Madame Blanc, who owns PDF, a large French oil company. Those are the basic facts."

"None of us is a moron, Ralph," the President said irritably. "We know all of that. The question is, what do we do in response to this situation?"

The national security adviser sucked in his breath. He was getting tired of being berated by the President and the press. After the first of the year, he planned to resign and to go back to his foreign policy think tank, where his views were given respect. But in the meantime, he had to deal with this crisis.

"I recommend we do two things. First, we send my deputy Wesley Scott to Paris in the morning. He'll present our evidence to the French government that one of their business executives was bribing an American general and plotting a conspiracy to overthrow the king in Saudi Arabia."

Margaret interjected, "Oh c'mon, Ralph, the French government's probably behind Madame Blanc, tacitly at least, right now. Even if they're not, they'll pretend to react with outrage while secretly encouraging her to make the effort to oust us from the dominant foreign position in Saudi Arabia."

Laurence raised his eyebrows. He was sick of her meddling in foreign policy issues, where she had no expertise. In a condescending voice, as if he were patiently lecturing a schoolgirl, he said, "You're far too cynical, Margaret. But that's only half my plan. Also tomorrow morning, I'll fly to Riyadh to talk to the Saudi king, to tell him everything we know about Colonel Khalid's planned coup, and to ask him how he wants to deal with it."

Bill Hayes interjected, "And if he wants American military help, what do we do then?"

Laurence responded, "I say we give it to him. Whatever he needs to stay in power. At least we know what we have. Who knows what we'll get if he goes, and with all of that oil at stake, we can't afford to take a chance."

Hayes fired back, "Have you estimated how many casualties we'll take in a Saudi civil war? Or what the state of preparedness is of our forces to deal with a situation like this on short notice?"

Before Laurence could reply, the President, clearly troubled by what he was hearing, said to the secretary of state: "Okay, Professor Frost, you're unusually quiet, what do you think?"

Visibly confused, Frost was running his hand through what was left of his thinning gray hair. "Right now, I just don't know."

"Okay, you get a pass." Waltham looked at Greg Nielsen at the far end of the table and said, "Nielsen, you're supposed to be an expert in this part of the world. What do you think?"

All eyes turned toward him.

"I start from a different premise, Mr. President," he said politely, trying very hard to speak slowly, rather than in his usual rapid-fire pace, which had annoyed Jimmy Carter. "I don't like the idea of French involvement in Saudi Arabia because it's our sphere of influence, and I want to keep it that way. But we've got to realize that the House of Saud is on its last legs as the rulers of that country. As they say on Broadway, 'We've had a good run.' We got about all we could out of the House of Saud, but it's winding down. It's not a question of whether, but when and how they'll be thrown out."

"Why are you so certain that they're on the way out?" the President asked.

"Because their corruption has achieved epidemic levels. Far too many people are unhappy. Regardless of whether the price of oil goes up or down, the vast majority of the Saudis are getting poorer while the royal family and all of its multitude of princes pull more and more golden eggs out of that goose. The plain fact is that enormous resentment against the royal family has emerged in all segments of the society as the economy has soured. At the same time, the religious fundamentalists, who hate the United States, are on the rise and becoming more violent. As Colonel Khalid demonstrates, the rulers have lost the support of much of the military. So the question for us is how to ensure that the next group of rulers who take over is friendly to us and will insure the flow of oil as well as our

other economic relationships. It might be nice if Colonel
Khalid and his supporters would do something to increase
democracy in the country if they gained control, but I'm
not so naive to think that will be their top priority."

Clearly taken aback, the President asked: "Are you telling me that I should support this Colonel Khalid against
the Saudi king?"

David took a deep breath. "Colonel Khalid's not perfect,
but he's the best available. If we make it clear that we're
behind him, I think we can lure him away from the French.
So I guess the short answer to your question, Mr. President,
is yes, I think you should support Colonel Khalid. I don't
think you want to be presiding over another situation like
the fall of the Shah, which left a critical and strategic Middle Eastern country in very unfriendly hands, continuing to
this day. Actually, it's even worse this time because with
Saudi oil we're not just concerned with the value of that
oil alone. They're the linchpin for the entire world oil market. If a fundamentalist regime should gain power in Saudi
Arabia and team up with the regime in Iran on oil policy,
then our problems will be magnified exponentially."

"But if we use our military, we can help the king defeat
this Colonel Khalid and shore up his regime? Right?"

"There's a catch-22 here." David started to move his
arms and pick up speed in his voice, but caught himself as
he continued. "You could help the king defeat Colonel
Khalid, but if the king's perceived by the Saudi people as
needing American military support to remain in power, the
opposition will coalesce. There will be constant hit-and-run
attacks on American troops, with resulting deaths. It'll be
Vietnam all over on a smaller scale."

The President got up and paced around the room, evalu-
ating what he had just heard. "The way you present it,
Nielsen, I don't have much choice. Do I?"

"I'm sorry, sir. It's not a good situation. It's not your
fault. Rather, it's a mess you inherited. This country's leaders have been in denial about what's been happening in
Saudi Arabia and to the House of Saud, as we were in Iran
and to the Shah. Even when we weren't in denial, we've

been too afraid of saying anything that would upset the Saudi king, as if he would take his oil and go home. Years ago we could have helped ourselves by persuading the House of Saud to change its approach to ruling the country. But it's too late for that now."

The President looked at Joyner. "What do you think, Margaret?"

She was nodding with approval, impressed with David's analysis. "I think that Nielsen here presents a good case. The fact that my station chief was just pulled out of a prince's swimming pool with rocks tied to his ankles, and that the protests our ambassador made are being ignored, demonstrates that the rule of law isn't exactly prevalent in that country. The last thing we want is another Iran. It's been a nightmare for us in so many ways. Besides, the fundamentalists could combine forces in those two countries on oil policy and cripple our economy."

No one else spoke. As a heavy silence descended on the Oval Office, everyone was looking at the man at the end of the table, who had been elected by the American people to make decisions like this.

"Okay, here's where I am," the President finally said. "The tax cut bill is my number one priority right now. The House has already passed the bill. The Senate will vote and hopefully pass it in two days. Then they'll recess for the election. If I make any move on this Saudi thing, regardless of whether I follow Ralph's recommendation or that of Nielsen and Margaret, I'll have to brief key congressional leaders. The press will be certain to pick it up, and we'll have a circus in town. Opponents of the tax cut bill will use that distraction to put off the Senate vote, which will effectively kill the legislation. I don't want that to happen. So for the next two days we'll go into a holding pattern about this Saudi business. That still gives me enough time to go either way before the 6th. In the meantime, Margaret, you and Ralph each give me something in writing presenting your respective positions. No more than two pages. Don't keep any copies. I don't want this leaking out. I'll shred the documents after I read them. Then I'll let you know what I decide. Anybody disagree with that approach?"

David thought for an instant about resuming the argument for immediate support for Khalid, but decided to bite his tongue. Nothing had changed in Washington, he thought sadly. It was politics first, second and third.

Sagit was waiting for David in the living room of a suite in the Hay-Adams Hotel just across Lafayette Park from the White House. They had checked in early that morning. She took one look at his face, and said, "I gather that you didn't get a commitment for supporting Khalid."

David mimicked the President. "We're in a holding pattern for a few days about this Saudi business." He looked disgusted. "Who knows where it'll come out? I hope you had a more productive morning."

She had a satisfied look on her face. "Well, as a matter of fact, I did. I've got a little surprise for you. It's in the bedroom."

What kind of nonsense was she up to? he wondered. "What are you talking about?"

"Why don't you stop talking and go look?"

As soon as he entered the bedroom, he saw her, resting on the bed, weary from flying all night from Israel. She jumped up and threw her arms around him yelling, "Surprise. Surprise, David."

David's mouth shot open in astonishment. "Daphna, what are you doing here?"

"Sagit arranged it all. You better ask her."

He turned to Sagit, standing in the doorway, grinning from ear to ear.

"Once I delivered the Zurich bank documents to Margaret, I knew you were vindicated and could resume a normal life. So I called the kibbutz and arranged for Daphna to fly over. I wanted to make it a surprise. I figured you two could spend some time together traveling around the United States now that this whole Saudi business with Khalid is over."

David's face rapidly turned sour. "I hate to be a killjoy, but it's not over."

Sagit didn't want to believe what she had just heard. Matter of factly, she responded, "Well, your part is over."

"Not the way I see it."

"No, David. No."

He gave her a tight smile, wanting to mollify her. Then he turned to Daphna. "Could we put off our U.S. tour for just a few days, and you and Sagit spend a little time visiting Washington sites?"

"So he can fly off to Saudi Arabia," Sagit said, her voice quivering with emotion, "and encourage Khalid to act now while the President's paralyzed."

"That's part of it."

Her body tensed. She knew what was coming next. "And the rest?"

"I plan to settle my score with Nasser, the terrorist responsible for blowing up the bus Yael was on." His words brought Daphna's tired eyes to life with hatred. "Don't forget, getting revenge against Nasser was the reason I got into this whole mess in the first place."

"And you're going to do all that yourself?"

"Khalid will give me some assistance," David said hopefully.

"You're dreaming. He'd never risk starting his new regime that way. He has to live with those people." Sagit had spent most of her Mossad career focused on the Arab world. She had no doubt that Khalid would be operating within limits, regardless of his friendship with David. "If you're really serious about getting Nasser, it has to be the two of us, and we have to try to kidnap him. If we fail and we have to kill him, that's one thing, but I'd like to try and bring him out alive to stand trial."

There was a knock on the door. Sagit looked up. "I didn't know when you'd be back. I ordered lunch from room service. Let me go see about that, while you come up with a plan."

Over lunch, David laid it all out for Sagit and Daphna.

At the end, he said, "All we'll need from Khalid is to lend us a helicopter and a Saudi pilot for about three hours."

Sagit replied, "He'll give us the helicopter. He'll never give us the pilot. Forget it."

"Then call Moshe. He'll give us a pilot."

Daphna nodded her agreement with David's assessment, but Sagit knew the Mossad director much better than either of them. "Moshe would never approve any of this in a million years. I'm going with you strictly on my own because Yael once saved my life, and I owe her that much." She gave a rueful smile. "Besides, I must be masochistic, but I've gotten used to doing these insane things with you."

Suddenly, Daphna spoke up. In a halting voice, she said, "I can fly a helicopter. Take me with you."

"That's not even an option," David said.

Sagit had read Daphna's air force file, and she knew what had happened on her last helicopter mission over northern Israel. "He's right," she said to Daphna. "You're not going."

By now Daphna was thinking about her escape in St. Tropez, and she was feeling more courageous. "Yael was my mother. It's my decision. Neither of you has the right to make it for me. You can't tell me what to do."

David was furious. "I don't believe you're doing this."

"You just said that without a helicopter pilot you can't get Nasser. Well, now you have one."

"I'm against it," Sagit shot back. "I know what happened when—"

"And it's time I got back on the horse. Isn't it?"

"No, it's not. None of us may make it out of there alive."

"Yael was my mother," the young woman said stubbornly. "I want to fly that helicopter."

"You really want to do this?" David asked.

"It's not a question of wanting. I must do it. I won't be able to live with myself if I pass up a chance to avenge her death."

David looked at her with pride. She had her mother's determination and stubborness. There was no point arguing with her. Like Yael, she wouldn't be denied. "Let her do it," David said.

"Not so fast," Sagit said to him. "How exactly do you plan to get us into Saudi Arabia? Except for religious pilgrims and those who have business, nobody gets a visa. This may be the only country in the world that doesn't permit tourists."

"I'll call Khalid. He'll arrange it."

"We'll never get in with Israeli passports."

"We'll use those United States Holt passports that got us into UAE. You used yours to go to Zurich, so it looks like Margaret Joyner didn't cancel them."

"True, but what about our helicopter pilot?"

Daphna reached into her purse that was resting on the floor. "I kept the Italian guy's passport I used getting out of St. Tropez for a souvenir. If I get some makeup, hair coloring and men's clothes, I'll be okay."

"This is insane," Sagit said.

David replied, "No more insane than kidnapping Eichmann, rescuing hostages at Entebbe or bombing an Iraqi nuclear reactor. I'll call Khalid and see how we can get visas."

When Khalid didn't answer, David decided to call again in an hour. Meantime, he sat down with Sagit and Daphna, and they mapped out their plans in greater detail.

Khalid wasn't answering his cell phone because he had turned it off as soon as Madame Blanc called and asked him to come immediately to suite 4800 at the Hyatt Regency Hotel in Riyadh. Khalid had been stunned by the call. He had no idea that she was coming to Saudi Arabia in person.

When he knocked on the door of the suite, she was smoking a cigar. She offered him one, but he declined.

"I'm very surprised to see you," the Saudi said.

"I decided to bring Greg Nielsen's report in person. Also, I have news. I wanted you to hear it from me first."

Creases appeared on Khalid's forehead. "What news? It's not good, is it?"

"I think it's irrelevant."

"Okay, tell me."

"General Chambers died of a heart attack yesterday in Geneva."

Shocked, Khalid sat down on a sofa and put his head into his hands. When she saw his reaction, she was now very glad she had made the trip to Riyadh to tell Khalid in person. He had no idea she planned to remain here until the coup occurred and then for the indefinite future. On his own, he might get cold feet. She waited for the news about Chambers to sink in. Then she said: "This doesn't affect anything between us. Everything can still go forward as we planned."

He was stunned by the cavalier way in which she had brushed aside the loss of a linchpin of their operation. "That's not correct. We needed General Chambers. He was the one who was going to persuade President Waltham not to intervene on the side of the king. Without Chambers, the U.S. will intervene, and we'll be crushed like bugs."

"The Americans won't intervene," she said confidently.

"How do you know that?"

"Because I have a second top American official working with me as well."

His forehead wrinkled with curiosity. "Who?"

"You don't need to know."

"I have to know, or I won't proceed." She relit her cigar and paused to puff on it. "Well?" he demanded.

"Charles Frost, the American secretary of state."

Khalid was taken aback. This woman couldn't be under-estimated. She was hell-bent on getting what she wanted. "You're kidding."

"Not at all. It doesn't take much money to buy a university professor, you know. I did it when I began to worry about Chambers."

"And Frost will persuade President Waltham not to act?"

"He damn well better. That's why he's being paid. I don't think he'll dare cross me."

He wanted to ask, Did General Chambers cross you? Is that why he's dead? But he kept that thought to himself. Instead, he said, "Give me Nielsen's report."

She tossed him a copy, and he immediately sat down on a sofa and began reading, nodding his head as he turned the pages. When he had finished the report and studied the maps at the back, he read it through a second time.

"Now you see why I wanted Nielsen," he told her.

"I agree, it's a good job." The compliment was grudgingly given. She had no idea where David was now, and what he was doing. She worried about that.

"I assume I can keep this copy."

"Correct."

"Now give me the codes to deactivate the automated systems."

She held out her empty hands, palms up. "I don't have them."

"You can't be serious."

"But I am. He's your friend. He promised to fly here on the fourth and to give me the codes then." Even talking about David made her angry. Victor had been right. She should have kept David under her control in Paris when she had him the last time, after he presented his report. "With everything that's happened since, he'll never do that."

Khalid sat back down on the couch. "So my forces will get blown apart by the defensive systems at the palace. Even if I win, I'll take over a country that won't produce oil for years."

"I think you're overreacting. Why don't you use Nielsen's report to modify your plan of attack?"

"What do you mean?"

"You've got control of the air force. Begin your attack under cover of darkness when the king's asleep, with a massive bombing on the palace so devastating that the king won't have a chance to activate those automated systems."

Shocked by her words, he jumped to his feet. "No," he said emphatically. "I won't do that. I'll be vilified for all time."

She was determined to use any argument she could to persuade him to abandon his gut reaction. "I can't believe you're saying that. With all of the pain and suffering the House of Saud's inflicted on your country, you want to wage a gentlemanly war against them. Get real, Khalid. All you'll be remembered for is the freedom you're bringing to your people. They'll erect statues in your honor in every town."

"I don't know."

She felt he was weakening, bending her way. "Great patriots have always had to make hard choices," she added.

He began pacing back and forth across the room, thinking about her words all the while.

"History rarely gives any leaders the kind of opportunity you have now," she said, and then appealing to his vanity, she added, "Great leaders, and I would put you in that category, seize the day."

She held her voice, while he continued pacing and thinking.

Finally, he said reluctantly, "I'll do it."

"Good. For the foreseeable future," she continued, "I intend to do all of my business out of this hotel. I've taken over this entire penthouse floor. They'll set up fax machines and computers. I've got a local firm, Global Security, hiring bodyguards and drivers. Several of my staff are coming to join me after the shooting ends and everything settles down."

He looked alarmed.

"Don't worry, my official cover is that I'm considering building a large petrochemical plant. I had no trouble getting visas for me and my people. The economic minister is planning a dinner in my honor. Of course, they hate the fact that I'm a woman, but I represent money and jobs. They'll look the other way. So much for principles. Meantime, I'll learn a great deal that'll help me hit the ground running to reshape the Saudi oil business once our coup occurs."

Khalid was taken aback. He had never envisioned such a broad-reaching role for her in the Saudi oil business. "But . . . ," he protested.

She cut him off. "Working within OPEC, we should be able to increase prices sharply."

Khalid left the suite shaking his head and very troubled. If he succeeded, how long would he have to deal with this horrible woman? And how would he ever control her? As he climbed into his car, he turned his cell phone back on. Five minutes later, David called.

"It's your friend from the steam room."

"Are you absolutely insane?" Khalid said when David told him that he wanted to come to Saudi Arabia with two women.

David chuckled. "That's what they told me."

"And they were right."

"But you're going to help arrange our visit because I have some codes that you need and because I was at the White House today. I know firsthand what's happening in Washington."

"You could tell me all of that right now," Khalid said anxiously.

The adrenaline was surging in David's body. He was back in his element, doling out information to achieve his purpose. "But I won't. Only in person. So I'll give you the three names on the passports we'll be using and you fax the visas."

David had tried deftly to avoid talking about what he himself wanted to accomplish in Saudi Arabia. That fact hadn't eluded Khalid, who knew that David wasn't coming merely to turn over information. "And what else are you planning to do here?"

"That I'll tell you in person as well."

Khalid decided that any further discussion was pointless. He would never talk David out of coming, but it suddenly occurred to Khalid that after his recent conversation with Madame Blanc, that might not be all bad. David could be of help to him in dealing with Madame Blanc. An idea was developing in his mind.

An hour later, Khalid called David back. "You'll have visas by fax within an hour. Use window number eight at Passport Control at the airport on your arrival. That one's been greased. When you arrive, rent a car, check into the Intercontinental Hotel and wait for my call."

In suite 4800, Madame Blanc replayed in her mind her conversation with Khalid. She knew that he was surprised by what she had said about her extensive takeover of the Saudi oil business. She had anticipated his reaction. She wanted to break it to him early and give him time to get used to it. Oh, he'll come around all right, she thought. Once his attack was launched, he'd be powerless to stop her. He'd be smart enough to realize that all she had to do was leak to the Saudi press and some key Saudi officials the extent of foreign support he'd received for his coup and he'd lose popular support in the country. If he didn't realize it himself, she'd explain it to him. No, she could control Khalid. She wasn't worried about him.

She tapped her fingers on the desk, thinking some more. But there was someone worrying her, and that was Victor. No one could ever incriminate her in the death of General Chambers, but that Israeli kid from Haifa was a different matter. Victor could incriminate her in that kid's death if he ever turned on her, and that was now a real risk. David had vanished since their last Paris meeting. Suppose he managed to get Victor back to Israel and charge him with the murder of that Israeli kid? If Victor turned on her to save his own neck, which he could do because she knew that scheming lawyer never really liked her, she could be charged with conspiracy to commit murder. She couldn't let that happen. No, she had to get rid of Victor to avoid that possibility, which would also have the advantage of eliminating the need to pay Victor his five-percent share of the Saudi oil profits. Yes, Victor definitely had to go. That conclusion pleased her for another reason. It was inexcusable how badly he had bungled Sagit's visit to Zurich.

She smiled sadistically, trying to decide how she would do it. Then she picked up the phone and called Javiar, the head of a Basque terrorist group headquartered near Bilbao, which had agents in Paris, cruel hard men who would take on any task that would generate cash that could be used to buy arms and finance their war for independence against the Spanish government. There was no risk that an action executed by Javiar could ever be traced to her.

After she made that call to Javiar, she felt much better. The last loose end had been tied up. Now she was in the clear.

CHAPTER 18

It was just past midnight when they landed in Riyadh. An hour after they checked into the hotel, the phone rang in David's room.

Khalid said, "There's a little café up in the hills east of the city, run by a blind woman and her husband. We used to go there."

"I remember it."

"Meet me there in an hour."

The streets of the capital were deserted in the early morning hours, but David drove slowly, taking back routes to avoid being stopped by the police. As they drove through areas familiar to him, they saw scores of huge construction projects on which work had been suspended, a clear testimony to the fact that the money had run out. David, Sagit and Daphna shrugged off the effects of jet lag and lack of sleep as the energy pumped through their bodies. They had come to the endgame. They would have plenty of time to rest and to sleep when this was over—if they survived.

Khalid was waiting for them in the parking lot, and he hustled them through a back door of the building and up to the second floor, where the blind woman and her husband lived. A girl of about ten brought in cups of pungent Turkish coffee and departed quickly. In the meantime, Khalid turned on a radio to minimize the risk of being heard, even though the café downstairs was closed. The sounds of a wailing Arab melody filled the room.

"Who are they?" Khalid demanded to know, pointing at

Sagit and Daphna, who was still wearing her Italian man's disguise.

David motioned toward Sagit. "She's an agent with the Mossad."

Khalid was horrified. "And you brought her here?"

"You'll understand when we talk some more."

Khalid sighed. "And the man with the Italian passport?"

"My daughter, Daphna."

Khalid peered closely at her, now noticing some resemblance. "Your daughter? I never knew."

"It's a long story for another time."

Khalid glanced nervously at the door. "By coming, and bringing them, you're putting us all at risk."

David tried to soothe him. "I know that, but we had our reasons. You'll find out in a few minutes. First, I want you to know that General Chambers is dead."

"I already know."

Now it was David's turn to be surprised. "How could you? Washington hasn't made it public yet."

"Our friend Madame Blanc is in Riyadh in suite 4800 at the Hyatt Regency. She told me about it."

David turned to Sagit. "That just proves what I suspected. She killed him. How else would she know?"

"She said it was a heart attack."

"That can be induced."

"It can?"

"Absolutely, if certain chemicals are administered to the body. The woman's diabolical."

"She claims that she also has the secretary of state in her pocket and that he'll oppose military intervention by the U.S. government."

David thought back to Frost's behavior in the Oval Office. "She may very well, judging from how he acted at the White House meeting I attended."

"What happened?"

David proceeded to describe the meeting in detail, including the fact that Frost was stunned by the news of Chambers's death and didn't support intervention on the side of the king, which would have been expected from the secretary of state.

When he was finished, Khalid asked, "So how likely do you think it is that President Waltham will decide to support the king and tell him about me and the coup?"

David shrugged, "I don't know Waltham, and I couldn't read him. I made the best argument I could for your support, but he was noncommittal. I'd say it's about fifty-fifty. Frost won't be a factor either way."

Khalid shook his head in disbelief. "So you mean there's a fifty-percent chance that my head will be hanging in a public square like that of Azziz five years ago."

"If you wait and do nothing until the 6th, that's about it."

Khalid looked dejected. "But what else can I do?"

There was a noise outside the building. It sounded like something scurrying across the ground. Khalid raised his right hand, signaling them to be quiet. Warily, he walked over to the window and stared into the night air—lit by a three-quarter moon and myriad stars. He looked in every direction, but couldn't see a thing. It must have been an animal, he decided.

David gave a sigh of relief, then resumed talking when Khalid cut back across the room. "That's one reason we came. Did Madame Blanc give you my report about the palace defenses and the oil field destruction systems?"

"As soon as she arrived in Riyadh. It was a great report, except for one thing."

"The codes?" David asked. Khalid nodded. "Well, you can't blame me. I needed something to hold over that monster. If I were to give them to you now, how quickly could you move?"

Khalid's face lit up. "You mean, advance the date of attack?"

"Yep, that's exactly what I mean."

The colonel closed his eyes, mulling over the details that would have to be coordinated. He liked David's idea. All of his people were ready and anxious. In some ways, a few days earlier would be better. That meant less time for someone to inform on him.

Finally, he said to David, "It'll be tight, but we can be ready to go as early as twenty-four hours from now. Tomorrow morning at first light."

"That should work," replied David. "President Waltham won't have made a decision yet, and you'll present him with a fait accompli. There's a good chance that he'll remember what I told him and not take any action."

"But what about Israel?" Khalid said, looking at Sagit. "What will they do? They usually make trouble."

Sagit bristled at his last comment, but bit her tongue to avoid taking the bait. "My government's had time to consider this issue," she said somberly, "because I briefed them after your meeting in London with David."

"And?" Khalid asked nervously.

"We won't take any action. The House of Saud's always been a bitter enemy of Israel."

"Okay, give me the codes," Khalid said to David. "I'll deactivate the automated systems tonight and launch the attack tomorrow morning."

David took a deep breath. "I need something in return."

"Saving your life five years ago wasn't enough?"

"Just a little something else."

Khalid's eyes narrowed. "What?"

"I want you to give us the support we need to kidnap Mohammed Nasser and to fly him to Israel to stand trial for the murder of the Israelis who died on bus eighteen last August, including my wife, Yael. The Americans may want to try him for the Khobar housing bomb five years ago as well."

Khalid was dumbfounded. "How do you intend to do that?"

"You don't want to know the details," said David. "We'll need the help of your mole in Nasser's organization to get us into Nasser's complex, and we'll need an unmarked helicopter. That's all."

"And if I don't give you those, you won't give me the codes?"

"I wish you wouldn't put it that way."

There was a long pause while Khalid studied David's

face to try to determine if he was bluffing. David's face showed no weakness, only determination. He could have been at a chemin de fer table.

Finally, Khalid broke. "I would be able to supply you with one of our MD 500s. We'll take off the Saudi markings. You'll have to fly it yourself, though. Can one of you do that?"

David pointed at Daphna, who nodded weakly.

Khalid shook his head in disbelief. "And if the three of you get yourselves killed in this idiotic effort, then what?"

"You didn't know anything about it. You can even behave like King Hussein used to, and act indignant that Israel carried out an action like this on your territory."

"What's the timing of your little excursion to Nasser's headquarters in the east?"

"Tomorrow morning. About six hours after you launch your attack on the king's palace, when there's still lots of confusion, but it looks as if you're in control."

David took a pencil and piece of paper out of his pocket. From memory, he wrote down the three codes and handed them to Khalid.

They spent the next day in the hotel and out of sight. At midnight, they drove to a small warehouse that the CIA had rented in the name of a phony U.S. oil company. In five years, no one had bothered to change the combination lock on the door, and David quickly let them in. "We used to call it the toy store," he said.

First, he located a pair of wristwatches that had a two-way alarm connection. If anyone wearing one of the watches pressed the tiny button next to the stem of the watch, it would set off an alarm on the other watch within a range of five miles. Next, he handed Sagit a small plastic bottle that was labeled LIQUID SUGAR in Arabic, but contained a powerful soporific. For several minutes, he rummaged through boxes of papers until he found what he was looking for: Iraqi government stationery with a perfect forgery of Saddam Hussein's signature, which the CIA had used to pass phony Iraqi messages before and after

Operation Desert Storm. He found an Arabic typewriter for Sagit, and above Saddam's signature she began to type the message: "Mohammed Nasser: Please receive my emissary . . ."

Suddenly, David gripped her arm tightly, and she stopped typing. "I can't let you go through with this," he said to Sagit. "It's too dangerous for you. I should be the one who goes in first."

"We've already been over this a thousand times," she said. "There were a lot more Israelis killed on that bus than just Yael. It's my job. Besides, this is the only way. You can't pass for an Iraqi. There's no alternative. It's that simple."

"But they'll never accept a woman."

"Hanan Ashrawi is a woman, and she's one of the top people in the Palestinian leadership. Besides, nobody questions Saddam. They're not surprised when he's eccentric."

"What if Nasser's people call Baghdad to check on you?"

"They'll be worried that lunatic Saddam would be offended by a call questioning his agent. Besides, there will be too much confusion as a result of Khalid's attack on the royal palace."

David wasn't convinced. He was worried that she'd never get out alive, but he could tell from the look of determination in her eyes that there was no stopping her now. Last year he had lost Yael, and this year it would be Sagit.

She resumed typing. ". . . Hanan Abdullah to discuss recent events in your country."

She put the letter in an envelope and sealed it with the official Iraqi government seal that David supplied.

He then handed Sagit and Daphna brand-new cell phones that couldn't be traced, and he took one for himself. "In case we have to talk."

The toy store had an inside locked closet with guns and ammunition that David easily opened with a pocketknife. He found an Uzi and a Beretta for himself, along with ammunition. He tossed Sagit a small pistol. "Put this in your bag in case of an emergency," he said.

"What about me?" asked Daphna.

"You shouldn't need it, but just in case," he said, handing her an Uzi as well.

Sagit tossed the pistol back to him. "It's too dangerous. They'll probably search me."

"So what? Tell them you brought it because you're in a rough neighborhood."

"It'll put them on guard. It'll make it more likely they'll make inquiries of Baghdad. It's a risk I don't want to take."

"Damn, you're stubborn."

"I understand these people. I know how they react. Besides, they'll have enough weapons in the compound for a small army. If I get into trouble, I'll take one of them."

"Yeah, just like that."

When he realized that he wouldn't be able to budge her, he handed her a small, thin black object that resembled a hair clip.

"What's this?" she asked.

"It's a poison dart, made of plastic so it won't set off metal detectors. You can wear it in your hair. If it penetrates the skin, the result is immediate death. It's something you can use in an emergency."

"You worry too much," she said, as she put it in her hair.

The tension was getting to him as he felt the full impact of what they were doing. "Too bad," he snapped. "I've gotten attached to you. I don't want to lose you."

An hour later, they met Khalid's mole on the second floor of the blind woman's café. They didn't ask his name. He didn't offer it. Sweating heavily the entire time of their meeting, he drew them a detailed map of Nasser's compound. Typically, defenses were light and there were very few people in the compound, the mole explained. The terrorist leader was a recluse. "He is moody and introspective. His compound is isolated. He dislikes having many people around."

The mole listened passively when Sagit told him in Arabic that two hours after Khalid's attack on the palace he should tell Nasser that he had received a call from Baghdad stating that an emissary named Hanan Abdullah would be coming in by helicopter. As David studied the map, he targeted the location where he and Daphna could drop Sagit outside the compound, and then the inside courtyard where they would pick her up with her prisoner, Nasser.

The helicopter was a spanking new MD 500, accommodating a single pilot and four passengers, powered by a powerful Allison turboshaft engine and equipped with TOW missiles. Though the Apache had been her usual helicopter, Daphna had flown MD 500s on a couple of occasions in the Israeli Air Force, and she felt a familiarity as they approached the helicopter. Suddenly, her knees began knocking, and she was perspiring. David sensed what she was feeling. "You can do it," he said. "You can do it."

Daphna saw her old copilot Yuri's face in her mind. She heard his anguished cries. She saw the back of his head flowing with blood. She was behind him at the controls of the Apache. It was spinning wildly near the Lebanese border. There were trees. A crash landing was the only way. She aimed for the tallest and thickest tree, and . . .

"C'mon, Daphna, you can do it."

"I don't know, David. I just don't know."

"Close your eyes for a minute and think about your mother. What she was like before Nasser and his men killed her."

"I'll try," she said weakly.

Sagit and David held their breath as Daphna climbed up awkwardly and reluctantly and sat behind the controls, fighting her demons all the way. They followed her into the helicopter and stowed their personal items under their seats. Daphna's hands were shaking, and her eyes were blinking. With clammy palms, she started the engine, and they both gave a sigh of relief.

Sagit turned to David and handed him a small piece of paper.

"What's this?" he asked.

"All of Margaret Joyner's telephone numbers. Home, office and cell phone."

"For what?"

"In case something happens to me, and you have to reach her."

David touched her cheek. "Nothing's going to happen to you. After this mission's over, we're going to spend the rest of our lives together, and you're going to wear that little orange bikini for me until it falls apart."

"That's a deal," she said, trying to force a smile, but grimly adding, "if I make it."

"If you don't think you will," he said, "we should stop now. Nothing's worth that price. Let's go somewhere, anywhere on this globe, and spend the rest of our lives together. When we were at St. Michaels, you made a list of places we should go together. Let's use that list starting right now."

Her face was unemotional, set in stone. She had returned to her role as the experienced Mossad agent. Nothing else mattered. "Sorry, that's not an option any longer." Her voice was cold and brittle. "At least until this is over. You missed your chance."

He looked at Daphna, who was more firmly in control of her emotions now.

"Ready to go?" Daphna asked.

"Ready," David and Sagit said in unison.

As they took off, he thought about what Sagit had told him in UAE. Moshe had recruited them about the same time, "Yael, myself and a girl by the name of Leora . . ." He glanced over at Sagit. He had lost her. She was staring straight ahead, in another world. He could read her mind. She was convinced that she would never be able to capture Nasser alive, and that she would die, but she was hoping to take Nasser with her.

Well, I won't let it happen, he vowed.

The helicopter roared and vibrated as Daphna lifted off into a perfect robin's-egg blue sky.

CHAPTER 19

James Knight, the President's press secretary, moved hesitantly to the podium in front of the White House press room. God, how he hated making these statements when he had so little in the way of facts. The press people would skewer him. Initially, he had hoped that the lateness of the hour, 2 A.M. Washington time, would mean that he'd have a small audience, but when he thought about the magnitude of the story involved, he realized how futile that hope was. There was pandemonium in the room.

In a voice smooth and polished from daily sessions with two different speech coaches, he began reading a prepared statement:

"At 5:10 A.M. Saudi Arabia time today, a military force led by Saudi Colonel Abul Khalid launched an attack on the residence of the Saudi king and royal family. Fighting was initially fierce, but within two hours, the king ordered his personal guard to surrender. The vast majority of the Saudi Army, Air Force and Navy have apparently joined Khalid's forces, who have now gained control of the palace and key facilities in the country.

"There has been no damage to the Saudi oil fields. Colonel Khalid has promised a democratic regime and has called for free and open elections as soon as stability has returned to the country. Thus far, Shiite and fundamentalist leaders have not made any public statement.

"President Waltham is watching developments closely. He has consulted with other major world leaders and warned other foreign governments against any intervention.

"And that's all I have to say."

Reporters were on their feet screaming out questions. The first one Knight heard was the first one he had expected:

"James, will we be intervening militarily on the side of the king?"

Knight was ready with the carefully crafted answer. "The President has ordered all American troops in the area to be on alert. Two of our aircraft carriers are on their way to Saudi Arabia. As of right now, no military intervention by our government is planned in what we view as purely a Saudi internal affair."

Half a world away, Sagit stepped out of the helicopter and gave David a small wave as Daphna lifted off to take the chopper back to the desert to wait for her signal. Sagit was convinced that she would never see him again. Walking the quarter of a mile to Nasser's compound, through blowing sand whipped up by the helicopter, she wasn't nervous. An eerie calm had taken hold of her.

She thought about Yael. She thought about the mangled bodies in the debris of Bus 18. She thought about the innocent pedestrians maimed because the bomb contained rusty steel nails inside to magnify the damage. She thought about children who no longer had parents, and a sense of righteous rage overcame any fear that she had. She thought about Yael and Leora. The three of them were "Moshe's girls." She thought about friends of hers who had died in Arab-Israeli wars and in other terrorist incidents over the years. She would be joining them in a portion of what her grandfather had called "Ha'alom Haba," populated by Jews who had given their lives so future generations of Israelis could thrive in the land of their ancestors. That thought gave her peace.

Then she compartmentalized and thought of Nasser and the mission at hand. All of her senses were finely honed. She knew what she had to do, and she would do it.

The compound was a château-like structure that had once been the winter home of a wealthy Saudi prince, before Nasser commandeered it for his revolutionary movement. With its gray stone walls and floor-to-ceiling windows, it could have been in the south of France, and perhaps it was a copy of a château the prince had seen there.

At the front gate to a high barbed-wire-topped fence, she met two guards armed with AK-47s. In the classic revolutionary mode, they had strips of bullets crisscrossed on their chests. They were young—no more than sixteen, she guessed. Sagit was wearing green military fatigues that were standard for the Iraqi revolutionary government, and her head was covered with a cloth. Yet since she was a woman, she could see the two of them undressing her mentally.

The mole had apparently done his work because as soon as she announced, "Hanan Abdullah," one of the guards opened the gate, and the other led her inside.

The compound seemed deserted, just as the mole had said it would be. One of the two guards led her across a dusty center courtyard, where David was hoping to land the helicopter. At the entrance to the château, two of Nasser's aides—the mole and a man named Hassan—met her. She held out the envelope with the letter from Saddam to Hassan, who opened it and read it carefully, while the mole searched her bag and ran his hands roughly over her body, pausing for just an instant on her breasts.

They led her inside the building, to a first-floor office where Nasser was sitting at a desk and writing. He was exactly as the mole had described: a man trying to emulate Saddam Hussein in appearance, but who had a charismatic look, and a smile beneath his thick mustache that offset the harsh cruelty in his eyes. He, too, was dressed in military fatigues with a pistol at his waist.

When Hassan handed Nasser the letter, he examined it momentarily and said, "Saddam is a friend. Any friend of his is my friend. Any enemy of his is my enemy." He said it in a matter-of-fact voice, letting the ominous words speak for themselves.

Hassan and the mole retreated while a woman brought in two cups of coffee and deposited them on a table in front of a sofa. Nasser pointed to Sagit, signaling that she should sit on the sofa, and he pulled up the desk chair to the other side of the table.

The thought that kept running through Sagit's mind was, How am I going to add the soporific to his coffee? There has to be a disturbance. He has to be called away, but how?

She decided to begin talking, hoping something would develop. "Saddam has followed closely what happened this morning with the Saudi king," she said, speaking Arabic quickly with a perfect Baghdad accent. "He wants to know if you're prepared to advance your own revolution. To move now before Colonel Khalid can solidify his rule."

A wary Nasser replied, "If I were to do that, how much support would he give me?"

"Whatever you need. He has money in French banks that can easily be shifted to your account to purchase arms."

"That's an attractive offer, but Tehran made a similar offer."

She pretended to be dismayed. "Their government is more unstable, less likely to be in power for future support."

Nasser was noncommittal. "Who knows?" he replied, enjoying being courted by the two bitter enemies.

"Saddam will help you with the Americans. He knows how to handle them."

"The war in Kuwait was not comforting."

"But since then we have been winning, slowly but surely. You must have patience and strength to persevere."

Suddenly, Hassan appeared in the doorway, and he signaled Nasser to come outside the room. As soon as he was gone, Sagit reached into her bag, took out the small bottle of soporific, and squirted a couple of drops into Nasser's coffee.

For an instant she felt relief, but that quickly passed as she overheard what Hassan was telling Nasser. He had called Baghdad for confirmation and learned that Saddam hadn't an emissary to Nasser, and he didn't even know a woman named Hanan Abdullah.

Quickly, she punched the alarm button twice on the two-way wristwatch—the signal to David that there was trouble.

When Nasser returned, his face was bright red, and he was furious. Hassan and the mole waited at the entrance to the room.

"Who are you?" he demanded to know.

"Hanan Abdullah."

"You're lying. Who sent you?"

"Saddam Hussein."

He pulled the pistol out of its holster and aimed it at her. "Who are you?"

"Hanan Abdullah."

"Shooting would be too merciful for you," he shouted. He walked over to his desk, put down the pistol, and picked up a sword that had been resting in the corner. As he held it menacingly above his head, he shouted, "I'll hack your limbs off one by one. First your arms and then your legs. I'll keep cutting until you tell me the truth or until you bleed to death. Well, what do you say?"

"I am Hanan Abdullah."

Slashing the sword through the air, he rushed across the room. As he did, she reached up to her head and grabbed the hair pin David had given her. She waited for the last instant, until he was so close to her that she could feel the air move from the sword. Then she aimed the hair pin like a dart, going for exposed skin so his clothes wouldn't destroy its effectiveness. She caught him below his left ear as he was preparing to bring the sword down on her arm. When the dart struck him, he was stunned, and he instinctively reached up to pull it out with his free hand. Then the poison did its work. In an instant, he dropped his sword and collapsed to the ground.

Out of the corner of her eye, she saw Hassan and the mole rush into the room, each holding an AK-47. As soon as she saw them, she raced for the desk and grabbed Nasser's pistol. While the astonished Hassan stood paralyzed, watching Nasser convulsing in the throes of the immediate death David had predicted, she fired and caught Hassan squarely in the heart.

Terrified, the mole stood still and stared at her with huge quivering eyes, not knowing what to do.

"I don't want to shoot you," she said. "I'll knock you out with a punch. You'll be okay, and your secret will be safe."

Quickly, he nodded his agreement, and she punched him in the head, leaving him dazed but conscious. Still, he kept his eyes closed.

Gripping Nasser's pistol, she ran toward the front of the château. The helicopter was hovering above the center courtyard when she stepped outside. She watched David jump out of the chopper and exchange shots with one of the two guards who had been on the front gate. But where was the other guard?

The bright sun and swirling sand were blinding her. She looked around searching for the other guard, hoping David had already killed him. Suddenly she heard the sound of an AK-47 firing. Instinctively, she whirled in that direction, shooting her own gun as she did. For an instant, her eyes locked on the eyes of the young man aiming at her.

She continued firing until bullets ripped into the right side of her upper body and shoulder. The pain was excruciating. Her knees buckled, and she collapsed onto her back on the ground.

From above, she heard more machine-gun fire. She was hallucinating . . . Yael . . . Leora . . . David. Then she drifted out of consciousness.

Her last thought was: Please God, don't let me die. Not now.

David's shots killed one of the two guards. Then he watched in horror, without a clear shot, as Sagit was ambushed by the other guard. "No!" he screamed, his gun raised in case the second guard was still alive, but the man wasn't moving. Sagit had killed him.

He bent over to feel the pulse on her left wrist. It was faint and thready. Blood was gushing from her right shoulder. She was unresponsive. He needed something to bandage her, and fast, to stop the flow of blood. There had to be something inside the château.

He dashed past the bodies of Nasser and Hassan, both of whom were dead, and into a bedroom. A woman was cowering behind a chair in a corner, and he ignored her as he frantically ripped sheets from the bed and ran back into the courtyard. Bending down, he hastily bandaged Sagit's wounds. As he did, he suddenly became conscious of a warm fluid trickling down his right leg and into his boot. Shit, I must have been hit, he realized. The blood was coming from his thigh, and he tore off a strip of one of the sheets and wrapped it around his leg. Then he scooped her up into his arms. As he hobbled with her across the courtyard, he shouted, as if his loud voice could penetrate her unconsciousness, "I'm not going to let you die. I'm not going to lose you."

Daphna had landed the chopper, and he placed Sagit down carefully on the floor in the back and covered her with a blanket.

"Start the engine," he barked to Daphna.

When nothing happened, he looked at her. She was sitting at the controls, staring into space, paralyzed and freaked out from the shooting she had just witnessed. From behind, he grabbed her by the shoulders and shook her hard. "Get hold of yourself," he said roughly, trying to shake her out of her stupor. "It's up to you. We'll all make it if you can get us the hell out of here."

His harsh approach worked. She snapped out of it.

"Don't worry. I'll be okay," she said. Her voice was still tentative, but she started the engine. As it sputtered to life, blowing sand on the ground, she asked him, "Where are we going?"

David tried to decide: where can I take Sagit? Israel was too far away, given the seriousness of her wounds and the range of the helicopter. Even if Khalid could have one of his pilots fly her there in a jet, it would take too long. A Saudi hospital wasn't an alternative for a Mossad agent, particularly now, after Khalid's attack.

No, there was only one choice. The big American military base at Dhahran had a hospital. The same base he had escaped from five years ago when he broke General Chambers's jaw. There was only one problem: how could he get in?

He directed Daphna to start flying toward Dhahran. Below the chopper was only desert, miles and miles of sand dunes and nothing else in the barren inhospitable terrain. Underneath all of that sand lay huge reservoirs of oil, but right now none of that mattered to David. All he cared about was saving Sagit.

David directed Daphna to jettison all of the MD 500's missiles, sending them crashing onto the endless sand below. Then he grabbed the helicopter's radio and called the Dhahran airbase's communications center. "Israeli civilian in unmarked Saudi helicopter carrying wounded Mossad agent requests permission to land and asks preparation of base hospital for major surgery." There was a long pause.

"Do you read me?" David called, trying to conceal the panic in his voice. "Do you read me?"

The American base gave David a two-pronged response. First, four F-15 fighter jets, which had been on Con Delta alert with pilots in the cockpits since the Americans received word that Colonel Khalid had launched his attack, shot down the runway and headed toward the helicopter.

Then the base radio operator replied to David in a firm voice, "Permission *not* granted. For security reasons."

"We're unarmed," David shouted back angrily. "All missiles were jettisoned. You can see that with your long-range scopes." David thought that they must have already observed the absence of missiles, but that still didn't cut it because the Americans were worried that he was on a suicide mission. "This is humanitarian," he added, softening his voice. "I told you I'm carrying a seriously wounded Mossad agent."

A gust of wind whipped the helicopter sideways.

Gripping the controls tightly, Daphna struggled to keep them on course. On the ground below, an encampment of Bedouins watched the chopper rock from side to side until Daphna had the helicopter leveled. The four F-15s were now directly overhead. David guessed that the pilots had their fingers on the buttons to fire heat-seeking air-to-air missiles the instant the order was given from Dhahran.

"Repeat. Permission not granted."

"You're making a serious mistake, you turkey," David said, displaying a confidence he didn't feel. "I want to talk to your commanding officer."

In a voice brimming with authority, the operator replied, "General McCallister, the base commander, personally denied the authorization to land."

"Then fuck the authorization," David shouted back into the microphone. "We're coming in."

"This is a warning. If you get within five miles of the base perimeter, missiles will be fired to shoot down the helicopter."

Daphna looked at him in fear.

"Slow your speed, but stay on course," he ordered her.

Then suddenly out of nowhere three American Apache helicopters appeared. They circled behind the MD 500. One remained directly behind, while one took a position to the left of the MD 500, and the other to the right.

The presence of the Apaches, each with the pilot in the rear and the copilot gunner in front, was too much for Daphna. She was over northern Israel again. They had been hit. The blood was running down the back of Yuri's head. She was trying to get back to base, and . . .

Totally unstrung, she lost her grip on the controls, and the helicopter veered sharply out of control, swinging wildly. Seeing the glazed look in her eyes, David realized what was happening. If he could have flown the chopper, he would have seized control and done it. But that wasn't an option. So he slapped her once hard on the side of her face, and then again. She pulled her head back with a start. "I'll be okay," she said, glancing at the Apache on her left, close enough so she could see the white USAF letters on the gunner's helmet.

David sized up the situation. He had no doubt that if they continued on this course for an unauthorized landing, they would be shot down, given the security that normally pervades the base and that had to be magnified after Khalid's attack. The Americans would never take a chance that he wasn't on a suicide mission. He decided to take a different tack.

"You tell Mac McCallister that Greg Nielsen's in this chopper. He'll remember me from five years ago."

"Who did you say you were?" the incredulous radio operator asked.

"Yeah, I'm the one who broke the jaw of that dumb fuck Chambers five years ago."

The stunned silence at the other end of the radio led David to conclude that the Dhahran radio operator had heard of him. He reached into his pocket and pulled out the slip of paper Sagit had given him before they took off.

Then he shouted into the radio microphone, "You tell Mac to call Margaret Joyner in Washington." He reeled off the phone number. "You tell him that the name of the wounded Israeli is Sagit, and if she dies I'll do a lot worse to him than I did to General Chambers five years ago."

The radio remained silent as the chopper moved closer and closer to Dhahran. Ahead, he could clearly see the base military structures, surface-to-air missiles ready to fire at a moment's notice, and the rebuilt Khobar housing complex. David looked over his shoulder at Sagit and was alarmed. Her face was ashen—devoid of any color and life. Her eyes weren't moving. If she was still alive, it was only by a thread.

They were ten miles from Dhahran. If they turned back, Sagit was as good as dead. The Israelis had a wonderful expression he had learned: *ain barera*. "No alternative." That described their situation right now.

Daphna was gripping the controls with white knuckles. She looked over at him in disbelief. "I think they mean business," she said in a trembling voice.

"Stay on course," he told her. "Start to cut altitude. We'll come in under the missiles." Even though he said it, he knew that would probably be futile because they would no doubt be heat-seekers. David held his breath as the chopper began to drop.

Suddenly, his radio crackled to life. "Permission to land is granted. Proceed to the chopper pad next to the base hospital. Do you need directions?"

David blew out his breath in relief. "Have you moved it in five years?"

"Negative."

"I know where it is."

As soon as Daphna touched down, a team of medics with a stretcher on wheels and emergency equipment ran out of the hospital toward the helicopter, ducking under the still-moving blades. David jumped out himself and watched breathlessly as they struggled to bring the moribund Sagit back to life. They placed her on a board, inserted a breathing tube down her throat, attached leads to her chest and hooked her up to a monitor. Then they assessed her, while a nurse inserted a catheter into her left forearm and hung IV fluids. All the while, a young woman was calling out orders for medication, and David moved up next to her. Her name tag said CAPTAIN DEBORAH MARKS.

"Into surgery now," the captain shouted, and they wheeled the stretcher into the building as fast as two medics could run alongside.

David grabbed the captain by the arm. "I want to talk to the surgeon who's in charge."

"That's me."

God, she's young, he thought. "Well listen, Dr. Marks," he said. "Please . . ."

And he started to cry, like he'd cried when he heard that his father had been killed so long ago, and when he heard that Yael had died in the bus bombing.

Captain Marks motioned to one of the orderlies to take care of David. Then she ran after the stretcher into the hospital and through the swinging double metal doors that led to the operating rooms.

A medic cleaned and bandaged David's superficial thigh wound. Then he and Daphna began the awful waiting for news about Sagit. Time went by slowly for them. He drank coffee, and she smoked cigarettes. For eight straight hours, exactly on the hour, because this was the military, someone emerged from the operating theater to give them a report, but it was always the same: "Surgery is continuing. No word yet on whether the patient will survive."

Shortly after the eighth message, General McCallister came into the waiting room. "Sorry about the confusion on your landing," he said.

"Don't worry, Mac. Your guys were playing it according to the book."

General McCallister was tall and thin, with wire-framed glasses. He had a kindly bookish face that made him look more like a university professor than a high-ranking military officer. David introduced Daphna to him, and the general said, "I wanted to get over here sooner, but things are quite tense after the attack on the Saudi palace this morning, as you might imagine. We've been on high alert awaiting orders from Washington to intervene on the side of the king, but so far they've told us 'sit tight.' None of us knows what the hell Washington's thinking, although I suspect that General Chambers's death complicates it. Well, regardless of any of that, after what Ms. Joyner said, no effort will be spared medically to save this Israeli agent. You can be sure of that."

"I appreciate that, Mac."

Suddenly, an orderly approached the two men gingerly, sensitive to the fact that he was interrupting a conversation of the base commander.

General McCallister looked at the orderly and said, "What is it?"

"Captain Marks would like to see Mr. Nielsen just outside the operating room."

As David followed the orderly through the doors that led to the surgery wing, he bit his lower lip and mumbled under his breath, "Please God, let her live. Please. I've buried my father and Yael. Not Sagit, too. Please not Sagit."

Approaching Captain Marks, standing alone with weary eyes, bloodshot from eight hours of surgery, David held his breath and thought, This is not good news. But suddenly the doctor cracked a small smile. He knew then, even before she said, "Sagit's going to make it. It was touch-and-go for a while, but she's a strong woman, and she has a fierce will to live."

He gave the doctor a bear hug. "Oh, thank you so much."

"Recovery and rehabilitation will take time. Something like three months, more or less, but she should be one hundred percent in all bodily functions after that."

"How can I ever thank you?"

She smiled broadly. "Oh, one day over a cup of coffee, while Sagit's still here, you can give me a firsthand report of your fight with General Chambers five years ago. It's taken on almost mythic proportions in the history of this base, but no one had the courage to ask General Chambers about it. So none of us knows exactly what happened."

"That's a deal," he replied. "I'll give you a blow-by-blow description. Now can I see her?"

"Just for a few minutes. She's still very groggy from the anesthesia. She won't recognize you."

He walked over and touched Sagit, stood silently, listening to her breathing, thanking God that she was okay. Tears of relief and joy rolled down his cheeks. After five minutes, an orderly nudged him. "Dr. Marks says to leave her alone now for a few hours."

As David walked through the doors from the surgery wing, an ecstatic Daphna was waiting for him. "I got the good news about Sagit from one of the orderlies," she said, and she threw her arms around him with joy.

Back in the reception area, General McCallister gave David a broad smile. "I hear she's going to be all right," the general said, having realized that Greg was in love with this Mossad agent.

"Your people are great. Especially Dr. Marks. I can't thank them enough."

"Listen, Greg, Colonel Khalid wants to talk to you privately on a secure phone." The general's frown showed his unhappiness at having high-level communications occur with a Saudi military official, to which he wasn't a party, but the White House had told him that Mrs. Joyner spoke for the President.

"Will you permit that?"

"Mrs. Joyner said I should give you anything you want. The telephone equipment's set up in the conference room across the hall." General McCallister pointed that way. "I assure you that we won't be listening in."

"I'll take your word, Mac. You and I frequently disagreed about policy when I was here, but you never lied to me." He could see the wariness in Mac's eyes, and he added, "Colonel Khalid and I still have a couple of loose ends to tie up. I assure you that none of it will affect this base or the U.S. military in any way."

McCallister snarled. He had enough loyalty to General Chambers, his former commander, to reserve judgment on the consequences of any action undertaken by Greg Nielsen.

David waddled across the corridor, with one lame leg and the other bandaged from his superficial thigh wound, into the conference room. He shut the door and picked up the red phone in the center of the table.

There was a great deal of noise and shouting in Arabic at the other end of the phone, but finally he heard Khalid's voice.

"How did you know I was here?" David asked.

"I planted an electronic device on the helicopter that emits a long-range signal. Just in case I had to rescue you."

"That's pretty impressive."

"You taught me well." His voice sounded full of appreciation.

"How's the battle going?"

"I'll tell you about that in a minute. First, tell me about Sagit. General McCallister said she was seriously wounded."

"After she killed Nasser, she was in a shoot-out with one of his guards. She was in surgery for about eight hours, but she's going to be okay. Full recovery after a few months."

"I'm so glad to hear that. She's a brave woman. What about your daughter? Is she all right?"

"She's fine. Now tell me about the coup."

"It's over," he said in a triumphant voice. "The three automated systems were deactivated. We subdued the king's guards. We didn't have to bomb the palace. The rest of the Saudi military has come over to our side."

"That's great. So little bloodshed. You've got to be pleased."

Khalid, normally reserved, sounded joyful. "It couldn't be any better. The shooting's over. Crowds are celebrating in the streets of Riyadh and the other cities. The princes are barking orders to their servants to get packed as soon as possible."

David was thrilled. "That's great. You're letting them leave?"

"Absolutely. The king and his princes can leave peacefully if that's what they want as we move toward democratic reform." David could almost see him waving his hand high over his head, signifying their exodus. "They're scrambling to get their assets into European banks. Oh, it's a great day here."

"And President Waltham didn't jump in on the side of the king? He let you win?"

"He sure did."

"I can't believe it."

"Did you ever consider that President Waltham found you persuasive when you were in Washington?"

David wanted to agree with Khalid, but he decided that modesty was the better approach. "I'd like to think that, but it was probably inertia on Washington's part. It's always easier to do nothing. But regardless, I'm thrilled for you at how everything has gone."

Khalid's voice now turned grim. "There is, however, one little black spot."

David wondered what he was talking about. "A little black spot?"

"Yeah, I have this French visitor," he said angrily, "who set up shop in the penthouse of the Hyatt. She's planning to run the entire Saudi oil industry, but that's not how I saw our deal. I planned to cut her in for a piece of the action. I never thought we'd be going back to colonialism again."

David decided that he and Khalid were close enough for blunt talk. He took a deep breath and said, "C'mon, Khalid. You were dreaming. The woman's a megalomaniac. You knew that from the start. You were unrealistic to think you could control her after the coup."

There was a long pause. Finally, Khalid responded. His voice was circumspect. "If she can change the deal, so can I. Besides, after the way the Americans behaved, by not intervening on the side of the king, I'd prefer to deal with them, but I've got to get rid of her in order to do that." He paused, giving David a minute to absorb his words and then continued. "Got any ideas about how I can get rid of her?"

This was the moment David had been waiting for. At last Khalid had seen the light about Madame Blanc. Now David could make sure that ruthless bitch lost the profits from Saudi oil she'd worked so hard to get. "You can't just expel her," he told Khalid. "If she's on the loose, she'll never stop until she's killed both of us."

"Agreed. What then?"

"Poison her water or food."

"I thought of that, but I've made this commitment to due process and the rule of law, and she hasn't broken any Saudi law."

David wanted to scream, Don't be a naive fool, but he knew he couldn't deal with Khalid that way. Instead he replied calmly, "She's responsible for the death of an Israeli, a kid by the name of Kourosh, when she was working to set me up. She also killed an American," his tone became sarcastic, "my good friend General Chambers. So why don't you lock her up in one of your bleak prisons for a while, then ship her out to one of those two countries?"

Khalid took a moment to frame his response. David was headed in the right direction, but he wasn't quite there. "That won't work. The U.S. would never try her for Chambers's death because it would mean airing all that dirty linen in the press. So she'd walk, and you're right, she'd never stop until she killed both of us."

Khalid took a deep breath before continuing. He didn't want to offend David by what he next said. "As for Israel, one of the things I intend gradually to do is develop relations with the Israelis much like Egypt and Jordan and Morocco have done, but that'll take time. Before I do that, I have to solidify my relations in the Arab world, and I won't be able to do that with a high-level extradition to Israel out of the chute."

"So let her rot in jail for a few years while you mend your fences."

"She's too well connected with the Sultan of Oman and the leaders in some other key oil states where she does business. They'll pressure me to let her go."

Khalid stopped talking and waited. It took David only five seconds to understand where Khalid was going with this conversation. It was obvious. David chided himself for being so dense that he hadn't seen it sooner. But now that he understood, he was ecstatic. There was nothing he'd enjoy doing more. His voice was somber when he responded to the Saudi colonel. "Your helicopter's still in good shape. I could refuel it here. How close to the Hyatt could we land?"

Khalid was relieved that David had taken the bait. "There's a helipad on the roof, just above the penthouse floor, which she's occupying. It's forty-eight stories off the ground. Plenty of room for you to maneuver out of sight."

"Who controls the skies from Dhahran to the Hyatt? We had a pretty harrowing ride getting into the American base. I jettisoned all of my missiles. So we'd be vulnerable as hell coming in."

"You don't have to worry," Khalid said in a voice brimming with self-confidence. "I have absolute control over the air force, and I'll make sure the skies remain clear for you. On the ground, my men control all the surface-to-air missile sites. You'll be okay."

"What about Madame Blanc's personal security in the hotel?"

"I found out that she uses a firm called Global Security, which specializes in providing support to visiting Westerners." Khalid glanced at a file on his desk. "It's run by a Saudi named Zamil. I'll tell him that if he wants to stay in business in the new Saudi Arabia, he'd better let me replace his guards with people I send, dressed in his uniforms, so she won't get suspicious."

David was impressed at how far ahead of him Khalid was on this. "When I get there, what'll these bogus guards do?"

"Whatever you want. They can do nothing except make sure she remains in the hotel suite. Then when you get there, they'll stay out of your way. But if you want them to help you, I can arrange that. You tell me."

David wasn't about to give up the satisfaction of doing this himself. "Thanks for the offer, Khalid, but it'll be a pleasure for me to tie her up in a tight little bundle myself."

Khalid smiled. "I expected as much. What do you want to do with that bundle? Will you need my help then?"

A plan was forming in David's mind. "Hold on a minute," he said to Khalid as he placed the phone down on the table and walked over to Daphna. "If it meant getting even with Madame Blanc, would you fly that chopper again?"

Daphna didn't hesitate for an instant. As she recalled her imprisonment in the château in Grasse, her eyes sparkled with hatred. "With pleasure, David."

"Good, then tell me the range of that MD 500."

"Four hundred and thirty kilometers. Four-fifty max, if I keep the speed constant. Figuring only two or three of us inside."

"Okay. Sit tight for a little while."

He returned to the conference room and picked up the phone. "Here's the plan, Khalid. We'll take the chopper to the Hyatt. Once we get our bundle inside, we fly to an airbase west of Riyadh. You pick one. Remote, but not too far away. We'll be pushing it on fuel. From there, I want a car with tinted windows and a military escort to take us to an isolated small port along the Red Sea. Say, around

Al-Wajh. I'll need a motor boat there, but no crew. That I can handle myself. From there, I'll be on my own, moving up the Red Sea and into Eilat."

Khalid thought about what David had just told him. "It's all doable. What else do you need?"

"Have your people set up a room service table with a bottle of champagne in a closet on her floor. Also a waitress's uniform."

"Will do. The hotel will have champagne around for Westerners. How soon are you planning to leave?"

David was now trembling with excitement. "As soon as they can refuel me here."

Dressed in Gucci leather pants and a pale blue cotton blouse, Madame Blanc sat at her desk in the Hyatt penthouse suite, hunched over papers that showed current production levels at each of the Saudi oil wells. In her position as Saudi oil czar, which she would be occupying starting tomorrow, all she would have to do was order those production levels down by twenty percent, and the price of crude oil would escalate by at least ten percent, driving up prices at the pump in the West by fifty or more cents a gallon. Her profits would skyrocket, not just from her oil concession in Saudi Arabia, but from all of her other oil interests throughout the world. And it could all be justified. She would get her huge cut, but the Saudi people would get the income to which they were entitled. It was their oil. It was her oil. The West's cheap ride was over, and her fun and profits were just beginning.

She was quite pleased with herself as she thought about what she had achieved. Her plan had been brilliant. Khalid had taken control of the Saudi government in record time. The crowds in the streets were celebrating his victory, but it was her victory. She would now control the ultimate prize: the world's greatest supply of oil.

Suddenly the phone rang. Who could be calling me? she wondered, as she picked it up.

"It's Zamil from Global Security," he said in a halting, tension-filled voice.

Immediately she knew something was wrong. "What is it?" she demanded, showing him strength.

"I have some valuable information for you. Information that could save your life."

"Tell me what it is."

"First, there's the matter of my fee for the information."

She was furious. "I'm already paying you a huge daily fee for your services."

"But, madame, this is above and beyond our arrangement. A special one-time fee. If I give you this information, I'll have to leave the country forever. My business will be gone."

"You're a thief," she screamed. "I'll fire you and hire someone else."

"As you wish, madame," he said coldly.

She knew from the sound of his voice that this wasn't a shakedown for more money. Zamil had learned something so critical that he was putting himself at risk for telling her. One thought immediately popped into her mind: that dirty bastard, Khalid, was double-crossing her. She had to know what Khalid was up to.

"How much do you want?" she asked.

He breathed a sigh of relief. "Twenty million U.S.," he said with confidence, now feeling he had the upper hand. "Wired immediately to an account in Switzerland."

"Ten's all I'll pay, and if your information's not worth it, with the friendships I have in the new government, you'll have your money, but lose your head."

"I'm aware of that fact, madame. Ten's not enough. It has to be fifteen."

Her face turned red with anger. "Twelve, or go fuck yourself."

There was a long pause. "Twelve it is," he said.

"Okay, what's the information?"

"You'll have to wire the money first. I can access my account by remote. I need to see it in the account."

He then gave her the information about his bank account, and she wired the money using her computer.

The phone was silent for a full minute. Then he said in a smug voice, "The money arrived."

"This better be good."

"It is. A little while ago, I received a phone call from Colonel Khalid's headquarters, from some captain telling me that within the next hour, my men who were guarding you will be replaced by guards being sent by Colonel Khalid. My people are to go quietly when the replacements came and not to say anything to you. This captain made it seem as if you will be receiving security provided by the new government." Zamil was perspiring heavily. He paused to wipe his forehead with a soiled handkerchief. "I asked the captain which unit will be providing your security, and he told me. I have friends in that unit, and by spreading around a little money, I learned that these new guards are supposed to sit back and do nothing if someone comes into your suite and takes you out, which means that—"

"I know what it means. I'm not a fool," she shouted, pounding her fist hard on the desk. Who the hell does Khalid think he is? I'll smash his balls.

Suddenly she had an idea. "How much would you want to have your people disregard this order and stay to defend me?"

He was breathing deeply now. His hand was shaking so much he could barely hold the phone. Outside, a car and driver were waiting to take him to Dubai and freedom. Don't be greedy, he told himself. With the money he now had in the bank, he'd be a fool to do what she was asking.

"I'm very sorry, madame, that's not an option."

She wasn't surprised to hear his reply. When she hung up the phone, she began thinking. What was Khalid up to? If he wanted to kill her or oust her himself, he'd send people to do that once the Global guards were gone. Instead, he'd set up an elaborate plan to let someone else come in and pull her out. Who? Why?

She closed her eyes, put her head in her hands and leaned forward on the desk, racking her brain for an answer. Suddenly, it hit her like a sledgehammer pounding on her chest. David Ben Aaron. Greg Nielsen. The man who had conveniently disappeared after he developed the plan of attack for her. She realized now that she had made

a blunder of epic proportions. Victor had been right. She
should never have gotten David into the plan, regardless
of what Khalid said. She should have persuaded the Saudi
colonel to work with her even without David. What struck
her now was that if David and Khalid had been so close
five years ago that Khalid recognized him by his limp and
knew the information David had, then there was always
the risk that David and Khalid would join forces against
her. The three of them were caught up in a vicious circle.
She was coming out on the losing end, and she should have
realized that from the beginning.

She grabbed a bunch of her hair in her hand, wanting to
tear it out. She was so furious at herself. Then she began
thinking again. From Victor's dossier and everything David
had done with her so far, she knew one thing: he was always the solo player, always acting alone. That's how he
would come for her, by himself. Somehow he'd plan to get
her out of Saudi Arabia and back to Israel, to stand trial
for the murder of that Israeli kid. She reached into the
desk drawer and pulled out a Beretta. With the gun in her
hand, she crossed into the bathroom and located a small
but extremely sharp switchblade knife she always kept in
her cosmetics kit. After slipping that into the pocket of her
pants, she returned to the desk, laid the gun down close to
her right hand and waited.

An hour later, Madame Blanc heard the unmistakable
sound of an approaching helicopter. Very good, David, she
thought. Neat and clean. No one on the ground to observe
what happens. She peeked out of a tiny opening in the
curtains. From pictures she had seen, she immediately recognized Daphna behind the controls. And there he was in
the back of the chopper. All alone. Of course, he wouldn't
want help. The solo player. Anxious to gain revenge. Well,
come on, David, she thought. I'm ready for you.

CHAPTER 20

Daphna landed the helicopter in the middle of a white circle in the center of the Hyatt roof. David jumped out and walked over to the three-foot-high metal railing that ran around the perimeter of the roof. He wanted to see what the situation was forty-eight floors below, in front of the hotel. All was quiet there. Several blocks away in each direction there were celebrations of the fall of the House of Saud, with people blasting car horns, and women walking freely in the streets with other women. He was relieved that there didn't seem to be any violence.

As he and Daphna walked down the inside staircase that led to the penthouse floor, each had a pistol in a shoulder holster under a jacket. David also carried a black leather bag that held two tear gas canisters, a gun for firing them and gas masks. He had gotten all of the weapons at the American base, courtesy of General McCallister, who was following Margaret Joyner's instructions to give David what he wanted.

Before opening the door that led to the forty-eighth floor, David grabbed Daphna by the arm. With a stern look and an even sterner voice, he said to her, "Now, let's go over this one more time. You speak good Arabic. Your job is to wheel the room service table to the door, make your statement in Arabic and once she opens the door, you run back to the helicopter and wait for me. Is that clear?"

"Absolutely."

"I'm not kidding, Daphna. I really mean it. If anything goes wrong in that suite, it's going to happen to me alone. Khalid radioed us the name and location of the base. You get your ass in the chopper and fly to that base. He'll get you back to Israel."

"I understand."

He wasn't convinced that she did. So he tried once more. "And the only point of you having that pistol is if someone tries to stop you from lifting off. You got that?"

"I got it."

"Then repeat it."

She did, all the while thinking to herself, There's no way I'm going to leave you alone down here.

David opened the door slowly and peered out at a penthouse floor, deserted except for two of Khalid's men, who had been expecting them. One of them pointed silently to a closet off the corridor which held a white waitress's uniform as well as a room service table with a bottle of Dom Perignon, some caviar and various breads and crackers.

Daphna changed into the uniform, then rolled the table slowly down the corridor. She tried to smile, to look pleasant like a waitress might, but she was gripping the sides of the table so hard that her knuckles were white, and she was wetting the clean white cloth with the perspiration on her palms. When she got to the door of Madame Blanc's suite, she rang the small white bell. Then David pushed her to one side of the door frame. He was on the other side, so that they wouldn't be hit if Madame Blanc decided to open fire through the wooden door. David was gripping his pistol tightly. The bag with the tear gas equipment rested on the thick brown carpet at his feet.

"Who's there?" a woman's voice answered through the door.

David signaled to Daphna to answer but not to move closer to the door. "It's room service, complimentary champagne and caviar."

"Isn't that thoughtful. The door's unlocked. You can bring it right in."

Now David looked at Daphna and pointed up to the roof. His message was clear: get out of here now. He watched her walk across the corridor and down about ten yards. He waited until she opened the door to the inside staircase and disappeared behind it before he turned the knob on the door to the suite.

He opened it a crack. He waited and then kicked it open with his foot, still hiding behind the door frame. From inside, there wasn't a sound. He glanced around the edge of the door and peered into the living room of the suite. He saw a huge desk which held a computer and piles of papers, but he didn't see Madame Blanc.

He was now very wary. This isn't what happens when room service makes a delivery. She had to be expecting something. Probably hiding in one of the bedrooms in the back and planning to ambush him. He took a look at the bag with the tear gas equipment, thought for a minute about using it, but rejected that option. He'd deal with her on his own. A louvered closet ran along the side wall that went to the rear bedrooms. Gripping his pistol, he made his way slowly and quietly on his toes alongside the closet. Suddenly, he heard a sound, just a tiny rustling in the closet, a few yards ahead of him, but it was unmistakable. He heard it.

Without waiting an instant, he raced across the room and dove behind a sofa, just in the nick of time. She came out of the closet firing at him, but the bullets went into the sofa or sailed over his head. She was out in the open now. He was totally in control. He'd wait a moment longer, until she used all of her bullets or until she moved toward the side of the sofa to get a clear shot. He'd tackle her and take her then.

Meantime, Daphna had crept back into the corridor as soon as he was in the suite. Once she heard the sound of shots being fired, she ran inside the suite with the gun in her right hand. Glancing over the edge of the sofa from his position, David spotted Daphna as soon as she entered the suite. He screamed, "No, Daphna, get out fast."

He was too late.

While Daphna was looking to her left, Madame Blanc circled up behind her from the other side. Using the gun in her right hand, the Frenchwoman delivered a powerful chop to Daphna's right arm, above the wrist, which knocked the gun from Daphna's hand. At the same time, Madame Blanc got behind the stunned Daphna with a powerful left arm around her neck and throat. Then she raised her own gun and held it hard against the side of Daphna's head.

"Okay, devoted stepfather," she called to David in a cruel, sinister voice, "if you even move from behind that sofa until you see the helicopter taking off through the window of this suite, I'll blow her brains out and fly that MD 500 myself." A feeling of victory lit up her face. "And don't think I can't."

"It's low on fuel," David called from behind the sofa.

"I'm sure it is. That's why once I'm in the air you're going to call your friend Khalid and find out where I can refuel."

"There's nowhere you can go," he said, stalling for time, hoping she would make a slip.

She squeezed her arm tighter against Daphna's throat. "Oh, don't you worry about that. I have plenty of friends in this part of the world." Then she gave a sadistic laugh. "And don't worry about Daphna. I'll either send her home first class on a commercial airliner, or I'll send her body, or all of its pieces, back to the kibbutz in a wooden box. I haven't decided yet."

"You won't get away with this," he said.

But she didn't even hear his words. "And after that, I'll send somebody to kill you. Sometime. Someplace. You'll never know where or when, but I'll do it."

From behind the edge of the sofa, he watched in horror as she made Daphna, looking terrified and abashed, still in the vise of her left arm and with a gun against her temple, walk with her, outside of the suite and up the stairs to the roof and the waiting helicopter.

David waited until he heard the metal door to the staircase slam before he made his move. He jumped up and ran to the doorway of the suite, where he scooped up the black leather case with the tear gas equipment. He was unzipping it as he climbed the stairs. By the time he reached the top step, and the door to the roof, he had one canister into the

tear gas gun and he snapped on a gas mask. He waited behind the door until he heard the engine of the helicopter start. Then he kicked open the door, took aim and fired into the open side door of the chopper.

The tear gas canister erupted in the confined space of the helicopter. Madame Blanc and Daphna both started coughing violently. Instinctively, they went for fresh air, Daphna in her white waitress uniform, rolling out of the helicopter onto the ground, and Madame Blanc stumbling out blinded, clutching and waving her gun erratically. David immediately went for the gun in her hand, but it slipped away from both of them, fell to the concrete floor of the roof and careened toward one side.

David went down on his hands and knees chasing it, but Madame Blanc had recovered enough of her sight to kick it away. At the same time, she grabbed the knife in the pocket of her pants and snapped it open. Once he scrambled to his feet, she came at him with the knife extended in her right hand, its stiletto-like blade gleaming in the bright sunlight. Tears were still running down her face from the gas. Her hair, which had been tied up in a bun, had come loose and was falling over her face. Her eyes had a crazed, mad dog look. This man had ruined everything for her, and she was determined to get even.

Terrified, he backed up as much as he could, until he felt the metal of the black parapet against his buttocks. With nowhere else to go, he stood his ground, raised his hands to shoulder level, waiting for her thrust, hoping to grab the knife.

She gave an animal-like scream, "I'll kill you. You bastard." Then she lunged at him. Mustering all of his strength, with both hands he grabbed her right arm and held it tightly, blocking her thrust. She kicked him hard in the crotch. As the pain shot through his body, he felt his hold on her knife arm weakening. Finally she broke free and raised the knife high. "Now you're mine," she screamed and lunged at him. At the last second, he ducked down to the ground, on all fours, like a blocker in a football game. Off balance, she flew over his back and over the railing.

She gave a bloodcurdling scream as she hurtled toward the ground, forty-eight stories below.

Tearing off his gas mask, he watched her head hit the hard cement of the driveway in front of the hotel. Her skull and body smashed into a bloody pulp. In the fresh air, Daphna had recovered enough from the tear gas to witness the end of David's struggle. She ran over and hugged him. As she tried to look down at the ground below, he turned her head away. "No," he said. "It's too horrible."

"I was so frightened for you, and it was all my fault. If I had only listened to you and—"

He clamped a hand over her mouth and kissed her on the forehead.

Pulling the cell phone out of his pocket, he called Khalid to tell him what had happened. "I'm afraid there's a mess on the sidewalk in front of the hotel."

"Then I think you better get out of town. Let me deal with it. We'll say it was an accident. She was up there with binoculars looking at the city, got too close to the edge and lost her balance."

David now gave a nervous laugh as the tension ebbed from his body. "Which is at least partially true. She did lose her balance."

"Where do you want to go now?"

"To your base for refueling as we planned. Then back to the American airbase at Dhahran to see Sagit."

Victor sat in his office with his eyes glued to the television set and CNN. Hour after hour they showed scenes of Khalid's military victory, of crowds celebrating in Riyadh and the hesitant and uncertain reactions of Arab and world leaders. But no one dared to send forces to challenge the victorious Khalid, Victor observed with pleasure. As he watched and listened to Saudi oil production figures, he constantly calculated and recalculated how much his five percent cut of Madame Blanc's profits would be. She had estimated that the deal was worth five hundred million a year for several years. That meant his five percent would be twenty-five million a year, but the figures he was hearing

made her estimate seem low. Each time he recalculated, his return got larger. He now thought it was closer to fifty million a year. That was some serious money. Definitely not chump change.

If he had that kind of money, Françoise would come crawling to him with her gorgeous golden bush. He'd buy a mansion in Cannes and drive a Rolls Silver Cloud. Maybe even buy a yacht with a helicopter, like her highness, Madame Blanc. Ah, those will be the days.

His secretary, a blonde in a short black miniskirt, stuck her head into the office.

Annoyed, he barked, "I told you I didn't want to be disturbed."

"I'm sorry, Mr. Foch. A package was hand delivered. The messenger said it was urgent."

"Then give it to me," he snapped.

The secretary handed it to him, and he turned back to the television set, tossing the package on the floor at his feet. As the secretary turned around, she raised the second finger on her right hand when he couldn't see it. Then she quickly departed.

At the next television commercial, Victor looked down at the package on the floor. It was a thick brown folder that would hold letter-size pages without having to fold them. On the front of the envelope were the words "Personal and confidential. To be opened only by Victor Foch." Also on the cover was a small sticker of a guillotine. The package must be from Madame Blanc, he decided. It had to do with Operation Guillotine. Maybe she was sending him a first installment of money, in cash, and that's why it was so heavy. Eagerly, he tore the strip across the top back of the envelope that said "open here." The envelope was padded with bubble wrap on the inside. As he reached in, expecting to find cash, his hand encountered a metal object. What in the world is this? he wondered. He began pulling out the metal object. He had it halfway out when it exploded with a force so great that it blew him across the room and cut a huge cavity in his chest where his heart had been.

*   *   *

This time Daphna and David's landing at the American airbase in Dhahran was nothing like the last one. Approaching the base, David radioed, "Greg Nielsen seeking permission to land."

"Permission granted, Mr. Nielsen, and your friend's resting comfortably."

Once they were on the ground, he cleaned his personal effects out of the helicopter, before it went back to Khalid and the Saudi Air Force, and he told Daphna to do likewise.

Reaching behind the seat, he pulled out a tan plastic bag.

"What's that, David?" Daphna asked curiously.

"Oh, just something Sagit left here," he said, and winked at her.

Playfully, she snatched the bag from his hand and looked inside. Then she blushed. "Oh, my."

He laughed. "That's the trouble with you young people. You never think a parent is capable of anything more than watching TV and rocking to sleep."

Her face was now bright red. "I never said that."

"Yeah, but you were thinking it."

Daphna waited in the hospital corridor when he went into Sagit's room. The patient was awake, but still groggy.

He came over and kissed her gently on the lips.

"David," she mumbled, smiling broadly. "You're okay. So glad."

"And you are, too," he said, breathing a deep sigh of relief. "It's all over, and there's no one to bother us."

She leaned forward and said anxiously, "Will you leave me and go back to the States?"

"Are you crazy? My life's with you always. I've got big plans for us."

Her face glowed with contentment. "What plans?"

He reached into the plastic bag and pulled out the orange string bikini he had bought for her in Dubai. Holding it up, each piece in one hand, he said, "Well, for starters, you can wear this in Eilat for the next couple of months, which will be a great place to recuperate this time of year. Then

in January, you can wear it when we go to Anguilla in the Caribbean for the winter. Spring, it'll look great on you in St. Tropez, and after that . . ."

She had fallen back asleep, so he stopped talking. Putting the bikini back into the bag, he noticed for the first time the handwritten note she had left inside. It read:

If I don't make it, here's something to remember me by.

Love,
Sagit

He tore the note into tiny pieces and dropped them into the wastebasket. Then he pulled up a chair next to the bed and caressed the back of her hand while she slept.

ACKNOWLEDGMENTS

I want to thank my wife, Barbara, who spent numerous hours reading each of the drafts of this novel, providing valuable insights about the characters and the plot. Equally important, Barbara supplied much needed encouragement to continue. Our children—David, Rebecca, and Deborah and Daniella—offered helpful suggestions based upon their particular expertise, thereby supplying partial repayment for their education. I want to thank Stacey Topol for taking the author's photograph that appears in this book, and Lawrence Rosenberg for supplying enthusiastic support for this novel.

Henry Morrison, my unique and extraordinary agent, worked long hours helping shape this project from its inception. As Henry commented on outlines and drafts, I was the beneficiary of his incredible storehouse of knowledge on all of the elements of a novel. He was determined that we would succeed, and he knew how to accomplish that objective.

Finally, I want to thank Carolyn Nichols and Doug Grad, as well as other personnel at NAL, who ran with the manuscript with enormous enthusiasm from its initial readings in the house. They devoted countless hours not only editing and offering superb suggestions, but finding ways to enhance and to strengthen the novel. It's a thrill for an author to have the support that Carolyn and Doug provided.